BREAKING LIVES

The Molly Turner Trilogy

J D Warner

Self Published

Cover design by: Art Painter
Library of Congress Control Number: 2018675309
Printed in the United States of America

THIS IS THE FULL STORY OF MOLLY, ORIGINALLY PUBLISHED IN THREE NOVELLAS: THE HARTPURY HORRROR, MOLLY'S CURSE, AND MOLLY'S END.

BOOK ONE

HARTPURY

"Is It True: No Good Deed Goes
Unpunished?" ~ Psalm 37

1. Evil Micra

Hello; my name is Molly Turner, and I am seventy-three years young, but I don't feel it—unless I am climbing steep hills.

An upright, bespectacled figure with pink tinted hair, most days you can see me wandering the roads and lanes with a litter grabber and a black bag ready in my hands.

You see, in this small Gloucestershire village called Hartpury, the A417 runs though from Gloucester, and you can actually see people just open their car windows and throw out rubbish.

Before I had started my litter clear-up campaign the previous year, the verges had hosted twice as much rubbish, but I realise it's not a thing that can ever be stopped. Each day, the litter I picked up the time before has been replaced by more. At times I imagine someone's peering at me through binoculars and saying, "That's it, lads. The road's clean now, so get down there and chuck out some more waste for the old biddy to clear up. It's our duty. We give meaning to her life."

In a way, my little task did give meaning to my life. I don't knit or crochet or paint or read much, but I do like gardening and walking. It's a somewhat solitary life, the bane of older people in our society, but in litter clearing I felt helpful; felt my existence validated.

Anyway, that day—*that* day—Wednesday, 5th September, with the bright year fading into wear-your-jacket chilly days, I was ambling past the old school buildings beside the A417, and poking at something in the hedge with my grabber, when I heard cars decelerating. It's a busy road where cars don't generally stop unless they're lost, so I noticed it.

A red car had pulled over, the other vehicles now

streaming past it. It had stopped by the gate of the field beside the old school and below the woods, a few hundred feet away and, as I watched, a man got out of the car, opened the field gate and went in.

I went back to litter picking. As other cars and lorries rumbled past, I tugged at a bag caught in the prickly hedge. Plastic bags are the worst. Sometimes they fight until their last shred.

Hearing the clunk of a car door, I looked up to see the red car by the gate do a rather dodgy three point turn in the road, and shoot off back towards Gloucester.

A few minutes later I reached where the car had been. Leaning on the gate, I gazed over the green pasture field where nothing stirred except long grasses in the breeze, and decided to call it a day. The rubbish bag was almost heavily full and that was my general criterion for stopping. Then I spotted a brown fast-food bag almost hidden to one side in the long grass. I unhooked the gate, went in and reached for the bag with the grabber. As it came up, I could feel its heaviness. 'Wastrels,' I thought, assuming left-over food weighed it down. But, when I looked into the bag, the image of tightly packed bundles of cash hammered into my head and made me feel giddy. It was a *lot* of cash.

I hastily dropped the bag back where I had found it.

So

much

money!

My thoughts tumbled over each other as I hurried back down the road. 'It must be drug money,' I decided. 'Something like that. Not lost, no, definitely placed there on purpose. Some bad guy will be along to pick it up. You don't want to be seen anywhere near it. Get far away!'

But how many cars had passed me in the short time the event had taken? How many people might have glimpsed my actions as they sped past?

Because, for a bare moment, the urge to keep it had been

there, the thought bright and sharp in my mind, but I wasn't brave enough. Neither hard up nor a wealthy widow, I knew that kind of money could break a soul in bad ways, just like lottery wins seem to work back on the winners. And after all the other pain in my life I wasn't going to risk bringing any more into it.

I would phone the police when I got home. Tell them all about it, hand the problem to them to sort out. I wanted nothing of it. I didn't own a mobile phone, or I would have called the police then and there.

No sooner had I reached the old school on my way back, than I again heard cars slowing.

'Don't look,' I told myself, but my head moved of its own accord, glancing back for just a second to see a pale blue Micra stop by the gate.

Now I was scared. By very dint of knowing about the money, I had impressed an inescapable dread in myself. "Home; coffee; cookies," I said, reassuring the frightened lady inside me. "Relax, call the police. It's not like you found a body, is it? Pull yourself together, Molly."

But maybe one can walk in a guilty way because, the next second, I heard slowing yet again and the little blue Micra appeared, chugging alongside me, a big, bearded man leaning over to glare at me from the driving seat as the cars behind overtook him and drove off.

The Micra passed by but pulled into the farm driveway a little ahead and, next thing I knew, the man was out and marching towards me like a guided-missile battering ram. I stepped back, hugging the litter bag to my chest as though it were a protective air-bag.

The man, eyes young and fierce in the bearded face, demanded, "Where is it?"

"Where's what, dear?" I asked, aware of the tremble in my voice, putting on a pathetic old-lady charade, hoping to appeal to his better nature. "Have you lost something? I can't say as I've—"

4

Without warning he lunged forward, wrenched the litter bag out of my hands and, in full view of the cars whizzing past and minding their own business, upended the debris onto the path and poked at it with his foot, then went *Huh* and walked back to his car.

I was glad I hadn't been wearing my backpack that day. He might have made a grab for that too, and spilled my snacks all over the place.

'Oh, he was definitely one of the bad guys,' I inwardly gasped, heart pounding with nerves, so glad I hadn't taken the money. But, if that was what he was after, why wasn't it back where my conscience had left it? Had I missed someone coming across the fields; someone sneaking out of the woods where they'd been waiting?

The evil little Micra and its burly driver who fitted it so badly drove off towards Gloucester leaving me peacefully alone, so I put on my gloves and scooped the rubbish back into the bag, knotted the top, and headed home with firm footsteps, halo intact, looking forward to biscuits and coffee and maybe something a little stronger.

'A lot stronger,' I decided as the Micra sailed past again, the bearded man looking at me a fraction too long, the car almost veering across the road as he gave me the evil eye. And five minutes later he passed by on the way back from the village, but I resolutely stared forwards, innocence in my bespectacled gaze as I hurried home.

2. Death and Life

I slept well that night, but that's the effect of my meds, not that I wasn't worried about my strange encounter, which I had tried to press to the back of my mind. I hadn't bothered calling the police. After all, if the bag was gone, I couldn't even prove I had seen it and, as Ozzy had said, 'If you don't *need* the police, leave them alone.'

So that Thursday morning, I had a good breakfast, then drove Ozzy's car out of the garage onto the drive and gave it the monthly wash. Technically, it's mine now, but I still think of the Mercedes as being his. It suited his temperament: old, distinguished and ostentatious. I kept it in good repair, fully intending to sell it one day and get something smaller. 'Not a Micra!' my wretched mind had to shout at me. But it's nice to sometimes meander down the lanes in the lovely blue Merc and get admiring gazes. I was, to be quite honest, more attached to the car than to the memory of the man who had bought it.

After picking some raspberries from the garden to chill for tea, I fed Misty, my old calico cat, for the third time that morning. Or was it the first time? I would be the first to admit my memory seemed to be slipping a little, the lines blurring with repetition. Sometimes I found something wasn't where I left it, so I'd laugh and blame 'the ghost', but I don't think there is one. Not Ozzy's at least; he might well have gone straight to hell.

Having had my elevenses, it was time for my daily wander. I left the Merc on the driveway to dry properly. There's nothing worse than rust to depreciate a vehicle. Ozzy had been depreciated by rich food, dying in his sleep. He'd been down in Bristol for a business meeting, and stayed for a party afterwards. I'd been invited but hadn't gone. His circle of friends was not my circle – and I just didn't like them. He'd complained that I never went anywhere with him and stormed out, and I'd never seen him again. The coffin came back, and the Mercedes, and my long lost freedom was re-instated.

Ozzy hadn't liked me driving—like many things, it wasn't in his world view of women. Does it sound nice to be cosseted and have everything paid for? I know women who envy me, but it's also a kind of prison, especially when your husband won't even let you watch what you want to on TV. And litter picking? Heaven forbid; he would not have allowed that. I could still hear him in my head disapproving every time I left the house, but the walking and the activity, that slight idea of helping the village to keep clean and pretty, were the things that kept me going.

Occasionally I would do different routes, down the side roads as long as they had paths, along to the petrol station and so on, but that day I found myself heading back to *that* gate; in *that* field.

Something had been going on there. The grass was trampled, turned up, scraped about, and I guessed it had been a rather serious game of hunt the very expensive burger bag. Or had the money gone and just the bag was left, empty? The bearded man hadn't specified the circumstances. Someone was going to be in trouble over that. I just hoped it wasn't going to be me, because—as you know—I didn't take it. Or did I? No, I was sure I hadn't, yet that image of the bank notes burned so vibrantly in my mind it seemed for a moment I could see myself lifting them out, looking all around, wondering if anyone would notice...

'You're going senile,' I told myself sharply and got on my way again.

At the edge of Hartpury, a wooded hill looms over the A417 and the old school and the fields, and there's a path beside the school leading up into greenness, where the first brush of autumn painted the leaves orange and red, conkers bristled on branches, and ripening blackberries festooned the brambles.

I went up the path, even finding bits and bobs of rubbish up there, puffing a little as I pushed myself on the steep slope. I wasn't ready to be old. There were many good years left in me yet if I played my cards right; kept taking the medicine. I'm mobile, feel good, and have some money behind me. I am lucky in many respects. I know that. Just unlucky in other ways.

The path opened out into an area of stumps and thin trees, brambles and ferns, and I walked off the trail and into the woods, eating a packet of crisps while looking down through the gaps in the trees at the field the money was no longer in. My gaze went across the A417 and off to the fields on the other side of the road, where my imagination changed the gently moving grass of the field to soft ocean waves.

I had always wanted to live by the sea. Since I had been a child, the call of the sea infected me, beckoning like a siren, but Ozzy was having none of it. I never had a career, having wasted university... but that's another story. I never had my 'own' money, not with Ozzy maintaining my place was in the home, caring for Gavin, doing needlework and cooking and croquet on the lawn – I'm kidding with the last one, but it gives you more idea of what kind of man he was. And, although cloistered, I had welcomed not having to go into the rat race I saw other people stuck in.

My husband's passing had given me freedom from his martinet ways, but no sense of peace. I often wondered if it was best to go quick like that, or to know you have time so you can say goodbye properly, to reflect on the good times—for there had been some—and to apologise for all the things that went wrong, find a feeling of settlement, especially over Gavin—

"Hullo there!" called a cheery voice, and I jumped and turned. A slim, elderly gentleman, wearing a fedora and an overcoat despite the warmth of the day, leaned on a silver topped walking stick, smiling at me from a good-looking neatly grey-bearded face. "Wonderful day, isn't it?" he said chirpily. "Nice views up here." He drew in an exaggerated breath. "Good air, too."

"Hello," I said, tentatively smiling back, morose thoughts slipping away. "The view is nice, but the air? Well, some days when they're cleaning out the barns the air has a real heavy 'country' pong to it."

He pulled a big smile; extended a hand. "Sanderson, major, retired. Pleased to make your acquaintance, Mrs…?"

As I gave his hand the briefest of shakes, a worried little voice asked, 'Where did he pop up from?'

I know a lot of people in this village, though one doesn't get to see many. Working parents, pensioners off doing Pilates and book clubs, none of it my scene, 'But you don't know everyone!' my suddenly panicked stupid brain yelled. 'He could be one of the BBGs—the big bad guys—
missing their money, checking up on you.'

I told my imagination to shut up. This man might simply be new to the area, and there I was, putting him in court with the bad guys, and yet…

"Molly," I said, not offering a surname. "I haven't seen you around before, Major. You new to the village?"

"Molly. Then you must call me Richard," he said, beaming again. "And I live over there, in Highnam." He pointed the stick in the general direction of that village over the Leadon valley. "I managed to get one of the older buildings with some residual charm. Even got a wine cellar and a functional well, would you believe. I generally walk in Highnam woods but today I decided I would like a change, so came up here."

A buzzard screamed high above us. They breed here; I've seen their nest, like a dinghy made of sticks. We both looked up at the raptor wheeling above the woods. "Have you seen the red kites?" Richard asked. "There's a new pair over Highnam woods."

"Oh, yes," I replied keenly. "I've seen a pair here, too, though could be the same ones considering the closeness. I *do* enjoy bird-watching. You too?"

"Indeed I do. Flocks of long-tailed tits bringing their broods to the feeders at the moment. Looks like it's been a good year for them."

"Yes, and the swallows' babies are up and squealing in the centre of the village." I was smiling too. Bird watching is a simple pleasure and the idea of shared enthusiasm was relaxing me in his company.

But abruptly he looked at his watch and went, "Aha, I'm out of time. You'll have to excuse me, Molly—business calls." He lifted his fedora in a polite old-fashioned farewell, grinned endearingly and said, "Until next time, my dear." Before I'd even got my *goodbye* out he had marched off down the path, walking stick click-clicking on the stones, and the last I saw of him he was withdrawing a mobile phone from his pocket.

'I am going to have to stop associating everything with that money,' I said to myself. 'There is no reason whatsoever that lovely man had anything to do with it. Just a nice man, out for a walk. Dapper, responsible, respectable.' I hoped we'd meet again. I wanted him to be a nice man I could talk to, walk with, and laugh with. I realised with a sudden pang how lonely I was. The conversation with Richard was the longest I'd had with a human in maybe a week. Age does not diminish your desire for good male company, and I don't mean intimacy, just yin and yang, people complementing each other. It had been just over a year since Ozzy had become not alive. Maybe it was time for me to make another effort to fit in with society.

Until next time.

I had liked that idea.

I walked home over the top of the hill, past the ridge cottages, then down the Old Road's steep slope, past the silent chapel and onwards to the not so silent new school. The playground bubbled with children, happy screams and shouts and laughter reminding me of what I had once had, and lost, and what I can never have again.

Some days I feel I am doing nothing but waiting for the end. The end of my story, of me, of the bad things that torment my mind when I am sitting at home, so I walked slowly, using any excuse to dally and make the walk longer. 'Check the ripeness of the elderberries. Might make some cordial this year. Let's see how the sweet chestnuts are coming along in the field down the bottom. Be nice to have a few for Christmas. So much tastier than those in the shops.'

Upon reaching my cottage, I was met with a piteous meowing. Perched high in the wisteria that half covers the building, Misty was claiming she couldn't get down. I wasn't surprised. She's getting on a bit now, still kittenish in some ways, but at ten years a cat is no longer young. I got her for company when Gavin—

Oh well, she was one of the few things that Ozzy approved of.

As I went to give her moral support, my eye caught a flash of dark blue in the back garden, someone shooting out of view, clothing flapping? A crow flying off? Not a person, surely?

"Oh, so is that why you're up the vine?" I asked Misty. "Did someone scare you?" Misty scrambled herself down and ran off. 'Tea and biscuits,' I thought as I opened the front door. What could be more cheering than Garibaldi and—

I froze in horror.

My house had been ransacked.

3. Custard Screams

My poor cottage!

Everything was everywhere. Drawers had been emptied, letters and newspapers scattered over the floor like patches of snow, the good cutlery spread around making strange silver graffiti on the rugs. Ornaments sat askew on the shelves and the china in the glass-fronted cabinet sat all lopsided. The settee and armchairs had been pulled out, cushions up-ended, while my precious books lay like dead birds with wings spread on the floor. Nothing but mess could be seen, all the cupboard doors swinging wide; a scene of chaos.

I had a strong suspicion of what they had been looking for.

'No, it's simply a random burglary,' I said to myself, digging under where I could see the phone cable like a snake hiding.

After I had called the police, I tucked the now-dry Mercedes back into the garage while thanking my stars no one had stolen *that*, made myself a cup of tea, then sat in the front room while I waited for the police to arrive. I took the brandy with me, for courage, and the sherry in case the brandy ran out, and I ate through a packet of bourbon biscuits I'd tucked away for visitors because, oddly, the biscuit barrel had also been burgled and all the Garibaldi and custard creams were gone. I'd been invaded by a biccy-scoffing burglar. I wanted to go upstairs to see what might be left of my jewellery, but I didn't want to—what's the expression?—*compromise* the crime scene.

The police turned up eventually, one Sergeant Williams along with a female forensics officer, and by that time I was a wee bit woozy. I'd taken what was left of the sedatives I had been given after Gavin's disappearance. They were well out of date and, in retrospect, maybe not the best things to mix with the alcohol, but they helped me feel calmer.

The police took photos and looked for fingerprints. No one had actually *broken* in. All access points to the house were still locked.

"Does anyone else have a key?" the Sergeant asked.

I shook my head. "No, no one."

"Not a cleaner, a handyman, a gentleman friend?" (I laughed at the way he put it. I suppose I am too old for a 'boy' friend). "Not an ex partner?"

"No one," I said again firmly, feeling I was not being taken seriously.

To my shame, it turned out I had left the tiny larder window open. And somebody who would have to be thin as a catwalk model had squeezed through it, leaving dirty boot marks on the inside frame.

"What did they take, Mrs Turner?"

I had no idea. I wobbled up the stairs to look. My jewellery, some of it gold—Ozzy's apology gifts had often been lavish—was still there in the dressing table drawer, and that made me think again about that money. That had to be what they'd been looking for if they'd turned their noses up at easy things like gold necklaces, and an expensive car on the driveway whose keys were hanging just inside the front door.

So I drew up my bottle-courage as the young policeman and I sat each side of the dining table and I began to explain what I thought was happening. The trouble was, you could tell from his frown that he thought the lady in front of him was crazy. It was quite likely the alcohol on my breath convinced him, not to mention the array of well-sampled bottles on the sideboard. Notes were taken, but eyebrows lifted. "You did right to leave the bag there," he said in a measured tone.

"Of course I was right, I'm a frightfully honest woman, but the point is they think I didn't leave it. They think I took it and it's here. The BBGs, I call them—the big bad guys."

As he looked at me as though I were mad, the

policewoman came in and handed him a note.

He looked up at me with a bigger frown. "The car in your garage, Mrs Turner; you are aware it's showing signs of being in an accident?"

"I…" My thoughts went fuzzy at the change of topic, the strange accusation, the nerves I was feeling. "I thought… I thought I got you here for a burglary. Can we concentrate on that?" I felt my face flush and took off my cardigan to try to cool down.

"I see no evidence of an actual *break*-in, and although the place is a royal mess, you admit nothing's been *taken* except biscuits." He glanced at the bottles. "Are you sure of your facts? Magically vanishing burger bags stuffed with money, mysterious bearded men accosting you, a distinguished looking man chatting you—"

"I never said he chatted me up. I said we chatted. Listen, I'm not making it up."

He sighed. His expression seemed to be blatant mistrust, mixed with old-lady-wasting-my-time fed up-ness. "Why didn't you call when you found the bag?"

"Because the bearded man—"

"So now there's a man with a beard too?"

"I did say that, didn't I?"

He scanned his notes. "No." He looked up. "You'd better start from the beginning again."

I was sure I *had* mentioned the man and that the policeman was double checking on my perceived notion of the truth, so I calmly repeated everything as he made more notes and nodded to himself.

"All right, so back to your vehicle," he said. "Can you explain the damage to the nearside front panel? There was a collision in Corsend Road earlier this morning, and the car fits —"

"Don't be ridiculous!" I declared, getting redder as matters cascaded even more out of hand. "I cleaned it off just today, and it was fine. I don't know why there's a dent in it, but it couldn't be from me driving it drunk."

"You were driving it drunk?" he asked in surprise.

"No!" I took a deep breath and said slowly. "I just assumed that was what you'd been thinking."

He scowled and wrote in his notes again. Probably something like 'old lady is now being snarky'.

I must have been so red by then that I could have been used as a stop light. "I don't ever drive it far. It's a kind of safety feature – a watchdog, so no one will rob the house if there's a car in evidence."

"But you say they *did* invade your house with the car there?"

"Yes, no, it was on the driveway this morning. I put it back in the garage before you came."

"And you didn't see the damage?"

"I didn't go round that side. I reversed it in. I always do. Ozzy—my deceased husband—used to say 'always park for a quick getaway'."

"Getaway? From what?"

"Not *literally,* for heaven's sake. It was just this 'thing' he'd say… " Between the alcohol rubbing my system up the wrong way and the policeman's disbelieving stare I was getting panicky.

"Listen," I said, leaning forwards over the table, trying for sympathy. "Everything I touch turns to trouble lately. My friends don't want to talk to me because I'm so miserable, even the vicar's avoiding my phone calls, and now you won't believe anything I say! I can't stand this. I am an honest woman! Stop making me feel like I'm not."

"Now, now," he said. "We do have counsellors, you know. Shall I arrange one for you?"

I shook my head as the young policewoman came back in. "The driver was ID'd male," she said to the sergeant and swept out again.

"Oh no!" I declared, full of sudden realisation. "*They* did it. Just something else to make me uncomfortable. They—the

BBGs. They must've got the keys out of the house, taken it off the drive this morning while I was walking, crashed it and put it back."

"Uhhh... Not too likely, is it, Ma'am? But you're off the hook if the driver was male."

I was mashing my hands together, my head ached and I sweated none too sweetly. *Was* this all connected with the money? I wished I *did* have it. I'd have given it back in an instant if they were going to frame me for things.

I heard mewling.

"I've got to let my cat in," I said, half rising as the policeman asked, "How many cats do you have?" and his gaze was on Misty, curled up on a nearby chair.

"I thought I heard her at the door," I mumbled, scaring myself with my confusion. "Look, I think you should just go and I'll have a lie down and stop worrying, all right? I do appreciate your coming. Long live the good old English bobby, eh?" I gave a wan smile.

"Anywhere you could stay for a while, Mrs Turner?"

"*Ms*," I said. "*Ms* Turner. I have nothing to hide. I'll stay and sort out, see if anything important's missing."

"And, just to be on the safe side, maybe consider getting your locks changed?" He raised his eyebrows, making it a request more than a suggestion.

I was left in peace to tidy up. They said they'd check in on me later. I suspected it more likely they'd send the social services to certify me, but no one turned up at all.

Now, whether or not Richard the dashing major was involved in all the oddness was anyone's guess, but, realistically, at the speed I walk, I reckon it would have been possible for him to arrange the ransacking of my house, and short theft of car, in the time it took me to walk all the way back. Hadn't I seen him reaching for his mobile the moment he'd left me on the hill? Hadn't I caught sight of someone fleeing the garden as I returned? They'd likely gone through the hedge, over the fence, into the field and run away. That's the trouble with having your nearest neighbour a field away. I could be murdered in my bed (nasty thought) and no one would hear me scream.

How did they know where I lived? I was pretty sure I could have been shadowed by the Micra the day before and not noticed it. Or someone could have asked at the Post Office: Who's that lady who picks up the litter?

However they'd found out, it had happened.

I called the workshop that usually did the car's repairs but they didn't have a space that week, so I booked it in for the next.

I called my car's insurers and asked what I should do about the accident I had not caused. They needed a police report. So there was something else to sort out. Wasn't it Shakespeare who had said, 'When sorrows come, they come not single spies but in battalions'? How right he was.

As the cold evening closed in, Misty came though the cat flap and nestled on me. But she didn't settle, wandering meowing, which is not like her. She was spooked, I reckoned. I almost fell over her as she slunk around the room, doubtless sniffing strange scents of BBGs and police-people.

After baking a batch of cookies to un-spook myself, I settled down to eat said cookies and watch TV, but after all the excitement and the booze, I promptly fell asleep in the chair.

At 02:15, according to the digital clock by the flickering TV, I was woken by a slight noise, and something in the TV-lit room moved. The good thing about wearing glasses is that it's hard to tell in half-light if someone has their eyes open or closed, so I peered around covertly.

A large shape was in the room with me. I couldn't recall for the life of me if I had locked the back door after coming in from the garden, so I was sure I had another burglar. He moved silently around. I faked a snore, trying to stay calm, to not gasp for air. He stopped, then I felt him pass by the back of the chair, go out to the kitchen, then I heard the faint clicks of the back door opening and shutting.

After a moment I got up and hurried to lock the door, heart thumping, wondering what was going on in my life. But the door was already locked and, through its glass panel, I could see in the garden, out by the flower border and outlined by the solar lights of its edge, a figure stood silent and still, just a blackness, no features discernible, though my prickling senses guessed from its mass that it was the driver of the Micra. And he had the ability to get in and out of my house! The key, which I always leave in the door, must have been copied during the first 'visit'.

'Yes, Mr Policeman, I do need to change the locks.'

I went back to the kitchen and leaned heavily on the work top as I recovered from seeing him.

Then I noticed the custard creams.

A new double pack of custard creams had been placed by the biscuit barrel. As an apology—or as a warning that they could get in any time they wanted—I did not know.

4. Plants Bite

It was early morning on that sunny day called Friday, 7th September, and I was well into the tidying of my violated house, trying to view it as a sort of late summer spring-clean. The door knocker sounded a sharp *rat tat tat* and I answered it to find Richard on the doorstep.

My heart jumped. It was surprisingly nice to see him again.

He took off his fedora as if it were a funeral and said sombrely, "Heard you'd had a spot of bother. Thought I'd come see how you were."

"That's very nice of you, Richard." My heart warmed to him. "Who told you? Is it all over the village already? I hope everyone battens their hatches."

"Indeed," he said. "The coal man said this morning as he delivered: 'Heard that Molly Turner's house got done over yesterday,' he said. He sounded obnoxiously cheered by it. Some fresh gossip to impart, I imagine."

I managed a wry smile. "They couldn't find anything decent to take, from the look of it, or my cat saw them off— she's part Rottweiler."

He laughed.

"Jack-the-coal tell you my address too?" I asked.

He gave a beautifully cheeky smile. "Couldn't resist asking."

I smiled back, though I doubt my smile was as breath-taking as his. "So, coming in for a cuppa, Richard?"

He came in, sharp, intelligent blue eyes looking all over, parked his silver-topped cane in the umbrella stand and sank gracefully into the comfy chintz-covered chair. I made up a tea tray using the new custard creams, buzzing around the kitchen, humming.

"I like that," he said.

"What's that?" I called.

"Reminds me of my late wife," he said, appearing in the doorway. "She would always hum in the kitchen. She liked musicals." Then he added strangely, "Every part of them."

"When did she leave us?" I asked, thinking how a poor lonely widower and equally lonely widow might, just might, make something quite nice together.

"Some time ago." He pursed his lips and looked sad and thoughtful, as though wondering whether or not to tell the story. I decided not to ask but he went on, "She went to London to see Les Mis, never returned, and then I found she had run off with an actor so I divorced her."

I coughed a laugh, not sure if the information was sad or funny. "Oh... I thought you meant she was deceased."

"She is. The rapscallion she favoured over me murdered her with a stage prop."

I stared a moment before gulping, "That's awful."

He gave a lopsided smile. "I call it poetic justice, my dear. Now, where's that tea at?"

"I've only got custard creams," I said hurriedly. "There were bourbons but I ate them all. Had a nervous nibbling session yesterday. That's hardly surprising given the circumstances, is it?"

"Just as well I'm watching my figure then, or I would be offended."

He laughed; I laughed. I wanted to like Major Sanderson, retired. He took his seat again as I brought the tray through and Misty jumped onto his lap.

"Scoot!" I said, reaching for her.

"No, no, it's fine," Richard replied, stroking Misty who purred her approval. I could have purred mine too.

But suddenly the cat sat back and hissed and grabbed at his sleeve with teeth and claws and I had to pull her off. Something flickered deep in the major's eyes. I'd swear another person glimmered in there, sending a tingle of fear into me for whoever I was opening my house to, and maybe my heart too. I should have listened to my senses, but I told myself not to be silly—anyone reacts badly when a cat decides to maul them.

I suppose we ended up telling each other our life stories over tea and biscuits, and what adventures he had experienced! I was enthralled, fascinated, really feeling the atmosphere from this man.

We got to talking about the Mercedes and its delayed repairs, and he instantly phoned a garage who agreed to come and get the car that very afternoon.

"I hold sway in some places," he said. "It's all in the manner. Act grand and they will treat you accordingly."

Almost two hours later, after cancelling the appointment at the regular garage, I watched the Mercedes being driven up the ramps of a breakdown truck by a young man still in his teens, while I chewed my fingers, nervous of his driving, and waved goodbye as the truck turned out of the lane.

"They'll take good care of it," Richard said, sensing my nerves. "Expensive cars make for expensive mistakes. They are very good with my Audi, though your Mercedes's worth two of mine, I'd say."

Back indoors, he looked out of the kitchen window at the garden's colourful sprawl and said, "I have to take leave of you now, Molly, but I hear there's a sale at Munchkins garden centre. And I hear they make excellent cream teas," he added with a twinkle in his eye. "Would you like to go tomorrow, social calendar permitting? Ten hundred hours good for you; for pick up?"

"Is this a date?" I joked, although my mind said, 'Please, let it be'.

"Definitely an assignation," he said. Then he took my hand and kissed it lightly. I drew away instinctively, hoping he didn't think me rude, but I was still touching it as he left.

~

In the night, the BBGs decided to empty my shed. They didn't make much noise as everything was carried out and

21

lain upon the lawn bit by bit—mower, strimmer, Ozzy's tubs of random screws and nails, the tool box, the old easel... everything. I stared at it all spread out, bedecked with dew, and tried to tell myself it was yet another sorting thing, something I would enjoy. I wasn't going to let myself get upset, I would turn the negative into a positive, and this time I wouldn't bother to tell the police.

So I spent a peaceful Saturday morning putting it all back in again and finding a couple of things I had mislaid, so it did have its uses. It all proved to me that the BBG thought I had their money hidden somewhere, though I also had to wonder why they were shy of outright threatening me, *we'll chop up your cat if you don't tell us* sort of thing. But I was glad they weren't like that. I began to wonder if one of them was someone local that I would recognise and that was why they kept hidden. And gave me biscuits. Odd.

Richard appeared at the side gate. "Ah, there you are, Molly. I've been knocking on the front door. Thought you'd come to grief. You need to get a remote bell."

"Is it ten already?" I sighed. "Sorry, I quite like sorting things out; got carried away."

The padlock was broken but I latched it on anyway and hurried inside to tidy myself while Richard waited patiently. I was only ten minutes.

"I approve," he said heartily, looking me up and down. "I like a woman who doesn't fuss around and waste half a day getting ready—and yet still manages to look so lovely."

I think I blushed the same pink as the flowery top I had on over slacks.

On my driveway sat a two-seater Audi convertible, a sporty little blue thing, even more interesting than my Mercedes. I sat in the passenger seat like a princess with the wind in my hair as we set out on the short trip to the garden centre.

Let me say, it *should* have been short, but he decided to take a scenic route, and go rather fast too, whizzing down lanes with no respect for other cars. We were hooted at twice. Three times if you include the tractor that was so busily getting out of the way that he didn't have time to hoot.

"Do you always drive this fast?" I asked breathlessly, hanging on to the grab handle for dear life.

"Live life the way you want to, Molly. That's my philosophy. Take it by the delicate bits and throw it the way you want it to go."

"Into a hedge?" I asked as we cornered and caught some drift on the wheels. I gripped the grab handle with both hands.

"Scared?" he asked, laughing all over his face. And for a second I felt that same misgiving as I'd had when Misty mauled him.

"Not in the least," I replied cheerily. "It's rather exciting, but I must warn you I might need *two* cream teas after this."

He laughed loud and happy, and slowed the car as the garden centre came into sight.

It was a great day of plant admiring, plant buying and cream cake eating. We were going to go Dutch but he said no, emancipation had its place but this was a cream tea date and he was old school, so he paid.

So it *was* a date. I went quiet. 'Just enjoy what fate throws at you,' I thought, but realising how I had easily resisted the money fate had thrown at me. I really had all I needed by way of belongings, it was just my soul that needed food. If I were to become firm friends with Richard, life might finally be fun. At our ages, he surely couldn't expect anything from me but platonic friendship, right? 'If he isn't a BBG.' How I wished I could quell that blasted little voice.

'Why, if he is a BBG, would he go to all these lengths to find out info?' I asked myself. 'Or is he playing some twisted game with me? Or is he simply an attractive innocent man who seems to like your company, you daft old biddy?'

Back at the house, after unloading my new green treasures, and over a cup of coffee, he sat on the settee beside me and told me what a wonderful time he had had and dropped a spontaneous peck on my cheek. I pulled away quickly, his touch on my skin the usual flash of fire I felt at any physical contact. The bane of my life. I smiled to cover any perceived rudeness because I have become good at hiding my feelings about such things, of pushing down a certain memory so I can function. Richard smelled of some male lotion, spicy yet sweet, and I wondered what he would make of my 'terms of engagement' should we get really friendly. Then he ruined the moment by pulling a piece of paper from a pocket and handing it to me. "Almost forgot. The contact for my cleaner: Katarina. I thoroughly recommend her."

My eyes automatically shot around the room. He thought it was messy?

He saw my startled glance. "Don't be offended, my dear. I thought, with all the gallivanting we two are going to do, it would be nice to come back to a spotless house."

"Oh, thank you," I said, now in awe of his consideration, looking at what Katarina charged. Not bad if she did a good job. These old cottages could get very dusty.

"Are you alright?" he asked. "You've gone a bit pale. Too much excitement for one day?"

"Exciting day. Definitely. Thank you. See you later," I gabbled, and I felt afterwards that I had pushed him out of the door rather rudely.

Because, you see, my wretched imagination had suddenly decided that Katarina was going to be a spy in this slow dance of suspicion.

Since it was Saturday, I reasoned a house cleaner wouldn't be working, so I called the number on the paper. A young, pleasantly-accented voice answered. She'd been cleaning for the major for over a year, she said. He always paid on time and was a charming man who had said some very complimentary things about me.

After that comment, I had to take her on to find out more.

5. Tree Tentacles

The sun came out through the morning mists on Monday, a truly autumnal spectacle. Still curious about Richard, I went to the Post Office and the nice lady there checked on him with her computer. He'd been on the electoral roll in Highnam for three years, she said, so that made me feel better. It didn't seem too likely that he had popped up on the BBG network just to seduce me into revealing the location of a considerable amount of missing money, but something still bothered me.

I wandered back up the path to the woods and sat on a tree stump overlooking the fields and the 'sea'. With that money, if I'd taken it, I could have bought a house by the real rolling and noisy sea.

I sat a while and listened to bird song, and tried to imagine the traffic drone as the waves below me. It was so peaceful,

For some reason it suddenly came to me that I wasn't high enough to do the view justice, so I looked the trees up and down and contemplated climbing one to get a better view. I stepped carefully around a capped well. There are two that I know of, hidden in the undergrowth, safe enough to stand on but the idea of what is below that cap makes me feel ill. Still water and I are not friends. The sea, rolling and passionate, yes, but dark lake/pond/well water, no way.

So why shouldn't I climb a tree? None of us are getting any younger. Why not climb a tree if I felt like it? I had climbed many in my childhood. It was not like I was a novice. There was no one to see; to laugh at me, but my inner voice tutted, 'And no one to take you to hospital when you fall!'

I told the voice to shut up as I looked around again and spotted a likely candidate.

About six feet off the ground, I looked down and got vertigo. The thin branches hooked in my jacket and seemed to pull at me. I imagined they were either telling me off for my silliness or asking me to stay and play, and I didn't appreciate either idea. So there I was, in the woods, trying to conquer my own reactions sufficiently to get down again, all the while calling myself more names than Ozzy ever had.

The sudden murmur of male voices from the direction of the path was a relief and I shouted, to my chagrin, "Help!"

Two men appeared through the trees, staring at the spectacle of a lady in a tree, hugging it for dear life. The younger of the two, a tall, gingerish man in his fifties, put out an arm to the shorter, greying older man, asking him to stay back as he approached me.

'More spies?' asked my head. 'Get out of that mindset,' I complained to myself. 'You'll end up in a psychiatric institution with full blown paranoia at this rate. They are coming to rescue you. You got that, Molly? *Rescue* your silly old hide.'

"Hi," the ginger man said with an amused smile. "Nice up there, is it?"

"Hello." I smiled back uncertainly. "I think I did a silly thing. Chasing your youth at my age doesn't seem to work. Could you help me down, please?"

I got down with a bit of help then went back to the tree stump for my backpack, litter-picker and black bag. "I was out collecting rubbish," I explained, "when the strange urge to climb a tree overcame me and I foolishly succumbed. I don't know what I would have done if you hadn't come by to rescue me." I took a deep breath, thinking how lucky I was they'd come along. "Would you believe there's rubbish up here too? People are so useless, ruining nice places so pointlessly."

"I was just saying something like that to Dad," he replied. "Aye aye, there's a green bottle poking out the ferns over there. May I...?" He took the litter picker. "Hang on, Dad. Stay here," he said like he was talking to a dog. He nipped into the ferns and returned with a plastic abomination for which I opened the bag's maw.

"I think I could do this twenty-four seven," I said despondently, "and it'd never be ending."

There was something about Dad's demeanour that puzzled me. He was placid, childlike, smiling vacantly.

The younger man saw me looking. "Head injury," he said matter of factly.

"I'm so sorry," I muttered.

"Happens." He shrugged. "Just have to deal with what life throws you, eh?"

He wiped his hands on his jeans and held out a hand. "Callum Bushey," he said as we shook hands. "And Dad is Joe. We live down at Copsely Ridge. Been there a few years now. Seen you walking along the road sometimes, good soul that you are. All the rubbish you must've picked up in your time, you deserve a knighthood or whatever it is they do for ladies."

"Sainthood?" I suggested and laughed. "Molly Turner, patron saint of litter pickers."

We chatted for a few minutes, my infernal internal suspicions dying and drifting away on the wind. Joe was not acting, of that I was certain, and Callum was nice; not as nice as Richard, to be sure, but I felt easy in their company in a way I hadn't for several days. I told Callum where I lived and offered him cooking apples any time he was passing.

I put on my backpack, armed myself with picker and bag, and walked back along the path and along the Old Road with them, chatting cheerfully. Even Joe joined in now and then, although his comments sometimes didn't seem to be related to what was happening in the moment, but when we reached Copsely Ridge, a small cottage rather like mine but with a wonderful view over the Cheltenham valley, Joe suddenly got agitated.

"Is Myrna there?" he asked, his eyes flitting from Callum to me and back again, panic in his poise. "If it's Myrna, I'm not going in."

Callum put an arm around his father's shoulders and consoled him in a touching reversal of roles. "It's okay, Dad. Everything's fine."

I was invited in for a cup of tea. Joe was seated at a table with a kids' thick jigsaw box. Callum tipped out the pieces and Joe immediately began to sort it.

"He's improving," Callum said with a slightly rueful smile, "but they said it'd be a long process." He beckoned me into the next room, a kitchen diner, where he made a pot of tea and took a cup through for Joe, with cookies on the saucer, before we sat with ours.

"Myrna's my ex," he explained. "She pushed him down the stairs."

"No," I gasped. "How horrid."

"She said it was an accident, but she and Joe had had a few run-ins. He reckoned she was a hanger on; like, not pulling her weight financially, buying stuff we didn't need, jewellery for herself, dresses, furniture even. One day I came home and found men moving in a new suite and the old one wasn't six months old. I mean, I do like nice things, but that was a bit much. We argued. Dad came round, we argued more. Then Dad went up to the bathroom and she thundered up after him shouting rather nasty accusations, and then Dad came down ass over tip over the balustrade, smashing his head on the corner of the hearth, and Myrna's stood there with her hand on her mouth going, 'It was an accident, I swear!'"

"Hence the *ex*. I am so sorry."

He sighed. "Been two years now. To be honest, it's been very hard. I can hire carers if I want to go off on my own; work, shopping, whatever, but Joe gets upset if I'm gone too long. And the other reason I don't think it's an accident is because he gets so agitated if I even say her name and... I don't know how to explain this, but he's very *defensive*. I mean, he reacts badly to loud voices."

"It brings back bad memories when he hears raised voices, that sort of thing?"

"Yes," he said slowly. "Maybe. I don't know. I choose to look after him so it's my problem, but Myrna got off scot-free. That's what rankles with me." He took a big swig of tea and looked grim. "Yeah, the authorities actually believed it was an accident. Honestly? I hope she's on the other side of the planet now, because if I ever see her again I won't be responsible for what I do." He looked at me in alarm. "Oh good grief, Molly, I'm sorry. I didn't mean to burden you with all this."

I waved a hand. "Not a problem. It helps to talk about things."

'And your own problems?' I asked myself. No, I wasn't ready to chat about Gavin yet.

I made sure I said goodbye to Joe when I left, and he smiled at me and said, "Bye bye," pointing to the half-finished jigsaw.

"Well done," I said enthusiastically. He beamed.

Outside, the sky had greyed and drizzle begun. I released the folding umbrella from my backpack as Callum said, "That was nice of you, with Dad. People don't generally bother once they realise how he is."

"Pfft!" I said. "We live in a world where people can't even take their rubbish home. They likely regard him as more rubbish than person. They think things have to have a use; know what I mean? They can't exist just to be nice or pretty."

"Do you have children?" he asked. "I think you must be a great mum with an attitude like that."

He felt the answer in my hesitation.

"Sorry," he said. I just smiled a thin sad smile at him, feeling tears I had thought were all gone welling up as I fought not to spill all my unhappiness onto this poor man with the wrecked father.

So I just said, "Make the most of what we have, right? Could always be worse; so many things to be grateful for, if we look for them."

"You're right. It's just finding them that's the problem."

The rain blew off again and I plodded away along the

ridge road, remembering what my eternally optimistic father had always said: 'Life is just a series of slight inconveniences waiting for us to deal with them.'

Deal with them? How? Unbidden thoughts of an incensed Ozzy found their way to the light. The old argument; whose fault was it? Gavin's for drinking too much, Ozzy's for not even trying to help him, mine for not standing up for my son and getting him into some kind of programme? When Ozzy threw him out a part of me had died, and when he'd drowned we had spent a lot of time blaming each other.

Maybe all this current madness in my head was because I still hadn't accepted his nothing-ness. Ozzy had destroyed all the photos of Gavin after kicking him out, even the baby ones. So if I hadn't managed to save one, of him in his twenties, all grown up and beautiful the way a son is always beautiful to his mother even when she's adopted him, it would be like I had imagined his existence.

I keep the photo safe in a drawer. Maybe one day I will be able to face having it framed, hang it on the wall, or up on the shelf and smile at it as I pass. But that time has not yet come. He'd have been forty this summer. It's hard when your child has no grave to visit. You could almost imagine he was still alive somewhere, very quiet, very busy, just forgetting to call home.

6. Katarina's Talons

Low morning sunlight flared into my east-facing front room as I drew back the curtains. The fields across from the cottage were white with dew, the sky flawless as a blue baby's bum, the trees standing high and proud in their late summer finery.

I will admit, I walked into the kitchen hoping my particular brand of fairy had delivered some more custard creams, but there was nothing on the side except a purring calico cat who wanted feeding.

Sitting in my armchair while I munched on my breakfast muesli, I turned the TV on to political things, flicked to old and boring programmes, and turned it off, wondering if I *should* make the effort to drag my old hide into the technological wonder-world of computers and mobile phones, but I had managed thus far without them.

But some days I felt trapped. Yes, I had the car, but it wasn't much more than a handsome stone around my neck. Even the weekly shopping run was done via my bus pass— would you risk a Mercedes in a supermarket car park? No, I didn't think so. I had friends, but either I had avoided them after my bereavement, or they had avoided me, and now any encounter seemed off; awkward. Most days I didn't speak to a single soul, but I'm happy in my own company most of the time.

Anyway, when people said, 'How are you?' it had faded from being a sincere question into a meaningless token wording. They might as well just say, 'Hello', and walk on by. Those I had wanted to engage with always felt like they wanted to escape my conversation, and those who took the time to talk to me, I ran from in case they touched on something I did not want to talk about.

Once, I'd even overheard someone saying how they thought I was odd. In this age, I can be proud to be odd. It's got to beat ordinary.

In times past I suppose someone would have yelled *witch!* and got me out of the village that way. But I do them all an injustice. They have their lives, I have mine, invigorated only by walking around picking up rubbish, making myself feel useful and less lonely.

No wonder I was making a habit of talking to strange men.

~

At five to nine there was a knock at the door and I greeted the new cleaning lady, who looked like a teenager with black curly hair, too much eye make-up, gold hoop earrings the size of handcuffs and the longest red nails I had ever seen. Oh yes, she was gorgeous, but looked like she was going to a party more than a cleaning assignment. How could she clean with those talons? Even her clothes, that hugged her like a lover's grasp, seemed unsuitable for the tasks she was about to undertake. But who am I, Ms Tweed-and-scarf, to comment on fashion?

I paid Katarina in advance then explained how to not lock herself out with the dodgy Yale. I showed the spy, ahem... the cleaner... around and then went off for my walk. When she'd asked for a mobile number in case there was a problem, I again thought of getting a phone.

To my surprise, as I approached the old school, I saw several cars parked up along the roadside and a spread of people out in the field with metal detectors.

Obviously, metal detectors do not respond to polymer banknotes, but my immediate thought was they were being used to cover up the reason for the BBG's searching. I hoped they would find that horrid burger bag soon. I'd had enough worry from its absence.

'Imagine how you'd feel if you had actually had taken it,' I pointed out to myself as I made my way along the path on the other side of the road, ignoring the searchers. "Good luck," I whispered to the pixies of fate. "Let them find it so this is all over. I want to hear a hurrah, a eureka, or something," but no sound came that I heard.

I arrived home just in time to see the cleaner out. She had done a good job. Much though I love Misty, chasing cat fur was never my idea of fun. It gets everywhere. I agreed she could come the next week, same time, and off her ample hips sashayed down the lane to wherever she had parked.

As I turned from the front window, I saw something out of the French doors. A large shape like a hulking man seemed to loom by the shed, but I realised it was just the plastic sheet blown off the cloche, caught on the shed door swinging in the breeze. But the door's movement meant someone had opened it again. Although the padlock was broken, it had held when I pressed the catch in. Since it was now out, that had to mean someone was still looking around my place. Had it been Katarina?

~

It wasn't until the evening I realised I hadn't seen Misty since I'd let her out after breakfast. I looked into her favourite places, her trees and hidey holes in the garden and house. I called and rattled the treat bag and checked the shed, but I didn't find her.

'Cats go walkies,' I told myself. 'No need to worry. She'll come back when it's dark, calling for her treats, mooching around the settee, trying to trip me up.'

But, as it got darker, I took a torch to check the road, fearing the worst, full of the horrid sinking emptiness of having lost something else I'd wanted to keep close. And when I got back it was very dark, and I had not closed the kitchen curtains, and there in the back garden I saw a man again. I would swear to it. But I pulled the curtains across forcefully and scuttled into the front room to turn on the TV, loud as I could stand, to drown out my feelings.

I woke at one in the morning, then three, then five.

Each time I got up and checked for Misty, calling through the open kitchen window into the black of the garden, shaking her tempting bag of treats. She had never gone off this long before. At five I heard rustling and called out hopefully, "Misty?" only to hear with some fright a deep male voice say, "No."

More than alarmed, I slammed the window shut and hurried into the front room. I should call the police again. Or maybe I had imagined the voice. It was just the one word, after all. It could have been tree branches rubbing in the breeze. How silly would I seem? And if it was a person, they'd likely gone away when they'd realised their error in answering the question without thinking.

I realised it was possible to be totally useless and talk yourself out of any situation.

I didn't sleep after that, just lay awake, praying for the return of a cat, asking forgiveness for hating my dead husband, begging a pardon for not being there when my son had needed me most; you know, all the silliness in life you couldn't control and wish you had. After seventy-three years there are a lot of old miseries you have to push down to act normally.

I realised the days had rolled around to it being Wednesday again, already a whole week since I had found the bag. A busy week full of new things, new worries, old regrets.

So, when the door knocker sounded at about nine in the morning, I dragged on my dressing gown and answered the summons reluctantly and bleary eyed.

Richard stood there, but not my nice smiling Major Richard of the finely cut beard... no, here was a fierce-eyed Richard look-alike who pushed past me into the lounge before he span and demanded angrily, "Where are my diamonds?"

"*Where are my diamonds?*" Richard had repeated angrily.

"What?" I gasped, not understanding the awful look on my friend's face. "What do you mean, Richard?"

"You will refer to me as Major," he said coldly. "And you know perfectly well what's going on, old girl."

He stepped closer. I stepped back so my waist touched the dresser. I tried not to look scared. I had stood up to Ozzy. I could stand up to this peculiar man.

"We have searched *everywhere*," he said, "and there's no sign of the diamonds, so I know you must have them."

"The only diamonds I've got are in my engagement ring," I snapped.

"Oh… feisty, aren't we?"

"I've been let down by someone I thought liked me," I complained. "Of course I'm going to be angry. Perhaps you'd care to explain just what's going on?"

"The burger bag."

"There weren't any diamonds in *there*," I blurted before I caught myself.

"So, you finally admit it?"

I sighed with heavy acceptance of my idiocy. "I saw the bag; yes. I saw the wads of cash in it too, but I didn't touch the money so maybe there *were* diamonds underneath the wads, but I wouldn't know, and don't ask me where that blasted bag is because, when I saw what was in it, I dropped it back *exactly* where I had picked it up like hot coals."

He *hmmd*, watching my face closely, seeing the hand pressed to my wildly beating heart.

"Any danger of you having a heart attack?" he asked.

"No. Why? Do you want me to? Fall down and die? Let it do your dirty work for you?"

He laughed shortly. "No, Ms Turner, I am actually, despite myself, quite fond of you; of your spirit. I just want to know how far I can push you to tell me where my diamonds

are. If you had a heart attack, I'd never know, would I?"
He stepped closer still. Scrunched up against the dresser, the
drawer handle dug into my back.

"Go away," I said, "and leave me alone. I swear by all
that's holy I saw no diamonds in that bag. The beardy man—
the one who grabbed me and spilled the rubbish out of the bag.
He must've told you I didn't have anything."

"Ah, yes, him. The fat prat. The new help." He thought
for a moment. "What did you think of him?"

"In what way?"

"Was he thorough? Did he search *you*?"

"I... I don't like where this is going."

"His name's Huggy. I hear he likes to hug people. Hug
people really hard, until they can't breathe."

I shuddered. "So...? You're going to make him squeeze
me until I give you ...what? Lies? Because that's all they can be."

He nodded slowly, the soft blue eyes I had liked so much
becoming cold marbles that made me feel unwell. "I think we'd
best search your house and grounds *again,* Ms Turner. I can
face losing the cash—it can be recouped quickly enough—but
the diamonds?" He shook his head.

"Are you sure the diamonds were even in the bag to start
with? Maybe you've been double crossed by your own kind."

He looked down his nose at me for a second, and I could
tell he was considering my suggestion. "No," he said. "No, I'm
sure that's not the case. So, as I was saying before you so
rudely interrupted, I've already spread it around that you're
having some work done on the house, so the neighbours won't
be surprised by any comings and goings. Huggy will be your
house guest for a few days, to keep a constant eye on you. A
distant relative, perhaps?"

"Well, there are definitely trolls on my husband's side."

"We will take this house apart brick by brick—"

"But you've searched already, and the shed, and I bet
your 'cleaner' had a good nose around too."

He smiled wanly. "Katarina—"

"She *was* a blinking spy!"

"More than that. The lovely lady is my wife."

"Mail order, I assume," I snarked. "So why'd you go on a 'date' with me?"

He laughed. "Obviously, I thought you might let slip the truth of you and the bag. Come on, don't you watch spy movies?" He glanced out of the French doors. "I think we might dig the garden too, while we're at it."

"Oh, goody. Can you get the potatoes up?"

"Your humour is barely humorous."

"I've nothing to hide, Major. How about you dig the whole garden, just to make sure?"

"So they *are* in the garden?"

"Oh, good heavens," I cried in exasperation. "I keep saying, I haven't got the fecking things!"

His eyebrows went up. So did his cane in a threatening manner. "I had hoped you would see sense, Ms Molly, for I am a reasonable man and you are an honest woman, but if you need more encouragement, I can offer it." He waggled the cane.

I drew in a breath and said, one word at a time. "I. Don't. Have. Your. Diamonds."

The cane smashed down on the coffee table, denting the corner, sending a sliver flying off. I jumped and put my hands up before me.

"So it is to be the total house search," he sneered. "You stupid woman. You will regret it. I don't make a habit of beating women, but I could make an exception in your case if I don't get what I want. You understand?"

I nodded feebly, he moved away, but he stopped at the front door and looked back, his eyes travelling up and down the tatty towelling dressing-gown I wore. "If I were you, I would get something on; maybe a suit of armour, before Huggy gets here. And we have your cat."

That did it. "Threaten me if you have to, but not my cat, you horrible little man!" I raged, my fists bunched. "How could I have ever thought I liked you? Taking a defenceless, innocent cat, hostage? If you hurt her there'll be hell to pay even if I have to come back from hell to mete it out myself!" I wanted to thump the truth out of him, trembling so much my heart started hip-hopping.

But he simply frowned, shut his mouth on some comment, and left.

I dressed hastily. A thick woolly jumper and denim trousers were pulled on as my cloth armour, not knowing what to expect from the horribly named Huggy.

But when he arrived, walking through the front door as if he lived there, having used some manner of master key—I shouldn't have been surprised—he grunted something then went to the kitchen and helped himself from the biscuit barrel, turned back as an afterthought and took the whole barrel, then sat heavily on the settee, munching.

"Coffee," he said, not looking at me. "Two sugars, don't scrimp on the milk. Cream if y' got it."

"Yes, sir," I said as sarcastically as I dared. He didn't look up, so I risked a curtsey too, but he didn't care, leaning over to grab the remote off the coffee table and turning on the TV, flicking through to the sports channel and football. Oh my, that was going to be worse torture than having my house ripped apart.

"Do you know where my cat is?" I asked.

"Hmmm," was the absent-minded reply with eyes fixed on the TV, then he suddenly leapt up shouting "*Goal!*" as he punched an arm into the air. It shocked me so much I fell back against the dresser.

"You okay?" He looked down at me from his wide height then offered me a crumby hand.

"Get lost," I said as I refused his offer and struggled up. "I'm not having any catnapper touching me."

"I haven't napped yer moggy," he said, frowning offended and slumping back in the chair.

"And I haven't got those damned diamonds he's on about. People are assuming things left right and centre, aren't they. When's the demolition crew coming?"

"They're not gonna demolish your house. You know that, right?"

"You know what I mean. Can we go for a walk or something? I don't want to be here to see them mess it up."

He shrugged, looking morosely into the tin. "Any more biscuits?" he asked, and then, "Where's me coffee, woman?"

"You do not speak to me like that." I glared. "Maybe you should buy some more custard creams."

He blinked. "How'd you know it was me?"

"I guessed and you confirmed it. And is it you who's been lurking in my back garden? Trying to scare me? Well, you succeeded. Hope that thought makes you happy. Scaring old ladies indeed! Where *are* your mann—"

A knock called from the front door. I went to open it, dread in every fibre of my trembling body, my knees feeling like they might give way.

8. Sharp Needle

Callum and Joe stood on the doorstep. "Oh," I said, taking a moment to calm down from anticipative panic mode, thinking their timing was awful, "have you come for apples?"

Callum pulled an embarrassed face. "I'm after a favour. Could you look after Dad for a few hours? I could tell he really liked you yesterday. If it's not too much of an inconvenience, you know, 'cause this work's come up in town and it's too late to get another carer today. The new bloke walked in and completely forgot what I'd told him about tone and said *Come one, get your boots on, Joe,* in a voice like a flaming foghorn and Joe went haywire— Oh, gosh, sorry, didn't see you had a visitor."

"Just a relative," I said, hurriedly dismissive before Huggy could say anything. If I'd thought this through, I could have written a note, passed it to Callum... No, there was still the hostage Misty to consider. "Of course," I said brightly. "Joe's welcome. Is he triggered by bangs, though? I'm having some work done on the house today. Or did you mean for me to come to yours? I can't."

"I was going to say mine, but here's fine, and he's okay with bangs. I'm so grateful, Molly. I can't afford to lose this work. In you go, Dad." He pushed Joe into the house and made a quick getaway.

Joe stood just inside the door on the *Welcome* mat and looked around, blinking as though the light hurt his eyes. I didn't have any puzzles or games of any kind for him, so I was about to take him into the sunny garden to find something to amuse him when the door banged open onto the doorstop.

Ah yes, this time it *was* my 'builders' or 'disassemblers', or rollicking nutcases depending on how one felt about the situation. I moved Joe aside and the troupe of four solid young men in paint-spattered blue overalls, really looking the part, walked in without even saying hello and went straight into the dining room with forbidding-looking toolboxes at the ready. I eyed the big van sat outside my gate with Vanker's Building Works neatly emblazoned on the side and changed it to wankers in my disrespectful mind.

Then I realised who one of the youths was, and my heart sank. He was the same youngster who had driven my Mercedes onto the repair truck. So they had that too; poor old metal beastie. Was it also being ripped apart in the search for diamonds and cash?

I steered Joe into the garden, not wanting to know what was going on indoors, picking up the fat-ball bucket on the way and filling the bird feeders while Joe stood and watched and seemed to want to eat one too.

Huggy, appearing from the kitchen with a slurping great mug of coffee in his hands, set it down on a side table and moved to the chintz chair to watch both the TV, and us in the garden, and the lumpy, scraping, thumping song of furniture being shifted began. I hoped they didn't damage anything in the dining room. There were many pieces of Lladró china, collected over the years, and some exquisite Waterford crystal. But what could I do to protect it? I had never felt so vulnerable.

I forced myself into another gear. "Can you help pick the apples, Joe?" I got two baskets from the shed and handed him one, and soon had him putting the apples in it as I handed them down from my perch on the ladder.

Huggy came into the garden. "Who won?" I asked out of habitual politeness.

He took a rosy apple from Joe's basket, bit into it, chewed once then spat it out.

I tried not to laugh. "They're cookers, Huggy."

"Huggy!" cheered Joe, doubtless hearing the word *hug* as an invitation, dropping the basket and flinging his arms around the startled man, who pushed him away angrily. I saw a sudden dangerous spark in Joe's eyes and calmed it hastily with a delighted, "Well done, Joe! You're doing a really good job. There's more on the little tree over there."

As Joe walked to where I had pointed, I cornered Huggy and said, "Joe's got something wrong with him, so be nice, you hear? If you want to be useful go and pick some blackberries." I gave him a big old margarine tub and pointed at the brambles. He looked at the tub then the brambles with little recognition. I took him to the hedge. "Green berries bad," I said like I spoke to a child. "Red better, but black nice. Okay?"

He began to pick them.

Joe was now by the pond, poking at the fish with a cane from the runner beans' support. It appeared that between the first-time berry-picker Huggy, and Joe the fish tormentor, I had two children to educate.

"Where're you from, Huggy?" I asked when I'd managed to entice Joe back to apple picking.

"Nowhere," he replied.

"Is it a bad guy thing; that you don't talk about families?"

"Ain't got one," he replied as he popped a blackberry into his mouth and continued gathering them.

"I had a husband," I volunteered. "He died suddenly. I have no children. I do have a sister called Lottie but I lost track of her some years ago."

Lottie had hated Ozzy. Said he was bad; that she could sense it. Looking back, she'd had the right idea, but I had been young and foolish and thought myself in love, so I had shouted hateful things at her and sworn I'd never talk to her again. And now I had no idea where she was. Maybe, when all the weirdness was over, I would buy something that could access the power of the internet and see if she was—

"He's at it again." Huggy indicated Joe, pond-paddling in his socks.

As I grabbed Joe, sat him on the bench and stripped off his sodden socks, it reminded me of little Gavin and how I had been an awful mother, unable to help my child. And Ozzy had been a worse father.

"Why d'you bother with him?" Huggy asked, watching Joe with a sneering not-understanding as I rinsed the socks under the outside tap and draped them on the washing line.

"Why not?" I replied. "He's someone's dad. He's loved. Don't I have a duty to care for someone else's loved one when they're in my care?"

"Right," he said thoughtfully, then, after a second of gears whirring. "What food does cats like best?"

"My cat liked fishy food."

"K." He went off down the far end of the garden, got out his mobile, and I heard his low voice in a muffled way, but one of the words might have been *fishy*. I hoped that meant he did know something about Misty, and that she was okay.

I spent the rest of the morning with my two boys ... ha-ha. Huggy was pitifully keen to learn everything about the garden. You'd think he'd lived in a cave all his life. While the workmen investigated my rooms and seemed to be having a really good time, laughing as they turned my life inside out, Huggy, and even Joe, listened as I pointed out the edible berries in my wild hedges, and the inedible ones, and tasted and spat out the ones safe to try but better cooked.

I was wondering what to feed them for lunch when Callum returned and took Joe and his wet socks away with many thanks. Just outside the door, Joe called back, "Bye bye, Myrna. Rot in hell!" with a cheery wave which dampened any hopes of a future in child-minding.

"Got chips?" Huggy asked.

"Umm, are there any in the freezer? Do I have to feed the other lads too?"

"Nah." He waved a hand. "They'll be off to the pub in a tick." He stuck his head in the chest freezer and poked around. "Bit empty. Peas, sweetcorn, frozen sprouts... bleurgh. No chips." He straightened up. "Box of eggs on the side here."

"Okay, I'll do egg and chips. There's potatoes in the garden. Could you be a dear and dig up some for me?"

"Taters?" he queried as though it were a foreign word.

"Spuds? What? I asked for chips."

"Which are made from potatoes."

"No way!"

I stared at him, unable to believe such ignorance. "You want me to show you? Go dig up some of those half-dead plants in rows this side of the apple trees. I need three big potatoes, like your fist, and I will demonstrate the magic that is cooking."

"Great." He rubbed his hands together as I directed him to the fork in the shed.

As he dug for potato-gold, I glanced across to the small coven of plants waiting in the corner to be planted out—the plants I had bought from Munchkins while on a happy date with a man I had thought liked me. If I was a vindictive woman, I'd have chopped them up and fed them to the compost, but that's like hitting your children when your husband has abused you, just passing on the pain to no good end.

~

As the evening darkness crept over the garden, Huggy started to look at his watch repeatedly. The lads had stomped off and gone in their van just after four. Despite their short foray to the pub, they had eaten almost everything in my kitchen—except the Brussels sprouts—and I was hoping they'd bring their own food the next day.

"Are you my gaoler tomorrow too?" I asked Huggy as he sat on the settee where a dent showed every time he stood up. "If you are, could you do some grocery shopping before you get here? Otherwise we'll both starve. Much though I adore your company, when are you leaving? Or do you have to tuck me into bed and read me a story?"

He snorted. "Oh, very funny, Ms Tur—"

"Just call me Molly."

"Nah, too close-like. Ms T. How's about that?"

"All right, but what about tonight?"

"You tread careful tonight." He looked grave.

"Because?"

"'Cause I'm gonna go when Needle turns up and takes night shift."

"Needle?"

"That's what we call him. Needle, 'cause—" He caught himself. "Yeah, so he's the guy got through yer window. He's that thin, y'see."

"So he's not as nice as you are?" I asked.

"Bloody hell," he said, taken aback. "Don't let anyone hear you say that. 'Specially the major. You're supposed to be scared of me; scared I'll hurt you if you put a foot wrong. He tell you why they call me Huggy?"

"You like to hug people *hard*."

"Yeah, but I don't *like* it. I do what I'm told."

"So... so... oh my." I backed away, a sudden cold fear enveloping me. "Seriously, have you killed people by *squeezing* them?"

"Nah, Ms T, they just pass out, but it's right scary and it helps get them to talk, you know, if someone needs some info. I just got shoved down this backwater from London. Ain't hugged no one here yet. Don't even know me way around the place. Too many trees."

"But... you're not going to *hug* me, I hope?"

"I don't want to, but if the major asked I'd have to. Reckon he's not asking in case, like, you're fragile and you pop all over me Doc Marten's before you talk."

I raised my eyebrows. "So old age does have benefits."

"You do see, don't ya? I don't wanna hurt you."

"I find that reassuring."

"But if he asked and I didn't, he'd do me in, 'cause I wouldn't be useful no more. That cane of his, it's a swordstick, and I hear he's fond of using it. Nasty."

"I think you're all terrifying," I declared. "You're like a swarm of wasps sitting on me, and I'm just waiting for one of you to sting me."

A gap appeared in his beard as he chuckled. "I like you,

Ms T, and don't tell anyone *that*, neither."

"So, if you like me, please tell me where my cat is."

His smile fell. He had just opened his mouth to reply when, without warning, the front door opened and the most cadaverous man I had ever seen in my long life crept in like Gollum, mousey hair long and lank, eyes big and round and cold as a shark's.

"You! You keep out my way," the skeleton ordered me with a pointy finger like a Halloween hand. "I wanna watch the movies. Got Netflix? Prime? Sky?"

"No internet here," Huggy said, up from his settee-nest, backing away towards the door.

I vanished up the stairs. Now there really was something in the house that I instinctively feared.

9. Bloody Nails

I found the un-builders had been in my bedroom. Just a cursory inspection from the look of it, nothing particularly out of place, but I could tell. I checked on Gavin's photo nestling safely in the drawer. The jewellery seemed to be all there, too. Maybe that would change when they had given the place a complete search, like they had in the dining room where I was happy to see nothing had been broken but, as far as I could tell, a few pieces of china were missing. I doubted that complaint would get me anywhere. Besides, it might annoy the lads, and who knew what they were capable of when riled.

Maybe this wouldn't be so bad. Maybe, once the major had been convinced there was nothing of his in the house, they would go away and leave me alone.

Later, when I went down for a glass of water, Needle lay with his feet up on the settee, fast asleep, TV tuned to the horror channel muttering dire things to itself.

But as I went into the kitchen his grating voice called, "Tea, no sugar, milk, any cake you got, crisps, crackers."

"Huggy ate it all," I replied as I went back out with my glass of water. "Gaolers should provide their own food."

He was up and had a hand round my throat before I could say another word. I dropped the glass with a thunk on the rugs, the horrid depths of his eyes defeated me and I whimpered a not entirely fake whimper. He let go. "Behave your fucking self, you fat old broad."

'Well now,' I thought, not showing my contempt, 'this one's very practised at being a BBG.'

I grabbed some tea towels and swabbed the wet rug in silence, threw the cloths into the washing machine then stuck my nose in the air and went back to my bedroom with a fresh glass.

Sat in bed, reading a thriller with a heroine in a much more dire predicament than my own who was coping quite well, which made me feel better in a way, I tried to turn off the fear-switch inside me and relax. But the whole scenario was so exhausting it wasn't long before my eyelids drooped.

I woke to a hand squeezing my left breast through my nightie. I supposed it was Needle but I didn't wait to find out. I did what the heroine in the book had done; I screamed and flailed madly in the near dark with my fingers bunched so nails would scour skin. They contacted, Needle fell back swearing loudly then scarpered. I rummaged in the tall boy's top drawer for the internal door key and locked it, as common sense should have dictated to start with.

I trembled. Then I cried from the shock. I felt so totally vulnerable and alone. I knew almost everyone in the village, but just knowing someone doesn't make them a friend, and I didn't need all those people who gave me empty sympathies. I had brushed them all away—maybe because I didn't want to admit how little I had cared that Ozzy had gone, when I knew people who still mourned their spouses years after.

Even if I had dared to run, the BBGs still had Misty, and she was the creature I loved most in the world. I would tolerate all this chaos, put up with all they threw at me, so that one day I could get her back safely.

So I lay there in my no-longer-feeling-safe bed, and shuddered and cried great sobs of unfairness, wanting to wash off the feel of the cold invasive hand, resolving to get drinking water from the basin in the en-suite in future, even though it always tasted odd, and maybe setting up a little store of food in there too.

I didn't venture out of my bedroom the next day until the workmen, and Huggy with two bags of shopping, arrived at nine. I decided I would not even offer to pay for them, on principle.

And the presence that had been a scratched-face Needle flitted out of the front door like a spectre.

I got Huggy on his own and didn't waste any time in telling on Needle. He looked at me with his upper lip rising in disgust. "I'll tell the major. He don't like that sort of thing from the lads."

When I thanked him, it was from the bottom of my heart.

~

But, and I am sorry that this story is full of *buts,* but things lurched from worse to worse.

A short while later Huggy's phone rang and he answered it. His eyes danced to me and away. Then I heard one of the louts' phones ring too, and a premonition came over me as the atmosphere in the house changed.

"Huggy?" I asked. "What's going on?"

"Sorry," he muttered, and legged it as the louts swept in and grabbed me.

Yes, they grabbed me. Three sets of strong young smelly arms held me back into the comfy chair while the scrawny one with the mean thin face produced a small pair of scissors. He began to cut my nails, hacking at them as I struggled because they were hurting me, reducing my only weapons to not-nails, skimmed to the quick and bleeding.

"That'll teach you to mess up our mate," the cutter said as he stood up, and they all laughed while I suppressed tears and said, "I can see you're only a criminal because you'd make a lousy manicurist," and the cutter waved his hand at me in a *get lost* kind of way.

"Come on, Jimmy," the one who had a bushy ginger beard said as the cutter dallied then leaned over me, hands on the arms of the chair and said, "Remember this, old lady. You bite, we bite back harder." Then he went away and I could breathe again.

I got up shakily and went to track down Huggy.

He was leaning against the apple tree doing something with his phone and tried to run when he saw me.

"It's all right," I said. "It's only nails, they'll re-grow."

"You ain't mad at me?"

"Course not. I asked you to tell on him. I just didn't know the major—I suppose it was the major who gave the order—would react like that." I gave him a close-to-tears smile. "I had worse from my husband, if it's any comfort."

"Your old man hit you?"

I sniffed back a tear. "Not exactly."

Funny how what a man agrees to one minute, he is willing to change when it suits him. Ozzy made me certain promises. He signed the pre-nup on the dotted line, well aware of my no-touchee problem when we married. I had thought I'd found safe refuge, but he kept wanting to change the rules.

The house phone rang.

"Leave it," Huggy cautioned.

"Are you sure?" I asked. "It could be important. The car insurance, or urgent scammers telling me my non-existent computer has a virus."

He huffed and muttered, "You'll have to risk it Ms T."

But not half an hour later there was a knock on the front door and, when Huggy peered out stealthily through the curtains, it was a policeman. Silence had descended on the house. I imagined the louts holding their breaths.

"What do you want me to do?" I whispered.

"Get rid of him," Huggy said.

"Oh my, I hate to think what that means in your line of business."

"Quit with the flappy mouth," he snapped. "Just make excuses. Get him gone."

I took a deep breath, opened the door a crack, saw the policeman who had interviewed me, and gave my best smile. "Why, hellooo," I said in my most charming voice. "I'm *so* glad to see you again, Sergeant Williams. Or may I just call you Willy?" I leaned against the door jamb in what I hoped was an old lady seductive way, making sure my butchered nails were hidden. "I'm sure you'd love to come in and have a drink, wouldn't you? Plenty of fun to be had here, I can assure you."

"Umm, no thank you, Ms Turner," the policeman said, frowning, stepping back. "Just, you didn't answer your phone, so I was concerned."

"Gracious me!" I was genuinely surprised. "So you've come to check on little old me. How *lovely*, but I can assure you I'm fine." I pushed my chest out and looked him up and down. "Just *fine*." I smiled again.

"Um, good to hear," he said. "Go careful with that booze, Ms—"

"Please, dear, call me Molly." I winked.

Something like horror crossed his face as he hurriedly backed off, turning away as I stepped back onto the mat and shut the door, fumbled my way to the settee and took some big breaths of calming air.

"Don't you ever make me do that again," I complained as Huggy stepped in from the kitchen. "That was heart-attack-inducing scariness. Lying to the police? I am a disgrace to the British monarchy."

"That was fucking great!" Jim said from halfway down the stairs, the other lads smiling behind him. "I changed my mind about you, Moll." They all laughed and I went to the kitchen and out of the back door, into the damp garden, girding myself with boots and rubber gloves, ready to deal with mockery and the fear engendered in me from my little act with the policeman, by burying them metaphorically in the ground under the new plants.

I'd just finished planting up the shrubs when Jim ambled into the garden, swigging a can of beer. He glanced around then said something to me I didn't quite catch. When I asked him to repeat it he marched over, pushed my back to the apple tree and grabbed my—you know—that part of me through my trousers and I was instantly enveloped in panic mode and cried out and struggled while he muttered something about old pussies. Luckily, Huggy had heard my yells and came out like a shot and, to my amazement, punched Jim to the ground.

"You okay?" Huggy asked me.

I nodded and said, "Thank you, Huggy," and sat there at the base of the tree all folded in on myself as Jim got up holding a hand to his face and skulked away looking daggers at the pair of us.

Huggy followed me around the garden like a lost dog after that. I asked if he fancied mowing the lawn and a flicker of excitement came to his eyes, but he wasn't interested as soon as he found it wasn't a ride-on, and he was strangely quiet so I guessed he might be feeling a wee bit guilty over my nails.

"It's all right," I said to him. "Honestly, come on, be a chatterbox again. I need the talk to calm me."

I put a reassuring hand on his arm. Big mistake. The louts had been emerging for a break.

"Going clubbing t'night?" Jim was asking the chunky one.

"Yeah, that hot chick'll be there. The one you shagged in the toilets, right?"

"Quit dicking around."

Chunky sniggered. "Maybe it's you that should quit with the dick."

It was at this point he had glimpsed my hand leaving Huggy's arm. "Oh, here's our newbie, a fuckin' granny lover," he sneered. "Huggy loves granny dry snatch."

I felt Huggy tense beside me before he snarled, "Strikes me, the way he's been carrying on, s'more like Jimmy boy here what fancies her."

Jim laughed aloud, the others joined in with the laughing, but Jim's eyes went mean and feral and, when they rested on me, I had to turn my gaze away until the louts moved farther away, wrapped in their smoky aura.

"Are they right in the head?" I asked Huggy very quietly. "Are they always like that? Do they enjoy it? Is it the way they were raised or something?"

But Huggy strode off into the house, and the louts looked at me and made obscene gestures that made me all the more determined to stoically take whatever they sent my way; to not let them win on any front.

Of course, fate had other ideas about that.

I was trembling deep inside. I could feel it like a subtle vibration and I didn't like it reminding me of that time—the time I had locked away deep inside and only let Ozzy see. The time that had steered my life off the path of study and almost certain success into illness and depression and, eventually, into a marriage of more convenience than love.

"I need to get out of here," I muttered and went to find Huggy. I thought it was funny how I had to hunt for the man who was supposed to be keeping an eye on *me*. He was in the dining room, leafing through a book on nature. Maybe I had sparked something in him. I could see tadpole images on the open page.

"Hey, bookworm," I said, as cheerfully as I could muster. "Can we get out of the house for a walk?"

"Reckon." He shut the book with a clap and shoved it back in its gap on the shelf.

"Okay. Do you want to see some frogs?"

He looked up, eyes widening. "Real ones?"

"Yes. I don't imagine plastic ones would be very interesting, would they?"

But, after trudging across the field, we found the bit of land adjoining the river was very muddy; too muddy for our shoes. We went back home and I dug out Wellingtons from the shed, finding both mine and the ones with Ozzy's initials stamped on—O.M.

"Too big," he complained, shaking his booted foot. I braved the house to see if I had any socks his size and returned to find him looking rather guilty, putting back screwdrivers onto the wall rack as if he'd contemplated stealing them then changed his mind.

"You can have any of those tools," I said. "I never use the things. The socks too if you like, and the boots."

"Wouldn't mind borrowing a few bits and bobs, now you mention it," he said, pulling on the thick woollen hiker's socks

I had brought down. He dragged the boots on over them and grinned happily. "That'll do it, Ms T."

~

At the boggy borders of the River Leadon, I took him across to the rocky place where the frogs lived in the day, and we lifted stones carefully, finding frogs, toads, and some tiny newts hiding there. He was laughing like a little kid as a slinky newt trickled through his fingers.

Then he stood and said, "I really likes you, Ms T. I bet you were a great mum."

I gulped, bit the bullet, and in a few painful words explained how my drunken son had been lost to the river.

He went very quiet, his thoughtful gaze back over the river, looking as if he had a similar story to tell, but then he sighed, muttered, "I'm sorry, Ms T. Really I am." And that was all I had ever wanted anyone to say.

On the way back, by the big lonesome pine, we met one of farmer Brand's free range chickens who had mastered escapology. We managed to corner her and I showed Huggy how to hold her. She was used to being caught so didn't struggle, and he stroked her with a kind of fascination as she gave slow *chuurrs* of approval.

"Lovely," he said. "Feathers are right soft."

I stroked her too and the memories flooded back—Gavin and the chickens, and the ducklings, and the butterflies and the worms and all the other little things he had loved, and all the heartache rushed back to me, and I realised I was trying to replace him with this overweight BBG.

10. Marsh Thing

It was still light, so we walked to the pond and stopped to watch the wild ducks paddling.

Huggy leaned on the railings betwixt pond and road and said, "Shoulda brought bread for the ducks. They like that. Right?"

"The fish eat it more than the ducks." I pointed into the clear water where small fish had gathered, anticipating food from the world above.

"Stupid man," I said, thinking distractedly. Huggy frowned at me. "Not you, Huggy; that major. What does he think an old lady like me could do with his blasted diamonds?"

"Take 'em to a pawn shop."

"Seriously? Just like that?"

"That's what he does... I think. Where else d'you think he'd fence them? Buck Palace?"

"Well, I wouldn't know, would I?" I said tartly. "How big were they, anyway? What's all the fuss about?"

"I dunno," he said. "Weren't mine. Even tiddly ones are worth a bit if they're nice and clear."

"And how many were there?"

"Crap, Ms T, you're asking the wrong bloke. Not my thing; pretty rocks. Now, cold hard cash, that'd do me fine."

Don't let anyone tell you the countryside is a quiet place to live. Apart from the ruckus the ducks were making, there were rooks and jackdaws calling noisily overhead, there were several mowers working up the road, a hedge trimmer chattered, cars came by constantly, a light plane zoomed overhead, and over the other side of the field a small JCB chugged as it cleared out ditches in preparation for winter.

Then a big yellow combine rumbled past us, first the main machine then the header pulled by a tractor. Huggy looked on in awe as the massive machines trundled past us almost within touching distance. "I'd like to drive something that big," he enthused. "Looks cool!"

I couldn't think how to divert his 'career' in that direction. "Look it up on the Internet," I suggested. "If you don't look into things you'll never find a way of getting out from under the major's boot."

The combine vanished up the road. The small JCB in the field fell silent, the ducks settled their argument, the mowers stopped, and a black cat paced over the now quiet road and vanished into the hedge.

I sighed. "I wonder how my cat is."

Wordlessly, Huggy flicked on his mobile then handed it to me. A video was playing; a happy little calico cat being tickled by a laughing black lad.

A tear sprang to my eye. "She's okay! You could have told me *you* had her. I've been so worried. The major wouldn't hurt her, would he?"

He shrugged. "I weren't s'posed to tell you, and anything's possible with that 'un, but I'll try to keep her safe. George, me roommate there, he and me take turns looking after her. What's her name?"

"Misty."

"Like you? Ms T?"

"I never thought of it that way."

"Why're you a Ms anyway? You was married, right? Though you ain't got no ring on." He put the phone away.

"Went back to my maiden name when Ozzy died. Took off the ring because I didn't miss him. It seemed appropriate at the time—new leaf sort of thing.

"You weren't happy. What went wrong?"

My mouth twisted as I wanted to tell, to spill out the whole disastrously captive marriage, but I didn't want to tell Huggy. I shook my head.

"Look," he said, sounding apologetic, "it ain't gonna take too long, then he'll be satisfied you haven't got his stuff and you'll be left alone."

"Not bumped off because I know too much?"

"Doubt it."

We continued our walk, me wondering how much doubt there was in 'doubt it' and chatting about the merits of owning cats—if one could own a cat or if the cat owned you— eventually coming to the church and its graveyard.

I went to Ozzy's plain granite-chipped grave and looked down at it, considering how helpful he might have been in this situation. He was certainly good at shouting, wheedling, persuading.

Huggy looked down at the inscribed headstone, then said with a question in his voice, "Oswald Marshman?"

"Yes. My husband. I changed my name when he died. I didn't like the surname. Marshman—I ask you! Like a marshmallow, all sticky-sticky. Or a monster that comes out of the marsh all nasty oozy muddiness. Marsh Thing. It's the sort of surname that leads to kids being teased."

"Bad name, yeah," Huggy agreed.

"My son should have been buried here too."

"Where's he at then?"

"No one knows. The river goes to the sea, the sea goes to eternity. His body was never found." I hadn't wanted to say those words. Not those specific words: *never found.*

I glanced at him. Under the beard it was hard to tell how he felt, but he folded his hands in front of him for a moment as though giving reverence to the dead, then he said, "I'll give you a moment," and walked off a short distance, reaching for his phone.

I stood silent, thought of Ozzy, and tried to not think of Gavin while Huggy kept a respectful distance. Then he finished with the call and came back, motioned for me to follow, so I did.

Back in the house, it was instant mood reversion; Huggy back to watching TV and pressing buttons on his phone, while still wearing Ozzy's boots.

"They're comfy," he said to my questioning glance. "And you said I could keep them."

"Mud on the carpet?" I asked.

"Nah, look, you could eat yer dinner off 'em. Washed 'em under the outdoor tap while you was taking yours off."

I shrugged. What was a little mud compared to the dusty chaos of the rest of the house. I watched his thick fingers dance expertly across the tiny keyboard of the phone. "I don't get the attraction of those things," I said. "Waste of time."

"Wanna play a game?" he asked.

"What? No." I laughed. As if I did that kind of thing. Games on phones, ha!

"Look." He waved it at me. "All you gotta do is move the little yellow light to bust the coloured rocks. Easy, right? Bet you can't beat my score."

An hour later, I was sat hunched up beside him on the settee, still battling Rock-Popper, and had learnt so much from him I felt humbled.

We were learning from each other. Maybe replacing missing elements of each other's lives. If it wasn't for the sounds of people ripping my house apart for something they couldn't possibly find, I could have felt contentment in that time. I had also resolved to buy a mobile phone when it was all over.

~

A spicy-smoky smell wafted around the house. The lads were upstairs and I dared to go see what was happening as Huggy went to make coffee.

In the jumble bag in my wardrobe, the monsters had found a raunchy red and black bustier. It hadn't been mine. I'd found it when sorting out Ozzy's stuff. It had likely been purchased for one of his women, but now Jim was wearing it over his clothes and prancing around like a moron. An effect of smoking the weed I had smelled, I supposed, though, it being Jim, it might have been just the way he was hardwired.

I folded my arms and stared at him in disdain. "Suits

you. Brings out the red in your eyes."

"Oh darling," the stupid youth lisped. "I am sooo ashamed of myself. I have been a *very* naughty girl; you must spank me." He turned his chino-clad rump towards me and wiggled it as the lads roared with laughter.

"This is not funny," I said stonily.

"Yeah, it is!" They laughed and laughed more.

"This funny 'ere, then?" asked Jim. His hands dived into the top dressing table drawer, lifted my one and only photo of Gavin that sheltered there, and shook it at me.

"Give me that!" I ordered, grabbing for it.

He swept it away. "So who's this, Moll? Eh? Speak up. No shame in having a boyfriend, and you like *boys*, don't you?" And he tore it into four before I could do anything.

Incensed, I scrabbled for the pieces as he let them fall. Could I glue it together again? I clasped them to my chest and glared at Jim to voodoo him dead.

"Ooh, you done it now, Jimmy boy," ginger beard chortled. "Gran's gonna have a right paddy."

I stomped down the stairs, tears pricking my eyes, went into the back garden through the French doors and sat on the bench still holding the pieces of the picture like precious flakes of gold.

Huggy appeared a moment later, worry on his face. "Thought you'd done a runner. Don't scare me. He'd have my hide."

I rounded on him. "Seriously? You didn't hear what was happening upstairs? You could have stopped them, couldn't you? Just walked in and said *stop*?"

He looked seriously confused. "Well, yeah, but no. I couldn't do nothing. It don't work like that. It's a higher-archy."

"Hierarchy! Honestly, sometimes I don't think people even try to better themselves." He looked pained and then angry.

"All right," I conceded. "I know there'd be no point complaining to Major Nitwit. Not that I imagine he's a *real* major, not really. With him being all highfalutin and posh and pretending every day. How can you do it? Do what a man like that says?"

"Don't shout at me." He glowered.

"My one and only picture of Gavin, my darling son, was torn up in front of me."

"But I didn't do it, you mad old bat, so calm down."

"And who's brought in weed?" I demanded. "I know that smell from times past. I don't want that in the house, the beer and cigarette stench is bad enough. Tell them to get their fingers out, quit messing around and get a move on."

"They wouldn't listen to me, that's what I'm telling you. Be grateful they're not doing heroin in the closet. Come on, Ms T, get yer boots on and we'll go down the river again. I know you like that."

I stared at him then put the pieces of Gavin's photo carefully into my handbag.

"Consideration at last, Huggy." I managed a slight smile. "There might be hope for you yet."

But a storm came on, so we sat in the Micra and played on the phone, and peace descended on me for a vague measure of time before the lads left and we managed to find food in the house and watch TV while gluing the photo back together.

"Ere, I know that bloke," Huggy said unexpectedly.

"My Gavin? How?"

He lifted the resurrected photo and peered closely. "Yeah, that's the bloke. The woman called him Rocky."

I felt my heart do a funny flutter of remembrance at the pet name. "Yes, he did call himself Rocky when he was a boy," I said as disbelieving excitement rose in me like the edge of a tsunami. "He had fancies of becoming a boxer, you see. Where'd you meet him?"

"Didn't meet him. At a pub in Bristol last summer—"

"No... you must be mistaken." I could have cried. "He passed nearly ten years ago."

Huggy stared at the picture, his face twisting as he

thought hard. "Nah, Ms T. It was him. That's my gift: I'm good with faces."

"But, Huggy, I told you he fell in the river and his body—"

"Was never found," Huggy jumped in. "And no body means he might not be dead. Listen, we was in the pub, the Battleship Royale just off the Bermin Road, and suddenly there's female-type whiny shouting and this woman is laying into her bloke, saying *that's your trouble Rocky Smith, you don't think,* and I saw her all blonde and pretty and him, this bloke here, all cross he jumps up and passes right by me, like, but—"

"Don't! Please, no more. It can't have been him."

A chaos of mixed ideas enveloped my brain: alive or dead, pubbing in Bristol or drowned? Rocky *Smith*? What was going on?

"But, but... *Why* would he do that? Not come home. Not contact me?"

"I don't go home 'cause me old man would kill me."

"Ozzy disowned him, which is extra tough when you've been adopted, I imagine, but I loved him and surely he loved me too. How can I ever find out the truth? The not-knowing is the worst. Afterwards—because this horror has to end eventually—I'll get on that Internet and investigate Rocky Smith for myself. Just how many men are called Rocky anyway?"

Huggy had searched on his phone. "Bad news." He showed me the scrolling list of Rocky Smiths. "All this lot's from a social network site."

I sat back in the chair. I had to accept I might never know, but for a few happy minutes I had thought finding Gavin might be the one good thing to come out of the chaos.

11. Fire Demon

The next morning brought more to worry about. No surprise there.

After the disgusting Needle had left and the un-builders had sloped in, Huggy paused on my front doorstep as though he didn't want to come in, and when I looked at him I gasped. His face was bruised, one eye puffy, cheek cut—the face that had lost the fight.

He only glanced at me, his face grim yet his eyes beckoning, before stepping back into the front garden. I went out too, leaving Jim and one lad wrenching my TV unit off the wall, while the other two found something else to rattle about upstairs.

I sat beside Huggy on the bench, reaching to turn his face to examine it, but he pushed my hands away. "Quit fussing, woman."

"Oh god, Huggy, you can't expect me to not be concerned. Who did this?"

He hesitated but couldn't stop his eyes flicking housewards, so I guessed. "Jim. Because you hit him, right? Because of me."

He put his hands together and leaned forwards but didn't reply.

"So it's my fault," I said. "Sorry."

"Nah..." He sighed heavily. "It's okay, Ms T. Chicks dig scars, bruises, missing teeth. This ain't nothing. Been stabbed before. Had a week in wiv the nurses."

"How gruesome. I think I'd prefer not to know your history after all."

I felt guilty. He'd been defending me and now his face looked like it had gone a few rounds with Tyson.

"Got summit for you," he said.

"Garibaldi? Custard creams?"

His meaty hand swam into my vision and offered me a phone. "For you."

"What?"

"I gone and got you a phone, so we can play Rock-Popper together." He looked very pleased with himself.

"I suppose you want payment for it?" I asked, heading inside for my purse. The food he'd bought had been a necessity, but the phone would reasonably cost a bit. But—surprise surprise—in the handbag hung on the coat peg, my purse was devoid of cash, the bank cards missing.

What do you expect when your house is full of thieves?

I extended the handbag's shoulder strap and wrapped it tightly around me. No way was I ever letting it out of my sight again.

"Never mind," Huggy said when I told him.

"*Never mind?*" I echoed, full of righteous anger.

"I mean, you can keep the phone, no charge."

"So kind," I growled. "Where'd it come from?"

He shrugged and I sighed. "Suppose I'd better cancel my cards before the monsters bankrupt me. No doubt they have ways of getting round the PIN codes. Permission to call the bank, sir?"

He harrumphed; I went indoors to call the bank on the house phone and wailed about losing my cards.

I did manage *not* to say they were in the wallets of some rogues in my bedroom. It would have made me sound like some kind of prostitute.

That done, I went back out to the bench and scrolled through the phone Huggy had handed me and found photos of unrecognised smiling children. "So you had the nerve to want money for a phone you'd nicked?" I exclaimed. "Just when I think you're half decent you pull this stunt?"

He shrugged, offended. "Leopards and spots. It's a good phone, Ms T, but it ain't really a phone no more. I took out the SIM so you can't call anyone on it, not even emergency."

"A phone that doesn't phone; how useful."

"I put the games on it for you."

"You went out of your way to steal some poor soul's phone just so I could play games with you?"

"Thought you'd like it," he sulked.

I stomped out to the driveway with Huggy hurriedly following me and eyed the evil Micra. "Give me the keys," I demanded.

"Nah," Huggy said indignantly, frowning. "I ain't giving you my keys."

"You stole a phone for me to play with," I said in a low hiss. "And I'm sure it ruined someone's day. Now you don't want me to steal your car. You see what it feels like? And someone stole my car and bumped it, didn't they?"

"Weren't me, and no one drives my baby but me," he said, patting the bonnet. "But I'll take you for a run if you want."

"So who took the Merc and pranged it?"

His voice dropped low and he vaguely indicated behind him. "One of them lads. Not saying no more. He—the Major—he just wanted to scare you."

"As ever. Calculating bastard." I hugged myself and pouted, thinking I wasn't going to be able to shame Huggy into becoming a good guy and rescuing me.

~

I suffered through the banging and dust and not-so-delicate moving of my belongings from one place to another. Rubbish and washing up, the grimy untidiness of an abandoned house, filled the kitchen. Beer cans appeared in random corners and I tutted as I moved things around, trying to keep a semblance of order in a muddled house. The place smelled like a pub before they brought in the no-smoking rule. The toilets both stank of men who could not aim straight.

Then they began attacking the kitchen so I wasn't allowed in there. No access to kettle or fridge or bread bin—

"Don't let them defrost everything in the freezer," I begged Huggy.

He went into the kitchen. I tried not to listen to

their uncouth voices using expressions I didn't for the main part even understand, then Huggy came back munching a Cornetto. He waved it at me as I made a *heaven help me* expression. "These are good, Ms T."

"So, I needn't worry about the food getting defrosted, just eaten." I threw up my arms in despair. "How can I do anything?" I demanded of him as he sat back in my/his TV chair. "These louts are practically un-fitting my fitted kitchen. I am starving. That obnoxious Jim—"

Huggy shot up and grabbed my arm which shut me up. He pulled me away. "I know, I know, but be careful what you say, Ms T. Come on, I got more stuff in me car if yer hungry."

I got in his Micra, such an innocent looking evil car. He squeezed in, definitely needing an upgrade—a promotion or whatever—or simply to steal a bigger vehicle.

He finished off the Cornetto and drew out a long vacuum flask and two mugs from a bag in the back seat. "What's this?" I asked. "Slow poison?"

He gave me a *mad woman* look. "Brandy-coffee. Figured you might need it."

I chuckled. "You're an angel."

"No one ever called me that before."

"Can't you get out of this business?"

He was quiet a long moment. "Not much in the job market for someone like me. Can you imagine me CV?"

"What did you want to be when you were little?"

He gazed at me then, his bruised face holding a look so full of remorse I wished I'd never asked the question, so I said optimistically, "What've you got for an old lady to eat, then?"

"Battenberg," he said, reaching into the bag and placing the cake on the dash.

"One of my favourites."

"I know. I got the idea from a receipt o' yours I found."

"Oh," was all I said, reflecting on how all the prying meant my home was no longer my castle. I hoped they didn't steal too much from me. My truly precious stuff, my diamond engagement ring, the house deeds, Will and so on, were in the bank.

Brittle, tinkling crashes issued from out of the front door. I grimaced.

Huggy fished a penknife from his jeans and sliced the cake into two, handed the smaller part to me in its wrapper and scooped up the rest, munching on it like a hamburger.

Suddenly I realised how much he ponged. The leather jacket he wore smelled of stale tobacco and even staler man sweat, so I suggested we moved to the seat under the front window. With coffee and cake on the garden table, I listened as various bangs and crashes and curses emanated from the cottage.

Gretchen Murr, a nearby neighbour I quite liked, came up the path to us. "Having some work done, I hear, Molly."

"Oh yes," I smiled. "You can definitely *hear* I'm having work done."

She laughed, her eyes flitting questioningly to the hairy man I sat beside.

"Lottie's daughter's boy," I said. "Had a wee car accident." I hoped that was enough of an explanation for his poorly face, but Sarah pressed on.

"And Lottie is?"

"My sister, so I suppose that makes Hugo here my grand-nephew? I never was much good with family trees."

"Me neither, but—"

One of the un-builder's dashed out of the door and barged past her on his way to the van. "How rude," she said loudly, looking to me for an apology.

I shrugged and smiled sweetly. "Young people. What can you do? It's all there is nowadays; rush here, dash there."

"Hmph," she said. "Still, must get on. Can't dilly dally all day. Bye bye, Molly; Hugo." She finger-waggled a wave.

With her out of earshot Huggy said, "Oi! The major been talking 'bout me behind me back, has he?"

"What *do* you mean?"

"How do you know me name's Hugo?"

"Is it really? I just used the first name that came into my head. You know, Huggy does sound a lot like the nickname of someone called Hugo, doesn't it?"

"S'pose." He swigged his coffee, finished off the cake and sat back saying, "How come you're so cheerful, Ms T?"

"Am I?" I thought a moment. "I suppose it's because I'm getting on and aware that I could drop dead from natural causes at any moment, just like my husband died in his sleep. But don't doubt I'm scared. Yes, I'm really scared, deep down. There are worse things than dying and all this messing up of my life is a horror. I wish I had never seen that blasted burger bag, which I didn't take, and that's all there is to it. I picked it up, I saw what was in there and I dropped it back in the same place. Why's that so hard for anyone to believe? I am quite innocent," I emphasised, "and this is going to be a story where the innocent survives."

I said it bravely. I didn't want them to grind me down. For all I knew, Huggy-Hugo could be playing good cop, but I doubted he had the wits for it. I wondered what crimes he had committed in his time, what possible future a man like him could find.

"It's alright, Ms T," he said after a moment's deep consideration that saw him staring into the distance as wheels turned in his head. "I believe you."

"Thank you, Hugo," I said, feeling sheltered by his words, but I should have known fate would spoil that moment of happiness. Ginger beard ambled out, turned and looked at the upper windows and said quite calmly, "The house's on fire. Sorry 'bout that."

I suspected a joke from his monotone voice, but then the other louts exited much faster, spinning around to look up, and I stood and saw in horror flames licking up the curtains in the spare room above us. "Shut the front door," I said loudly, but no one moved from their spectating. "Keep it contained," I said angrily and managed to shut the door despite Huggy trying to hold me back. Damage limitation was foremost in my mind, dulled by panic, my thumping heart, the shaking and nerves and jelly legs of a woman about to lose everything.

"Don't just stand there, call the fire brigade! Get them here fast!" I gibbered as the louts just stood and stared like my blazing house was a firework display. Then I heard Huggy talking to the emergency services on his mobile.

We stood back farther as sparks flew out of the chimney like swarms of fireflies.

I lost it. I totally lost my cool. "Did you do that on purpose?" I screeched as I grabbed Jim by his clothing. "Did you torch my house on purpose, you scum?"

He pushed me off violently. Huggy caught me before I fell.

The flames had a grip. We all ran to the lane and I watched, helpless, as the crackling hiss became the roar of an animal eating my house. It was a blessing Misty was 'safe' elsewhere, a double blessing the repaired photo I treasured resided safely in my purse, and even a triple blessing that the Merc was in another place.

But the sirens sounding from the A417 and the crackle of the fire hid my impossible to repress sobs.

12. Dark Well

When all the fuss was over, when the louts had done a runner and left Huggy and me alone, the house was just a dripping, smoking square with a roof bent and buckled, held on by splinters. The fire had taken hold quickly and zoomed from room to room, so only the fire brigade's swift response had left anything recognisable. It had busted out through the windows and scorched the wisteria to a skeleton plant, bounced its fat fire around the furniture until it was naught but black wood, smashed the delicate china as surely as hammers, and flame fingers had read all my beloved books into ash.

"Still got yer hubby's boots," Huggy said quietly, stood beside me out in the lane as we watched the firemen efficiently go about their jobs. "Don't tell me you want them back 'cause me Doc Marten's were in *there*."

"Oh Hugo, I can't tell if you're trying to make a joke to cheer me or not," I muttered. "Keep the boots. I don't care. Where do you live? Can I come and bug you for a few days?"

He gave a dull chuckle. "That'd give me neighbours something to talk about."

They were out there now, my neighbours, some gawking, some walking up and passing by, watching the fireman as they rewound the hoses. No one had offered help or even the standard British cup of tea that cures all ills. I leaned into Hugo. He put an arm round my shoulders. He was the first man I had let do that in many years, and I didn't care what anyone thought.

"I guess I'll have to find somewhere to stay for a while. That little hotel on the Newent road, maybe? The major can't want any more of me now the whole house has gone, surely? Can you keep Misty for a while, until I get sorted?"

I heard a familiar tapping and, "Well, well, well; what have we here?" asked the major, swaggering up.

"Did you arrange this?" I said with venom in my voice. "So help me—"

"Botched work," he jumped in. "No malice aforethought, I assure you. My fault entirely for hiring those undisciplined idiots. Molly, you can come spend a few nights at my place. Katarina would love to see you again."

"I'd rather not," I said sharply. "I'll find somewhere for myself, thank you very much."

He leaned towards me, eyes sharp and forbidding before saying, "Yes, you will come to my place. Don't think this is over."

"Crap, man. Just leave her alone," Huggy said, moving in front of me. "She ain't done nothing. She's just a nice old lady."

"Huggy, what happened to your face?"

"Had a disagreement with the lads; bit like this one. You hurt her, I'll break your fancy stick over your head."

"Oh?" The major lifted his swordstick, glanced behind him to the positions of the firemen, said, "This one?" and before we could move he whacked Huggy across the head with it so hard he fell, and I jumped back in angry surprise.

The major looked down at the man holding his head then at me. "Do not run or call for help, Molly," he cautioned in a soft voice. "You'll only get someone else into trouble. Now, Huggy; you've had a disagreement with me too. I brought you onto this team for your subtle skills, so you work to my beat, not your own." Another look at the firemen and another whack as Huggy tried to squirm out of the way. "Not your day, is it?"

Calming, the major pulled his coat around himself, tidy and upright, every inch the respectable gentleman again. "The car's parked by the pond," he said. "Walk there now, Molly. Peacefully take my arm, act natural and try to smile, because if you don't I will use the other mode of my swordstick on your friend Huggy, and I can assure you it will hurt him a *lot* more."

~

Less than a half hour later I found myself locked in a dark, cold, windowless cellar, with only a bucket for company. Loud rock music played continuously to annoy me, and I had nothing to sit on except the tiled floor. My shoes and handbag and glasses had all been taken, but I could smell something bad and was sure it was old blood.

Feeling around, I found the room was vaguely circular, and in the centre was a low brick wall that was also circular; the functional well the major had spoken of that happy day in the woods that seemed so long ago. I dropped a loose piece of tiling down it to hear the splash, and it wasn't a long drop to the water, though I may have misheard the splash in the cacophony of sound that vibrated painfully in my ears. I ran my hands over the bucket support, but I wasn't going to feel any farther for fear of unbalancing over the low wall and falling down. And it was the well that stank, oh how it stank, like corruption, rotten, diseased.

The music cut out, light flashed in as the door opened, leaving me blinking. The major stood there, just staring at me.

"I don't know where anything of yours is," I said with a fed-up sigh in my voice. "I wish I did, to get this over with, but I *don't!*"

"Hmm… we'll see. Four days without water. Enjoy. Or I could get Needle to try the heroin on you. You might talk that way. Which do you prefer?"

I was speechless for once.

"There's a bell up there." He pointed to a button. "Ring it when you're ready."

And with that he was gone, and I was alone in the darkness and the music returned, even louder, so the walls and floor vibrated and everything made me feel ill.

I investigated every little corner again. I fell over my bucket and cussed and yelled and screamed at the music. I wondered if I stood very, very still, I could meld with the wall and become invisible, but it was my tired mind playing tricks on me again.

I rang the bell, hoping at least it would shut off the music. It did, but the major was not amused. I had disturbed a meal for nothing. After that I rang the bell and disturbed him several more times, for fun, for five seconds relief for my ears, but on the next occasion he hit me with the stick. Hell; that hurt.

The major leaned on the door jamb and folded his arms over the stick. "Did you know," he began, and I wondered what amazingly inciting detail he was about to impart. "My Katarina, has she told you about that last night, at the dinner after the business meeting in Salveston Manor?"

"The night Ozzy died? No, what of it?"

"My Katarina is beautiful, desirable, no?"

I blinked. "Are you saying not so subtly that she and Ozzy had relations?"

He chuckled. "Relations. Such a nondescript word for casual sex. Very much so, behind my back too. Naughty Oswald; naughtier Kat. I know I cannot satiate the minx—"

"Yeuk; no more verbal torture, please. Not that I believe you anyway. I can't imagine Kat seeing anything in him."

"Maybe it was because he didn't see anything of *you* on that side of the marriage," he countered. "Had that occurred to you, Molly? I knew Oswald well. He said you were an ungrateful woman. He said all you ever did was complain. Now I've met you, I must say I see his point. You are entirely self-absorbed. Think about that while you enjoy the music."

The major left. He didn't know that I hadn't cared what Ozzy did. Much leeway been signed for on his side of the premarital agreement. Mine simply said that he could never have a sexual relationship with me.

I married a man who would be my saviour, and I would be the pretty thing on his arm who would turn my face from his many dalliances. It had seemed a great idea at the time.

The door opened, the lights flashed on as the music cut off and Katarina crept in. I hoped she'd brought food, but she hadn't. She closed the door behind her softly until just a shaft of light illuminated the room.

"He leave you here until you tell," she said quietly. "I know his ways."

"Why didn't he do this first?" I asked. "This is what I would have expected, not the gradual destruction of my home."

She shrugged. "You are old lady and he wanted to be... gentle. He imagine you give in easy. But Huggy tell him you were Oswald's wife—"

"Widow," I cut in. "But what's Ozzy got to do with this?"

"You pretend still? You did not know? He was my major's boss."

I sank back to sit on the floor, head pounding, a kind of final puzzle piece clicking into my mind. That was why Kat and the Major had been there the night Ozzy died. They were in the same business. The monster! The unutterable monster I had married. The Marsh Thing was real! Keeping me in the dark for years. Me in my sacred gilded tower while he dealt in... I assumed it was drugs; no one had actually said. But if I hadn't hated him before, I did then. Trying to keep me safe had done the exact opposite.

And Hugo, there he was dropping me in it again, though he'd likely have been punished if he hadn't told. What a horrid system to live in.

Her head tilted a little as she read my face. "You did not know. Interesting. My major, he wanted to get stuff gently, but now he knows you were Marshman's woman he thinks you are good at hiding—that you were taught things by him, so he do this hard way. Tell him, old lady. You want to exist here until death? You die from lack of medications? I know old ladies take a lot of medications."

"I am *not* an old lady and I won't die without my meds, but not having my glasses is a bit of a nightmare and my bottom hurts. The bastard hit me with his stick." She was staring at me with a frown. "Someone will look for me,

Katarina. People don't just disappear."

A slight rueful shrug lifted one shoulder. "All the time they disappear."

"He should have tried this to start with," I said bitterly. "Then he'd have soon discovered I don't know anything, and my house wouldn't be burned to the ground and—"

"It is not his style. The burning. I doubt he had hand in it."

"But if the louts hadn't been there, the accident would never have happened, so he's still to blame, isn't he? What *do* you see in him?"

"He is my husband. I do what he tell me, as you did with yours, no?"

"Ha!" The dumb innocence of her broke my heart. "I did that for years, young woman, and believe me it won't get you anywhere. Ozzy could sleep with anyone he wanted to; yes, I let him. It was an agreement we had."

She looked baffled, and suddenly I was telling this bruised flower how I had been broken, and she was nodding in sympathy as I explained the attack, the STI, and the subsequent damage that had blighted my life since my teens.

She rubbed a hand across her nose. I think she was sniffling. "You..." She sighed again and I heard the hurt of years in it. "You nice old lady. You deserve better. I tell you, my major, he is scared to hurt you. Hurt me, yes, because no one care about me, but you? Marshman's widow must have many, many people in the organisation who care about her..."

'I do?' I thought in surprise. That was news to me.

"... so he wants only his diamonds; you give them, all okay. But you don't give them..." I saw her shrug. "...he keep playing with you, like cat with mouse, but he dare not hurt you too bad for fear others hurt him worse."

The door opened. The major appeared, his features shadowed by the bright light behind him, a vampire coming to feast on my innocent blood. "Kat, Kat, Kat," he said in a tired voice. "You should not be here. More dissent in the ranks?

What is my world coming to? Leave."

As she passed him he grabbed her arm and said, "I will deal with you later."

Jim and Needle traipsed in after him. Needle handed the major a cat basket. Misty saw me, cried out to me, turning round and round.

He attached the basket handle to the bucket winch and, even as I saw what he was planning, I was up and the lads were holding me back as I cried out in horror.

The winch creaked, the basket could be heard shaking, the cat's terrified *mewls* echoed up the well, then were silenced.

The major looked at me, no emotion in his gaze. I now saw his little grey beard was the beard of Satan himself, and the horrid louts were demon attendants. I had no words. Nothing I could say would save Misty. There was no truth to tell and a lie would soon be found out.

He turned the handle and the basket was raised from the water. Misty called to me, I sobbed, he lowered her again, watching me, my wretched old face contorted with grief.

I sank down, limp against their grasps, and began to choke as my heart finally complained enough to black me out.

13. Rotting Corpse

The shock of hitting the cold well water brought me around to full comprehension. Light glowed from on high, the bucket rope was tied around my waist and I was still clothed, but my bare feet found oozy mud and sticks beneath them and I wanted to howl myself out of the nightmare.

Then a hand touched my shoulder and I uttered a high pitched wailing cry, a pure full-blooded terror enveloping me. The hand was black and rotting, attached to an arm, maybe once attached to a body. It was bones I stood upon too scared to move, my toes sinking into the vestiges of a corpse.

His face looked down, then Needle and Jim's joined in, the unholy trinity of demons gazing at their terrified victim.

"I am not sure," I gasped, spitting out the vile water, "what you think this is going to achieve." My teeth chattered so much I could hardly speak. "I h-h-have collapsed once, and I'm likely to c-c-collapse again and drown."

"No begging," Needle observed. "No *mercy, mercy, I'm just an old lady.*"

"No denying the charges either," Jim said.

I reasoned there was no point anyway; they didn't believe me. They would never believe me. I could pretend to show them where the stones were, but then there would be no stones and it would all go round and round and...

I thought of dear Misty, a victim of this monster who had his elbows leaning on the well wall while he watched me like a Roman inspecting a dying gladiator.

I thought of darling Gavin, a victim of the man he had grown up calling Daddy, drowning drunk one starlit night in Bristol.

I thought I was going to be a victim too. It might be easier to let go, wait for that time when I would feel warm and drift off as my body heat was sucked out by the frigid water. Feet lifting out of the mud, I did a desultory doggy paddle, heard voices receding, the lights went out, and I was left in the darkness with only loud rock and roll and a corpse for company. "How'd it work out for you then?" I asked it, and I was so far gone I wouldn't have been surprised at a reply.

I figured I wouldn't last half an hour. Confusion came on quickly. If you ask me what I remember most it was the odd lights that sputtered in the darkness, the vile scent of the corrupted body, the odd illusion that I could hear Misty purring in the rhythm of the music, and I said softly, "I'm coming, Sweetie. Mummy's coming."

Then I was out on the floor and choking while Needle and Jim looked very concerned. The major had gone, and I guessed I was not supposed to actually drown or they'd get into trouble. As it was, I thought I was likely to be poisoned by the water.

"Oi, Moll. You still with us?" Jim asked.

"No," I said.

"Huh. Got some spark, this 'un," Needle said.

"I haven't got the diamonds, boys. Please believe me," I begged, my pride almost gone.

Jim shook his head. "Not us you gotta convince, Moll. He'll be pulling out your toenails soon, since I cut your fingernails too short, you see, so can't get the pliers on them."

"Just chuck me in the well again," I groaned.

"So tell us where these fucking diamonds are," Needle said. "I have never met a broad as dumb shit as you. That's all he wants. You wanna die for them? What good's that? You's dead, you can't use them."

The major swept back in. "Any luck, gentlemen?"

"Listen," I said as fiercely as I could muster. "Just because I was Ozzy's wife doesn't mean anything. He managed to keep me in the dark for years, and I hated the man in the end and it was wonderful to hear he'd died. There, now I've said it. I blamed him for everything wrong in my life; my lack of friends, for persistently trying to renege on our pre-marital agreement, the death of our son, of refusing to adopt any more children—everything."

"Fascinating," the major said, though he couldn't have looked less fascinated if he'd tried. "Is that it, Molly? Yes? Good. Jim, go find me a hammer."

Jim gave Needle a look that I couldn't read. Confusion?

"What?" the major roared. "In my day it was a good thing, a mark of confidence, of acceptance into the group to be asked to get the hammer."

He glanced at me, a strange smile curving his lips. I hated to think what he saw as I lay there hugging myself, teeth chattering, my clothes stinking and wet, my hair muck-matted.

The louts did not move. "What's got into you two?" he demanded. "I have had enough of this stupidity, both hers and yours. If she still won't tell after a little light hammering you can dig the grave; and I can tell you, lads, there is no higher honour than *that*. I was the fastest digger in my group."

I sniggered at his pomposity and his attention flew back to me.

"So you still have life for humour," he said. "So how about laughing at this. I was only joking. I have no intentions of hammering you—not after what Kat told me."

He waited a beat until I showed some recognition of what he meant. Could I trust anyone? Of course not. Kat had revealed my painful secret. Maybe she thought it would save me from the well, but I doubted it would save me from madness.

He must have seen the anger in my eyes, for then he said, "Oh, don't fret so, she's still on your side, you know. I had to... drag... that info out of her. She's round the back now, whimpering like a little bruised puppy. I will cheer her up later with the charms you denied Ozzy."

"Bastard," I spat.

He laughed and crouched beside me, sniffed and stood

78

again. "I didn't think this through, did I. Still, I doubt a bit of mud will put off the lads. I could kick myself for not seeing the pointers earlier—when I tried to kiss you on the cheek, when Needle grabbed your breast and Jim fondled your nether regions, your reactions were so extreme. I imagined it was because you are old and not used to such things any more, but it's more than that, isn't it, Molly? So much more." He crouched beside me again as I sniffled and looked around for hope. "Is there a name for it?" he asked. "This sexual aversion you have?"

"Trauma induced spontaneous combustion."

"Heh. What more could I expect from you. Now, I have explained the situation to these gentlemen and they are very keen, despite your age, to study your reactions in a purely clinical trial."

"Please don't." I began to curl into a ball, protecting myself.

"Or you could tell me where… Finish the sentence."

"They're up your arse."

"You are remarkable. Even knowing what the lads are going to do, you don't lay up on the sass."

"And there fades the Molly we know and love," I said faintly, beginning to hide inside myself, withdrawing, letting myself become only a body without a mind.

I was scanning the floor. When it had happened, all those long years ago, I'd had no warning, no chance to look for a weapon beforehand. What was here that I could use? This time it was two lads, then it had been two lads. Their actions had scarred my life forever. What did I have now that the young Molly had not had? I had tried learning Tae-Kwon-Do since then, but was pretty useless at it, and at Uni I had used my wooden sandal to strike out—though I had been hit back with it and I had no shoes on now at all, so that was no good either.

And the answer came to me. An answer I didn't like because it would hurt me as much as it hurt them, because either I could let my fear weaken me or I could use it to empower me.

"I will leave you to your play, gentlemen," the major said, standing to leave. "I do not think I have the stomach to watch *this* kind of torture."

Jim grabbed me and I started kicking, while Needle ran his hands over me, pulling at my revolting clothing, his clammy hands stroking my skin, and it was unbearable, like flames rippling across my body. Did I scream? It was more of a groan, panic and all the flashbacks, hot horrid images of *those* boys back then and now *these* boys, and in between the safety of a sexless almost loveless marriage, yet it was easier than breaking down the barrier, for there was no counselling in my youth. You got on with stuff. So your attackers gave you an STI that likely rendered you infertile? Deal with it. You buried the bad, or hurt others to cover your own feelings.

I had collapsed into myself as a teenager and never stepped out again. I can't even look at a man without thinking about that day, about what they did to me, remembering the hard hands and the male smells and young Molly's tears and the boys' laughter, and all the other tiny things that can ravage my dreams some nights. Now a simple kiss on a cheek is a bad enough trigger, so to have these lads' hands pressing into me, squeezing and prodding and trying to force my body this way and that, here was the horror that would hold me and freeze me until I had regressed far enough inside myself to not react at all.

If my plan didn't work.

"Stop!" I squealed, back arching as I forced my thighs to clamp together. "I'll tell you where the diamonds are."

"That didn't take much," Jim complained. "No fun at all." He adjusted his trousers and sat on his haunches, watching for me to change my mind.

"I don't want *him* to have them," I said in a low, conspiratorial voice. "Do you think he deserves them; that stuck up nitwit? Give me something to write on and I'll draw you a map; show you where I hid them, but please don't touch me again. Deal?"

They looked at each other, a greedy silent agreement passing between them. Jim took his inflexible, grasping hands off my arms as Needle rummaged in his massive pockets then shoved a small crumpled notebook at me.

I found myself tensing, fear in every pore, my breathing short and shallow as I fought my own body's reactions. The pain in my chest was real, the thrumming of my heart bad. Could I really do this?

"Pen?" I asked. "Pencil? I'm not going to write in blood, you know. Where's a writing implement? Are you telling me you carry a notebook but no pen? Hurry up."

I was frantic inside. It was taking all the energy and confidence I had built up over the years from arguments with Ozzy to keep my body still, to maintain the illusion of calmness because, once I moved on them, I would have to keep going, seeing it through to the harsh end of either them or me. I was about to find out if forty years of heavy gardening work had paid off in the strangest possible way.

"Here; this do?" Needle handed me a wax crayon, well chewed. My heart missed beats. This could ruin everything. I stared at the green crayon and moved it into position as I asked tentatively, "You got kids, Needle?"

"Nah, it's me nephew's."

"And, excuse the question, but have you ever killed anyone?"

"Not that it's any of your business, but yeah. Me and Jimmy here, we've done our bit for population control."

At his words, I could feel an anger rising in me that was greater than the fear.

"Good," I said, "because I'm about to kill *you*." And I lurched forwards to plunge the crayon deep into his eye. As he fell backwards wailing, I managed to push the shocked and slow reacting Jim backwards against the well wall where I grabbed his ankles, heaved, and unbalanced him into the well as easily as lifting a mega-bag of compost.

I turned back for the agonised gibbering Needle and cracked his head against the floor until he shut up, then dragged him to the well, yanked him up and tipped his skinny arse over the edge like a knobbly sack of potatoes. I heard a clunk. I hoped they'd knocked their stupid heads together.

I thought I was going to faint. My heart was complaining again; racing, hopping, missing beats. I was breathless. My back was killing me from the exertion, and I had to get out of the cellar and away quickly. How?

But I needn't have worried. That day, Fate had angled everything my way.

The door shocked me by opening quietly; so quietly I thought I was hallucinating, but I ducked behind the well to hide. Then Huggy's hushed voice said, "Ms T?" and I saw his wide shape in the doorway. He held a jemmy in one hand and the other reached beckoningly towards me. We crept out of the house, into the dark and cold and peace of the night, far away from loud music and cold-blooded Majors and hot-blooded Katarinas and wells containing far more than water, and he practically carried me down the road to the waiting not-so-evil Micra.

14. Hell's Boots

"Are *you* safe, Hugo?" I asked as the Micra wound along the lanes connecting Highnam and Hartpury and I snuggled deeper into the fleece Huggy had thought to bring for me. I pressed him to reply. "Come on. It won't be good if he realises you helped me escape."

He shrugged. "I take my risks, Ms T. So does Kat. It was her turned off the alarms for five mins so I could get you out. 'Rescue poor old lady,' she said. He'd beaten her, poor kid. She needs to escape as much as anyone, but she won't risk it, so she reckoned the least she could do was 'elp you." He gave a heavy sigh then went, "Sorry 'bout Misty, George had to hand her over when he asked. You know how it goes."

Yes. I did.

"Oh crap, I forgot." He pointed to the glove compartment; I opened it and found my glasses.

"You didn't happen to get my handbag too?"

"Nah, sorry, Kat didn't give me that. Had your lad's pic in it, right? Shame, but come on," he said, turning where I directed him into Over Old Road, "you go shelter with your mates. I don't think the Major'll bother chasing after you—"

"Not bother? Hugo, I think I killed Jim and Needle."

"What? How? Blimey!" he spluttered. "Still, couldn't happen to a more deserving couple of vermin. Nice one, Ms T."

"You needn't be so happy about it. If I've killed them I'm down to the major's level. Not what I wanted for my life." I pointed widely to Copsely Ridge and Huggy parked a little away from it.

"Major won't know where you are," he said reassuringly, "and I sure ain't gonna tell."

"That'll be a first. You've told him about other things, Hugo. And Kat told him something I had expected her to keep quiet. So... this time, please *do* keep quiet."

He chewed on his lip. "You know what it's like. Threats and punishments. It's not easy."

"Look, stay here for a while. You'll be safe with my friend. We'll find something for you, somehow."

He sighed, hands running loose around the wheel as though he were turning a corner. Was he considering my offer? I wanted to rescue him since I had failed to rescue Gavin.

"Nice you caring, and all, Ms T. Appreciate it. I'll think on it. Now, I gotta go get an alibi for the time, and get your lad's pic back to you. We can talk then."

~

My horror was over. All was well. I could risk breathing again.

And, because it was all over, I found the overwhelming urge to tell someone about the major, so I told the startled Callum, who had answered his door in his dressing gown at three in the morning to a stinking, dishevelled old lady, illuminated by the security light into a scrawny spectre.

After a warming shower, a change of clothes—his jeans, shirt and jumper fitted me well—and over a cup of tea or three with marmite sandwiches, and a good dose of paracetamol for my bruised and aching head and back, I told him everything that had happened.

"Bloody hell! Forgive my French, Molly, but how long've you been stuck in that nightmare? And that hairy man at your house, your watcher, was he a danger to Dad that day he stayed? You should have slipped me a note or something."

"I think slipping you a note would have been far more dangerous for Joe than picking apples with Hugo. He wasn't even a threat to me. He doesn't want to be on the bad guys' team, I'm sure."

"Okay, so what's the next thing to do? Call the police. We can do that now."

"No! No police. Too dangerous. Let me lie low. Just let me stay awhile. I mean a few days until I sort out somewhere else to live. Somewhere a long way from Hartpury."

He was frowning. "But that major, he lives over in Highnam, you say? Can't you get the police onto *him*?"

"Callum, which bit of *dangerous* don't you get? Hugo said he'd seen the major kill someone with his swordstick." I touched my bruised head. It didn't hurt so much anymore, but I would have a black eye, for sure.

"So he should be reported," Callum was saying earnestly. "With this Hugo as a witness we could get him out the way."

"No. Stop it!" My thoughts whirled in that dusty old bin called a brain.

Joe appeared at the top of the stairs. "I want cocoa," he said.

I whirled on Callum, pointing to his father with a shaky finger. "*That's* what you should be focused on: Joe. He's improving in leaps and bounds, isn't he?"

"Yes, he's definitely showing shows of improvement."

Joe came down the stairs and waved at me, then went into the kitchen.

"Then focus on Joe," I said, "and ignore the problem I *had*, because it's over now, okay?"

He looked dubious. "You owe it to the villages to get that major out of circulation."

"No," I said, all determined to put the past behind me and forget it. "Let me go on as if life hadn't had a massive hiccup."

"You are really blasé about this, you know. Mad majors running around isn't going to do anyone any good."

"But it isn't going to be just him, is it? Report the major and someone else will step up to take his place, and they might get *you* if they know you're the one reporting him. Isn't this how it all works? By keeping people too scared to do anything? I had my cat murdered, so imagine if they threatened Joe."

There came a crash from the kitchen. "I dropped it," Joe said as he came back to the living room looking abashed.

Callum shook his head and got up. "Sorry, Dad." He went

into the kitchen and, as I heard him sweeping up broken china, Joe patted me on the back.

"There, there," he said kindly. "It's all right, Milly. We all make mistakes."

"You are feeling better, aren't you?" I asked. He just smiled.

"So one thing puzzles me," Callum said, loitering in the kitchen doorway as the kettle hissed behind him, "Where *are* the money and the diamonds?"

"I've no idea, but I hope they're somewhere the major never finds them. Somewhere someone really hard up finds them by accident, and gets to have a nice life because of them."

~

The next day was spent struggling to sort both the car and the house insurance over Callum's phone. Enough to drive you mad when you've not got the details they want and me getting all flustered and forgetful. I also hoped the phone calls weren't enough to lead anyone to me that I didn't want to see.

But in the afternoon while Callum was out getting the medicines I'd managed to order on the phone, and Joe was peacefully watching YouTube, and I'd had a mooch in the house—admiring its layout and lamenting the loss of my lovely cottage—I went to the door as the bell rang, peered through the peephole, and saw it was the major.

"Molly?" he called. "Are you there?"

'Damn you, Huggy!' I thought, then yelled, "I'm calling the police."

"My dear Molly," came his silken voice. "Please don't phone the police just yet. Let me say my piece."

"Lord above, shut up with whatever you're playing at now and scarper."

"I came to give you some good news."

"So give it then leave me alone to call the cops."

"I don't think you will call them. You are as deep in this as I am. They investigate me, they investigate Molly Marshman, am I right?"

"Get lost." I walked away from the door. He hadn't mentioned the lads down the well. That, I presumed, had to mean they had survived.

"I have my property back," he called. "Most of it. Turned out the culprit was close to home after all. And you don't want me to get lost. I have your handbag here."

"Leave it on the doorstep then, you sicko!" I spluttered. "I don't ever want to see your face again. You froze me in that well, had me assaulted and you *killed my cat!*" The tears flooded out again. "And… and… I will probably be traumatised for years to come, just because you wouldn't believe the word of a lady."

"Listen, Molly, quell the fires of your indignation. Maybe you can help me. It was Huggy."

"Huggy who told you I was here? Yes, I'd figured that out."

"He took the money bag."

My vision blurred for a moment. Oh, of course it was him! Who was it saw the opportunity to take the money and blame it on the old lady passing by? That was why he'd been so moody around me.

"And I would never kill a cat."

"What? What are you playing at?"

"I let her go. Outside my house. Just ran off free as a bird. Haven't seen her since, but then I haven't seen my diamonds at all. I was wondering if Huggy might have given them to you, for safe-keeping, out of some misplaced sense of friendship. You see, he couldn't tell me where they are."

"*Couldn't?*"

"I was a bit over zealous, shall we say. I didn't have Needle to advise me, for some reason."

I felt dizzy as the import of his words sank in.

"He was quite a bad guy, our Huggy, but he liked you," I heard the major say through the door and my ears rang with a strange dizziness. "He told Needle not to touch you, dared to stand up to me."

"All in the past tense," I murmured to myself, leaning on the door as tears came and my heart trembled, reminding me I hadn't taken my meds in days. Maybe the major would be the death of me after all. I felt my heart was breaking.

"You have to understand," the major's irritating voice went on calmly from the other side of the door, and if I'd been capable of it I would have opened the door and hit him with the table. "Since I still don't know where the diamonds are, there's still a problem."

"Well, at least you can't take my house to pieces again," I erupted. "You and your bloody diamonds can rot in hell 'cause I have no bloody idea where they are, you utter fecking idiot-monster!"

"Actually, if you think about it, *you* killed Huggy," came his muffled voice, still annoyingly calm. "If he hadn't gone back to get *your* handbag, and if *you* hadn't incapacitated Needle who understands the drug administration far better than I, I believe he might still be alive."

I heard the click of his cane as he walked away, heard the distant sound of the car starting up and leaving, then I sat on the settee while I tried to calm my wildly palpitating heart. He had managed to blame Huggy's demise on me, the bastard. But, oh no... why was I still so sympathetic and missing the man who had caused the whole wretched mess? I had liked Huggy. I had hoped for him. I felt I could have taken him in and looked after him like a surrogate son. Set him on the right path—

I stopped. He was gone, just like Gavin, and that was that.

So I made myself a cup of tea, drowned it in brandy, and comforted myself by planning how to look for Misty. I'd ring the RSPCA and report her missing, and call both villages' Post Offices to put up adverts. After all, there was a river between Highnam and Hartpury. I couldn't expect her to get back on her own.

I found myself, for a funny mind-slipping moment, wondering if Huggy would help by driving up and down the local roads looking for her, and then my tired brain stuttered back into gear and reminded me he wasn't just lost, he was gone forever, so I sat and dripped tears into my tea as I cried for them both.

15. Death-watch Beetle

I was watching the local news that evening when it was announced.

...body of a man identified as Hugo Jenkins, a known Cheltenham felon... believed killed in a gangland hit, was discovered in a Hartpury field by.... The newscaster said it with a grim and sincere face.

The picture... no...!

The image burned into me. I could hardly focus through a deluge of tears.

With the yellow ditch-digging JCB showing half in the background, a pair of Wellingtons were shown sticking feet first out of the mud. The striking O.W. on the boots told me who it was.

"Oh, Hugo!" I wailed.

Callum was sat at his desk on his laptop, but he looked over at the cry that flew out of me, saw the image on the screen, jumped up and turned off the TV and sat beside me on the settee.

"Callum, that was the lad who helped me. How could the major do that to him? Bury him like that? Thank god he was dead before they did it."

I was shaking to my core. Had the boots been left exposed as a hideous message to me?

But that would mean I was still a suspect. I supposed if the diamonds still hadn't been found, I had to be, but worse still was the idea that if I'd let Callum go to the police when he'd suggested it, perhaps Huggy's murder could have been prevented.

Callum's mobile rang. He jumped to it, listened to the voice on the other end and just said, "Yeah, sure, no problem," but I didn't care what it was about. I was in my own uncomfortable, mentally damning myself world. Maybe Callum would end up looking after both Joe and me, both invalids of life.

Joe was sat at the dining table watching his personal DVD player, jiggling and making small noise of excitement like a teenage boy. Oblivious to the world around him, for a second I envied his state.

Callum sat beside me again. "Poor sod," he said, and I assumed he meant Huggy. "Didn't he give you any idea where he'd hidden the diamonds then? We need to get that cat murdering major out of your life."

"Oh come on, Callum. I really don't want to talk about this now. Poor Misty deserved her fate less than Hugo."

"Okay, okay," he said in a calming voice. "I'm around if you do need to talk. But didn't he give you any clues? If he had the cash it follows he had the diamonds. And it sounds like the kind of thing you could do with right now, now the house is burned down and you need to get back on your feet and so on."

"Clues? No. We caught newts and a chicken and talked about edible plants and the merits of owning cats and played on mobile phone games, that was all we did, not discuss where to hide diamonds. If he did have them—and I agree I suppose he did—the answer's gone with him and, like I said before, I hope someone who really needs them finds them."

While Callum returned to his laptop, the grandfather clock tick-tock, tick-tocked and I was warm and comfortable and all was peaceful in that tiny world. Callum had picked up my heart meds from the doctor earlier, plus a hefty packet of antibiotics to take because of the well water, and all would soon be fine inside me. And all would be okay outside me too, I told myself.

Eventually I said, "I need the loo now. All that crying triggers it."

"Tears are natural," Callum said. "Cry all you want, Molly. Losing Huggy and Misty, I can understand the grief."

As I went up the stairs to the toilet I heard him on

his mobile again. 'I really must get one,' I thought. 'One that actually works, not like the one Huggy gave me.'

And then I was sad all over again.

I stopped at the landing window on the way back, and drew the curtain aside. I gazed at the stars, bright and lighting up the sky alongside the almost full moon. I wondered if Misty could navigate home by stars, or the moon. I had no idea.

Then something struck me

Huggy.

I had never told Callum his nick name, just called him Hugo, I was sure I had. But minutes ago, downstairs, he had distinctly called him Huggy. The last thing I wanted was to suspect Callum too, but the more I pondered on what had been said, or what I had not chosen to say, the more confused I became.

Then the answer to my wondering come in the most undesired way.

Car headlights swung into the drive. I opened the window and craned my neck to see round the corner, but I didn't have to see. After the clunk of a door shutting, I could hear the *click, click, click* approaching like a death-watch beetle.

I heard the front door shut and his hideous voice wafted up the stairs.

Callum had let the major into the house, and known Huggy's name, and asked about the diamonds in a rather persistent way.

Ergo, Callum was also a BBG.

I wanted to run, to hide, but within the house there was nowhere to do either, but boosted by the healing chemicals now coursing once again through my veins, I stepped down the stairs like a duchess, head up, eyes ablaze and said, "Hello, Major Nitwit. Fancy seeing you here."

"Aha, Ms Molly. Fancy seeing *you* here." He beamed.

"I've nothing for you, you know that."

"Oh, but my dear, I'm just visiting my friend Callum. Callum, my boy, didn't you tell her?"

I stopped on the middle stair. "What now?" I said in disgust and weariness. "Are you his brother-in-law or something? A transgender long lost aunt? No, I don't care, nothing would surprise me. Just go, Richard. Don't be a dick, although I suppose you can't help it with that name."

The major laughed. "Got quite a tongue on her when she gets going, hasn't she."

I stood still and looked across at Callum miserably. Finding out he was also one of the BBGs seemed par for the course my life had taken that month. And Joe? He couldn't be bluffing, could he? Would he jump out from his chair any second and all three men would join in with laughing at me?

"I don't care what you mindless manipulative morons are up to now," I said, "but I'm going to go for a walk to get the stench of you out of my nostrils."

"Hmm, a nice bit of alliteration there," the major said. As he turned to Callum an idea leapt into my head. Risky, but maybe…

"So, Callum," he said. "You're convinced she doesn't know where the diamonds are?"

"I would say it's a safe bet she doesn't, sir," Callum said, fixing my agonised eye.

"Well then, time to tie up the ends, wouldn't you say?" He drew his sword from the cane smoothly.

'Well practised,' I thought in dread, and took a step backwards, upwards, trying to stay calm before I executed my escape plan.

"Sir, is that really necessary?" Callum said, shooting me worried glances. "She's only an old lady."

"She's not just an old lady, she's a mouthy old lady who would have no trouble telling the police everything she had seen and heard now it's all over and she feels safe, am I right, Molly? She's also Oswald's old lady and I wouldn't mind betting she knows a fair few things about our business, eh?" He smirked at me, voice suave and calm and even. "I doubt the elders will mind me despatching her, all things considered.

Shame you weren't at that meeting, Molly; the one where I poisoned Oswald. Could have been rid of the two of you. Saved all this fuss and mess. Anyway, don't pretend to care, Callum. It wasn't that long ago you were begging me to get rid of your old man, and a useless job Myrna did of that; made him even more of a burden."

"I promise not to say anything," I said, pleading, the idea that the major had somehow poisoned Ozzy not surprising me at all.

I stepped back again.

"Wait!" Callum said, facing the major head on. "You *told* Myrna to push Dad?"

"You wanted Joe 'off your back'." The major said, his voice no longer calm, rising angry as Callum challenged him. "Your words exactly, man. You wanted to move up the ladder and his criticism of our lifestyle was holding you back. You don't get too many choices, you stupid—"

"No, Myrna!" came the great cry as Joe launched himself at the major. "No no no!" Joe yelled and he flattened the major as Callum yelled for him to stop, but as they tussled I turned tail and fled to Joe's room, clambered out of the window onto the low roof beyond. I looked at the drop. I had climbed a tree and got stuck, but this was life or death, so I dropped inelegantly onto the plants below as yells and crashes rang from out of the open window behind me, and I fled a new horror.

16. Haunted Woods

Joe had saved me with his obsession over Myrna, or Myrna had saved me by hurting Joe to the point where Joe was obsessed with defending people.

My head span as I limped up the road, ankle complaining where I had landed badly, my back muscles upset again, and soon I was staggering. I heard a door slam behind me and assumed the major was coming for me, so I put on another spurt, but I wasn't going to last long.

I stopped and looked back, hands on knees, panting, and there he was in the moonlight, coat flapping like evil wings as he ran towards me.

Damn that there were so few houses and cars on that road but, if I alerted anyone, they would be in danger too.

I ran into the woods as soon as I reached them. Stopping to get my breath back, surrounded by the sweet innocent scents of trees and bushes, I felt the woods to be mine. My friendly trees; my haunts. I knew all the twists and turns of these woods, even in the pale moonlight. The bushes reached their branches to me as if to comfort, and I padded on, hearing him follow me, hearing the crashes and cracks as he tracked me. As I stopped, so did he.

I don't know how people in movies can move so quietly. It is virtually impossible. Also, I had no doubt that his strides were longer than mine, and he likely didn't have heart problems, but I would push on until the game was won.

I took him around in a circle. A calculated circle. I hoped he was wondering just how big the woods actually were and feeling lost, though he had a torch. I could see its feeble beam as I crouched to one side in a thicket and let him pass by.

He was far enough away again so I pressed on, trying to keep to the clusters of scrambling brambles and red-hipped dog roses where my skin and clothing were caught and scratched, but it meant the same would happen to him and hold him up. And annoy him. It was worth it just for that.

When I came to the main path bisecting the woods, I hopped-ran downhill and then nipped back into the darkness. I found a sturdy stick, one that would not break under strain, and waited for the pompous dick behind a tree trunk, and clobbered him on the back as he passed. He went sprawling, the torch flying out of his hands, but still lit, so that plan to remove the torch hadn't worked.

"Molly," he roared into our silent arena. "Come out and fight fair."

I think he hoped my snarky nature would make me answer, but I didn't, busy considering another plan to deprive him of torchlight.

Or maybe it didn't matter.

Finally reaching what I had been heading for, I used the sturdy stick to lever off the heavy metal cap. I was lucky it hadn't been concreted on. I couldn't look down. I had no idea how deep it was or if it even held water anymore, but I was pretty sure the hole would be too much for him to climb out of easily, if at all. With the major out of the way for even a short while, I would risk going back to Callum's to call the police, if Callum hadn't done it already, going from the anger in his voice over the major's machinations. Could be, he'd had enough and was ready to see people punished.

I hastily gathered some smaller sticks and pushed them across the gap, black and scary in its emptiness. Every five seconds I had stopped and listened, beginning to think he'd given up, then hearing his footsteps a little closer each time.

I stood and panted quietly, listening, waiting for my moment to drop the major down the well.

"Hello there, Mollykins," he said, scary as a spectre in the woods, the failing light of his torch making him a dim figure across from me. I stepped backwards; he stepped forwards. I looked left to right as if planning a new escape route and he laughed. I sank to a crouching position with a fake sob-sigh of weariness and he lifted the sword.

"End days, I think," he said. "The elders will understand when I say you were going to tell the police everything Ozzy had told you."

"Sure," I said. "Mysterious elders understand about things like that."

"You can become a mystery yourself," he said. "The Hartpury horror. Children will tell the tale of how a murdered woman haunts these trees, and spook themselves for generations to come. How is that for a legacy?"

"You know the divide between us. I don't half-drown kitties or scare children."

"Now, now, don't lie. Jim and Needle are about a third of your age, Molly, and look what you did to them. Threw them down my well. And now I have two men in hospital, Jim with a cracked head and Needle minus an eye. Get it? One-eyed Needle?" He chuckled a ghastly sound. "That crayon move was clever. I didn't know you were so resourceful, but that's what makes you so dangerous."

I waited for him to move, the stick behind my back in case I needed to hit him again. I could see in my mind's eye him falling straight down that hole, screaming and then begging me to get him up, asking me to forgive him, making empty promises and still yelling as I walked away to call the police on his miserable hide.

I will admit I felt a visceral pleasure in that wait. But when he did step onto the brittle sticks and lurched forwards, his body half down the hole and half up, he dropped the sword and his hands grabbed for my ankles, trying to drag me down with him, and I filled with pain and fear, my howls waking the woods and sending pheasants clattering with fright.

I had to reach one hand into the nearby flesh-ripping brambles to save myself, while with the other hand I beat at him with the stick. I hit him again and again, bashing him until he relinquished his grip and slipped and fell, and I heard the deep splash.

"Molly!" came his plaintive echoing cry. "Mollyyy!"

I walked away, nursing my bramble-savaged hand, limping up the path and back to Copseley Ridge for the phone, full of a perverse pride. Not pride that I had dumped another man down a well, but pride that I had bested another of my demons. I felt neither guilt nor grief nor shame, only a vast relief that I could be freeing many, many, people from his evil influence.

Then I reached Copsely Ridge and had to scream again. Both Callum and Joe were in the front room, almost where I had left them, but underneath all the blood that covered them it was hard to tell who had been who.

17. Graveyard Meeting

I don't know what became of the major's body. The police had come to me at the local hotel I had booked into and told me he'd been dead by the time they'd located the well. I was questioned relentlessly over the next few days, but never charged with anything.

Katarina gave herself up to the police. If I'd still had a house I might have been tempted to have taken her on as a housekeeper, because she did me a great favour. She had been looking after Misty, rescued from the major's garden and kept hidden in the big house.

Callum and Joe were cremated in Gloucester and I was the only non-press person who went to the service. I had hoped the mysterious Myrna would put in a show, but she didn't. She hadn't been a silent partner, though. Since she was still married to Callum, she had sorted the funerals and put Copsley Ridge on the market before you could say Jackanory.

I claimed Hugo's body as no one else had come forward, so he's interred in the village graveyard, and I got him a nice headstone because I could never have one for Gavin.

Finding out that Ozzy was a BBG was liberating. I no longer felt bad about hating him. Gavin fell into the river after a drunken fight with mates; that's what we'd been told. Now I think it likely that Gavin, a strong swimmer, was not drunk as they'd claimed, but hopped up on drugs, which made sense now I know what his father had been. And I had not seen any of it, living my life blinkered by his adamant 'women stay at home and don't have technology' attitude.

Since the fire, I had reaffirmed my relationships with many people in the village. To be honest, I suspected the many invites for a chat in Hartpury were mainly to get me to talk about my story, but I felt the place was less hostile to me, more giving, and I liked that. The imagined hostility was my fault, I could see that now. Locked in my own perceived miseries, I had driven people away.

Life is like the sea, I had decided, from gentle waves breaking down castles built in the sand, to storms breaking lives that could never be repaired.

However, the story wasn't over yet.

One chilly day in late October, I had walked to the churchyard, and I was looking at a new headstone erected a few days before at my cost. It read, 'Hugo Jenkins, taken too soon, stone dedicated by Molly'.

He deserved more than he had been given by life.

Someone approached me. I heard the damp tread of footsteps in the overgrown grass, so I turned and there he was: a tall, middle-aged man, wearing a grey raincoat and a stern face.

"Mrs Marshman?" he asked abruptly.

'This is it,' I thought with an odd kind of acceptance. He was a hit man, sent to kill me. So I drew myself up tall and acted as if I didn't care. No one was going to say I hadn't met my end with courage.

"Yes." I managed to smile. "Though I haven't gone by that name in a while. Can I help you?" I met his eye and kept on smiling.

As he put a hand inside the coat, I think I did squeak in fright because he put out the other hand in a placatory way and said, "It's alright, Ma'am," and he withdrew a warrant card and flashed it at me, though whether it was real or not was anyone's guess. "D.I . Courtland," he said. "C.I.D."

I swallowed hard. "Nice to meet you."

"There's a car out front of the church. I'd be grateful if you'd accompany me to it."

"I'm sorry," I said. "I don't think I trust anyone after what I went though. I don't want to go in a car with you. Where do you want to take me, anyway? The police station; a big deep hole?"

He pulled what could have been an amused face. "Castle

Carron churchyard."

"That doesn't... er... cheer me at all. Sounds like you want to bury me outside of Hartpury."

Now he smiled. "I can appreciate your hesitation, Mrs Marshman. I am familiar with the situation you've survived. Now I am following *police* orders to take you to Castle Carron, maybe a half hour run. Back before tea, I imagine."

"And why are you taking me to this place I've never heard of? What's there for me?"

His smile evaporated as he said, "Your son."

18. Death Fails

I sat in the back of the not-so-comfortable unmarked police car as it sped down the motorway. It certainly looked official on the inside, with a police radio and lots of other instruments on the dashboard, so I tried to relax.

I was full of a nameless sad-joy. They were taking me to Gavin's final resting place, on the coast just past Bristol, where I suppose his body had washed up. That raised the question of how they'd known it was Gavin. Then I realised it must have been Ozzy's plots and schemes at work again. He had known but kept the location of the grave from me; the final denial of having raised a child who had defied him. The final insult to me, for refusing to even try to make a 'real' son for him.

I drew a great sigh. 'All right, deal with what you have now, Molly. No point in forever thinking about yesterday. Today will be the start of a new chapter.'

The car drew up outside the gateway of a picturesque little church in a tiny quaint village, and the trees and bushes around the graveyard were all a glory of gold and red, shining with the dampness of recent rain and shaking in a strong breeze.

I walked behind D.I. Courtland as he entered the churchyard and we came up to the first row of upright stones, then he nodded to me by way of farewell and went back to the car.

I pulled up my coat collar to keep off the wind and looked around. Which one was it? There were so few I could look at them one by one. The row at the back looked newest, so I walked that way, but none of the headstones said anything like I would have expected. Puzzled, I looked up and around. The police car still sat by the gate, and there by the church wall the big D.I. stood in his raincoat.

But it wasn't him; this other man was bearded.

'Huggy?' I said to myself, puzzled.

I walked quickly towards him but the man walked off and, as the wind rocked the trees around me, I rounded the corner of the buttressed wall and saw him enter the main door of the church.

The heavy door was slowly closing as I got there, so I pushed it open again and stepped inside. Damp and musty carpet and old book smells hit my nose. I shivered a little.

Where was the man? I looked over the short rows of polished pews and saw no one. For a jarring moment I thought I had followed a ghost.

I walked a little down the aisle then turned and looked back, and there he was, in the corner by the font, the play of wind-dancing lights coming through the stained-glass windows playing tricks on me.

"Quit playing around, Huggy," I said, ecstatic to see him alive. "I'm *so* relieved to see you again. Come here and give me a hug, why don't you?"

The man stepped into the light.

He wasn't Huggy.

"Oh, come on," he said in a voice I had never got out of my head. "A few years and a beard and you forget all about me?"

I stepped towards him, arms out. "If the seas froze over and the world caught fire, I could never forget you, Gavin."

~

It turned out that Gavin had heard all about my escapades on TV. Four deaths in a little village was big news.

We sat in the church and talked a while. He hadn't run away those long years ago. He hadn't fallen into the river, no, not at all. He'd been in his despicable father's drug group and decided to go undercover for the police when Ozzy kicked him out for taking those same drugs. Although he hadn't managed to take down Ozzy's group, he had provided valuable information that had taken much off the market and convicted many people. My son; the spy. And, when he'd done enough, he was taken into the witness protection scheme, and left his old life and me behind.

So when he'd told the police he wanted to see me, it was safer for me to be taken to the church than for him to come to me.

~

Misty and I moved out of Hartpury to live with Gavin and his family on the coast, in a house a stone's throw from the sea, just like I've always wanted. The blonde girl Huggy had seen in the pub is Gavin's wife, a charming creature, and their three children are amazing! Instant grandmother-hood!

Gavin hunted down for Lottie for me. She passed some years ago leaving two sons, but although I can rest happy in the knowledge I have some relatives left, I cannot, of course, ever meet them. They wouldn't know me from Adam anyway, and I doubt I'd feel anything for them; I just needed to know.

So here we are, a separate little flat for me, the freedom of their garden to potter in, a pond with goldfish, a gardener to do all the heavy stuff, and children to play with. Heaven, for both me and Misty, who has settled in well.

I landed on my feet and, although terror had gripped me for a lot of my life, I was healing from the inside out. I could hug my grandchildren, my daughter-in-law, my son, and not feel like I wanted to scream at the contact. That was progress. Old dogs (not me, because I am not old) can learn new tricks.

I had felt like a piece of rubbish cast aside to moulder socially throughout my life because of one horrible incident. Beating Jim and Needle and the major taught me I could fight back and, believe me, the new Molly will fight back for the rest of her life. I had discovered that even in the meekest heart there is a power to call on. It may not be a nice power, but its name is survival, and that comes down to the fittest mentally as much as physically. I'm off the radar. Mrs Marshman became Ms Turner, became Ms Smith. I don't pay tax, don't draw my pension even, have no involvement with the social services or show up anywhere—after all, I don't know who's left that might want to still play hunt-the-diamonds.

Which I have.

You heard right. I have the diamonds, ghastly little uncut things that look like nothing really, like crazed beach glass. I can't believe people died for them.

Gavin's growing family absorbs money, so I gave them to him, because I wouldn't know the first thing about how to sell them and he does.

The major had slipped up and overdosed Hugo before he could spill the beans, and because Major Nitwit had been so keen to make a point to me and left the initialled boots on him, and because I chose to see to Hugo's funeral myself—receiving the boots in his effects—the system efficiently handed back what the BBGs had searched so long and hard for.

I won't say I *knew* they were there, but I did suspect. Seeing Hugo with the tools in the shed, and the fact I'd noticed he'd worn the boots all the time, favouring them over his Doc Martens, made me examine them very carefully.

He'd borrowed tools to carve out the inside of the boot heels, creating compartments.

Poor Hugo; I still feel sad for him, but I like to imagine that my big, bearded friend would be happy to know it was I who found the stones.

~

My grandchildren listen to my latest attempt at a poem with big eyes, while all I can think is, 'Last laugh's on you, Major Nitwit, not me, not the woman whose friend you killed, not the woman you dropped in a well so vile she had to have a fortnight's worth of antibiotics, not the woman you pursued murderously through the woods... No, it's you who the children will mock forever... *You* are the Hartpury horror.'

~

"In Hartpury woods, there is a bane
a crazy man with a greying mane
who brandishes a fearful cane
and scares the children who call his name.
Major!

105

Major Nitwit! they cry,
Pursued by the devil, his spirit to blacken
he's in through the bushes, and out through the bracken
though scratched by the brambles, his pace does not slacken
'til tripped in the well to die."

BOOK TWO

KERTON-ON-SEA

"Love in action is a harsh and
dreadful thing compared with love in
dreams."~Fyodor Dostoevski

1. Cliff Capers

I was woken abruptly from a dreadful dream, one full of loss, longing and pain, so maybe it was just as well that at the tender hour of 4.30am someone had entered my bedroom and was rummaging in my drawers.

Getting up onto one elbow, I gave the back of my son's head a disdainful look before asking, "Gavin, what are you doing? Do you know what the time is?"

"Sorry, Mum," he muttered without an apologetic syllable in sight, moving down a drawer and peering through my petticoats and panties.

"The frilly ones are at the back," I said, flopping back down, one arm over my face to keep out the light from the corridor. "Is there something you want to tell me regarding this underwear obsession; to tell your lovely wife?"

He grunted a laugh. "I just think when Vana emptied these drawers for you to move in, she must've missed something, 'cause I can't find it anywhere."

"It?"

"A notebook," he said, turning his attentions to the bottom drawer. "Tiddly thing, half A6 size, whatever that is. You haven't seen it around, have you?"

"Gavin, I've been here a while now. Any notebook, tiny or otherwise, would have come to light by now, don't you think?" I yawned widely. "Perhaps the kids took it to draw in. How important can it possibly be if you haven't needed it until now, and why's the info not in your lovely shiny computer?"

"Some things are safer *not* in a PC. It was a client list for the last place I worked. Kept it just in case, and now the boss needs something I think's in there. Actually, I thought it was in the safe but..." His stressed voice faded out and rummaging ensued in the tall boy instead.

"Have you asked Vana yet?" I sighed. "Your father always lost things and I always found them. June says Henry's just the same. So pop off and shut the door on the way out, there's a darling." Rolling onto my front, I closed my eyes into the pillow, though I doubted I'd get to sleep again.

"Vana?" His voice echoed down the corridor that connects my flat to the house. Then the door clicked shut as I longed to hear him say, "Love you, Mum," like in the days of old, but the words never came.

"Love you, Gavin," I whispered into the early morning's waking drone, missing the loving child he had once been, lamenting the man who had grown up out of my sight. Time could not be reclaimed.

On the really quiet nights back in Hartpury, the silence could get so thick your heartbeat was your only company, but outside my seaside window the world was beginning to wake, seagulls up since first light. Every morning here in Little Kerton-on-Sea, I had to deal with family activity, people's loud voices, Gavin and Vana rushing around to go to work… It was another noisy world entirely.

I was glad to be under Gavin's aegis, but I pined for the peaceful presence of Hartpury woods. But one rarely gets everything one wants in life, and this seaside town had to be better than where I had lived, because my family was here, my grandchildren, my new life safe from harm.

'Let me sleep a little more,' I prayed, 'for soon my three grandchildren will whirl into my bedroom like the winds of wrath, and leap onto me if I'm not up to get their breakfasts.'

I've been here over a year now and, despite that overwhelming urge to get here and live here and have a new life here, what I have found is that what you want is not always what you need, and desire for new-ness and safety can quickly fade.

In my mind's eye I had seen the seaside as sunshine, blue water and softly lapping waves, but Kerton's not like that at all. What I now experience daily is the sticky-salty sea spray in my hair the moment I step out of the house, and permanently having to dress like it's deep mid-winter, not to mention the new rash of wrinkles I have garnered from walking with my face scrunched up against the prevailing wind-blown sand.

Yes, sand at the seaside—how dare it be there.

It gets everywhere. I care for my grandchildren and I could call all of them *Sandy*. Here is lovely sweet Myha, six-years-old with café-au-lait curls, and Minnie, her identical twin. Collin is much taller, older at eight, a rather awkward child who thinks he knows everything and hates being corrected, and talks back to me all the time. He runs me ragged but I do love his spark.

The children like nothing more at the end of a school day than to eschew the village playground with swings and fancy apparatus and instead run down to the beach and build frigid castles and raid rock pools that still have a thin sheet of ice on them at 3.30pm. And I am the one who cleans up after the children, who vacuums the sand out of carpets, and shakes beds and the boy's pockets and everything.

Vana is a fiery woman of whom I am too polite to ask the whys and wherefores of her family origins. Her English is natural but finely peppered with words of her own language, and if you get her mad she'll spout incomprehensibly. I think Collin gets his awkward attitude from her.

He's making me miserable, that grandson of mine. I wanted to love these children, to hug them and play with them, to make up for so many lost years, but instead I have to face his overt cheekiness along with my disillusionment with the seaside. I've even gone so far as to get a hearing aid, sans battery. My hearing is fine, you see, but the family doesn't know that, so I can leave it on the side and hear Collin's plots and plans without him knowing I can hear. He also likes to run off with it to annoy me, though it's become more of a game lately. It's just my way of getting one-upmanship on the child. Am I a sneaky woman? I prefer to think that what I do is all for the good of the children.

Gavin says I have to accept that Collin is Vesuvius, boiling with hot words and ideas, and Little Kerton is Antarctica, four months of sunny activity and eight months of the cold, cold wind that comes off the sea, and I know he just wants me to stop complaining.

I suspect he is fed up with me already, even though I have taken on the task of housekeeper and childminder while he and Vana work. I feel I am Nana-the-irreplaceable, the mighty organiser without whom this family would fall apart, and I wonder every day how they managed before I came back into their lives. I arrived with a lot of money in uncut diamonds, so I don't think the cost bothers him, but I am trying to figure out what's wrong. There is something about his attitude, the odd small remark that hurts me. I had been dumb enough to imagine us running into each other's arms to the resounding chords of movie music. But although we had hugged then, conversation nowadays is sparse. Hello and goodbye and let's rummage in your drawers at an ungodly hour—and even when I ask what's wrong, he has to 'rush' and the issue is never resolved.

My mother used to tell me I was destined for greatness. I could never believe that. I felt at the time it was something that all decent parents said to encourage their offspring, but the best 'greatness' I ever felt was when I dropped a man down a well, and I'm pretty sure she didn't mean that, or that she would have approved of it—even though it had been to save my own life.

~

At the end of the school day, the children walked in front of me, filled with chattering post-school excitement, and traipsed down the wooden cliff stairs to the rocky beach. It is at least fun to beach-comb while they play, the twins throwing sand at each other—which I have told them not to do a thousand times and have now given up saying. They'll have to learn the hard way.

I like the way you can walk to everything here. The shop

sells a good selection of items, including fossils, and is also a Post Office at select times. There's a lovely pub overlooking the sea, and a spectacular new village hall, and I really like that there are very few residents out of season. Fewer people means less rubbish, though I know that will change once we get some tourists as the weather warms up. Not many visitors, because the beach is hardly Costa Del Sol, and we have no town novelties to hold anyone, though the fossil hunters like the cliffs; no joke shops or souvenir huts or ice cream parlours. The old restaurant will likely have to shut this year if the spring storms cause more landslips in its area, and if the shop doesn't have what you want you have to drive or bus to the bigger towns inland.

While the girls set to their favourite occupation of building sandcastles, Collin wandered around on the cold beach, his thick brown hair ruffled by the wind, finding more stony things for his collection and filling his school bag with them; and with sand. Did I mention the sand that gets everywhere? It would be in his schoolbooks too, and I'd have to shake them out onto the porch when we got home. I cannot deny I found looking after the children hard work. I loved the interaction with them but, not being as young as I used to be, my energy levels had dipped—but Lord knows I will never admit to being old.

The winter waves were grey and foamy, and the sea roared like a petulant bear to the accompaniment of shrill gulls' cries. I shivered despite my coat and scarf and all the other warming woolly stuff.

Then I heard a voice from above me.

The cliffs over the beach are not majestic towering stacks, they're a sloping thirty-degree angle of messed up rock falls and slippage and mud and clay and sand and everything else. On the cliff top above where I stood, dozens of feet away on the angle, the spire of our small abandoned church could just be seen. Coastal and cliff erosion has taken down most of the graveyard and the sea literally carried away its bones, the sweet little church replete with *danger: do not enter* signs. A dozen more years and its own stony-bones will rest in the sea.

I looked up at a second loud voice. Way above me, on the edge of the graveyard and between two lopsided box tombs, I could see two figures. One looked to be a lanky man in a heavy coat, the other a blonde woman waving her arms, scarf flapping madly in the air, from her stance arguing loudly but the wind stealing the sense of her words. I couldn't recognise either of them from that distance, but the evident tone of the argument disturbed me on a deep level. Man versus woman has always ended badly for me, so I stood and sent her positive vibes while I watched whatever relationship drama was being acted out above me while also watching my grandchildren.

I looked back at the children, then back up the cliffs, and in that instant of inattention the couple had gone.

2. We All Fall Down

"Ice cream, Nana," yelled Myha. A demand, not a request.

"Brrr. Too cold for ice cream." I gave an exaggerated shiver. "I can see ice in the mud ripples over there."

"Yes, ice cream's for *any* weather," Minnie joined in, then Collin ran up and grabbed my hand.

"You taught us that, Nan," he said with his cheeky grin. "Ice cream, ice cream, we'll all scream for ice cream," he carried on, and I was soon being dragged to the steps and pushed up playfully by children chanting, "Ice cream, ice cream, Nan wants some ice cream."

I will get so fat. What's that? I don't have to eat it, you say? But that's torture, keen and true. If they eat ice cream, so do I.

As we came out of the shop, licking ice cream cones, a woman with no coat on despite the temperature, was marching down the path on the other side of the road. Arms and scarf hugged around her to ward off the chill, face red with cold, or fury, her usually neat blonde hair lank from windy salt air, red painted nails flared against the grey of the world as she swiped a hand across her nose. She was the woman from the cliff top. Now I recognised her: the local publican's wife—Lisa Gilroy.

But she had passed on by, not noticing or not caring that I was staring at her with this huge need blossoming in me, an almost overwhelming desire to run over the road and take her in my comforting arms and get her to spill all her worries to me. I fought it down. I can't cure everyone's emotional ills; look how much it took to 'fix' mine.

I gathered up my wards and went home, trying to push Lisa from my mind, trying to concentrate on house duties and homework to do and dinner to get, but how I wished I had gone to her then. How I wished it later.

~

That evening, someone hammered on the front door and rang the doorbell too for good measure. I hurried to the peephole and saw Lisa Gilroy's husband, Terry, standing agitated under the outside light. He's a tall chap, and as he stood there in his long coat he had rather the shape of the person Lisa had been arguing with on the cliff top. 'Suspicious much?' I thought.

Even as I opened the door he was saying, "Have you seen my Lisa, by any chance? I can't find her anywhere and I'm getting a wee bit worried, like." Gavin arrived before I could answer and Terry went on hopefully, "You seen her, Gav, mate? Getting right worried, I am now. Not answering her phone, neither."

"Last time I saw her she was in the pub with you," Gavin said.

"Invite him in, you two!" Vana said from behind us. "*Bozhe mir*; it's freezing with the door open."

"No, no, I gotta get off, thanks," Terry said, and I wondered why I was stalling. If I admitted in front of Gavin that I'd seen them arguing, Terry might be very embarrassed, but that wasn't the point. I *had* seen her fine and well after that cliff top debacle, hadn't I?

So Terry was walking smartly up the path as my slow clockwork brain finally worked through a way to answer and I called, "I remember now. I saw her walking in Church Street towards the pub at 4.15."

He span. "What? That's like four hours ago. I'm going to coppers," he declared and ran off, literally chuffing off into the darkness of the unlit road.

I told Gavin what I had actually seen. "I didn't think Terry needed to know he'd been seen arguing with his wife. He might think I'd spread it all over."

"Now, now, Mother," Gavin said in an unwarranted weary voice. "Remember my rule. No adventures here at the seaside."

"Pft; was hardly an *adventure* last time, was it," I retorted. "Nearly died." And a nasty memory flared in me so suddenly that tears welled in my eyes, and Gavin held me until I had pushed down the ghastly thoughts in the way the Witness Programme psychologist had advised me, and all was peacefully hidden inside me again.

~

Once I had dropped off the children at school the next morning, I made my way to The Smuggler's Joy pub, which is set on a slightly hillier part of the land, far enough back to not feel the effects of the slipping cliffs that ate the other pub some years back. The Joy overlooks the sea, the beer garden one of our attractions in the summer with a huge tent-like covered area shielding customers from the sea air while affording them glorious views.

Fellow pensioner and grandma, June Bailey, intercepted me at the end of the road and we walked together. June was the first person in Kerton to befriend me, then came others, but June was undoubtedly my *best friend*, something I had not had since high school. I had found a need to fit in, to be wanted, and with my family's rather waning interest in me June had kept me afloat with her humour many times.

Other than that she believed in fortune telling and the afterlife spirits guiding us, things I had little faith in, she was a perfectly perfect friend.

"Have you heard?" she said, with all the excitement of a gossiping Gerty. "Lisa Gilroy's missing."

"Yes, Terry came round last night looking for her," I said. "So, no luck, poor man. I know what it's like when someone vanishes and you don't know where they are."

"Police were there last night," she said, indicating the pub we were approaching. "I gather they went all over the cliffs."

"That sounds like they fell off the cliffs."

She tittered. "You know what I mean."

"I expect they'll be coming to see me soon, then."

"Why?"

I told her I'd seen Lisa walking up the road with no coat, looking angry.

"Ooh." Her face lit up at the idea of scandal. "Wonder if the little lady had an illicit boyfriend and she broke it off and he's really broken it off with her, final-like." She opened her eyes wide. "You know what I mean."

As we reached the Smuggler's Joy car park, I stopped and stared at her in a deprecating way. "Honestly, June, I wish I hadn't told you. What a horrible thing to surmise from so few clues."

"Hmpf." She adjusted her fur hat and plumped up the red scarf around her neck. "Wouldn't be the first murder round here," she said tartly. "Human nature, isn't it?"

"You should ask the spirits where Lisa is."

"Spirits only speak when they want to," she said, "and well you know it."

"I only know what you tell me."

She gave a hesitant laugh and fidgeted. "So, you want I should ask my cards if Terry had anything to do with Lisa's disappearance?"

"I was thinking more along the lines of just asking where she is, but yes, why not? Give it a go."

I had become distracted by the sight of a police car outside the pub and was looking across at it.

"Hmpf, I can tell you're not listening to me," she said, following my line of sight. "Police cars more interesting, are they? Oh well, I could give the crystal ball a go, I suppose. No harm in asking."

As we stood there talking, a policeman exited the private gate of the pub—the gate that leads to the publican's back door —and he stopped to look across at us. He stood there and, as I looked over at him, I realised with a start he was gazing at me, rubbing his chin and frowning.

I excused myself from the curious June and hurried over

before he let the cat out of the bag by using my old name. She stood and watched.

My hair is no longer so short and pink hued, I have garnered another year's worth of wrinkles and even bought different glasses, but Sergeant Williams was a proper copper and had recognised me nonetheless.

"Fancy seeing you here, Sergeant Williams." I smiled as I met up with him. "Oh, hang on, you didn't get shunted to a lower dominion on my account, I hope?"

"Not at all. Transferred to Poole on account of the mother-in-law's problems. Nice to see you!" He beamed, shaking my hand avidly like he'd just met a screen star he followed. His voice went lower as he leaned in. "Errr... what name you going by now? Don't worry; know all about the Hartpury case. Knew you'd been moved off somewhere for safety, didn't know it was here, though."

"Molly Smith. Has no charm to it." I smiled ruefully.

"Ahh, so, are you the Mrs Smith I'm s'posed to be interviewing in the case of the missing Mrs Gilroy?" he said, suddenly all unsmiling. Though, to be fair, a missing woman is as unsmiling a thing as you can find.

"Yes. Look, can we go inside? It's bloomin' freezing out here and my friend stood staring at us over there will assume we're having an affair, if I know her."

We sat ourselves in the snug where the wood-fire was blazing, and I told Sergeant Williams what I had witnessed on the cliffs and in the street, not that my wobbly descriptions were much help. I didn't add that I thought the man arguing with her might've been her own husband. It would be too embarrassing if I was wrong. When it was all over we said our goodbyes and I left, hoping Lisa would turn up soon.

~

That afternoon the children dragged me down to the beach as usual. It was fine and bright with ice in the air— bracing, as the walkers like to say. I strolled backwards and forwards, looking for any interesting things in the sand or the flotsam that collects after each tide, skimming rocks into the grey-scummed sea while the twins remade their washed away castle in the same place as the day before and the day before that, and Collin found them new pebbles for the windows and steps, running backwards and forwards like a maniac.

I think they all have Gavin's mindset of *don't do anything unless you have to, unless you are nagged to*. I thought it was just teenage boys who got like that, but Myha and Minnie at just six tender years were terrible to control. No, I don't mean control, I mean to care for, to point in the right direction, to offer help to. Or maybe I was just lousy with children other than as a watch dog, or is it I am just too old in the generation sense. Collin loves to mock my non-expertise on the PC, though he lets me play on shared games sometimes.

I have a mobile now in case of problems, but every time I look at it I am reminded of the picture on my lounge wall: a pair of boots sticking upside down out of the mud, the only image I have of a man I befriended, who helped me... Hugo.

I must stop thinking backwards.

Positives: food really does taste better when it's eaten sitting on the sand, out of the wind, on a not-raining day. Summer days are glorious, the views over the sea are spectacular, the neighbours are nice and there's not much litter until the tourists start to arrive—

"Nan!" came Collin's shout from down the beach, enough anxiety in it to make my heart sink. "Come look what I found."

I glanced back at the sand-playing twins, then hurried to where Collin stood, agitated, farther along the beach than he was allowed to be, at the base of some slippage, all rocks and mud and sand slumped down off the friable cliffs like a sloughed skin. There used to be smuggler's tunnels in the cliffs, hence the name of the pub, but falls had covered them all.

"Be careful," I said looking at the high slumps in concern. "Your father would whip me if anything happened to you. Go back up with your sisters now; scoot."

"But, Nan," he whined, "look there." He pointed to

something in the pile and my heart jumped.

A hand, slim, white, with red painted nails, was lolling out of the mud bank.

3. Bang Bang

Collin's wide eyes were fixed on his find, and he seemed to be panting, nervous breath clouds condensing around his head like mist. I stretched and leaned and prodded the pale hand with my gloved finger.

"Plastic," I lied glibly. "A mannequin. You know, a shop model sort of thing. I'll call the council; get them to shift it so no old ladies have heart attacks."

He looked at me and I saw doubt on his face, but he shrugged and ran back up the beach, so I took out my mobile and dialled the emergency number. When it was promptly answered, shielding both the microphone and my mouth from the wind, I said in a voice trembling with nervous tension, "Hello. I just found a body under Church Cliff."

~

Gavin and Vana were not happy to come home and find a police car outside the house.

"Dad, Mum!" Collin yelled happily, running to them the moment the front door opened. "I found a body, a real live body on the beach."

Vana must have taken him to another room, as only Gavin came into the lounge where I sat with two policemen; Sergeant Williams and another chap, so young and fresh-faced I'd have taken him for a schoolboy.

"Mum," Gavin said with a frown and a voice that implied I was the naughty child, "what did you do now?"

"I didn't do anything on purpose," I said indignantly. "Collin found a body on the beach. Likely, poor Lisa Gilroy."

Gavin sort of nodded a 'Hello' to the policemen before he asked me stonily, "And how much did my son see of this body?"

I stuck my nose in the air. "Honestly! Don't fret so. Only her poor white hand was sticking out of the mud fall, and I told him it was plastic. It's not like we danced on her bloodied corpse, is it?"

Sergeant Williams, used to seeing bad things, I would have imagined, reassured the still unhappy Gavin. "She was almost entirely covered by a recent landslip, so quite possibly the fall killed her, but we'll know more after the autopsy." He stood up. "We'll mosey off now, Ms Smith; thanks for your help." He nodded goodbye to Gavin and the policemen left.

Seconds later I had Gavin on my back. "It's attracted to you, isn't it, Mum? You're like a magnet to trouble."

"Don't be silly. Don't be nasty. It's like the man said, Collin only saw a hand. Why such a fuss?"

"I don't want my kids involved in *anything*."

"Who's involving them? I told Collin I thought it was a mannequin's hand, got him away from it, called the police then brought the children home and they were oblivious until that silly policeman mentioned 'body' on the doorstep."

"What?" said Collin's voice as he came in, eyes alight with childish fervour. "You can tell me about bodies, you don't have to lie, Dad, I'm a big boy."

"You're eight, Collin. That's too young to be seeing bodies."

He shrugged. "I do look on the Internet, you know. There are hundreds of kids living in places at war. I've seen—"

"Maybe not so much Internet," Vana said as she came in, frowning.

"You can't hold back information from them," I complained. "Children need to learn. Their brains are like sponges, soaking up information, or so *I* read on the net."

Vana folded her arms and challenged me. "And when he gets around to the nasty stuff?"

"You can't control children, only what they read, and even that control's wrong in its own way. They need to know the bad as well as the good to make up their own minds."

"Not about dead bodies at eight," Vana snapped.

"Then when?" I asked.

"I am not having this conversation," she said, "with an

old lady who half the time can't remember her own name! Rocky," she wheedled, using her pet name for Gavin like a bargaining tool, "this is your family. You tell her how it goes."

Gavin sighed. Vana realised she'd lost the battle and stormed out, slamming the door behind her.

"I think you're a bit too liberal, Mum," Gavin said.

"Oh really," I said, the words copiously laced with sarcasm. "So maybe, if I am so dangerous, such a magnet to trouble suddenly after the last year's *peace and quiet*, I'd better go find somewhere else to live before aliens come down and abduct us all." I stalked out.

"What we need," Gavin's tenor voice boomed from behind me, "is a family discussion, not a bloody mass walk out!"

But as his angry cry faded I was already in the connecting corridor and reaching for my flat's door handle. Misty, asleep on my sofa as usual, stretched and yawned when she saw me, showing all her sharp little cat teeth. I wanted to borrow them and bite Vana but, being civilised, I chose to sit and stroke Misty, a calming constant in my life, who promptly asked to go out.

I should pack up and go; go somewhere, I don't know where. But despite everyone having issues with me, I could be mature and deal with it. I really had no authority to say how the children were to be raised. I was basically their guardian, their cook, their escort to and from school, a helper with homework, plaster-bearer ready for scratches.

Reviewing that list in my mind I could see my value to the Smiths. And I didn't forget things. Vana was just being Vana.

If I were to leave, how complicated their lives would become, reverting to the chaos and juggling they'd had before I'd arrived. Vana would have to give up her job again as she'd never find a minder who did all I had done for them—not at my low price of, oh yes, *free*. I was surprised she was even risking chasing me off. I expect she assumed I wanted to rest in this comfortable yet well-earned bed forever, so I wouldn't walk.

I sighed in discontent and went out to the balcony and the testing early evening sea breeze. I had adored that little balcony from the moment I had first seen it. Yet, that time, as I gazed out on the darkening view, in a strange twist of the mind I looked across the grey mass of the sea lit only by a few lights from the town and a half moon, and I saw instead the fields of Hartpury. Life, eh? Homesickness: the last thing you can control.

It was time for the children to go to bed, so I went to that task from force of habit, feeling love for the children but speaking politely and tersely to my son and his wife when I encountered them in the kitchen, then I made sure Misty was back in for the night and went to bed after my cocoa and fell asleep quickly, slipping into a bad dream of dark wells and wet faces.

~

After the school drop-off the next morning, I decided I ought to go see Terry Gilroy, offer condolences or something. I knew from past experience that the bereaved often need someone to talk to but won't admit to it; especially men, who thought they had to be big and tough and hide their emotions.

The pub's front door was shut, and I wouldn't have been surprised to find a note saying, 'Closed until further notice due to bereavement', or something like that. So the chances were he was still in bed or on the phone. I remembered how much sorting out I'd had to do when Ozzy had died. Perhaps I was remiss in coming there. Terry would more than likely have neither the time nor the inclination to see me.

In the quiet-for-tourists months, some repairs were being done to the main doorway's porch, a pile of cut white stones neatly stacked by the half-dismantled archway, and a small skip of rubble on the other side. As I walked into the car park and along the side of the building to see if I could see anyone moving through the kitchen window—yes, I am that nosy—an off-white Clio with a chugging exhaust drove into the car park. *No luck here, sir; no beer today, or did you come to pay respects?*

I was looking at the budding bushes around the car park, wishing them to bloom and give some colour to the place, when I heard the car door open and shut and a tall, thin and heavy-coated man called over, startling me, his scarf obscuring his face as he said, "'Ullo, love, you know if anyone's home?"

"I don't know," I said. "There's a problem in the family."

He nodded, giving me a long measuring look, and I half expected him to say, 'Here, I know you, don't I?' but he wandered off as I turned around the corner of the kitchen extension to face the cold sea view. The wind—oh, that blasted eternal wind. I adore the summer days and nights; hate any other season.

Litter, a crisp bag, rustled and scurried away from me like a dry leaf. I leaned over and grabbed it before it escaped, thinking: note to self, petition the town council for more lidded waste bins.

A sudden *wheep wheep wheep* and the pub's alarm was going off. I hurried around the front of the building to see the be-scarved man emerging from the private gate and carrying a sack of knobbly-somethings. "Wasn't me," he said in strange apology as he spotted me. "It just went off."

I shrugged; maybe time for me to shift too before I got the blame for something.

The alarm shut off into blissful silence, then Terry Gilroy, dressed only in plaid pyjamas, rampaged out of the private gate yelling, "Stop, thief!" at the man now starting up the Clio and, as the moving car's window wound down, a revolver was being pointed at Terry.

I turned tail and hastily scurried up the earthen bank of the footpath, hiding myself in the bushes while the shots I had expected to hear never happened, but sharp *whangs* came instead. I peeked out and saw in admiration that bold Terry was pelting the car with stones from the skip while the car attempted a very feeble twenty-three point turn to get away with much yelling and cussing emanating from within it.

A half-brick impacted the windscreen and a shattered hole appeared. The driver stalled in shock and fired the pistol. And Terry, still bombarding the car with stones as fast as he could, staggered, blood appearing on his upper arm, falling to his knees as the car drove off with its messed-up window and pummelled paintwork like it had been caught in a meteor shower, and I hurried to Terry while calling emergency services for the second time in two days.

Gavin would have a fit over this.

Then I thought of how the driver had looked at me. What if he'd recognised me? How much worse could the day become?

Gavin would have a double fit if I was silly enough to mention *that*.

4. Nice Men

"She was murdered," Terry's cracking voice said as I crouched beside him in the car park and wrapped my scarf around his bleeding arm. "My Lisa," he said bitterly, eyes damp, lips trembling. "They murdered her."

"Who's *they*?" I asked the bereft man sitting in the open on a cold day wearing only his PJs. He started to shake, from cold or shock or both.

"Oh," he said sadly with a tiny huff of black amusement. "That's a tale and a half, that is, Molly. You don't wanna know."

And I really, really didn't.

Well, yes, actually; I did.

I managed to get him up and helped him round the back of the pub and in through the private door, until he sagged onto a bench in the snug and I took off my coat to place it around his shaking shoulders.

I unlocked the front door for ease of access for the ambulance crew then listened to Terry's sad tale while we waited. I heard how Lisa had been trying IVF, and failing, and failing again, and she'd sold all her jewellery and all their savings were gone and it had run to the point where she was ruining the future of the pub. He'd backed her up as much as he could, but then she'd really got herself into trouble by borrowing money from a loan shark—which he'd not known about until too late.

He sounded such a nice considerate man that I could have wept for him.

"Terry, if you've nothing valuable left, what did the man who shot you take?"

"Well that there mad woman, the one she borrowed money from, she wanted the money repaid, you know? The only things we had left of value were a few old collectors' dolls, but Lisa wouldn't sell *them*, you see, said they were her dollies, like her babbies, and we had to keep them for the kiddies, for the future." His lips trembled. "What future now, eh?"

I waited in silence while he composed himself, listening for the distant sounds of a siren. "But the mad lady had said she wanted 'em," he went on. "Wanted the Sasha dolls from the 60s and the German bisque-headed things that looked like devil dolls to me. I guess an argument with the woman went bad. Sal had been bashed about the 'ead before she was chucked over, the coppers said." He suddenly broke into huge man sobs and I patted his back like he was a great big baby, not knowing what more I could do.

He sniffed and wiped his nose on my coat. To be fair, he was in a state so had probably forgotten it was my coat. It has a lot of dire stuff from the children on it anyway. "Yeah," Terry went on, "so them dollies was only in the back room. On display shelves I made for them, for her, so the bugger got 'em easy after he'd busted the lock and triggered the alarm. Only took the time it took me to wake and get downstairs for him to snaffle the lot." He sniffed hugely.

"Okay," I reassured him, the first fluctuating wail of a siren reaching my ears. "You're doing well, Terry. You keep saying 'the woman', who's that?"

"I dunno. Never got her name. Sal said she just turned up, said she'd heard she wanted to borrow some money and she could arrange it, and my Sal dealt with her, but she had these eyes, Molly... piercing dark eyes, like she was going to kill you just by looking at you. Course, with eyes like that I wouldna trusted her from the get-go. But Sal, nah, she wouldn't listen to me." Tears rolled down his cheeks. "I said I wanted her more than a babby, but that weren't right thing to say, apparently, so we'd had a few arguments. It were like wanting a babby was pushing us apart, not together, and now I ha'nt got Sally neither." He put his head in his hands and shook it slowly. "You know, I hopes they come back, I does; come back and burn the place to the ground and all me memories with it. Then I'll have nothing more they can take from me. So I can go off and start again"

I sat there not knowing what to say, just being with him as the sirens came down the road and the ambulance swung into the car park. I left everyone to their parts in the great tragedy that is life and went home. The police knew where to find me if they wanted to talk to me... again.

~

"Lord above, Mother," Gavin said. "How do you manage it?"

I hadn't wanted to tell him, but I realised policemen turning up out of the blue to question me about the pub incident would give it away. And as for the burglar recognising me... I couldn't be *sure* he had, so I'd keep quiet about that.

I stuck my nose in the air. "It's not like I *make* these things happen. Just wrong place, wrong time."

"Just promise me this: you will not get the kids involved in anything."

"What a stu—"

"Promise!"

"Of course I promise. I will have adventures all on my own. All right? And, as much as is possible with my magnetic personality that attracts bad guys to me like moths to a flame, I will not even have any adventures. Honestly, Gavin, there I was thinking I brought you up to be a nice considerate man and now this!" I flounced out of the dining room with him no doubt glowering behind me.

~

June rang me that night.

"I was just consulting the spirits, asking about Lisa— and no joy on that—and Moira phoned to tell me about your exploits at the pub earlier, with guns and ambulances and car chases. How come you never phoned to tell me yourself? Spoilsport. It's such fun having a dramatic friend like you. And friendly with that police officer I saw the other day?"

"There wasn't a car chase. She's exaggerating again, and the coppers just an old acquaintance. Don't be nosey. Oh, that's your middle name, isn't it? June Nosey Bailey?" I said a bit cattily.

She laughed then became serious. "Listen. I had a nap after dinner, and I think I got a dream message for you."

"Me? Dream message? What are you talking about?"

She exhaled heavily and the phone hissed. "*I* believe, even if you don't. I 'felt' it was a message for you. 'Finders keepers, losers weepers.' That was it, the voice clear as a bell, then I woke."

"It's interesting having you as a friend, too," I said. "Has it ever occurred to you that the wine talks... or the Vodka? That's a spirit, isn't it?"

"Oh, ha ha jolly ha. Don't mock my beliefs."

"I'm not. Could you ask your spirit buddies what I have to do to find a nice man?"

In the background of June's phone call a male voice began shouting for her.

"Look at that," she said in a partially amused despairing voice. "My dearly beloved can't find his golfing shoes for the morning... again. You want a nice man, Molly? I love Henry but I wouldn't call him *nice*. Now, I'll have to go before he has an aneurysm. Speak again soon. Ciao."

5. Finders Keepers...

Thursday dawned veritably spring-like; clear skies, bright sun, fat buds on the flowering hedges, a few sheltered daffodils opening their trumpets, dandelions and daisies blooming in the verges.

Abandoning the children to the maw of the school, which they moaned about but liked really, I went to the beach on my own to plod along and listen to the gulls and the waves and hug myself against the wind trying to run off with my hat.

Wrapping up warm and walking on a deserted beach in winter is an invigorating experience, I will admit. No smell is better than the salty sea air to clear your head and brainwash you into thinking life's not so bad, as long as it's not messing up your hair quality.

And there is definitely no sound in the world better than the smooth lapping of waves on the beach, jostling the pebbles into chatter, talking to each other about what has happened since they last met as rocks millennia ago.

I walked around the cliff fall where blue and white *police-line-do-not-cross* tape, ripped by the wind into shreds, still fluttered in the breeze. Even they couldn't tidy up behind them. I looked up to the graveyard and tried to remember what the man Lisa had been arguing with had looked like. Taller than her, short brown hair, heavy dark coat, possibly glasses, that's what I had told the police and, now it was settled in there as a firm memory, I couldn't pull anything else out of my head.

The beach gets narrower after a point. Tourist signs warn of sitting too close to the cliffs. The signs are not there for fun, I can assure you. It's a point of no return, where the slips are more likely, a place that needed a bigger, more demanding sign saying, 'do NOT walk here after a storm for a week or so until the land settles'.

I ignored the signage, of course, and walked on.

And stopped.

There, around the corner, hidden by the slip, on its roof in the rocks and debris of the cliff, was the smashed-up Clio from the pub burglary. 'Oh', I thought. 'Dare I look inside?' Of course I did, though it was terribly flattened. I peered in and spotted only one thing that was useful and I thought…

'One should never lose the childlike delight of finding and collecting pretty shells, or nice stones polished by ages of wave-tumbling… Or the nerve tingling excitement of taking pistols from wrecked cars.'

What had June's spirit voice said? 'Finders keepers'? Whether this was what the voice had meant or not, I felt sure the gun would be safer in my handbag than being left on the beach for someone more vulnerable to find, especially since I could see some of the chambers were still occupied.

~

After school, at the village playground, Collin was sliding in the mud, making it worse for everyone else who might want to walk that way. The ground used to be recycled rubber stuff but the council took it up when it was found to be dangerous, so now the playground's a hippo-wallow in wet weather.

Collin slid like an ice skater and landed with a *whomp* on the bench.

"Maybe you shouldn't do that," I said. "You'll hurt yourself, or someone else," but he went off and slid-slid-slid under the climbing frame.

"Honestly, Collin," I said as he defied my suggestions yet again. "You are a very headstrong boy. I think you will go far if you can be eased into the right direction. Anyone would think your grandfather had really been your grandfather, your behaviour is so—"

"What's that mean? Why wasn't my grandfather mine?"

"Because we adopted your daddy as a baby."

"You did?"

"Didn't he ever tell you? Well, I suppose he didn't have to. It's not like *you* were adopted."

"But if he's not my granddad then you're not my grandma and I don't have to do what you say," he crowed, jubilant at his own logic.

"Even though I am, indeed, not related to you by blood, I am still your carer and here to help."

He pursed his lips, deciding. "No. No, I won't do what you say."

He grabbed my handbag, laughing, calling to his sisters, and ran with the bag towards them as I yelled for him to stop. The girls detached themselves from the group of sensible children playing on the green top. "Myha, Mins," Collin cheered. "We don't have to do what the old lady says any more. She's not our real nan."

"Give me back my bag," I demanded as I caught up with him. "That was very rude."

"No, *this* is rude," he said, the ultimate horrid little boy, and he upended the contents of my bag onto the ground as I gave a small shriek quite expecting the pistol to go off. It didn't, but Collin's smile fell abruptly. He looked up at me, then back at the pistol by his feet. The girls stepped back.

"Don't touch it," I growled. "You know it's dangerous."

"Cool," Collin said, beginning to smile. "Nan's got a gun, a real gun, super cool! Can I have it when you die?"

I rolled my eyes at him, gathered up my possessions and put them back in the bag.

"So now you know," I said with a severe look. "I am not just Nana, I am *dangerous* Nana, so don't mess with me, and do not *ever* tell your parents about what you saw, okay?" I waggled a bony finger at them, really feeling the part of the wicked witch. They nodded, tight lipped.

One up for Nana Molly, child carer extraordinaire. That might fix Collin's attitude problem.

This finder was definitely keeping.

~

In the night I woke sweating and shaking, the memory of that autumn in Hartpury two years ago upsetting me. So when June intercepted me after school drop-off the next morning, the end of the week and freedom beckoning for the two days of the weekend, and she asked why l looked so glum, I surprised myself by starting to speak and then being unable to say anything as tears rolled down my face. Sometimes you can hold it all in until the wrong question is asked, and then the flood gates open.

I went back to her house and, over several cups of well-fortified coffee, I told her what I had told so few people in my life: my PTSD problems with men; the attack at Hartpury. From her spontaneous *oohs* and *ahhs* as the story unfolded I think she found it more entertaining than her soaps, but she was considerate and attentive.

"Why'd you not tell me all this before? I could have been holding your hand all this time," she said, handing over the tissue box when she saw how soggy my hanky was.

"As you can see, it wasn't easy to tell. I've been burying it for years. Hoping it would fade out with the counselling. I'm trying to write a book about it, but... "

"Yes, you must. No matter how hard it seems, battle on. It'll help. Cathartic." She leaned forwards. "Is it that you're... you know, just incapable of feeling attraction? Desire?"

"Oh, it's not *desire* that's the problem. I have plenty of desire. Just put me in a room with some hunky male strippers."

She laughed, but was still puzzled.

I drew in a great breath and leaned forwards, my hands open as if imploring understanding. To me it was simple. If the first time you met a snake it bit you, then you're going to be scared of snakes forever, right? I was simply scared of men because the first ones had hurt me; badly.

"It's just that when a man touches me—" It always sounds so lame out loud, though. "It's like those first men all over again—like electric shocks in my system, bad ones that makes me want to run or curl into a ball and pass out." I flopped back in the chair. "Oh God, it's impossible to explain."

Everyone on the witness protection scheme has access to a psychologist because of the traumas they might have experienced, but I felt like my clinician hadn't understood the problem either.

For a woman like June, who'd been happily married for forty years and had two sons, my warped viewpoint was probably inconceivable.

"Have you tried online dating?" she queried, showing she understood nothing.

I tutted. "I'm sorry, I wish I'd never said anything, but you did ask."

Her hand rested lightly on mine. "Molly, I'm your friend and I'm glad you feel you can confide in me."

I began to drip tears again. "June, you're the person I trust most in the world. Your friendship means so much to me."

"Aww... " She hugged me awkwardly, saying, "I love you, Molly. I want to help you. I *will* help you, somehow."

I managed a sad little laugh. "If you turn out to be one of the bad guys I'm never going to talk to you again."

She laughed hard. "Molly! I've been in this village since '62; ask around."

"I wasn't serious."

"You were; even if you don't realise it, you were. You've been traumatised on top of your trauma but you won't admit it.

I stared at my feet.

"Anyway," she said, "I don't think old ladies get to be what you call Big Bad Guys. We get to be NNGs, right? Nice Nutty Grans."

I laughed at her cheerful dismissal of my life's problems and thought, 'I suppose she's right. Older ladies are never BBGs, we're just their victims.'

6. Muddy Molly

"Letter for you, Mum," Gavin said at Saturday's breakfast after collecting the post. He held a buff envelope, turning it around and around as if the action would make it talk to him, then he frowned at me. I took the small envelope from him. It had the address right, but I was referred to as Ms Turner, my old name, my bad name, the name I would never dream of giving anyone. I looked at it in horror.

"I think you'd better burn it," I said, putting the envelope on the table and standing back as though it were a snake about to strike. "Anyone who knows where I am, *shouldn't* know where I am."

"You sure you told no one where you were going?" Vana asked, her porridge spoon halfway to her mouth.

"No one at all, not even the postmistress so letters could be forwarded. We're incognito. That's the whole point, isn't it?"

"So," said Gavin, "it's someone from here who knows your old name."

"And that's not likely either is it?" I stood and lifted the snake-letter by its tail and angled it in the light, trying to make out the blurry postmark.

"I don't know," Vana said sternly. "Is it likely? Too much sherry? Chatting to the schoolyard mums a little too much? Gossip in the shop?"

I stared at her, hardly believing my ears. "Why are you being spiteful, Vana? I never drink to tongue-loosening levels, and I'm the last person to be accused of gossiping. And, Gavin, honestly, why would anyone want to send me a letter if they live here?"

"No one is going to know until you open the bloody thing," he exclaimed.

I opened it, butterflies filling me, and saw...

"Oh..."

I wilted into my chair and handed the letter to Gavin.

His eyes ran over it. "Not good, Mum," he said and handed it to Vana.

She glanced at it, drew a huge sigh, looked daggers at me and placed the letter on the table, tracing a sign on it with one finger and muttering something in her family's language. "This is what grandmother would do to remove the curse from it," she said, "but I doubt I can for you."

"I'll pack my bags," I said, sighing with resignation. "I am not sticking round here and putting you at risk. I'll book some tickets to somewhere obscure."

I went to get up but Gavin put a hand on my shoulder to stay me. "Mum, I know this is bad but I am *not* letting my mother go through shit again. I'm calling the cops. Vana, you sort the kids—"

"That's what we have her for!" she complained. "C'mon, Rocky!"

"Tough; you know Mum needs help." He picked up the house phone and called the police.

"You're cursed, Molly," Vana said with no sympathy. "Accept it. My grandmother used to say once someone suffers misfortune, bad luck will always follow."

I went to my room but, back there on the breakfast tabletop, if you had been a fly on the wall who could read, you would have seen the words...

"Revenge will be mine. S Sanderson."

A relative of the man I had accidentally killed was after me, knew where I lived and knew how to scare me. I had no idea who they were, but I was pretty damn sure now the burglar *had* recognised me.

Now what could I do?

~

The cliff tops most likely to slip next were fenced off with expansive stretches of orange *danger* tape. I suppose there's no point in using real fencing since in the autumn it would likely travel to join its old friends halfway down the

137

cliffs.

I stood there motionless, watching the sea, feeling age—not just mine, the age of all things, the passing of time, seeing the children growing, and then great-grandchildren if I was lucky enough, the cliffs crumbling until the sea had claimed much of the village, including Gavin's house, my flat, the pub and the little B&Bs dotted along the top road. The cliff top church was never used now due to its structural instability, the stylish village hall now licensed for civil marriages and christenings instead, until such time as finances permitted the building of a new church. Most likely sometime in the next century.

Everything would come to its end in time. But we humans like to feel, often wrongly, that we have some control over that time, build fences around ourselves with medicines, shore up the inevitable, try to live lives long and full, thinking it matters. In fact, my dying today would leave no echoes in the future of the hungry sea.

I looked back for a moment at the tall man dressed for the weather with a thick camel-coloured coat, scarf, gloves and peaked-cap with ear flaps pulled down; he followed me wherever I went. He still looked cold despite his attire; something about him was hunched. I suspected he had underestimated the wind and the way it creeps into a body.

You see, later in the day, another letter had been pushed through the letter box for my trembling fingers to open, but I needn't have worried. Inside was a police-headed missive telling me I had been appointed a custodian, which I took to mean a bodyguard.

Aware that just about anything would upset Gavin and Vana after the events of the past few days, I decided to keep quiet about the new development. Especially because, to my mind, giving me a bodyguard meant I was bait; an old lady dangling on a hook over the pool of bad guys.

The gentleman in the camel coat was Mr Quoit, my watchdog, who simply followed me around at a discreet distance. I was not supposed to talk to him, or give any indication that I knew him, but the letter had mentioned he was booked in at the Glendenning Hotel, room 6, should I need to discreetly contact him.

But I am Molly, she-who-refuses-to-act-her-age, so I couldn't resist playing with him.

I went home to get my Wellington boots, him following a fair distance back, then plodded along another path to the line of orange warning tape, ducked under it and went slip-slidey down the first bank, looking in the sludge and crumbly clay for fossils for Collin. It's safe enough. I'd fossil-hunted there before, but at that time of year and with the recent rain it was, to say the least, muddy. You had to double-check where you walked.

I glanced back. Poor Mr Quoit stood watching me from the safety of the orange line, the wind whipping at his scarf tails as he hugged himself and I didn't have to see his eyes to tell he was glaring at me.

'Will he follow me down?' I wondered, daring him psychically. I spotted some nice intact turritellids—tower shells—and reached for them, and farther over I unexpectedly saw something that would send Collin into fossil-hunter raptures and get me back into his good books: a perfect shark's tooth.

I moved over and crouched a little, wary of the mud sucking at the boots, grabbed up the prizes that lay scattered around profusely and straightened up, went to move away...

But I couldn't lift my feet. The vacuum of the super sticky mud held fast my boots.

I closed my eyes. "Stupid old woman!" I muttered to myself.

Looking up to where the ramrod straight Mr Quoit stood watching the sea in a studied display of nonchalance, I waved a hand and shouted, "Yoo hoo! Excuse me!"

His head turned and, as I lifted one foot out of the boot to demonstrate my predicament, I overbalanced, twisting sideways and landing in elbow deep mud.

As I remained immobile, fearful that any further movement would see the mud swallow me even deeper, a male voice said, "Here." He was stood a good few feet away in a mud-puddle and held one of the thin fencing stakes towards me, being too sensible a man to approach closer. Managing to get a hand out to grab it, I was inelegantly drawn out of the muddy area by Mr Quoit's pulling and my stepping out of the boots to leave the poor things behind. I plodded up the rise, following where Mr Quoit led, my socks now plastered too, feeling rather ridiculous to say the least.

Back at the top and safety, I sat down on the coarse grass —too dirty to care about getting dirtier—and said, "Thank you, and hello, I'm Molly Smith." He, of course, would know my name, but I decided to play things as though he were a stranger. The cliff area looked empty but you never knew who might be around, hiding. I decided I was paranoid, took a big breath and, as he stabbed the stake into the ground so hard I wondered if he was imagining stabbing it into me, I went on, "I don't know what I would have done if you hadn't been there. Sunk down to Australia? I won't offer you a hand to shake."

"New Zealand," he said in a cultured voice.

"Pardon?"

He uncoiled his scarf from around his neck and I saw he was much older than I'd assumed. He had neat, short grey hair and a moustache to be proud of, and was around my age. "It is a common misconception that Australia is opposite us, when in fact New Zealand is our antipode, the land you would encounter were it possible to sink right through the Earth from England."

"So I have learned something *and* been rescued, lucky me." I saw his posh brogues were, like my socks, suffering muddiness incarnate, laces encrusted with gunge and mud spatter extending all the way up to his trouser's knees.

"Your poor shoes," I said contritely without really apologising. "I did make a mess of it all, didn't I?"

He didn't smile as he said, "I am Mr Quoit, as you well know, I'm sure. I've been warned what you're like. I was briefed on your capers back in Hartpury before I took on this assignment."

"Fame at last," I said, smiling in the hope that he'd smile back and magic the long, good-looking face into a handsome one. "So, now we know each other, could you please escort me home?"

"With pleasure, Ma'am," he said stiffly. "As long as there is no more mud along the way." We walked slowly, slopping muddily, some puzzled looks flying our way from residents, with me chatting happily to my taciturn rescuer, back through the streets and up to the back door of my flat.

7. Playing With A Quoit

"So, I have an actual bodyguard," I said to Mr Quoit later as I sat in clean clothes in my lounge and had coffee and raisin scones. He had on his shirt, but only a fleece blanket wrapped around his waist sarong-style, while his trousers tumbled through the super-fast wash cycle with my clothes. I'd had the option to redress, so had done so, but none of Gavin's trousers were going to fit this lanky man.

"You look funny," I said, trying to make conversation to soothe his bear. "It's like you're in a dressing up parade as a poorly attired Caesar."

"Hmph. You had taken a slight diversion, you say?"

"Yes, that's right." I smiled and offered him the plate of scones. "Have another, why don't you? I made them fresh this morning."

"Appeasing me with scones, are we?"

"Well, it *was* just a slight diversion to collect fossils for my grandson, Collin. He's mad over them, and there's quite a good range along these cliffs, and I never really thought I'd get *really* stuck."

"Still an ill-conceived notion, Ma'am," he said, grey eyes critical, no sign of relenting to humour. "I can appreciate the getting fossils for your grandson part, but why the risk at your age? Doesn't the local shop sell fossils garnered from these very cliffs? What if, instead of getting stuck, you had tripped and broken a hip?"

I grinned. "Because part of the value of fossils is the joy in finding them yourself, and I knew you would rescue me."

"So you have technically wasted police resources on a whim?"

"I don't know. Are you technically a police resource?"

He twitched his moustache and said officiously, "I am, madam, a retired officer of Her Majesty's Metropolitan police force. I volunteer for simple duties such as watching—"

"Ladies make fools of themselves?" I winked.

His smile was strained and polite. "Very much so, Ma'am" he agreed. "And, to be honest, though I fully understand the thrill of finding one's own fossils, a little research is called for. The Chama deposits of fine sands and silts hereabouts can produce treacherous quicksands, in which from time to time people do indeed get stuck. You see, I have been an ardent amateur geologist all my life."

"Oh! Really? How wonderful. What a coincidence," I gushed. "Would you like to see what I found in the midst of my cheery muddying, then? I managed to get them into my pocket before the er... stickage. Hang on."

I rushed to check on the washing and popped his damp trousers into the dryer on their own so they'd dry quicker. Retrieving the shells from my coat pocket, I returned to the silent, monolithic Mr Quoit to show him the ancient prizes.

He was on the settee, back to me, and my heart stopped when I entered the room and saw him with his hands in the air as if someone had a gun trained on him, but it was just Misty's contact he was avoiding. She had decided his blanket-clad thighs looked like a comfy place to sit, but he was obviously not a cat lover in the least, so he sat with his hands as far from her as possible and was too polite, or too scared, to shoo her away.

"I believe it is my turn to be rescued," he said drolly. "Cats and I have never seen eye to eye."

I removed her soft lump and put her on the floor. She ambled off. At least she hadn't hissed at him like she had with the major, the action which should have been my first warning sign that he was a ne'er-do-well.

"So you don't like cats, but are you a bird watcher?"

"No. I am a ferroequinologist."

I stared, playing the unfamiliar word through my studious brain. "Iron horse...? Ah, you're a trainspotter?"

He grimaced. "If you insist on the banality."

Not the answer I had expected, but to each his own passion.

He perused the turritellid shells with no sign of interest, but held the big shark's tooth delicately between index finger and thumb. "If I am not mistaken, Ma'am," he said, "this is a fine, well-preserved specimen of Jaekelotodus trigonalis."

I blinked at the long words, and I'm usually good with such things. "Sounds like a magic spell."

He twitched a smile. "It is a tooth from an extinct species of sandshark. In these local Barton beds you could also find..." He rattled off a whole collection of scientific names.

He reached to the side table where the contents of his pockets waited, including a cigarette lighter with an engraved crest. He saw me looking at it and said, "I do not smoke. It is merely a keepsake from a relative." Picking up a small, black police notebook with integral pencil, he carefully wrote in it the names he had spoken to me.

"So," I said, well impressed, "you know your fossils then. Collin would *love* to have a talk with you."

"I don't think that's advisable. I am supposed to be undercover, if you recall, Ma'am."

"Molly. You must call me Molly." He looked doubtful. "Look," I pressed on, "Ma'am and Molly start with the same letter, so as your mouth forms mmm, just switch your brain mid-word to Molly. Ma...olly. See?"

"Hmm," he said, but I thought I detected a glimmer of humour. "You certainly have an interesting way of looking at things, Maolly. I suppose this means I should let you call me Stanley."

"And will you?"

He seemed to think about my question for ages, all of twenty seconds, then he decided, "Very well. You may call me Stanley in certain situations, and I believe you are sensible enough to know which circumstances I mean."

I beamed at him, a smile that was not returned although his moustache did a little jog around his upper lip, but we chatted on for a while nevertheless. He certainly had a rather officious, unsmiling manner, but I was determined to break through his shell with my charm. To be fair, I knew I'd put him on the spot. He wasn't supposed to talk to me, let alone be seen or come into the house with me. 'Oh, Molly,' I berated myself, 'you really are a silly billy. You might have messed up things for Mr Quoit with his employers. Or, maybe, since he's a 'volunteer' it doesn't matter. Anyway, what's done is done. Try to behave in future.'

But I jumped straight in the deep end again. "And what does Mrs Quoit think of all this spying on people?"

"Personal protection detail, not in the same league as spying. And Mrs Quoit..." He cleared his throat.

"Oh golly, I'm sorry, I know I tend to be a bit forward sometimes. Divorced or passed on?"

"Both, and that leaves one with..." He looked lost for a second, eyes downcast.

"A kind of regret tinged with guilt, I am guessing."

He exhaled sharply. "Regret, certainly. Very much so."

I wasn't sure if I liked Stanley or not. Although he obviously had a dry sense of humour, and a sharp wit that he wasn't ashamed to use against me, he still couldn't grace me with a smile despite appearing relaxed in my company. He was an unknown factor, and I found myself wary on the one hand and feeling a draw to his honesty on the other.

It didn't help that I was constantly reminding myself that the last man I had rather liked had turned out to be some kind of drug baron and almost killed me. I doubted Stanley was going to turn out that way; after all, he was a policeman. The man was only doing his job, keeping a safe eye on me. He might not like me at all. He might actually hate me. It might all be pretence for the sake of duty. A mindset of, if I was happy in his company I was less likely to misbehave?

I heard the children screaming somewhere deeper in their house and pulled an apologetic face, glad I was free from them that weekend.

He showed no response to the noise so I carried on questioning him. Start as you mean to go on, and go on I did. "But you know all about rocks and so on, so come on, tell me all about these cliffs and don't skip the gory details."

"They are primarily composed of unstable eroded deposits of Eocene marlstone."

"Wow, it's like you're speaking a foreign language."

"On a historical note, you know about the smugglers' caves, I presume?"

"Hence the pub's name. Yes, though I do wonder how you can have caves in such loose cliffs."

"The underlying marlstone rock *was* hollowed out by the sea, but it was men who added to the size of the caves by carving out the relatively soft stone to make storage spaces for their contraband. The Eocene detritus, the 'loose stuff' as you call it, gradually erodes and falls so there could be many caves hidden in those cliffs, just beyond our reach, filled in, collapsed."

"Ooh... exciting. Collin would love to hear all this, though I suspect he'd get straight down there with his Dad's shovel and start digging. So, perhaps he'd better *not* hear."

A while later it was time for him to leave, dressed, smart again, shoes cleaned mainly, and trousers nice and clean. I had enjoyed his company. But I remembered thinking that when I first met the major. That slightly disconsolate yearning for male companionship had filled me back then and was now creeping into me again.

As we parted company, Stanley advised me he would be having Sundays off so another chap would be taking over his duties. "Do not play with him," he cautioned.

"I would never dream of it," I said.

I let Stanley out the back door and tidied up. I was sure there would be no end of teasing or disapproval if Gavin realised I had let a man into the flat. Maybe it was because I was thinking that way and tired after my time with the mud event but, as I went to close the curtains in the kitchen, it was not my face that gazed back in the dark reflection, it was the major's. I swept the curtains across furiously. *Just tiredness. That's all.*

~

I had wondered how good Sunday's security replacement would be; if he would keep a little farther from me than Stanley had managed. But I'll tell you this, he was way better than Stanley at the covert observation lark because I couldn't spot him. At all. In fact, because there were quite a few early visitors to the town—partly because of poor Lisa; murder makes for good tourism figures—I found it impossible to figure out who was watching me, so anxiety drove me home.

After a worrying while, becoming bored by midday, I began to consider if the police could have made a mistake; forgotten to send someone over and now I was extra vulnerable. I decided the best thing was to go to the Glendenning Hotel and ask Stanley, just to be on the safe side. It couldn't hurt, could it?

8. Painting Passion

"He's asked not to be disturbed," the young woman behind the reception desk said, hardly making eye contact, flicking a long skein of brown hair over her shoulder with purple-painted nails. I'd never seen her before so I couldn't even try my wheedling cry of 'But it's just me, Molly Smith who lives in Ardeal House', and she had turned away and picked up her conjoined mobile before I had even finished speaking. And they say customer service is dead.

I was turning away when she left her post, phone still her main focus, and she moved into the little room behind the desk, so I shot up the stairs as quickly and quietly as I could. Stanley might well be tired after our jaunts, but surely he wouldn't mind me popping in to check on my own safety.

I gently knocked on the door. There was rustling from within the room then his angry voice called, "Do not disturb!"

Not put off by his tone—I'd had worse from Collin in the past few months—I knocked again. "Stanley; it's Molly. I've got a problem."

The door opened a crack and his face peered through. "Molly," he said in surprise, more surprise than I had yet seen in him. Maybe it was because he was relaxing, hair mussed and moustache awry, so I pulled an apologetic face.

"I'm so sorry, Stanley, but I'm really rather worried. Are you sure there's someone else out here to look after me, because I can't see him."

He almost laughed. "That's the point, Molly."

"Yes; yes, I know," I went on, embarrassed, "but you were pretty obvious and now I can't see anybody. Are you sure he didn't go to the wrong seaside or something?"

"That is highly doubtful. I briefed him myself on the phone this morning." He gave a big sigh and opened the door a little farther so I could see clearly that he wore a paint-

148

splattered apron over a short dark-blue dressing gown. His hairy legs showed equally hairy feet and I felt it gave him a kind of boyish charm; the innocence of a half-naked person.

"I'm painting," he said, opening the door more to show the inside of the room, waving a hand at an easel stood to one side, the canvas facing away from me so I could not see the picture. "I asked the receptionist that I not be disturbed."

"Oh, is that what the girl said. I thought she meant for me to come up. Wretched Collin's hidden my hearing aid again. Can I admire the picture?" I said, and skipped into the room before he could shut the door on me.

"No," he said firmly, moving to shield the canvas from my prying eyes.

"But I don't care what it's like," I said. "I mean, I do care. I'm sure it's good. Just a little peek, pretty please?"

"I would rather you wait until it's reached full glory," he said, "so please take your leave, don't worry about the watcher, and I will let you see this when I have finished. Agreed?"

I heard something then. In the silence after his words, a tiny creak issued from the wardrobe. I doubt it showed on my face that I had heard anything, and I had already mentioned that my hearing aid had gone walkies, so Stanley wouldn't realise I had heard it, but I kept my pleading smile frozen in case.

His artist paraphernalia was all over the top of one cupboard, and discarded clothes were in a heap on the bed; he didn't appear to be the tidiest person when he was on his own, and he caught my critical glance at the clothes so picked them up to move them.

As he lifted them, a pair of pale pink panties slipped gracefully out of the pile and fell to the floor. He grabbed them up.

"Each to their own," I said, amused.

"They are a component of the painting." His eyes jittered around in embarrassment, as if he were looking for other items he would rather I did not notice. A brassiere, maybe?

"A... still life featuring underwear," he said lamely. It was odd to hear such nervousness from him. "I can assure you they are not what I wear."

"I wouldn't think any less of you if you did," I said. "A still life with underwear. That's a new one, I must admit. Quite novel. Can't wait to see it."

The wardrobe creaked again; it must have been uncomfortable in there.

Then I saw the reflection in the mirror on the small dresser, which confirmed I was certainly persona non grata. Small but clear, the image on the canvas was reflected: a naked woman, half turned away from the painter, from the waist up barely painted, but her legs and ample derrière were well executed and plainly those of a well-endowed lady.

It was only a glance, but I had seen enough, so I mumbled a contrite, "See you tomorrow," and kept up the smile as I left hurriedly.

I stopped to take some deep breaths on the landing, wondering exactly who the (probably) still naked woman in his wardrobe was and why she had felt obliged to hide. Was she a local I would recognise? I am not the kind to gossip so her identity would have been safe with me even if she were married. How embarrassing for them both. I was a git. But I still wanted to set up camp in the foyer, do some spying, see if I could catch her leaving. Tempting though the idea was, it could realistically be ages before anyone emerged. But as I stood there silently, I did hear the murmur of voices from beyond his door, and I sighed deeply, sad that I had read the situation correctly.

Then came the other noises. Noises that... you know... meant they were enjoying each other's company, so I tiptoed away, resolving to stay at home for the rest of the day.

Despite Stanley's reassurances, I was not comfortable with having a watcher I could not watch back.

9. Teacup Tragedy

Curiosity, jealousy, and a kind of lament over the hotel 'scene' built up in me for the rest of the day until I felt like a volcano about to pop, until I just *had* to tell someone, so I chose June, of course. Tucked safely in my bedroom that evening, I called her on the mobile.

"How absolutely wonderful," she said, and I could hear the cheeky smile in her voice. "Things are really looking up for you, aren't they?"

"I just said there was a naked woman in his wardrobe, and I left them having nookie. What's good about that?"

"Oh, that bit's not good, it's your reaction that's good. You like him and that's *really* good."

"No, I don't," I said hastily. "Not like that."

She chuckled and the phone made her sound like a chicken clucking. "Ooh, yes you do. You're jealous; that's *very* good."

I managed to hold back a degree of anger at her insistence, loving phones for the fact you can mouth curses and not be seen. "I've only just met him, so, no, I'm not—"

"Yes, you are. Don't argue with me, young lady. The painting was a nude, and you're envious as hell. It doesn't matter that you've only just met him."

"Hmm. I see why you need the spirit guides. You're incapable of logical reasoning off your own bat."

After another spate of chicken clucking she said, "So, what was she like, this naked painted lady?"

"All I saw was her bum and thigh, a bit pink and on the chunky side."

"And that really doesn't make you mad? You don't want a man to care enough to paint *you* that way? To have you as his muse? Girl, you're way more messed up than I thought."

I wasn't sure what her annoying questions were making

me feel; awkward, exasperated, waking up something I hadn't realised I felt towards the taciturn Stanley, yet I didn't cut her off. But I did take too long to reply and she came on again with...

"You do fancy him, you minx. I know it, you know it, and you just have to admit to yourself that you fancy the pants off him. That in the end you wanted to rush into that room and drag Madam Chunky Bum off him so you—"

"God, no! You're a very odd person, June."

"I'm very empathetic. So... still life with underwear? What an excuse! Sounds like he has a reasonable sense of humour, at least."

At that I choked and laughed, but my laughter ended with a tear in my eye. I said in a more restrained voice, "Yes, okay, you win, I do like him just a little bit, but only 'cause he's the only man I know."

"Pah! Bob Elliot, Tom Heastings? Nice eligible males."

"No! Old widowers with bad breath and collapsed biceps. I do have standards, you know."

"Tell you what..." she said slowly as a plan formed in her addled brain, "I reckon I know that purple-nailed receptionist. Marissa's her name, used to work at the garage in the summer, so why don't I go and ask if she'll let me into his room when he's out?"

"What? You'd get the girl into *huge* trouble."

"But you got me all excited now, Molly. You can't do that and expect me to calm down quickly. Come on, he doesn't know me, I can hang around for a bit and see who comes in, or leaves; get a sneaky picture."

"No. It's his life. It's his choice. Do not go to the hotel to spy on him; promise me?"

"Spoilsport."

I said goodbye and flung myself back on the bed, true lovelorn teenager style. Life was so very cruel, bringing Stanley into my heart now, not 50 years ago when I had needed him most... not even a year ago when he would have easily defeated Major Sanderson for me. I needed a champion in my life, but I was realistic enough not to believe it was going to be Stanley, even if he was a widower with not bad breath and, from what I had seen, some pretty nice legs. And now I had discovered that I did actually quite like him, I wondered if I was going to be able to keep him. The chances were that I wasn't, since he felt obliged to hide nude women in his wardrobe. Now I got to thinking that she wasn't someone local at all, that he had actually 'paid' for her company. That was, of course, his choice to make, but I knew that kind of intimacy was something I could never give him, and my poor old heart shrivelled up again.

I was just dozing off when the mobile rang again, June all excited and bubbling with a new idea. I don't know how Henry keeps up with her zest for life. Sometimes she reminds me of me—two old(ish) ladies who gossip and plot. We should call ourselves the Wrinkly Twins.

"Let's ask the wine for guidance and have some tea," she enthused with the slightest hint of a hiccough. "I mean, ask the tea leaves and have some wine. The night is young, Henry's out with his cribbage team and I'm all alone with my bottles. Come on over, girl!"

~

Fifteen slightly out of breath minutes later, having moved as fast as I could in case my police watcher had gone off duty, I was taking off my coat in June's house and eyeing the white teacup and pot waiting on the dining table, which was spread with her best lace tablecloth in deference to the practice.

Tasseography, as she says it is named, is an ancient art which June has practised for many years, and she claims some success with, so despite my natural reservations I was curious as to what would show in the tea leaves.

We sat either side of the table, and she gently spooned a few tea leaves into my cup and poured hot water on them to steep for a few minutes.

"Remember," she said softly, "it's your emotions that guide the combinations. So, think about the questions you want to ask and let the universe help."

I drank the bitter black brew contemplatively, thinking all the while about poor Lisa, Stanley-who-I-liked-too-much, and my future overall.

Then I swirled the delicate white china cup counter clockwise and upended it onto the saucer, leaving the last of the water to drain, then turned the cup back up the right way to show the pattern of tea leaves.

The ritual completed, I passed the cup to June to read. My heart missed a beat as she looked at me almost fearfully.

"Upheaval. Chaos. Death," she said quietly, "followed by heartbreak or grief."

"No, *no!*" I didn't want to hear what she said. "I don't believe it anyway. I was thinking of Lisa, so if anything those symbols represented her rather than me."

"Let's go again, then," she said, back to being chirpy, and poured me another cup of tea while she supped from a huge goblet of wine. "Cheers," she said. "To wine, women and righting wrongs." If she were to drink any more, I would no longer be certain if she spoke, or the wine.

On her reading of the second cup, I had to give a short huff of disbelief. Lovers and deception. Unsurprisingly, they represented relationships and choices. Then the death symbol was seen. "Again?" I said in dismay. "What are the odds of it coming up twice in two readings? Could it be I haven't swirled the cup enough?"

"It's definitely a coffin," June said. "Look." But as she shoved the cup and its sinister leaves towards me I recoiled. "Don't look so down," she said, her attitude still bright, but the 'predictions' weren't about *her*. "It's a good read as readings go. I've had some that I've had to think twice about saying. You know, your husband's having an affair, sort of thing."

"Really? Death and deception is better than affairs?" I muttered, remembering that fleeting ghost of the major's face in the window. Had he come back to haunt me? Not that I believed in ghosts any more than I did the tea leaves, or Tarot, or walking under ladders or the evil of black cats.

"Got anything else you could ask quickly?" I enquired. "A cross-reference kind of thing? To see if the projections agree."

She gave me a horrified look. "One does not play with such powers," she said stiffly.

Since, in my opinion, playing was exactly what she was doing, and upsetting me needlessly, I asked, "How about sacrificing a chicken and reading its entrails?"

She snorted loudly. "It'd mess up my lovely tablecloth," she said pointedly, and for a second I wasn't sure if she was serious or not, but then her eyes twinkled. "Molly, accept fate is rampaging towards you no matter what I do, but getting a hint of what's to come can help you through it."

I shrugged and yawned widely. "Oh, excuse me. Time for bed. Enough excitement for one day. The children are off to the Maritime Museum with the school tomorrow, so I'll have to get up even earlier to sort them for the early coach. They exhaust me."

"Not surprised," she retorted, downing the last of her drink then looking sadly at the empty bottle. "You do too much for that family and they don't appreciate you. My lads would never ask me to look after the grandkids that much."

"You don't live with them. Anyway, that's for me to say. If I feel put upon I can assure you I have enough energy left to move on, find a new place."

"Well, have a drink of something other than tea before you go," she insisted. So after a few glasses of another of her many bottles of wine, I left her on good terms. I always leave on good terms, even though we don't always see eye to eye. BFF. Best friends forever, as the children say nowadays.

Walking home was not exactly nerve-wracking, but there were quite a few people about that I didn't recognize and again I moved as fast as I could.

I had the gun in my bag. It lived there. Whenever I

left the house I would tick off: purse, pillbox, hankie, loaded revolver. There, the essentials all in one place.

But, if pushed, could I ever use it? If my family was threatened, maybe, but I didn't want the chance to find out.

Turning the last corner to Ardeal House, I caught a whiff of scent that stopped me in my tracks and I looked around.

A couple had passed me, the woman quite tall and bundled in a thick coat, the man also tall and appearing younger by dint of his fashionable jacket, possibly her son, and I guessed it must have been his cologne I had scented; the same as the major had worn. He didn't have to be a ghost to haunt me. Never mind how much counselling I had, I would forever carry little pieces of that awful time in my head, and I was glad of the gun snug in my bag.

10. Spying

After the earlier than usual morning school run, I collapsed into an armchair. I was tired already, but happy I had spotted Stanley back on duty.

I dropped off to sleep again, or maybe the wine from the night before was still singing in my veins. Either way, June woke me at 9am by calling my mobile. "You won't *believe* what I found," she said, her voice excited and bubbling with the urgency to tell someone of her adventures.

I sat up smartly, startled into being wide awake, alarm bells ringing in my head. "What? Don't tell me you went to the hotel. I told you not to go. You promised!"

"Er, no, I don't think I did, but listen. I didn't need to go into his room, I had a mooch through the bins out back. Wasn't that a good idea?" She sounded like she wanted a badge for enterprise. "I saw the maid chuck stuff into them so thought I'd do a bit of bin-diving."

"Gross!"

"I only skimmed the new stuff. Had a quick shufti and guess what I found?"

"I don't know," I said, disgruntled. "Pink silk knickers?" It was bound to not be anything good. Not good for me, at least.

"I found three notes that had been started then screwed up."

"Written by Stanley? How could you possibly know that?"

"They started with 'Molly'. Who else would have written them, daftie? Come on round this morning. Henry's gone to town for a meeting... you know, a consultation kind of thing, so more time for wine, women and righting wrongs for us."

"No, thanks, just tell me what the notes said—as if I could stop you from telling me."

"Oh, gosh yes, you'll love this, Molly."

"I will?"

"I don't know the order of them, but I'll do them in order of *actio effectus*—"

"What?"

She drew in a sharp breath of annoyance. "Dramatic effect, you uneducated woman. Now, this one..." I heard some rustling. "This one starts 'Dear Molly': that's all it says. He must've been unsure of how to address you."

"Well, that's nice... I guess."

"Hang on, it gets better. The next one says, '*My* dear Molly'."

I waited for the punch line with bated breath.

"And the third crumpled note starts... Ready for it?"

"That's what it says? 'Ready for—'"

"No, get your head out of the clouds! No, it says, 'My *darling* Molly'."

"You must be joking. All that from a man I only met a few days ago? You've made this all up just to get me interested in *him*."

"No, I haven't, you daftie! He's just been smitten with you. You don't give yourself enough credit, Molly. You may be getting... more mature... but you're still a good looking woman. And he's, you know, the strong silent type wondering how to make the first move on you."

"No." My head was spinning. "He... Oh, I don't know. I'm scared more than enchanted."

"I read a wonderful article that said men fall in love way faster than women, so that's what's happened. That's why he called you darling."

"I cannot get my head round this."

"Come over and you can see the notes for yourself."

"It makes no sense. If he's calling me darling but sleeping with his model—"

"Of course he is!" she broke in with her voice of illustrious wisdom. "He just used her as a substitute; probably called her Molly when—"

"Stop it!"

"Honestly; I don't know. You try to help a friend and this is all the gratitude I get?"

My heart was thumping. In that moment I was so angry with her assumptions I felt I would never talk to her again. But I breathed deeply and swallowed words I didn't want to say to someone who was usually my rock.

"I am grateful. And I would come on over, but Gavin and Vana are out and—"

"You can't be babysitting. What's the excuse this time?"

I don't want to see Stanley Quoit following me until these feelings settle down.

"I was going to sort the sock drawer," I said, not even convincing myself.

"Right, of course; theirs or yours?"

"There's a lot to do here, you know?"

"Oh, alright, slave. Go ahead and sort the sock drawer to your heart's content and ignore real life. I can take a hint. Pop round after school tomorrow, if you can lower yourself to my level. Meanwhile, I'm going to have a teensy tipsy alcoholic day in on my own *sob sob*."

"And keep away from the hotel," I said. "Promise me that. Go on, promise me properly this time. I don't trust you."

"I promise. There! What an absolutely delightful friend you are, Molly," she said in a faux scolding voice, but I imagined her smiling sneakily, and it scared me.

11. Who Watches The Watcher?

The skies were cloudy, but the clouds were at least white and high and scudding merrily inland, not threatening rain. With the children safely deposited in school I was walking to June's place to see the mysterious 'Molly' notes for myself when, to my surprise, Stanley walked straight up to me from the pub's car park.

"Hello," I said smiling, nervously sweet. He slipped his arm into mine in an unfamiliar yet pleasant way and *darling Molly* sang in my head. I wondered why my instinct hadn't been to pull away. Maybe the counselling had been working away in my mind and I hadn't even noticed. I smiled to myself. Yes, Molly did quite like the feel of this arm around hers, but I had to ask, "Are you being weird, or is this important?"

"We have a problem," he said, turning me around so we walked back through the car park.

"I was on my way to see June," I complained.

"June?"

"Yes, my best friend, June Bailey, she only lives by the old forge. Can't this wait?"

"Visit later," he said shortly. "There's a man following you."

"Is his name Stanley Quoit?"

"Be serious, Molly. *I* am being serious. I saw him watching you on Saturday, my colleague spotted him yesterday and he's following us now, as we speak."

"Maybe he's just another policeman, from another department or something."

"Highly unlikely. I would have been informed of any extra help assigned. Besides, I don't think you're so important that you merit two watchers at any one point."

"Gee thanks, Honey," I drawled in an affected Southern twang. "Now ah am truly offended."

He harrumphed, which might have been his way of laughing, and we stood by the bench at the farthest end of the car park, where the breeze tickled my ears through my scarf and my knees through my slacks and made me want to walk on to escape it. Stanley appeared to be admiring the sea view, though I had to assume it was something policeman-y that he was doing, looking for clues on the faces of the waves.

"What does he look like, this man?" I asked, readjusting my scarf, pulling my coat closer. In a minute, if he didn't get the hint I was cold, I would walk on.

"He reminds me of Oliver Hardy."

"Of Laurel and Hardy fame?"

"Exactly. Somewhat round with a small moustache."

"All right, if he's portly, let's go on a long, long trek, all the way down the coast-walk and give Mr Hardy some exercise."

"I think heading for the Cliff-Top café is in order. I am famished. Not breakfasted yet."

And what were you up to last night that kept you abed long enough to miss breakfast? No, no. He's mine now. Go away bad ideas.

We set off, his arm around mine again. I wanted to see the man following me, but I didn't dare turn and look.

"Sorry about the hotel thing," I said, as we began to walk smartly along the cliff path. "I didn't mean to be so rude and disturb your private time."

I felt his arm tense. "What do you mean?"

"Sunday private time," I said. "You doing-your-own-thing time."

"Don't mention it," he said. "The problem is past."

I wondered in whose arms he might have been that day, and why he was even holding my arm now.

And why, if he was with that nude-modelling woman, was he writing me notes with *darling* in them? Was June right in her assumptions?

Finally, it occurred to me that any man would likely

want to hide his naked model/prostitute/whatever from the woman he... liked. I didn't want to attribute myself with any more esteem than that. There hadn't been anything romantic going on with her; he'd just been embarrassed at my incursion. *Embarrassed enough to shove the poor dear into the wardrobe?* I will admit the idea amused me. The note most likely was an attempt to apologise for being abrupt with me. I sighed with relief at my incredibly astute observation and looked at the arm wrapped familiarly around mine.

"Why *are* you holding my arm, Stanley?" I asked cheerfully. "Rather forward, isn't it?"

"I want to make it look like we are together, so that our shadow doesn't think you're an easy target."

"Why'd you have to say that!" I squeaked. "*Target.* Let's walk faster. I'm scared now."

"Molly, calm down. I am sorry you're scared, but I am here to watch over you. Nothing will happen to you while Stanley G Quoit is on duty."

I gave a shiver. "Right. All calmed down. What's the G for? Graham?"

"You need distracting. Try again."

I held his arm even tighter as he marched on and I guessed at his middle name, failing each time, but it was a good distraction technique. I would have to try it with the children sometime.

When we reached the café, some brisk walking minutes later, I sank gratefully into the seat of a double setting in the busy place. Stanley ordered an extra-large breakfast platter for himself while I just asked for coffee and alternated looking out of the side window with watching the TV news on the flat screen over the serving area.

He took out his phone and sent a message to someone. "Just checking in," he said quietly.

He had seated himself facing the door, so my back was to it, protected by the heavy rear of the padded bench 'But I could be shot in the head!' I thought with more than some alarm, and

162

I slid down in the seat so my head was below what I imagined the line of sight from the door would be.

"What ails you?" Stanley asked, his face showing a cross between amusement and concern.

"I... Can we move? I'm scared someone's going to... you know..." I raised my finger pistol-like and tapped my head. "I feel very exposed."

"I consider that scenario highly unlikely. It is only in Hollywood that a killer would shoot someone in a café, in broad daylight, with so many witnesses. The beach is far more likely."

"And that's supposed to be reassuring?" I hissed. "Can't I just go hide in the flat? Have coffee and make scones while you keep guard?"

I heard the door open and saw his eyes flick up then down.

"He just came in?" I guessed, so tense I could have broken a cup with my grip.

"Yes," he said, keeping his voice low, masking his words by shuffling the sauces and condiments on the table. "He looks a little puffed. No—don't turn to look."

"I'm happy to help him get fit. A kindness I am well known for, Geoffery."

"Incorrect. After this repast we could try going farther down the coast. Are the tides amenable, do you know?"

"You just said to keep off the beach."

"No, I said you were more likely to be attacked on the beach."

"Isn't that the same thing?"

The door bell dinged. "He's gone," Stanley said. "Likely waiting for us outside. Don't fret so, Molly. Just keep with me."

As I felt fear creeping into me again at the words 'waiting for us', Stanley's food arrived, a huge plate's worth, and he tucked in like he'd been starved for a week not just a night. I have always wondered at the ability of men to consume so much food so fast, even Collin ate at twice my speed. Vana had often complained, with only a slight measure of humour, that Gavin could empty the fridge at one sitting. Must be a man thing.

He ate steadily as I quietly sipped my coffee and gazed out of the window, hoping to get a glimpse of my follower—I felt that knowing my enemy's face might make him less scary. But although several people passed by, none of them matched Stanley's brief description.

"Gustav? Grayson? Geronimo?" I offered.

"Wrong, wrong and certainly wrong." He was smiling over his fork.

Stanley finished eating, wiped his mouth with the paper serviette, belched and apologised, then paid for the meal while I went to the ladies. On the way, I couldn't help but look outside again, and I wanted to stay there, in the safety of the café while Stanley went out and chased away my pursuer like a knight in shining armour.

As I returned to the table I cried, "I have it. You are Galahad, my knight!"

He steepled his fingers, looked over them and said, "No."

"Is your name even English?" I asked.

"Time to go. Keep guessing. Give your mind something to worry about more than you-know-what."

But I had to give myself a firm talking to before I was ready to leave.

As we went out of the café's door, the sun came out from behind stacked cumulus clouds, spreading an uplifting light across the area like a monochrome picture changing into glorious colour. In the distance the waves' tips sparkled in the new light, and for a second my spirits soared. I grabbed Stanley's arm and he looked startled. "Are you all right?" he asked.

I smiled like the sunshine warming my face.

"Oh Stanley," I said, "can't you see? Sunshine, sea, a handsome man on my arm..."

"Hmpf," he said, but I could see the smile lurking behind

that moustache. 'I am his darling,' I thought. 'He can't say it, but I know it. Is this what I have been looking for? Is he the man I have literally dreamed about?'

I laughed and leaned into him a little as we walked together down the twisty switchback footpath to the beach where we stepped over rocks and shingle to the sand. I didn't think about who was behind me, only about who was beside me, and my fear kept quiet.

"Giovanni?" I suggested.

"No, but I quite like that one."

A half hour's stiff walking on wet sand and my legs were definitely going to complain later. Stanley stopped a moment and glanced back the way we had come, then ran his eyes over the sea view in a nonchalant I-am-not-checking-on-someone-tailing-me way.

"Is he still there?" I asked. "Anyway, are we trying to lose him, Griffin? Outrun him, Gunnar? What are we doing... I can't think of any more Gs?"

"Since you are the target—"

"Stop using that word!"

"I am trying to keep you alive by keeping you at a distance from him. Where is the next path up?"

"Another half mile or so." A shiver ran through me. "Why's he just watching, not doing anything? I mean, I feel safe with you, but what if he starts shooting at me or something?"

"Then we had better move faster."

"If we go up too fast, it'll be my legs that struggle," I complained as he hurried on.

"Legs or life, Molly. Your choice."

"Seriously, now. Do you really think he wants to *kill* me?"

"Quite likely me too, given half the chance. You wouldn't believe the characters I've come up against in my time."

After that, I couldn't talk because I was getting breathless and my heart was starting its odd beat—the one the doctor said was fine but I didn't like. It would always remind me of running from the major.

"Wait!" I said and reached into my handbag for my pillbox. Just to be on the safe side, I popped one little tablet under my tongue to dissolve. Stanley frowned but didn't ask what the pills were for.

Up the steps we went, Stanley bounding along like a man half his age. He had to keep slowing for me to catch up. I had given up his arm, not wanting to pull on it as I pushed myself, pushed my aching legs, pushed through my fear, and then we were finally back on the cliff tops and on a branching footpath wending its way through a caravan park.

We stopped. Stanley got out his phone and made a call.

"What are you doing now?" I panted, hands on knees, ashamed to be so feeble and breathless in the face of his superior fitness. At this rate no hit man was needed to get me; my own body would kill me. "Calling for a helicopter, I could hope."

"Taxi," he said, and I thought it was almost the best word he'd ever uttered. "Mr Hardy will take a long time to get here and he won't know where we've gone."

"Don't forget the children," I said. "I have to be back by three."

"How did they manage before you came to the family?"

"I don't know."

"Then they'll manage if we're a tad late. Your life or theirs?"

"Never give me *that* choice," I gasped, and I must have sounded cross because he fell silent.

12. Is Love All Around Us?

We met the taxi on the other side of the caravan park and Stanley ordered it to Castlepoint Shopping Centre. I leaned back and rubbed my burning calves and thighs through my trousers. Even the children hadn't exerted me to the point of leg-aches.

Stanley used his phone, the conversation sounding like he was reporting the situation to his superiors, and the taxi shot along the bypass, past Bournemouth hospital and into the shopping centre in less than twenty minutes.

We indulged in some window shopping. He found a model train shop that I had to drag him out of, and I found a massive bookshop that he had to extract me from with promises of dinner in one of the many restaurants.

As we were leaving the shop, a rather large man barged in and for a moment I thought he was my doom as he seemed to bump into me on purpose. I gave a squeal of surprise, and Stanley put an arm around my shoulders, saying soothingly, "Don't worry. That was not anyone of consequence. Now, deep breaths, and I think it is time for sustenance."

This time I was really hungry and he smiled as I tucked into pasta formaggi. "I like a woman with a good appetite," he said, bringing to my mind the image of the rather chubby lady he'd been painting. "I was worried when you declined breakfast."

I managed a droll smile, the food not really calming my soul, only my belly. "You never have to worry about me and food. We are good companions. Though sometimes I prefer my calorific intake in a good wine."

Thus we wandered for a couple of hours, chatting about this and that, and I jumped every time a man came close to me, whether he was fat or thin or looked like Mel Gibson, I was so on edge.

"Gibson?" I squawked.

Stanley laughed aloud, a chuckle really, but the best I had gleaned from him yet. "No," he said.

The most awkward moment was when I gave money, only some small change, to a homeless man sitting all forlorn on a faded quilt by the elevator. Stanley seemed quite contemptuous of him, so I felt obliged to lecture him on man's need to be humane to fellow man. We sat in another café, me with hot choc and marshmallows, and him with an espresso that had cost almost double what I had given to the homeless man.

As I went on about how we should be nice to each other and help where we can, an amused smile trickled over Stanley's face, his head tilting to one side, and I fully expected him to tell me I was too idealistic and out of touch with the way the world works. I know too well how it works, which is why I try to be nice to people.

When I stopped to slurp my hot choc, Stanley said, "I like you, Molly." I bit my lip, a habit when I am too excited to speak, and he put his hand around mine holding the cup on the table. I stared at it, a comforting hand, warm and strong, no scary electric shocks from it at all. "You are a good woman," he went on, and my heart melted like the marshmallows.

~

Window shopping, bad guy avoiding, and me trying to stop flirting all done, we got another taxi back to Kerton and he said goodbye at Ardeal House's gate. I was suddenly and inexplicably filled with the urge to hug him, to take that one step forward and launch myself into a world I was so unfamiliar with. But, to my utter surprise, he made the first move and leaned to kiss me, a quick peck beside my ear. I forced myself to stay still.

"Thank you for such an interesting day," he said.

"Interesting? You could call it that. I was scared, excited and full of enjoyment all at the same time. And that name guessing game, pure genius."

"I enjoyed it too, my dear."

"Stanley, you said 'my dear'."

There was the briefest of pauses. "Did I? Slip of the tongue, I'm sure. But I will put you out of your agony. I am Stanley Graham."

"But... that's what I said first—Oh, sneaky!"

He gave me a slight wink before he strolled off, and that was enough to make a not-so-old lady's heart flutter in the nicest of ways.

~

When I went to pick up the children and managed to talk them into going to the village hall playground instead of the beach, I spotted Stanley come in the playground gate, sit on a bench, and set to fighting the breeze to read a broadsheet. "Just use the phone," I muttered to myself. "Silly man."

"Who's that?" Collin asked, picking up on my words and angle of view.

"Is he your boyfriend, Nana?" Myha asked, and all three children laughed at the absurdity of the idea.

"He's a friend. He's Mr Quoit and he knows all about rocks and fossils," I said, hoping it might get me some Brownie points with Collin. "Do you want to meet him?"

I don't think Stanley approved of my breaking his cover just for Collin, as he gave me a tilt of the judgmental eyebrow. He sat awkwardly on the bench with Collin, while the girls played with other children and other parents barely passed a glance over his presence. But, after a few minutes, I saw him drawing diagrams or pictures in his small notebook while Collin, uncharacteristically still and quiet, sat engrossed in tales of rocks and fossils. How much he understood, I had no idea, but there was no doubt he enjoyed it, his face aglow.

"Back to the beach now, Nan," Collin demanded after at least half an hour, leaping up and waving goodbye to Stanley with a great big smile. "Got some fossils to look for."

"No," I said, "we have to go home and do homework now

or tea will be late."

"I want to go to the beach!"

"Who am I, Collin?"

His eyes fell, his mouth turned down. "Dangerous Nan," he grumbled and stood placid. I wondered if I had done wrong in calling myself that, but if any mention of the weapon silenced Collin's tantrums, that was a blessing in itself.

Stanley had moved off. I wanted to yell, 'Come back. You are ten times more interesting than these children are,' but he vanished around the corner of the hall, presumably to wait until he could trail after us back home.

~

Another morning came around quickly, children bounced in onto Grandmother's bed, and I heaved myself up to get them sorted. Vana had already left for work. Gavin was on his laptop organising something before leaving. So much for my money helping this family to have more family time.

I was feeding the children breakfast, the TV burbling in the background like it always does, when the eight o'clock news came on with its classic fanfare.

Two seconds later I was staring at the screen like an animal transfixed by headlights, unable to move.

A man and a woman had been found dead on the beach beneath Clifor's rock, a precipitous cliff a mile or so down the coast from Little Kerton. *A suspected lover's tryst,* the newsreader said. When the facial composites were shown I gasped into a squeaky-screamy sob that silenced everyone in the room.

The man was no one I recognised, but the woman was June.

13. A Friend Is Forever

It was me; my fault; I had done it again with my curse. The way I saw it, I had told June not to go to the hotel again, made her promise not to go, but she had gone anyway and that had got her killed. Her death was nothing to do with secret trysts or mutual suicides, she loved her Henry, and Henry adored her. I was sure of this because she had told me so many times how wonderful he was to the point where I just wanted her to shut up about her good fortune. I would bet all my money on the fact that one cannot fake nearly forty years of happy marriage when talking to a best friend.

I was sure someone had seen her poking around at the hotel, meddling somehow, discovering more than she should have about... What? What could she have discovered, uncovered, realised? Had one of the bad guys thought her a policewoman with her nosing into the business of others?

What of the mystery man who had perished alongside her? My mind ran overtime. Could he be her killer; a man who had accosted June on the cliff top, gone to throw her over and fallen too? I couldn't imagine what she would have been doing there, anyway, a half hour's walk or more along the cliff top road.

She must have been taken there to be thrown off the highest point on the local coast.

I hoped she'd been unconscious before she fell, like Lisa Gilroy had been.

However the scenario had really played out, I was inconsolable, my tears floods, my speech gibberish, wondering how I was going to face Henry, when would the funeral be, what could I say honestly to her two sons if they spoke to me... ? Such a mess of reactions. I lurked in my room, neglecting my 'duties', all my optimism gone, finding no way of awakening my usual capable self.

Gavin had to take the day off to get the children to school, then whisked me off to the doctor for an emergency appointment; he was that worried about me. But the doctor simply gave me some tablets to calm me. I doubted they could cure consuming guilt. Vana was right; everything I touched fell to ashes.

I went back to bed at 10am, headphones on, playing strong classics, blocking out the world as words swam into my head, images of the major and the cellar and nasty things that I knew were only visiting me because of the tranquillisers, but I had no power over them. I had to pull myself together again, I had to fight again. There was S Sanderson to deal with. He was the one doing all this. It had to be him. Hadn't the police stopped him yet?

Stanley phoned me at 10:20. He'd seen Gavin take the children to school, then me driving off in the car with him and returning, and he was consequently enquiring after my health, disturbed at my non-appearance. When I thanked him for his diligent concern he managed to turn the compliment on its head. "Much of this job is about observing patterns," he said, "knowing the routines of a person so you are alerted if that pattern is disrupted."

"Ah, so if I always take the kids to school for nine and I don't show one day, you'll wonder where I am."

"Exactly what happened this morning, though seeing you with Gavin didn't trip any alarms, and I assumed you were worn out from our jaunt."

"No." I started to explain about June but couldn't finish, gabbled a *sorry* and hung up.

~

Later that afternoon, the door bell rang, and moments later Gavin knocked on the bedroom door before coming in with a bouquet. "Someone thought to send you flowers, Mum. I'll get a vase."

I stroked the flowers' petals, inhaled their soothing scents; freesias and carnations, alstroemerias and delicate

172

gypsophila bound in a bright, colourful bouquet not exactly appropriate for bereavement.

Spotting the gift envelope tucked down the side, I flipped it open and almost fainted.

It was printed, not handwritten, but the impact was the same as if she had written it herself.

I seem to recall this is the anniversary of the day we first had 'wine, women and righting wrongs' Cheers! Many more wine-ing years to us!

She must have ordered them a couple of days prior, before she had been dragged to a cliff top and pushed over. My lovely friend, kind to the last.

On the bottom of the card it said:

"To love is to lose.
But a friend is forever.
June."

By the time Gavin had returned with a vase the flowers were on the floor and I was a sobbing mound in the bed.

~

After that, Gavin and Vana were somewhat nicer to me in my grief and let me do my own thing, though Gavin would call in or phone me every half hour, or so it seemed, to make sure I was okay. He had arranged to have as much time off as was needed—and was enjoying it, I could tell, the children cheered by having their father caring for them. I didn't tell them I was wandering off with Stanley. To be honest, I wanted something apart from them, someone of my own, to not feel accountable to Gavin and have to tell him everything I did every hour of the day.

It had crossed my mind that June had been mistaken for me. In a way, that made sense. To some people old ladies all look alike, and the fact she'd been at the hotel might have enforced that idea. That made me feel even more guilty, and more scared for myself, so keeping away from home might help safeguard my family, and keeping close to Stanley would safeguard me.

So I walked on the beach to meet Stanley and I had literally cried on his shoulder, and he had held me and not said a word. Nothing he could have said would have helped, to be fair; I just liked the feel of his arms around me.

That dozen or so days after June's death was a bad time, and I don't recall it all; the fogging of the tranquilisers, I suppose. I know I felt I was going crazy, in a little heavenly hell, bemoaning the loss of June's company and enjoying Stanley's.

He would update me with little comments designed, I was sure, just to calm me, to make me less frightened for myself. There was a strong criminal investigation going on in Bournemouth, he said, a bit of a fracas that he considered meant no one would be bothering with me for the while. 'For a while' was not a particularly reassuring phrase, but I didn't tell him that. In a way, I'd rather the police were looking for June's murderer than worrying about me.

"Who is S Sanderson, anyway?" I asked. *Better the devil you know.* "Do you have a picture of him, so I know to run the other way?"

He fished out his phone and tapped and scrolled, then showed me an image of...

"A woman! I didn't expect that. Wait—" I homed in on her dark, beady eyes. "I bet this is the woman who ordered Lisa Gilroy's demise."

"Quite possibly. She is Major Sanderson's sister and, how shall I say it politely...?"

"A murderous bitch like her brother?" I offered.

"Indeed," Stanley said. "But she's busy in Bournemouth now; the focus of the investigation I mentioned, so I think you can relax a little, Molly. She'll get her comeuppance one day."

"I'll happily pull the switch," I said bitterly, and we walked on in companionable silence.

If it was damp we strolled in the weather, and if it was fine we sat on the beach blanket and watched the sea that had eaten a million souls and, along with his closeness and the medicine, it all served to get my mind back into order. I felt the bond between us strengthening as we talked, about anything that came to mind, classic trains and litter picking, the way the world was now compared to the world of our youths, our hopes for its future, and gradually the shoulder to cry on became the arm to lean on and the hand to hold.

~

"The man killed alongside Mrs Bailey has been identified," Stanley said one day.

"And...?"

"Freddy Crathbourne. A small time crook, known for burglaries. Did time for money laundering."

"Do you have picture of him?"

"Do you really want to see it?"

I sat on the rocks and firmly held out my hand for his phone. "Show me."

I looked at the mug shot on the screen. He didn't look the same as the artist's-impression shown on TV, so I suddenly recognised him.

"This is the burglar from the pub. I'm pretty sure of it. I won't say he's the one that tipped Lisa over the cliff, though. He looks way too hefty to be that person I saw with her." I stared at his face, wishing him in hell. "June would have put up a good fight, if I know her, so I suppose she could've pulled him over with her."

"Unlikely," Stanley said. "She was struck from behind so would've known nothing about it, if that is of any comfort." He took back the phone, seated himself on the rock beside me, and stared out to sea.

"I wish I could've killed him myself," I managed to say through the lump in my throat, the pain in my heart.

"Pardon?"

"Well, what do you think? He bashed her, heaved her over, overbalanced or something, so fell with her; serves him right."

"There is no direct evidence for that."

"Stop being a policeman for a bloody minute! Sympathise with me. My best friend's been killed and I... I'm... just so shattered with all the absolute shit that's happening in my life." I wailed and his arm came round my shoulder so I cried against him.

As I calmed I dried my face and went on, "I'll assume Mr Freddy didn't jump voluntarily, and I really, absolutely and totally don't believe he was carrying on with June like the news said, so I say he found June snooping around the hotel and decided she was up to no good and got rid of her."

"And what was she snooping for?"

"Oh—" I had driven myself into an awkward corner. I couldn't say: *She'd gone to spy on you, Stanley, and see who your muse was.* So I said, "She just had this funny idea that there was something spooky going on at the hotel."

"Do ladies get odder as they get older?" he asked.

"I think we might. Bear in mind, June was really into the mystic arts. She was always 'feeling' things, so who knows what she was up to."

Finders keepers, losers weepers. The words rang in my head, just as I imagined they'd rung in June's dream. I had found, she had lost.

Gulping back tears, I stood and we walked on. Again the guilt washed over me. I had told June not to go to the hotel, made her promise not to go, told her not to be nosey about Stanley, but she'd ignored me on all fronts.

At that moment, I don't think I would have minded too much if someone *had* jumped out of a bush and shot me.

~

For Lisa's funeral a week later, almost the entire village attended. Buried in the next town, as there was no longer a graveyard for Kerton, her plot was covered in flowers. One of the 'wreaths' was a rose teddy bear, which I found most poignant knowing how it was her efforts to get a child that had led to her death.

And the pain didn't end there, for then it was time for June's funeral. Her family had come from Taunton, so we attended the crematorium there a fortnight after her dramatic end. Henry, flanked by his two tall sons, was silent and stoic until the very last second; that awful moment when the coffin takes its final ride along the rollers into the furnace, then he had collapsed and I, among others, had gone to him and I became a wreck again consoling him.

I didn't go to her funeral reception. Not with the size of the guilt-stone hanging around my neck. Gavin drove me home and I don't think I managed three words the entire journey, then I sloped into my bedroom, put on my walking shoes and headed for the beach while calling Stanley on the mobile to begin to cheer me again.

I was in love with him. I felt it so strongly I scared myself. This was nothing like I had felt for Oswald even in the heady first days of our romance. This was something deeper, almost spiritual in its intensity, and when I thought of all the troubles being over, everything settled and my world safe again, I realised I would be Stanley-less again, and I wouldn't be able to deal with that. Not ever.

14. Fateful Friday

Gavin and Vana had both taken a day off work and gone into Bournemouth early one Friday morning, to shop, to have some time away from nursing the old woman (I'd heard Vana say that) to be together for while, planning to be back by 6pm. That was the ending time of the after school birthday party I had been asked to take the children to, and for afterwards Gavin and Vana had planned a film night with pizza and ice cream and I was invited.

Our village hall is a construction of great beauty. I don't know who the architect was, but he might have been into creating cathedrals before. With its high ceiling and exposed rafters, mammoth windows and curtains fit for a manor, it was the best thing in the whole village and I loved it. Its elegant curves made me happy in a way I can't describe, and the newer parts where religious symbols had been carved into the woodwork to make it more churchlike for weddings and christenings and such like, had created a transcendent quality to its splendour.

And that day it was full of the beauty, and noise, and chaos, of children.

Kerton primary school is small enough that all the children tend to go to all the parties just to make up numbers. There were only six children in Myha and Minnie's class but any child would whine it was no fun having a party with just six children and get their parents to invite the whole school. This, from the screaming horde that met us as we walked in, appeared to be exactly what the birthday girl, Dani Weaver, had done. Thus did I discover that forty excited children have the sound-load of a crowd of four hundred.

With the thumping disco music, the gaily coloured balloons that floated all over like giant soap bubbles, the decorations hanging from the beams and the big birthday banners, it looked to be a splendid event. I had my eye on the tables, piled high with tablecloth-covered food. I hoped they had my favourite: egg sandwiches. *It's for the children*, I reminded myself, not that that would stop me from snaffling some.

Stanley had tagged along to the hall with me, perhaps to watch out for children who might be hit-men in disguise, as he wasn't the most cheerful party goer I'd ever seen. He was very much on edge that day and, even when I leaned against the wall and watched the games with him and tolerated the loud dance music, he hardly smiled.

"I love this place," I said above the music. "Don't you think it's divine; the construction, the workmanship? It's one of the best buildings in the village; one of my favourite things."

There came no reply, though his eyes did look up and around so I knew he'd heard me.

I was getting used to his quiet times, to be honest. Better a man who knows when to open his mouth, than one who talks on and on about nothing. I was aware he knew something of my past life from police records and, although he had told me of some of the adventures of his life, he had never mentioned his deceased wife or any children. I began to wonder within his silence if he might have children he missed. He could have lost a child, and the party brought back bad memories.

You know me; I had to inquire. "Do you have children?" I asked into the beat that made me want to move my feet.

"Never had the fortune," he replied. "My wife hated the idea. Nowadays, I prefer snakes. Frankly, I see little difference in the two species."

I almost choked. *Oh dear. I should have asked sooner.* The children were an essential part of my life. It wouldn't do to have a partner who—

Oops, I was thinking too far ahead.

"I'm sorry that happened to you," I said, really meaning it. I could not have imagined a life without children, hence our adoption of Gavin. "Children can be vile, that is true. I have to

179

agree on that, but they are also adorable if they're your own."

He looked at me askance and arched an eyebrow with a look of *are-you-sure?*

"Oh come on, you enjoyed talking to Collin about the rocks and things, didn't you?"

He managed a begrudging nod. "Grandchildren," he murmured. "Something I could never have dared to imagine."

"So, do you keep snakes? Who's looking after them while you're looking after me?"

"A good neighbour."

"Could I see them sometime? I actually love snakes."

I felt the hesitation.

"I suppose," I said cautiously, lowering my voice in a quieter moment, "that when this is over, this watching me thing, you have to go home and leave me here and I will never see you again."

He didn't reply but his lips pursed with deep thought.

I watched the happily milling, chatting and excited children, and their excitement filled me too, so I leaned a little more his way to say, "You could stay, you know."

"Stay?"

"I mean, I'd like you to stay. Wouldn't you? The flat's big eno—"

He abruptly pulled away from me and vanished out of the swing doors that separated hall from corridor. *Had the question really been too forward?* I sighed. We'd been getting on so well it seemed, to me, to be the perfect next step in our relationship. There's not time enough for any of us to wait for *the* right moment. I'd had to jump in and ask or spend the rest of my life wishing I had.

But I was kidding myself, wasn't I? Stanley was into thick-thighed women, and a sexless marriage would not be his idea of heaven.

I was about to follow him out when the lights dimmed and the doors swung open at the ceremonious entry of Moira Weaver carrying her daughter's birthday cake, all the bright

180

little cake candles flickering upon it, counting up a child's life, symbols of hope for Dani's future. I wished her well.

I found Stanley in the kitchen. With his back to me, he leaned on the kitchen counter, talking to Dani's father, Nigel, both men with beer glasses in their hands. *Beer trumps Molly,* I realised.

"Time's up, gents. Your lady friend's hunted you down, Stan," Nigel said with an amused grin, raising his half-pint to indicate me in the doorway. "Don't you be blaming him, Ma'am, it's a tad noisy in that there hall."

"Doesn't worry me in the least," I said. "Happy to see him having a good time."

"Ooh, nice attitude," Nigel said. "Got yourself a keeper there, Stan-my-man." He winked.

"I'm just going out for a breather," I said. "My beer-less way of relieving my ears."

Outside the door I found myself laughing inside: *Lady friend.* Was that how Stanley had referred to me with Nigel? How sweet. I liked it.

Now, wouldn't duty oblige him to follow me out?

As expected, the hall's door swung open and a beer-less Stanley emerged. He pulled his coat around him and glanced at the clear sky. "Frost again later," he said.

"I do wonder if summer will ever come. It feels like it's been winter for the past six months." I breathed deeply. The air was pleasant, in the distance the waves sang on the rocks, it was all peaceful.

"Molly..." He coughed as if he had something hard to say and stepped up to me. "I have... in there... when you asked... I'm sorry I dashed out. I was quite fazed by what you were saying about the flat being big enough—"

"Oh no, no." I twisted away in embarrassment then turned back. "I didn't mean to discomfit you. Umm... think nothing of it. Just a lady looking for her last... something or other. Now you've got *me* all tongue tied."

"Nigel gave me a few pointers. Some advice. I am too

old for this game so I will just say... " He gave a meaningful hesitation. "*Could* we make this work?"

"*What?*" On paper the word looks little, but it was expelled from me forcefully enough to blow a metaphorical hole in the page.

I looked at him, he looked at me, and for few trance-like minutes both of us were unsure what should come next.

He raised a hand to my cheek. "Should I kiss you?"

"I don't know," trembled my voice. "This simple touch is bold new ground for me."

"I do know what you mean. In all sincerity I do. I have read all your files now."

I started to cry; from happiness for a change, but then I remembered the painting, the sounds I had heard from that room, and wondered if he truly understood what he would be losing in a relationship with me. "Do you *really* understand my problem? Do you know what you're letting yourself in for?"

"Molly, it's your soul I'm after, not your body."

I found myself taking huge gulps of cold air to calm myself.

"Molly?"

"Oh Stanley, do we have a lot to sort out!"

"If the flat is unsuitable, we could buy Chapel Cottage."

"Did I tell you I fancied that house? Reminds me of the one in Hartpury. The one the major's idiots burned down. Oh, now you've done it, you've got me all excited and I won't be able to stop talking—"

"Sssh..." He put a finger to my lips. A shiver of anticipation ran through me, but he took it to mean I was cold and opened his coat to wrap it around us both.

"So," he murmured against my head. "Are you happy?"

"Oh yes," I sighed, listening to his steady heartbeat. "Happier than I ever imagined I could be. I just wish June were here to see this."

"Then my job is done," he said.

Only later did I find out what he meant.

~

Party over, egg sandwiches successfully snaffled—along with some birthday cake—the children rushed out and I went to get my coat. Coming out, I could see neither my grandchildren nor Stanley, not that I was too worried. Ardeal House was but a few minutes' walk away, and Stanley was likely with them. We had an announcement for the family, so it was apt that he should take them home. I smiled. What a day!

Moira Weaver exited the hall and locked the door behind her.

"Have you seen my three?" I asked. "Lost sight of them in the crush."

"That man friend of yours took them off," she said. "Nige said he seemed a nice chap." Her eyes sparkled with feminine glee. "Nige says he told him to—Oh."

She stopped, probably suddenly realising Stanley might not have taken her husband's advice and she'd be putting her foot in it.

"Get real and propose?" I suggested with a slight smile.

"Did he?" she asked, eyes wide. "Oh, come on, Molly, do tell."

I shrugged. "After a fashion. He's not that good with romantic stuff."

"Show me a man who is!"

"Funny he took the kids off without waiting for me, oh well, Collin knows where the spare key is, so they can get in okay."

Moira congratulated me and went off. I wouldn't have to tell anyone about my new relationship. It'd be all over the town by the next week.

Gavin's car pulled into the car park. I was itching to give them my good news, but my excitement waned as I saw Vana and him looking around, puzzled, then Vana jumped out of the car and marched up to me. "Molly, where are my children?" she demanded. "Tell me you haven't mislaid them!"

"God, Vana, get off my back, will you? I have never lost the children. Why do you have to be so mean? A friend took them back to the house."

"We just came from the house," she said, stone-faced. "We didn't pass them on the way."

"Oh..." A flicker of panic hit me. "Maybe they... they went down by the crossroads."

She said something foreign and angry, gave me the 'look' and hurried off with Gavin. I felt a real stab of anger. I kept thinking Vana and I could weather the storm of my settling in, mother-in-law versus headstrong daughter-in-law, but here it was being laid bare again. It was a shame their trip to town hadn't lasted longer or they could have just come home and the children would have been bathed and ready for film night, and bursting full of stories of the party.

Gavin would likely be angry enough when he got home and found them in the care of an undercover policeman. A policeman who could become Gavin's stepfather. I laughed at that idea.

Families!

Smoke hit my nose. An inconsiderate bonfire to ruin the lovely evening?

I looked around for the culprit.

And through the windows of the hall kitchen I saw flames.

No!

At least *this* couldn't be my fault, though I couldn't imagine what had started it. I hurriedly called the emergency services, asked for the fire brigade, watched as the blaze ran amok, lapping up the curtains, smoke filling the rooms I could see into, red flames trickling up walls. I stood way back, the horrid hypnosis of the fire affecting me, making me stand trembling with stress. This was not the way I wanted to remember the day Stanley had proposed.

Passing cars stopped; people asked if the fire brigade had been called. I couldn't do anything more so I hurried home full of painful remembrance of my little cottage in Hartpury going up in flames, and I needed to see Stanley and the family to sort out many things with them.

Vana leaped on me as soon as I walked through the front door and grabbed my upper arms in a forceful grip. "Where are they?" she demanded in the fierce and fearful voice of a haunted mother. "My kids? Where's your bloody so called-friend taken them?"

15. Church Of Secrets

"I don't know where the children are." There was no escaping the fact; I had to admit it. Getting out my phone with shaking fingers I said, "I think my friend must've taken them to their place instead."

Before I could call Stanley, the phone trilled so unexpectedly that my fearful confusion made me almost drop it.

"Hello?" I said to the unknown number with Vana stood in front of me, eyes afire, hands on hips.

A deep male voice I didn't recognise said, "If you want to see the children alive, get to the church on the cliffs *right now*. No police or they die."

Click

"What?" Vana shouted. "I can see your face, Molly. What's happened now?"

She'd call the police, endanger her own children.

"I'm just going to get them," I said truthfully. "I know where they are."

She slapped me across the face. *"Suka!* You *did* forget them!"

"Hey!" Gavin pulled her back. "Calm down."

"If anything ever happens to them I will kill you!" she raged at me over an accusing finger.

'Overreacting much?' I thought. 'We need to have a good sit-down discussion when this is all over.'

If I make it back.

I ran to my room, checked the contents of my handbag, grabbed a torch and rushed out of my own back door, thinking how the neighbours could probably hear the argument now raging between Gavin and Vana deeper in the house.

Hurrying down the darkening roads toward the cliffs,

my whole body shook. Pulling my tweed coat tighter, I couldn't help but wonder where Stanley was, my quiet knight, my almost partner? He had taken the children, but now the BBGs had the children, so where was Stanley? Had they killed him? Was he captive? Was this my curse again? The fate he'd earned from consorting with me?

'You should have called the police anyway!' my inner-self argued as I sweated suddenly, hot and panicking.

'I couldn't risk that. Not at all,' my conscience agreed firmly.

Leaving voice messages for Stanley, begging him to contact me; I was in dread as I strode down the roads, a dark hint of frost in the air. I had to get the children but I needed backup. Where was the silly man? I was sure he would do his best to help—as soon as he got my messages. He was a policeman, after all. He had probably been in sticky situations before.

As I came within sight of the cliff tops I called him again; got voicemail again. "I *need* your help," I said in the fiercest, most despondent tone I could muster. "Someone's kidnapped the children and I can't rescue them on my own."

I looked behind me, hoping to see someone coming to help, but all I saw was the sky glowing where the burning hall and the flashing lights of the fire engine reflected on the low clouds. I heard voices calling, the lamentation of the town as one of their treasures burned. At least I was not responsible for the death of a building.

Drawing a deep breath of courage, I carried on walking to the church on my own, torch in one hand, handbag in the other, holding it as tightly as a drowning man clamps onto a piece of wood, wishing I had someone to whack with it, or the guts to use the weapon inside it.

When the bedraggled church came into view there were dull lights flickering in the stained-glass windows, blessing them with a final glory soon to be gone forever. I hoped the children were okay, not too scared. I hoped Collin was regaling them with tales of fossils and giant sand sharks.

I didn't want to go in, but I had to. I didn't know if I was going to be killed on sight and the children released, or if they would kill the children too after I'd been disposed of. What kind of animal was S Sanderson? Psychopathic tendencies ran in the family, evidently.

Terror stopped my breath. My heart flip-flopped. I didn't want to get any closer. Flashbacks assailed me: the cellar, the well, the major—

And my legs got weaker and wobblier the closer I got to the building until it felt like my limbs were blades of grass. What was I walking into? Was there even the faintest glimmer of hope I'd get out? Or would I be thrown over the cliffs like June and Lisa?

As long as I can save the children.

I didn't have to worry about walking in, because in the next second the church door squeaked open and two goons, to refer to them politely, rushed out. One grabbed the handbag I was clutching like a drowning man clutches a straw, then they both took an arm and practically lifted me off the ground to frogmarch me inside.

"Nanny!" the children yelled, tied up little souls, sitting in one of the broken box pews.

Two other heavies were sitting on a shattered pew, one each side of a woman whose eyes seemed to glint in the candlelight. Getting to her feet gracefully, almost elegantly, as if she thought she was the most important person in the world, she took my handbag from the goon.

A few inches taller than me, with a mean, middle-aged angular face, she was heavy-hipped, likely attractive once, but now with untidy short chestnut hair heavily streaked with grey, her pretty days were well over. Sporting thick drab trousers and a chunky jumper, she seemed to me a woman who wanted to hide any vestige of her femininity. And those eyes, hooded and evil and reflecting candlelight in their depths. This wasn't just S Sanderson, it was the 'man' on the cliff top with

Lisa. The woman with evil eyes, hardly recognisable as the woman in the photo Stanley had shown me.

"Hello, nasty person," I said, polite to the end. "Major dickhead's sister, right?"

She glared, looked in my bag and found the pistol, took it out and angled it so the candlelight reflected along the length of the barrel. "Freddy's old bashed up pistol," she said, almost to herself. "The one the nincompoop left in the car and wasn't there when I sent him back for it. What did you imagine you were going to do with it, Molly Marshman?" She dropped the pistol back in my bag, handed it to the goon, then took a step forward so I thought she was going to hit me and I moved back sharply. Instead, she gave a nasty, victoriously vindictive grin.

"You killed my brother," she said flatly, and a scent wafted to me; the major's cologne. Was this the woman of the couple I had passed in the street on that evening after leaving June's house?

"And it couldn't have happened to a nicer guy," I said cheerily, "you know, what—"

She backhanded me then, and I realised how gentle Vana's tap had been. Sanderson's strike knocked me almost off balance, my spectacles shaking on my head.

Where was Stanley? I couldn't help but wish for him to appear, and hoped he was arranging for cavalry to come charging in.

"What?" I asked, one hand to my painful cheek, "no hardy henchmen drugging me, half drowning me, messing with my life the way your brother did?"

She tilted her head to one side and malice spread on her face like hideous sunshine. "Shut up, old woman. You took the only thing I valued."

"Nothing original to say then? Full of clichés?"

"Shut up!" she yelled in my face, ugly in her hatred, fists bunched as she appeared to resist hitting me again.

"So now you're going to say..." I battled on, talking as much as I could while letting a part of my brain try to figure out how to escape, "that you're going to take something of mine in return, am I right? Listen, everything bad started off as good. It's life that messes us around."

Her face was mocking now. "Oh my, my, my, what a little old moralising old woman you are. Did you never have any naughty fun in your teensy weensy little life of do-gooding?"

I spoke slowly, hoping the words might sink in; might affect something in her addled and distorted brain. "Revenge is a dark and lonely road. Once you go down it, there's no heading back. The question is, how far are you willing to go?"

She beamed. "All the way, of course. I want to see the look on your face when you realise what I've done; what I'm doing."

"As in?"

"You liked that building, didn't you, the hall so sleek and —"

"You set the hall alight? Pathetic woman," I sneered.

"Yes... Because you liked it." *And who had told her that?* "I am taking all the things you like, love, care for. Wait until you find out what I am going to do ..." She indicated behind her. "... to them."

I expect she enjoyed my look, because it was a genuine spontaneous mix of horror and disbelief and panic that I couldn't hide.

Her smile thinned. "Oh yes, yes." She stood back and made a sweeping movement with her arms to show the sniffling children. And Collin, who understood precisely what was going on, began to shout and wriggle against the rope that bound him, setting off the twins who bawled a harsh cacophony of childish distress.

"You're more of an animal than your brother ever was," I said in pained disgust. "Hurt the chil—"

"*Kill* the children," she said, waggling a finger. "Let's be clear on that."

"And did you kill June; the woman found on the beach?"

She shrugged. "Women. Beaches. Which one? When?"

She grinned into my confusion. "Lisa Gilroy, who wouldn't pay the bill or even agree to try to pay her bill?" She shrugged again. "I hit her a couple of times and she went *phewwwwww* down the cliff. But June Bailey, who nosed around the hotel and I met bin-diving one night? Odd woman. No, not personally, but you did love her too."

I fell to my knees, not believing what I was hearing.

She gave a mean laugh and I just stayed there, cowed, head suddenly ringing with a stress headache, mind whirling, terrified, misplacing where I was for a second, feeling outside of myself, my fear for the children so great.

"Please," I begged. "Please. Not the children. Me, okay, I'm just a stupid old woman, but not them."

"Oh, *yes*," she said in a satisfied voice. "Yes, this is more like it. Now put your wrinkly hands together like you're really praying, really begging me." I did. "So much better in a church," she smirked. "More fitting."

I bowed my thumping head into my praying hands. '*Help me!*' I yelled to anything in the universe, an atavistic call to powers beyond my ken, a plea for mercy for the children.

When she'd finished enjoying the spectacle of me on my knees, the two burly men heaved me up by my elbows.

"Please," I begged again and fell down, a deadweight sack of potatoes against their hold. Anything to give me time to think. I had escaped the major, escaped the cellar, saved myself once before. I would do it again. This time the stakes were even higher.

16. Caving In

The door creaked open and Stanley walked in.

My throat constricted, trying to form a combined cry of, 'Get out, you're in danger but come and rescue us!' but as he approached he said, "Sarah, this does not look like what we discussed."

So the cry that emerged from me was a strangled, "*What?*"

He took a step closer to the two of us, looking at me with contempt on his face. "Scaring her? I approve. She needs taking down a peg or two."

My mouth fell open. Not my Stanley, not my nice well-spoken Stanley with whom I had fallen in love; please no, he couldn't be on the bad guys' side.

"But not the children." He carried on. "To threaten—"

"Oh, I am not threatening, Stanley," Sarah said haughtily, "I am *stating*. For Richard, all she loves will die: the woman, the hall, but not her son and his wife, no, she hates them so I have seen. But these little monsters she feels for so they will die alongside her." She hooked her thumb at me. "Isn't that fair, Molly?"

"No!" Stanley said angrily. "You can't do this, Sarah, I won't let you. Crush Molly, yes, that was the deal, win and break her heart, I did that, but you are not to harm the children."

"*My brother*," she roared, "was worth the whole town!" Her cheeks flamed with anger. "Don't block me, Stanley. You know I'll make you regret it."

"I still think it unwise," he said, jaw tight. "You will have the might of the entire police force down on our heads—"

"Then what's the point of having you as my pet policeman? But no one will ever find them, thanks to your brilliant idea," she said pointedly as I knelt there listening in horror, wondering how she was going to make us disappear.

Stanley snorted. "I think—"

"You think too much. I'm in charge. Do as I say."

"Stanley," I said with my nose in the air, trying to focus the fear from the words 'only if they are found' into something else, something I could use. "You're a great disappointment to me."

"Ha!" Sarah said, her face piggish in victory, so undeserving of what I thought a pretty name. She grabbed Stanley by his coat lapels and pulled his face down to kiss him, span back to me and stuck a finger in my face. "And *you* will never look at my husband like that ever again." She sniggered. "And that is a fact."

'Oh gawd,' my poor heart lamented. 'Her husband'. I didn't *want* to look at him ever again. *Break her heart?* Well done, you did that, Stanley. Sarah had been the woman in the wardrobe, of that I was now sure. Those solid thighs painted so lovingly had given her away.

"I hope you enjoyed our little show the other night," she said with twisted lips. "Oh yes, I knew you were outside listening. Did you hear what he did to me? You'll never know that kind of pleasure, will you, Molly? Old and frigid as you are."

I refused to listen to her baiting. *"Darling Molly,"* I whispered to the floor. "Was that some kind of mean set up too?"

"Oh, the notes; they were found?" She squealed like an excited schoolgirl, aching to elaborate further. "My clever idea. Intimate little notes for the maid to pick up, to wonder about, to gossip about, to feed back to you, and it worked. Nice. I will have to try small town tattle-tales again."

Stanley walked off. "Wait," Sarah called after him. "You haven't told her the best bits, Stanley." He stopped with his back to us, in the stance of a man who does not want to talk.

"Come on, Stanley, the last straw—she needs it to break her completely. Get up, Molly. I want to see you fall down again when he tells you." I didn't move so I was pulled up by the goons, like an old cow at a meat market. "Now, fess up, my dear husband."

His sigh was a hiss in the echoes of the old church, then he said, "I killed June."

As I slumped again, seeing Sarah's disgusting smirk, Stanley sidled into the pew to sit beside Collin and got out his notebook, beginning to write in it casually as my mind reeled and I felt I faded in and out of existence.

Sarah looked at her watch. The candles flickered all around us in the draughts. The two big ruffians shuffled their feet and rubbed their fat hands together for warmth, while the children mewled like lost kittens and the creeping cold wrapped itself round me like a shroud.

She looked at her watch again. "It's time," she snapped.

The two men dragged me bodily to the altar end of the church, beyond the pews where the children were seated, who squirmed in anticipation of rescue as I got closer, and I saw a hole in the floor exposed by the shifting of another pew. The scratch marks on the floor showed where it had been forcibly moved aside, and steps went down steeply into the carved yellow-red rock beneath.

"Stanley," I yelled, "do something. You can't just sit by and watch *children* murdered. What kind of man are you?"

His only response was to lean over and put his head in his hands. "Coward!" I shouted at him.

One of the men went in front of me with a flashlight and the other pushed me after him. I staggered, one hand on the damp stone wall and one holding onto my glasses, without which I would be blinder than a bat, desperately trying to keep my balance on the steps pressing me into a small space where my head grazed the roof and shadows from the torchlight showed the slant steep and long and twisting into the cliff underneath the church.

It was a long way down, the route switching back and forth as it ate into the marl bedrock, slippery in places, and

I stumbled and slid until, by the light of the goon's torch, I saw the place open out into a cave. No, not a cave, there was no opening, the rock having fallen in and closed the entrance. Now it was a hole in the ground; an inescapable hole. We were to be entombed.

Moments later the children came stumbling in after me, herded by another of Sarah's monsters, tripping over their own feet in fear so I caught them one by one as they screamed and sobbed.

"You bitch!" My agonised voice ran up the narrow walkway as the men receded and the place was plunged into darkness, but she was too far away, laughing no doubt, her vengeance close at hand. "And tell your bastard husband to drop dead," I roared, wondering if I could go back up the tunnel, or if I had the strength to shift the pew they would move back into position to hide us. It had to be worth a try. I heard the children getting up and felt around until I could untie them, and they all hugged me. More than a hug, really, a collection of desperate grabbing hands like I was a lifebuoy who could just float them back to the surface of their ordinary world.

Someone else was coming down the tunnel. I looked up hopefully into the descending torchlight, but only saw one of the big men with a pry-bar. In no time at all he had forced a thick-hinged grid off one side of the tunnel wall and attached it to a clamp on the other side with the bar, blocking the way back up.

He vanished. All light vanished too. We were alone in a hole of dripping noises, the scents of seaweed and salt and decaying vegetation and some other noxious stench pervading the place. This had been a sea cave, once. Now it was our condemned cell.

"It's alright," I said, lying and reassuring as hard as I could, even though my fear was freezing me into inaction. "I'll get us out of here, I promise."

"Like how?" Collin muttered grumpily, his hand clasping

mine in an iron grip for one so young. "It's not a video game, you know. There's no secret hidden exit and that woman took your gun so you've got no power now."

"Guns aren't power, they show weakness, an inability to fix things except by force."

He pulled away roughly. "No, it's all your fault. You should have hidden the gun in your pants or something then you could have killed that woman and we wouldn't be here now and it's all your fault!"

"Collin, really, that's not helping." My lips quivered with the guilt he was shovelling onto me.

"Dad says everything's your fault," he raged on. "Mum too. It's why they argue so much. And now we're going to die because of you!"

17. Trickster

I leaned against the wall which dug into my back like sharp fingers, and closed my eyes, steadying my mind after Collin's hurtful outburst, yet knowing nothing he said would matter if we couldn't escape.

From what I had seen of the place before the darkness covered it, the hole was about the size of my front room, all of 20 feet square-ish, all rocky slimy prominences.

The girls held onto me making small fearful noises. Again I said, "It'll be alright." I couldn't say anything sensible, anything *true*, could I?

Water sloshed somewhere close, a melodic noise that might have been quite pleasant under other circumstances. "There must have been a way in, or out, once, if it's a smuggler's cave," I said aloud. "They didn't store stuff here if it's tidal, just came in from the beach and took their contraband into the church up the passage. Likely the local vicar was in on it."

"Great," scoffed Collin. "We're stuck so we can't avoid history lessons."

I bit back a reply. Water suddenly licked at my ankles, then was gone again, the tide inching up with each wave.

"What are we going to do?" Myha suddenly cried, panicking, stamping her feet in a staccato.

"I want Mummy!" Minnie raged.

"So do I," I muttered.

"Are we going to die?" Minnie demanded. I could hear Myha sniffling.

"No. I won't let you, sweetheart. I need you to jump on me in the morning to wake me up, don't I?"

"Good, Nana, 'cause I don't want to die. I want to see Dinosaur Valley."

"Right. Dinosaur Valley. Duly noted. I wish I could see; it

would help a lot."

"Umm... Nan, I've got a lighter," Collin said in the wary voice of a child who expects to be told off.

"Great. Give it to me."

"Are you gonna yell at me?"

"Like you yelled at me just now? No. What else have you got that might be useful?"

"A penknife."

"Wonderful. I need that too."

As I felt the lighter pressed into my hand, I felt like joyfully singing, 'Boys, boys and all their toys', but when I felt the penknife my stomach did a flip flop. It wasn't a penknife by any definition. In the lighter's glow I could see it was a handle hiding a spring-loaded blade. The boys used to call them flick knives in my day. Whatever its name, it was a pretty big and dangerous knife for a little boy.

"I'm not mad, Collin, not in the circumstances, but wherever did you get this knife?"

"Errr..."

"If you stole it, you'll have to return it when we get out of here, okay?"

"No!" he said indignantly. "I don't steal things. It's a present."

"Collin, come on now, don't lie. Dad wouldn't ever let you have a knife this big."

"Not Dad, that man, that Mr Quoit who told me about the fossils, he winked at me and slipped the knife and the lighter all wrapped up in a piece of paper into my pocket while we sat in the church."

"Good grief! Okay, sorry, Collin." But why had Stanley, murderer, deceiver, husband of my enemy, done such a thing unless...

Unless he had, in his own weird way, a conscience that wouldn't let him kill children because he'd never had a family of his own.

And these strange gifts were because he knew there was

a way to survive the hole.

"Nan, do you want the piece of paper too?"

By the wobbling illumination of the lighter, I read what Stanley had hastily scribbled as he sat by Collin: *My darling Molly please forgive me I didn't know she was going to attack the children, HOLD ON, the knife can cut marl, the light can only help. Stanley.*

I shut the lighter and leaned against the wall. A chuckle came from me; a demented little chuckle for the sadness of my world. Stanley had lied to me; he was married though it certainly didn't sound from the short conversation earlier that he wanted to be married to *her*, so I should hate him. But on the other hand he was trying to help. 'Hold on'. That had to mean he was going to rescue us. Now I loved him even more, wretched man, and hated him to the point of desiring vengeance because he had killed June. This was conflicting, to say the least. What a trickster!

So, should we just wait to be rescued? Or should I be scouring every inch of the frigid hole to find some obvious means of getting us out with the knife? In any event, I had to act faster than my cold limbs wanted me to.

I hugged the children, water surging against my calves. The tide was coming in fast.

"Collin," I said with urgency. "I've had an idea. Keep the girls close. I'm going to investigate."

I stood him against the wall to brace him then managed to pass the twins to him one at a time, little hands clutching feverishly at any contact, grabbing onto my clothing then having their fingers disengaged and placed where they needed to grasp on him. I flicked on the lighter and looked over the walls to see the algae levels; maximum high tide markers. The slimy thick green line was about level with my chest, which meant the hole was not going to fill, but I wasn't ready to cheer yet. Any water was cold at this time of the year, and since we had no way of avoiding the incursion of seawater, we would get wet, we would get cold, we might well get hypothermia

—especially the skinny twins—and we could all die just as thoroughly as drowning.

"All right. You won't like this but take off your coats and jumpers."

"Then we'll be even colder," Collin complained. "You're not dangerous, you're pathetic."

"You think I don't know that? Feel free to share *your* escape plan, Mr Know-it-all." I was wrestling off my coat, moving to the girls to take theirs. "Listen, if we can keep the coats dry then, when the water goes back down, we'll have something to bundle up in to warm ourselves. Do you understand? We'll get wet, that's a given, and wet clothes will drag us down and make us even colder, so give me anything you can to keep dry, and we'll huddle up and keep sane and warm each other until the tide turns. It's quite fast, you know that."

I held the reluctantly shed clothing over my head and moved to the metal grille, forcing the coats into the gaps at the top to keep them secure and dry, and suddenly had an epiphany. Of course, 'The knife can cut marl', so I got going, scraping, sawing, working at the rock around the hinges' pins. We could get out and sit on the steps well away from the water and wait for our rescue. Job sorted.

Ping!

The blade snapped off in the hinge as I slipped the knife in the wrong way.

I bit back on a swear word but Collin heard it. "What have you done wrong now, Nan?" he asked, his lack of trust in me painful but merited.

"Nothing," I lied as my mind flitted from one idea to another, dismissing my plans one by one, trying to find something else workable with the stub of a broken knife as I stepped back to the shivering children, and I turned off the lighter to hold and hug them, to pray, to beg help of the forces June had believed in so firmly, to think alone in the dark, holding Collin's hand that had never held mine so firmly before, almost feeling his demanding thoughts coming through it: *Save us, Nan!*

Abruptly, one of the girls started shouting. "Nana Nana Nana! Someone's touching me! Someone's touching my bottom!"

I instantly snapped on the lighter, only to see a blackened dead hand tapping her, its arm in the water, connected to a body drifting face down.

"Just seaweed," I said, lighter off, steering the floating corpse to the other side of the cave and putting a rock on its chest to weigh it down. I think the rock sank through the rib cage but I didn't use the light to check.

Water rising, I hoisted the children onto my shoulders, like monkeys grabbing and chattering, trying to keep three cold, semi-naked children out of the water's way, wondering if I had done the right thing, but what other course of action could I have taken?

My chest tightened, a feeling of nausea swept over me; an angina attack approached and I didn't have my pills. I couldn't die there, I wouldn't, I refused to, but this was something I could not control.

When was Stanley planning on rescuing us? It had to have been an hour already.

Or was it—God forbid—a nasty joke? Were Stanley and his not-so-lovely wife laughing at the idea of us sitting in the cold water, waiting... numbly waiting for a rescue that was never going to come?

The cold was attacking my insides like a frigid cancer, constricting my blood flow, starving my heart...#

Nan! Nan! *Naaan!*" a panicked Collin squealed distantly.

With a snap, I regained consciousness as water enveloped me. No hands were on me as I stood and spluttered sea water and yelled, "Children!" fumbling for the lighter I had tucked into my bra for safety.

Collin was clambering up the grille, holding on for dear life. Minnie was on his back like a baby lemur, arms around his neck; blue arms, shaking arms, a child so cold she wouldn't be able to hold on much longer.

"You fell," Collin said, his words slurred, accusing.

"Myha?" I said, casting around in the water and finding her floating face down. Guilt and grief assailed me as I grabbed up the dead fish of a child.

The terror that had enveloped me in the major's well of corrupted water filled me even more now, a terror not for me but for the children, and all I could hear in my head was Vana screaming and Gavin's condemning voice saying, 'Mother, how could you let this happen?'

18. Hold On

I held Myha to my chest, no heartbeat in her, no breath, no place to put her down so I had to try CPR with her cradled in my arms, awkward, frightened beyond my wits, not knowing the proper procedure, never having done it on an adult, vowing to do a Paediatric First Aid course, promising those empty promises, the bargains with a god I didn't believe in. *Let her live and I will never drink again, I will give more money to charity, I will help build a new church...*

Holding her awkwardly with one arm, I pressed down on her chest with my hand, over and over for what felt like long frigid minutes, then rubbing her, trying to get her to breathe like a newborn puppy that looks dead, stimulating it into action. My heart staggered again as she mewled then threw up water.

"Myha!" I cradled her close, waded to the others and we all held each other, crying with fear and relief. Water now up to my chest, death had been beaten for the moment, but how many more moments did we have to survive?

The water had gone down a fraction. I felt it leaving, like a sucking on my clothes, like being licked by a very large dog.

As the water receded, I encouraged the freezing children to strip and put their dry clothes on and we all found some relief; but the coldness was not our friend. What would happen the next time the tide came up? How many times could we stand the torture?

For now, the children put their coats back on, we hugged, rubbed each other's arms and legs, and we huddled in a warming clump of bodies under the tent of my coat, and tried to be brave.

"The tide won't be back for a good few hours, so..." I heaved a big sigh, "all we have to do is make a tunnel through the front, and for that we can use Mr Quoit's knife as a digging tool."

"Until you break it again," Collin muttered. How the child sounded like his mother.

"I'm still all ears for your escape plan," I reminded him.

He didn't answer.

"I'm keeping you alive, isn't that enough?" I asked.

"More like you're trying to kill us, fainting like that."

"Collin, I am getting old and so is my heart. It doesn't like the cold. It could give out again if I don't watch out. My medicine's in my bag, my bag's with the bad guys. I am doing my best so stop complaining, for Pete's sake."

After a second his contrite voice said, "I didn't know you were ill. You should've said. I'll rescue you."

"Umm... that's kind of you," I responded, wondering if there was a hidden meaning to those brave words, or whether it was an attempt at sarcasm. "Now, the beach, I guess, has to be in this direction. You sit here, all tucked up, and build up each other's warmth and keep an eye on Myha."

I was cold, trousers wrung out but clinging damply to my legs, with only my blouse and cardigan to actually warm me, but I hoped the exercise from trying to dig would keep me warm. I felt my way around the rocks and bumps to the theoretical opening of the cave and set to work. Loose stones I shifted to one side. The knife saved my hands from the scouring sand and finer pieces of stone and I huffed and puffed with exertion and knew my shoulders would ache diabolically later.

Then I moved another stone and a rain of them showered down, glancing blows to my head and my back, making me squeal in a most unseemly way as I scrabbled backwards.

"Nana!" came a chorus of sharp little cries followed by Collin's, "Are you alright? Are you hit?"

"I'm fine," I said hurriedly, "just fine." *I feel cuts on my face. There will be bruises too.* "Don't worry, everyone, I have this in hand."

Setting to it again, elbows chafing on the wet sand, the small stones under my chest felt like boulders.

I laboured a while, the children silent under their warm pile, but I was the one suffering now. The exertion that should have warmed me froze me instead. Although I could feel the gap getting wider, deeper into the pile, I worked slowly because I knew that any second it could lose stability and come crashing down again.

Then, a wind, sharp and familiar, sudden and unexpected despite being desired, gusted into our would-be tomb and swept around the scent of salt water and the stench of the body in the corner and I felt physically sick.

Swallowing hard, I looked towards the hole I had made to the outside, darkness out there as the hours had sped on. But it was nothing helpful, unusable, a space a small troll might have navigated, but not me. I had to go extra carefully now, stone by stone—my fingers frozen, fumbling, body weakening...

"Not long now, sweethearts," I murmured. "I've made a small hole, just got to make it bigger and we can get out of this mess, okay?"

"Nan, Myha's breathing funny," Collin said.

She was panting. I rubbed her arms and legs and held her to my chest, the temperature inside the coat tent barely staving off the eternal chill. Minnie held my side and we rested there, a moment out from trying to escape, a moment needed to get my strength back as much as Myha's.

We all jumped in fright as a great groaning clatter of rocks on rock sounded, and I realised my tiny tunnel had succumbed to the weight above it. Back to square one. I could have cried, my despair was so total.

So, in the end, I got you after all. The major's mocking voice seemed to echo off the walls.

"Go away," I said aloud.

"Who, Nana?" Minnie asked.

"No one," I said.

"So where's Collin?"

I was up with the lighter on in an instant of heart-stopping, blood draining realisation. He had gone. He had tried to go through the hole and it had fallen on him! Or had it fallen when he'd got out? I didn't know anything anymore.

Near exhausted, I huddled with the girls, all of us sobbing. I knew I had to move, but I couldn't. My energy had gone out with the tide, out with Collin's possible demise. I was empty. Though this particular tide hadn't killed us, the next might, or the next. Something would get us one way or the other.

Minnie's head moved sharply. "Someone's shouting."

Yes, they were. I crawled to the wall and yelled as loudly as I could then flopped to the ground, thinking of outside, in the real world, the warmer world, the world where I would be cursed and hated by my child, but at least I had the girls; they were safe. Was that enough? *No, never enough for Vana*; my thoughts tumbled over each other. I was afraid of being rescued. I didn't want to be found lacking a child, I didn't want the rescuers to find his body, I remember that so keenly in those last seconds as the wall of debris was defeated, and all I could think was of my guilt in losing one, not saving two.

~

They say that it is when the battle is finally over that you collapse. I know I did. I vaguely remember the man, the hard-hatted rescuer who broke through first and said, "Thank god; do you know how hard it's taken to trace you?" but I don't remember how we got to the hospital. I only know I woke and I was warm, some kind of hot air puffer blanket on me, monitors attached to me. I reached for the red buzzer and a nurse appeared. "The children?" I whispered.

I saw her face drop as the monitor declared my heart's stuttering rhythm.

"The little girls are going to be fine, Mrs Smith, but the boy is in intensive care."

"What?"

The monitor beeped madly. The nurse eyed it cautiously as she went on, "I understand he was caught in a rockfall? He sustained head injuries. Some brain swelling. He hasn't woken yet."

"He's in a coma?"

"Yes, and he'll be kept that way for a while, best way to heal, you see." She placed an encouraging hand on my arm. "Now don't you worry, there's nothing you can do and he's in the best place."

"Take him to Bournemouth."

"You don't trust our nursing experience? It wouldn't do him any favours to be moved at this point."

"*Is she awake?*" came a yell, and the Vana-missile was incoming, right on target. I think if Gavin had not been with her she would have beaten at me with her sharp little fists. As it was, the nurse had to call for orderlies to remove her for upsetting me, for sending the monitor into a crazed representation of the storm inside me, where my head rang with her vileness.

And the most awful thing was I knew I deserved it all

~

When the girls and I were released from hospital two days later, the police had come to the flat and quizzed me as to what was going on, so I'd told them to talk to Sergeant Williams who would have all the details and to come back if they still needed more.

Need I mention that Gavin and Vana were still mad at me? Very, *very* mad at me. The children had been put at risk—almost killed—by their grandmother's shenanigans, an involvement Gavin had specifically told me to avoid. And, when Minnie decided to blurt out about the gun and the knife, Gavin didn't even wait until the sentence was over before assuming it was *my* knife and *my* gun I had been wielding.

Even worse, both girls had heard me telling the voice of the major to go away, and they had turned it, in their stressed minds, into an instruction for Collin to go away, thereby causing him to try to wriggle out. I was pretty sure the voice had come after the collapse of the tunnel, but I was getting battered on all sides and arguing made me question myself. In truth, I think he had finally done something noble: he had heard me say I was ill. He heard me say there was a hole, and he had tried to rescue us.

Then came the bombshell. Marching orders for Molly. There I was thinking I had done a good job in keeping the children alive, and there were the parents disregarding the fact they were still alive... even Collin was *alive,* expected to make a full recovery. Fear made them angry, and the thing they feared was me.

Vana wanted me out. She'd had enough of living in fear. Gavin very regretfully sided with her. Part of me could see her point of view. It seemed senseless to argue. The crazy Sarah and her husband were still out there somewhere. Chances were, the moment she heard I'd escaped the hole and arrived home she'd come and burn down the flat, and Misty-cat, and the twins.

So I simply nodded at Gavin and Vana, looked at the twins who avoided my gaze, and went into the flat to pack. Where could I go? Somewhere interesting. The biggest problem was, I didn't have a passport so couldn't go abroad. Unlike Gavin, I had chosen to vanish completely. With no driving licence, no pension and no passport, Molly Smith was a no one.

Still, I had never gone to the Lake District, or seen Ben Nevis, or Loch Ness. That sounded interesting, and there were always bus tours to investigate.

I should have known it wouldn't go to plan. Even packing my bags turned out to be something I soon regretted.

19. Enough Is Enough

While packing my bags, I took out the bottom drawer of the dresser as I saw clothing slip down the gap at the back, and right at the bottom of the drawers, tucked under the edge, I found the little notebook Gavin had been looking for right at the beginning of this story.

It was small and black with an integral pencil, just like Stanley's, just like the average police notebook, and when I opened it and leafed through the pages I was struck dumb and then became very angry—incandescent with the pain of deceit and the things people put on me when it was not my fault at all.

The tiny book contained accounts of *people of interest*. That's what it said on the first page. There were many names and a few lines of description for each of them. One of them was Sarah Henders née Sanderson.

Another was Stanley Henders, tall with grey hair, grey eyes and a bushy moustache.

There were a lot of names and descriptions in that book. It appeared Gavin had been working with the police. It would have helped matters if he'd come clean about his involvement, or maybe he'd forgotten who was in the book, and of course I had kept Stanley out of his way for fear of comment, but the last date was only the year previously. Nevertheless, I was still angry.

I was so angry that something popped in me, a mental break of outrage and despair and unfairness.

I stormed out of my flat and found Gavin in his office. He looked up as I marched in, a frown forming; and a guilty-pinched expression spreading over his face as I slammed the notebook down with as much noise as a tiny notebook can make.

"Explain this," I demanded. "You've known about these

horrors for a long time. Don't you think it would have been a good idea to warn me of them?"

He waved his arms apologetically. "I couldn't, Mum. It's all supposed to be secret stuff, you know?"

"Secret?" I hollered. "From *me*? *You* have risked the children, not *me*. By not telling me what you knew about this organisation working in Little Kerton, you effectively precipitated all of our trouble. Even the death of June! If I'd known what was in that book, I would have never even... anything. *Anything.* Your silence caused it all."

"What you moaning about now, Granny?" Vana's tired voice said from the doorway where she leaned against the jamb, a study in not-caringness. "He does his job. I do mine. You watch kids. That's the deal. Not our fault you're useless at watching kids."

I rounded on her. "Did *you* know there's a group of thugs working in Kerton?"

I knew the answer from the fact that she glanced at Gavin and he shrugged.

"You *both* knew? So how could I be expected to keep the children safe against an invisible enemy! All you do is make me feel more and more guilty over something I had no control over because you two idiots thought granny was too thick to understand or keep a bloody secret."

"Yes," said Vana.

"No!" Gavin said shooting up to face her. "Stop this blaming. Now. Get back to the girls, Vana. I'll deal with this."

But a huge tidal wave of what's-the-point-of-anything was sweeping over me. I felt it drowning me, killing me more thoroughly than the cave.

I fled back to the flat, ignoring Gavin's call after me. I'd had enough. I couldn't rectify anything. Gavin and Vana hadn't been honest. If I couldn't expect it of Gavin, just who could I expect it from?

I threw a few things into a bag then threw the bag into a corner and sobbed on the bed. I felt unworthy to be liked in any fashion. Angry son, wary grandchildren, fierce daughter-in-law; what was I to do?

Just an old woman—yes, an *old* woman—who has tried and failed to find her place in the world.

I left a short note saying I'd decided to leave them in peace and move on, then I took all the remaining medication with almost a whole bottle of wine. I looked for Misty to apologize to her. Yes, apologize to a cat. She might miss me, she might not, but she would be fine with the family. The children were very fond of her; she was tolerant of them, never peed in corners or ate the plants or scratched anything. Yes, she'd be fine.

Then I left everything, walking off down the road without a coat or a handbag, away from my cosy little flat and the new life I had in truth begun to doubt within months of moving in, and certainly after chaos had yet again descended on me.

Coming to the main crossroads, I took one last look back, and then walked resolutely through town, along the roads in the semi-darkness and down the path to the beach in the cold, letting the discomfort wash over and into me. I'm not brave enough to wade into the sea or jump off cliffs, so I hoped I could just sit on the beach and fade out from the drugs I could feel fizzing and fading my brain, and exposure would take me. No one would miss Molly who was cursed. Molly who got people killed. I hoped June might come visit me at the end, take my hand and lead me off, saying something sarcastic like, "See? I told you there was an afterlife. Now, come and meet some new friends."

More likely, the major would come and sit gloating, waiting for me to slip-slide away so he could drag me to hell. If I'd been killed by the major, so many nice people would still be alive.

I perched upon some cold, smooth rocks. Past crying. Past everything. I had fallen in love and found it all a trick, though the man had at least had the decency to call the coastguard to rescue us, even if it had taken so long we'd almost died anyway, and Collin could still die, realistically, and I wondered how that rescue would go down with Sarah if she ever found out. She'd gloat when she saw my demise on the news. Maybe have a party. Finish off the nude painting to celebrate...

The sea hissed on the sand, the clouded sky hung dark and stormy, and farther down the beach I saw pin-point lights dancing, torchlight, night time beachcombers, and then I heard a voice from above.

"Oi, Ms T, wotcha doing down there?"

"Oh, Hugo," I breathed to the imagined voice. "I didn't think *you'd* come for me. But I suppose I did love you in my grandmotherly way. I am so sorry about what happened to you."

The clouds twisted, stars shone through, Hugo's face loomed in the half light as he extended a phantom hand.

"Come on, let's be getting you in the warm. Not good for old ladies to be out in the cold, is it?"

"I'm alright now you're here, dear." My voice seemed to flutter. "Just sit by me. I guess it'll all be over soon. Peace; that's what I want."

"Oi, Georgie," his voice called, rattling my ears. "Come give us a hand. It's Ms T, but she's acting right weird."

A dark figure appeared outlined against the sky, a spectral man, Hugo on the good side and Georgie on...

No. Wait.

George was Hugo's roommate. He'd looked after Misty during that fracas in Hartpury. He wouldn't be on the bad side, and why was he dead too?

"No," I sobbed, tears turning to ice on my cheeks. "Not another victim of the curse."

Somebody took my head gently and a blurred bearded face peered into my spectacles. "Come on, what you taken?"

"I wanted to go."

"Go where?"

212

"Heaven," I murmured, and smoothly slid into oblivion.

20. The Nice Psychiatrist

I woke on a cloud. A nice soft fuzzy white cloud that smelled a bit like disinfectant. I kept still, listening to an alarm going *beep beep beep* nearby, vaguely wondering where I was and, if this was heaven, where were the harps and angels, Hugo and George and June?

A second later my brain kick-started into cognizance, and I realised what I heard was a heart monitor, the world only fuzzy from lack of spectacles. 'Hospital; again,' I thought as I lay in the crisp, white-sheeted bed with rose spattered curtains around my cubicle. Had I dreamed of Hugo and George or had I been so close to passing over that they'd been able to visit from the other side? June would have been ecstatic to have heard about that. The blurry memories made me cry again. I rubbed the tears away with the back of my hand and felt the cannula in my arm shift a little, and I cried more, feeling useless and done in.

A dark-haired nurse side-twisted through the curtains, a cheery smile gracing her pretty face, but it dropped when she saw my wet cheeks. She offered me water and a tissue then hesitantly smiled again when I asked for chocolate cake. She went off and came back with a lidded cup of water. Sitting half propped up, squinting at the IV line running into my left arm (the bag said sodium chloride), I drank the water through a straw as she checked on the machine beside me, noting details on the chart she unhooked from the end of the bed rail.

"Where am I?" I asked.

"Royal Bournemouth," she said. "Do you know why?"

"Not the faintest," I lied. If I admitted to an attempt at suicide, no matter how feeble, they'd cart me along to the Pysch ward.

"Do you know your name? Why you were crying just now?"

"Umm..." I was wary, nervous. The other thing to consider was, who else might be knocking around that might want a piece of me? Where was the awful Sarah hiding? Where had Stanley vanished to? What would Gavin and Vana think of me now? Did Gavin have the power to shove me into an old folks' home on the basis of mental infirmity?

"My memory is very blurry," I lied. The nurse removed the empty water cup, gave me a mechanical cheerful smile and left, opening the curtains to a blurry view of other beds, other faces, all old ladies. "I am in the wrong ward," I said aloud. "I am not old."

Somebody with a sense of humour laughed.

I managed to wriggle around to get my chart, and squinted at the words: Jane Doe. Of course, I'd had no bag, no ID.

"Look in the locker," crackled a very old voice from the bed next door, where a grinning white haired blob could be made out. "Glasses," the blob said. "I know that look. You're missing your glasses."

I thanked her and retrieved my spectacles from the locker.

"I'm Joan," the perky owner of the old voice said, and held out a hand to me.

"Jane," I responded without hesitation, and took the offered dry and wrinkly hand for a bare second.

The nurse reappeared. "Making friends?" she said. "That's good. Now, umm..."

"Her name's Jane," Joan said, brightly helpful.

"Okay, Jane, there's a consultant here to see you. Would you prefer to be in the day room for your assessment; out of the public eye? We've got no private rooms at the mo. I'll get a wheelchair for you." She went off before I'd even replied.

Me, in a wheelchair? How undignified.

But there I was, in the wheelchair, hospital dressing gown over the other gown that has only ties at the back so everyone can see your bum if you're not careful, and the tall stand thing with wheels that runs along beside you with a saline drip feeding into your arm. I felt as presentable as a dead mouse.

The white coated man waiting in the dayroom was very nice and young and polite, and introduced himself as Doctor Kellow, the consultant psychiatrist.

Uh oh, be careful, Molly.

He plonked his lanky frame down in a padded chair and took up his clipboard and a pen from his jacket.

Reading from the clipboard, and calling me Jane, he told me in a solemn, serious voice that he was there in response to another doctor's request due to concerns over my toxicology report. It had showed alcohol and benzodiazepine. He said how I'd been delivered into A&E at 23:32 hours by evening beachcombers after being found unresponsive. My stomach had been pumped, which likely saved my life.

"Was it a sincere attempt to take your life?" he asked over the board, pen poised to write my response. "Or were you hoping to make a point to someone? A cry for help, maybe?"

It had been concluded from the state of my face that I might well have been the victim of some abuse. So, how much did I actually remember? Did I want the police called? Would I like to discuss my feelings?

When I didn't immediately reply he leaned forwards, his expression pleasant and caring. "You're in a safe place, Jane. My role is the assessment and management of all patients for whom significant risk is identified, including patients who are at risk of harming themselves, harming others, or are vulnerable to neglect."

All I could think was, this meant no one had connected me to the same woman who'd escaped a hell-hole and been questioned by police in Kerton cottage hospital the day before. Was it really only the day before? I was a bit confused.

I still didn't know if I should say my real name. Hadn't Gavin missed me yet? The clock high on the pale green wall said 10:02 am. If this was Sunday, it could be everyone at

Ardeal House thought I was sulking in my room so they weren't bothering with me. Or they could think I'd upped and left already and didn't care. When they noticed the note, though, they'd be sure to contact the police (wouldn't they?) so for now I played the fuzzy memory card. I didn't want to go into all the explanations, it was too much for me, and without even having to fake them I collapsed into tears again.

Ignoring my distress, Dr Kellow scribbled on his clipboard, then said quietly, "Jane, I'd like to have you transferred to my clinic. It's only in the new annexe. I'll take you down to the concourse myself if you like; call a porter to take you the rest of the way?"

"Like this?" I spluttered, drying my face on the gown.

"It's all hospital grounds; no one will bat an eyelid."

"Not on your Nelly," I blurted. "Unless I'm unconscious I'm going out with clothes on. Nurse!" I hollered, and a different one came to my call. "Please take out this drip, I'm off with Dr Kellow and I don't want it banging into anything as it hurts anyway, and do you happen to have any clothes I could have? Are mine around? I'm not gallivanting down the road in this inelegant ensemble."

She gave Kellow a look. He nodded and she removed the drip, saying, "I'm sorry, but there's nothing else to wear. Maybe you can call a relative to bring something in later."

"Fat chance," I muttered.

She twisted the chair's foot supports around from the sides and placed my feet in them firmly. "There, all ready for the Grand Prix now. I'll see to your paperwork" She pulled a quick smile at me, positively beamed at Dr Kellow, then slipped out.

I was breathing heavily. Some sixth sense was prickling me, though to be fair it could have been simply the idea of being confined in a wheelchair that made me feel incredibly defenceless. I wondered if fear was something soldiers got used to, and old ladies simply couldn't. Yes, I said *old*. I did feel it then. Old and vulnerable.

The original nurse reappeared with what I took to be transfer papers. Dr Kellow signed them, then she left with an almost genuine, "Good luck, Jane."

"Actually, I really would like a blanket," I said, looking at Dr Kellow hopefully. "It looks chilly outside."

He glanced out of the window at the grey-sky day then turned back to me with a weird smile. "Don't worry, Molly. Where you're going you won't feel the cold."

21. Hellchair Ride

Dr Kellow took a hypodermic needle from a pocket and waggled it before my face before jabbing it through the gown and into my thigh.

"Just a nice little local to keep you down," he said. "So you can talk and yell all you like, but not run."

"So who are *you* in the miserable band of bad guys?" I asked as I felt numbness chill my leg. I wasn't going to give him the satisfaction of trying to run and falling all undignified with my petite derriere showing.

"So you *are* in there, Molly Marshman," he said. "I knew you were faking. My real name is the same as my dad's. Richard Sanderson Junior at your service, you pesky murderous old bitch."

It's funny—depending on your definition of funny—how many people thought I had murdered the major when in reality he'd done it to himself while trying to kill *me*.

"Nurse!" I yelled.

"They'll just think you kooky, Molly."

He took the wheelchair handles and whisked me out.

"He's a fake!" I shouted to the nurses at their station, who looked at me with sympathy before looking away. "He's a fraud, I tell you. Call the police!" I yelled along the corridor, a little old lady pushed by a strapping white-coated psych-consultant. Ha! What was the likelihood of a gang boss's son becoming a psychiatrist? Diagnose your own father as a sociopath, why didn't you? That's if he was a real shrink, and from the nurses' reactions they'd certainly seen him before. But had the nurses even been real nurses? Was I even Molly?

I threw myself out of the chair, sprawling, catching myself with my arms. He got a passing porter to help get me back in the chair as I gabbled, "He's not a real shrink, you know. He's kidnapping me." But the man looked at me as if I were really mad and hurried on.

"Keep going, Molly," Junior said jauntily, his steps even as he marched along. "I am really enjoying this. Should have got it on camera for Aunty."

Little did he know I was enjoying it, too. All the shouting was kind of therapeutic. I was finding the will to fight returning.

"Stop this chair right now," I bawled at the top of my lungs to the hospital audience, "you lily-livered coward who only beats up old ladies 'cause he hasn't got a dick!"

Down to the open expanse of concourse we went, the crazy old lady in me loudly calling to anyone around that I was being abducted, kidnapped, stolen, nobbled, shanghaied... Of course, no one listened. Many ignored, some gave glances then looked away. I had expected no less. People don't want to get involved. They assume everything's being handled by someone else.

Where was I being taken? A quick death, to my mind, would have been lethal injection in the hospital, to mimic a heart attack, drawing no suspicions at my age. But being taken out and away could only mean something far worse was waiting for me. It wasn't going to be anywhere nice, of that I was certain. Somewhere I wouldn't *feel the cold.*

"You're a ghastly excuse for a son, you know?" I said loudly. "You never visit your mother in hospital and now you're dragging her out to kill her. What will everyone think of you now?"

That got a few puzzled looks.

I tipped out of the chair again, cussing silently as it bruised my bruises.

"Shut this or I'll fucking handcuff you to it," he growled as I was hauled up again, kicking best I could and yelling until a porter ran over to help.

"Get your hands off me," I hollered at him. "He's molesting me, everybody. This man just put his hands on my tushie."

"Kerrist," Junior swore and shoved me roughly back in the chair. "Bad day for er... challenging patients, eh?" he said to the porter and walked on.

She was waiting for us outside the main doors. All dressed up in a beige silk trouser suit and with make-up on, Sarah honestly didn't look too bad as she greeted her nephew with a pat on the cheek and a big, toothy smile.

"What, no Stanley?" I said in as sarcastic voice as I could muster. She whapped me across the back of the head. "You'll never see him again," she snapped.

Taking over the wheelchair's handles, Sarah began to push me along the path skirting the hospital wall.

"Aliens!" I shouted as loudly as I could. Heads turned. "I'm being abducted. Help!"

Sarah laughed. "I'm actually happy to see you alive and well, Molly," she said chattily, "because now I can really have some fun with you. This time we'll try something a little more permanent; more thorough, without the complication of small children."

I wondered how much she'd cackle if I told her I'd tried to kill myself the night before. Now I knew what impending death felt like, if that was where I was destined to end the day, it was nothing to fear. Friends would be waiting for me.

A piggy snort managed to escape my nose as I inwardly laughed. She thwacked the back of my head again. I assume no one noticed or, if they did, no one came to the rescue of the crazy old lady who'd recently been shouting about aliens abducting her.

I was also thinking she ought to shut up and get on with it. In all the movies, the bad guy spends far too long telling his victim what he's going to do with them and subsequently gives them to time to escape.

Around the corner the wheelchair and I sped under her guidance, past the services' entrance, past A&E where the ambulances stood waiting for calls.

I was practising flexing my thighs, fighting for some

control as the short-acting drug Junior had administered showed signs of already wearing off, when someone shouted, "Gerroff!"

The wheelchair jerked up and back and down again with a rattling jar that almost sent me flying, and Sarah was no longer pushing me, her silk-trousered legs inexplicably sprawling in the road beside me as I sat numbly in the wheelchair trying to understand what was going on and a *whomp*—

A shriek...

A crashing bang all behind me, and people were running and screaming around me.

Someone took the wheelchair handles, whispered, "It's all right, we gotcha," in a soft male voice, and smartly wheeled me along and, as we crossed the road at an angle to the hospital, the chair was turned so I could see why people had acted that way. Sarah's body lay under the wheels of an ambulance that had crashed into a pillar of the A&E's portico.

"Clever, huh?" my male pusher said. "Runaway ambulance, handbrake left off, rolled off; no one'll suspect a thing."

"What?" I squeaked.

"Not far now."

"Who...?"

"Later, later. Just round this corner..."

I was pushed through an unofficial gap in the hedge that surrounded the car park and came face to face with the smiling expression of a sunshine yellow Micra's bonnet, looking rather like one of those friendly anthropomorphic trains in children's shows.

I reached a floppy hand to the Micra as we moved alongside it.

"Hello, nice Micra. You remind me of someone I used to know."

Then the person who jumped out of the passenger door startled me so much that, had I been standing, I would have fallen over.

"Lo, Ms T, long time no see." He beamed a friendly and delighted smile into his beard. "Let's be 'aving you on board the magical mystery tour then."

"Hugo! You're not dead?" It was feeling like an hallucination. "How can you not be dead?"

The small time crook who had helped me in Hartpury shook his head firmly. "Not the last time I looked, no. You saw me and Georgie on the beach, 'member? Come on, let's be 'aving you. Explanations later."

He and George hoisted me up and pushed and pulled me into the Micra, while I tugged my dressing gown around me and tried to hide my scraggy bum from their sight.

22. Old Friend, New Friend

By the time I was safely bundled into the back seat of the Micra, and we had driven sedately out of the car park after paying at the gate machine, my leg's power had almost returned.

"Same car?" I asked. "But it's not blue?"

"Just a re-spray to confuse people," George said easily.

"You changed the reg-plate, I hope?"

"Nah," Hugo talked over his shoulder at me. "Too much 'assle. Just keep it dirty so can't be read."

"That's an offence."

"That's my Ms T," Hugo laughed.

"I would have said it was a good idea to bring me to Bournemouth hospital not Kerton, but I guess 'they' just always know where I am."

He nodded. "Did think you'd be safer 'ere."

"Fail in all directions," George said.

"How come you escaped the major's wrath?" I asked George.

"I scarpered when Kat said Major Pissed Off had grabbed Hugs. Hugs had to track me down later."

"Kat was worth her weight in gold." I thought of the young woman who'd been practically held captive by the major. "Hope she did okay."

"Deported," Hugo said dolefully.

"That's sad. Oh, clothes?" I asked suddenly. "Or is Molly to stay mainly undressed for life?"

"We'll go get yer togs."

"And Misty," George said. His smile was all white teeth in his handsome black face. Take a few years off me, around fifty, and I would be enamoured of him.

"Misty in a car? In a *Micra*? The basket alone would hardly fit. Wait—Are you running off with me?"

Hugo nodded. "Yer'll be safer with us than with anyone, since half the bloody population round 'ere seem to be in the cartel's pocket."

"Hmm... yes, even the shrink that got me out of the ward, a chap calling himself Kellow, claimed he was the major's son."

Hugo frowned and shrugged. "No idea 'bout that. And, Georgie, well done on taking out Madam Sarah the bitch-cow fuckwit. Nice moves, man!"

"It was an accident, honest," he said with a devilish grin. "That ambulance wasn't locked and the handbrake was dodgy; just an accident waiting to happen."

"And was her falling an accident too?" I asked.

"Of course." He rotated his shoulder and grimaced. "That was one hefty lady. Likely had trouble with her centre of gravity. Think that accident nearly put my shoulder out."

We all laughed, then George said, "Fate, Ms T, only fate, only karma seeing to it that people get what they deserve. Nice things as well as bad."

As he said those words, I caught something in the look he gave Hugo.

"What *are* you two doing here anyway?" I asked.

Hugo drew in a deep breath and crinkled up his beard in a smile reflected in the rear view mirror. "Been keeping half an eye on you, after hearing some stuff on the grapevine. Since George and me, we got evicted, 'cause the landlady... well, she found out that..." He hesitated.

"Found out you're criminals?"

George shot me a worried look. "Well, yes and no, but that wasn't what she was worried about."

"How many guesses do I get?" I asked.

The two men exchanged glances and I made an inspired guess. "You're a couple. Congratulations. Can I be a bridesmaid? I've never been a bridesmaid."

"You feeling alright there?" George asked me.

I smiled the biggest smile I could, thinking how this

little revelation made me happy for them, after the pain of the cave and everything that had happened to me, I was going to be saved by this loving couple.

"I'm happy for you," I said. "That's all."

"So the homophobic landlady chucks us out and you want to be our bridesmaid," George chortled. "You're amazing, Ms T."

"Thank you, kind sir. I believe in the philosophy that one loves who one loves." *Stanley, Stanley, how could you hurt me so much?* "So come on, tell me, boys, how'd you survive? Escape the group, cabal, coven, whatever they were?"

"Drug runners," Hugo began. "The lot you an' me upset —yeah, not like me, I was just muscle and I didn't deal with dirty stuff. Needle and Jim and the other two lads did, though. Anyhoo, they work in a messy world full of fear, hurt an' pain; sure you noticed that." He glanced at me, then his eyes went down again beneath his beetling brow as if he was ashamed of the things he was telling me. And he might well have been.

"Damned if you tell and damned if you don't tell," he said and went on sadly. "All the time, constant on the edge of yer seat kind of fear, of being bumped off, of being arrested, of doing something boss man don't like, all wears on yer nerves. Not a good way to make money, to live. Sitting back and watching them destroy your life..." He shook his head. "Yer mates' lives too. Nah, I couldn't deal with it no more. I was trying to escape when I took the dosh bag in Hartpury; me retirement fund I reckoned. I wanted even more to escape when they caught you, 'cause that was all my fault."

"But the major said he'd overdosed you. The boots, sticking out of the ground?"

He sighed heavily. "He sent two blokes out to bury me —you know 'em, other two from searching yer house—but they realised I weren't dead and cause they sorta knew me they didn't want to bump me off final-like and took me to the hospital where some coppers 'appened to be for something unrelated, but taking me in was so suss the lads got nicked.

They told on what the major had wanted them to do with me, so the cops buried the boots and put out that I was dead as a way to lure him in, or summit."

"Ah, I see. Would you believe, I have a picture of you on my wall?"

"How'd you manage that?" he frowned. "Mug shot?"

"I got an evidence copy from the police," I said. "It's just the boots sticking out of the mud. But I don't need it now I have the real thing."

I leaned back in the seat.

"There's just one last question now," I said quietly, almost to myself. "Where's Stanley, and is he likely to come after me? He saved us from the cave but, now Sarah's been killed—at least, I suppose she's been killed; being run over by an ambulance likely has that effect on a person—will he want to get back at me for *that*?"

23. "The Wheels on the Bus..."

The Micra drew up outside Ardeal House. Neither of the family cars were there, so no one was in. I unlocked my back door with the hidden spare key and found my stomach sinking as I walked in. No one had even bothered to look in my room. My goodbye note was still anchored to the bedside table by my phone. I could have died in my sleep for all they knew; been on the way to becoming a mouldering corpse like the one in the cave.

I gathered some clothes and slung them into my smallest suitcase, tore up the old note and wrote another. I simply said I had gone to stay with friends. No lie there.

I considered keeping the phone but it was full of memories of Stanley.

And just where is he?

No, don't wonder, leave that subject well alone and go off on another adventure. Remember: friendships trump love. Okay?

Misty made her presence known. I gathered her soft fluffiness into my arms and knew I could not take her with me, no matter how much George might think it a good idea, so I put her outside and locked the cat-flap so the family would have to let her in later. Then they'd look for me.

I went back out to the Micra dressed and ready.

"Where's Misty?" George asked with a look of intense disappointment.

"I'm sorry, but I honestly can't see her travelling with us. A dog might, but not a cat."

He pouted. "I am... bereft."

I slung my belongings into the boot, climbed into the back seat and said, "Wagons ho!"

"Wagons wot?" Hugo said.

I am so going to enjoy educating these lads.

"Wagons ho was what the wagon train leaders would

yell to get the settlers' wagons moving when the west was first being colonised."

"So..." He started the engine. "Micra ho!"

~

We stopped at the cliff-top café because I was very hungry, and I'm ashamed to say I ate like a horse (or a man). In between bites I filled the boys in with what had happened to me, though I couldn't help but keep looking around, nervous, suspecting everyone who came in of intending ill towards me. I had attempted to disguise myself with a headscarf and really red lipstick. I'd have done the dark glasses bit too, but I didn't have any.

I borrowed a phone to call the local hospital, to check on Collin, but no one would talk to me other than to say he was still alive, but that was some comfort. George patted my back. He was into patting. "Don't fret so, Ms T. Lad'll be fine. My mum, she got kicked by a horse a few years back. Right in the head. Out for a week, she was, fine as rain after."

"That's reassuring. Thanks. Now, shouldn't we be getting out of town?"

"Slow and steady-like," George cautioned. "Rushing around is suss." He let his hand stay on my back like calming a cat.

Filled with foreboding like an evil doughnut, fear crept into my system and made me feel sick, though it could have just been the food I'd eaten too fast.

"I need to be somewhere nicer," I complained, "not full of bad memories. Let's go now. Please?"

'Where's all your fire gone, Molly?' I asked myself. 'It wasn't that long ago you were promising yourself you'd never be scared of anything ever again.' And I suddenly realised I wasn't scared for me, but for these two lads who had seen fit to rescue me just because they liked me. Family isn't just blood; it's people who grow on you.

"Okay," Hugo said. "Got a little job to do. You look after Ms T, Georgie, and I'll be back in two shakes of a lamb's tail."

"Pick up my special backpack while you're at it, right?" George asked. "You know, just in case?"

"You're not gonna need *that*," Hugo scoffed as he stood up. "Bet you fifty you don't need it."

"You're on," George winked at him.

Hugo stood and looked down at me with a curious expression I couldn't read. "See ya later," he said, and off he went.

"What is he up to?" I asked George quietly. "Is it something illegal? It's something illegal, isn't it, the way he looked at me, like he wanted to apologise for doing it before he did it?"

George huffed a laugh. "I dunno. Might be he just wants to get a crate of beer for the trip. I love him, but he baffles me too sometimes. You want pudding? I fancy pudding. They got apple pie?" He stared up at the menu board.

A shiver ran through me as I remembered the last time I had been in the café, scared of being followed, wanting the security of Stanley beside me, all a lie. I doubted there ever had been anyone following me. The danger had been beside me all the time. I was a fool. Maybe I was also a fool for trusting the lads, but I would never know until afterwards and I just felt that I was... almost one of the gang, somehow.

I ordered a pot of coffee and stared at the brown stuff circling in my cup more than I spoke to George. He made up for it by talking, on and on, about the adventures the two of them had been on together in the past year, how Hugo had actually, *really*, fancied Katarina and was distraught when she'd been 'thrown back over the sea', as he put it.

"Hang on," I interrupted. "I'm confused now. If he's with you, how can he have fancied Kat?"

He shrugged. "You can love more than one person, right? He'd have moved her in with us, given half a chance."

I decided I was stepping out of the bounds of my knowledge of modern love, so let the matter drop.

Then George went on about how he'd wanted to get a

kitten, in the hope it'd cheer Hugo after Kat had gone, and I saw he was a caring young man, no matter what his past crimes might have been.

About an hour and a half later, after drinking too much coffee to perk myself up, and too much apple pie with cream to make myself full-belly happy, Hugo returned with a backpack that he handed to George, and a new, startling appearance. To add to the crescent scar I had noted on his cheek before—maybe the result of his argument with Needle in Hartpury—he now had bruising on his bearded face. I looked at him in alarm as he eased himself into the seat opposite me, squeezing George over.

"And what in heaven's name have you been up to now?" I asked.

He gave a pained laugh and raised a finger to his battle-wounds. "Not sure, but the other geezer's unconscious, so reckon I won."

"Why and what the hell, Hugo?" *Great start to the relationship.*

I turned to George. "Does he do this often?"

"Lady's asking, Hugs."

Hugo lowered his head and said quietly, "All in the name of honour, Ms T. That doc, the shrink what gave you grief. I nipped to the 'ospital, found 'im, gave 'im a few love pats and chucked 'im in a nice big waste bin."

"Oh Hugo," I cried, clapping my hands together. "I do love you!"

"Yeah," he said, a light coming into his eyes as he saw my approval. "It was *boof!*" He shot out his arm in a punch. "Then *bash!* That's for Molly, you rotter, and *bosh!*" He play-punched George. "That's for Molly, too, you stinking bastard."

"Excuse me," said an annoyed, cautioning voice from behind the counter, "but could you gents keep your voices down. You're disturbing the other customers."

"Nipping to the loo," George grinned, and left with the backpack. I would find out eventually what was in it; 'just in case'.

24. True Love

We left the café, and drove to the town's bus rank, where a big green out-of-service bus waited.

I watched in confused fascination as Hugo began to attach the Micra to a tow bar on the rear of the bus.

"Isn't that rather a giveaway, if anyone's looking for you?" I asked.

"Nah, I'll just get it sprayed another colour later," Hugo said. "Wotcha think? Pink next time, for a lady, huh?" He laughed, and as I stood there with my mouth open to lecture him on the foolishness of thinking the BBGs wouldn't be able to track him 'somehow' through his precious little Micra, George prodded me and mouthed, 'Don't bother,' then unlocked the bus door and we boarded.

"A bus *house*!" I exclaimed as the internal conversion was revealed. "It's beautiful."

"Yeah," Hugo grinned and winced as the action caught his bruise. "Amazing what you can get off internet auctions, innit?"

I laughed. "Still, it must've cost a pretty penny." I admired the kitchen section at the front, almost as nice as my own—as my own *had* been, I revised with a jolt. Just as I was wondering how much a single-decker bus and its conversion ran to, George said softly, as if the world was listening in. "He's still had some of the major's diamonds, you know? Didn't all fit in that hidey hole."

"Well, I think this is amazing. Where are the beds?" I asked. "I'm done in. Just need a power nap."

"Past the bathroom; that slidey door." Hugo pointed to the back of the bus, so I walked up the middle with my bag and dropped it on a settee as I passed.

Stanley emerged from the sliding door like the xenomorph appearing in 'Alien'. It had about the same effect on me. I staggered and reached to a wall cupboard for support.

I glanced back where Hugo and George were as frozen as I was, because Stanley held my pistol loosely in one hand.

I took a deep breath and jumped in. "Oh, thank you, Stanley, that's mine." I extended a hopeful hand. "Can I have it back, please?"

"Get off the bus, Molly," he said coldly, his eyes on the boys more than me.

"How'd you get on? The door was locked."

He gave me a deprecating look. "Did you imagine a simple door lock could defeat me? Come on, Molly, get off this effrontery to British style. We have places to go, things to see."

"What?"

"Sarah's dead; a traffic accident. We're free. Where shall we go?"

"Fucking hell," George whispered. "He wants to run off with you, Ms T."

"What's the idiot saying?" Stanley demanded. The pistol raised its ugly snout.

"Listen," I said in a gently placating voice, "I don't want to run off with you, because I have decided to run off with my friends here."

"These simpletons?" he asked, astonished. "These raging homosexuals?" His mouth curled in disgust around the word. "Huggy showed some promise at first, but once he set up with that black thing—" He indicated George. "He was lost to our cause."

"Stop insulting them," I said, hard put not to rage at this pompous and bigoted man I'd thought I'd loved. "You haven't been honest, Stanley, and I can't be with yet another dishonest man, and put that wretched pistol down. You're not going to shoot anybody. That would be rude."

His face crumpled. I actually thought he was going to cry. "I love you, Molly," he said. "Sincerely and utterly, it is no lie. Your kindness, your humour, your open humanity; so much more than Sarah ever had. You treat me as an equal, not a slave. Let us be each other's company into aging. We deserve each other."

"There's another great big problem, Stanley. A really *enormous* problem. You killed June. I can't forgive that."

"Sarah made me do it."

"Made you?" I was incensed at the passing of blame. "Like, she stood there with a gun on you and said 'Push her off or *you* die'?"

"Freddy was supposed to—"

"The burglar, right, and why'd he go over the cliff too? Was there an orderly British queue or something?"

He glared at me. "You do not know how things are."

"If the major's shenanigans were anything to go by, then by golly yes, I do."

"Then you will understand that Freddy did not do what he was told. He refused to kill June, so I had to remove both of them, but I did not enjoy my duties."

My hand had covered my mouth in horror. "Wha... what the actual hell, Stanley! You are stood there asking me to run off with a *murderer*. How do you think I could ever do that?"

"Because the group will never stop looking for you, and you can be safe with me, I assure you. I would be no worse than your first husband. I knew Oswald well, and wondered at the undeserving way he spoke of you."

"No, no, my head is spinning," I complained, fitting all the pieces together like a warped jigsaw puzzle. "Was there ever a man following me?"

"Of course not, the ambition of that exercise was to bond you to me."

With a crazy laugh I declared, "An unfortunate success."

I looked back at the lads, who stood stock still with blankly despairing faces.

"I must be crazy," I said, beginning the show I had come up with in a millisecond, "but if you'll keep me safe, okay. You have intelligence, style, and I did fall for you, so you win. Now give me the gun, just to be on the safe side, and I'll come with you. See there? I have a little bag packed already. It'll do."

Stanley gave a suspicious growl.

"You're going with him?" George squawked. "I wouldn't trust him as far as I could throw him."

I said gently, "I'm a big girl, George." Then I whispered, "I think he'll shoot you both to get me."

"Stop whispering," Stanley ordered.

"So give me the gun," I repeated. "I'm coming with you; once I get over all the horrid things you've done, we can have wonderful days on the beach together, talk about rocks and trains and anything we like, right?" I held out my hand to receive the gun and his eyes flickered over all of us.

"You're giving me the chance of a new life, Molly," he said. "I cannot express my gratitude adequately. But one of the rules of my world is, no loose ends."

He shot George.

I cried out and leapt in front of Hugo, shielding him, saying tightly, "Keep still. He won't shoot me."

I hadn't managed to save George, but I'd be damned if I didn't protect Hugo.

"Georgie..." Hugo whimpered.

"Stay. You can't do anything for him."

"Molly," Stanley ordered. "Step away. If you truly desire a life with me, accept the bearded oaf's life is forfeit."

"No!" I snapped over my shoulder. I span round, my arms out wide, still trying to shield Hugo. "If *you* truly desire a life with *me,* he lives. Get it?"

"Whatever *do* you see in him?"

'All of the things I don't see in you', I thought, but I said, "Go on, Hugo, off the bus with you, and I will follow in two ticks."

Hugo and I retreated to the front of the bus, Stanley walking slowly towards us, the pistol still raised.

"Get off, Hugo!" I whispered. "He'll be out in a min. I saw a big bin alongside the toilet block." He got my meaning and reached for the door button as I tried to distract Stanley with,

"Did you know, Collin's in the ICU, in a coma? The rescue came too late for him."

Hugo jumped out.

"I did my best," Stanley said defensively, the pistol loose at his side again. "It's the fault of the rescue services. I gave them as much information as I could and assumed they'd have some kind of ground penetrating radar, infra-red or the like."

"Maybe he'll wake if you tell him fossil stories."

"I might make a terrible grandfather, but I shall be a most excellent husband, I guarantee." To my surprise and relief, he turned the pistol round and gave it to me, handle first." A peace offering," he said.

As I accepted it, I looked at the fallen, beautiful George. I thought of Hugo out there waiting to deal with Stanley to avenge him. I thought of June, my lovely friend, beaten and thrown over a cliff; Lisa Gilroy, who had just wanted motherhood and paid the price with her life; bereaved husbands, terrified soaking children, injured children who Stanley-the-deceiver thought were less than snakes...

So I shot Stanley Quoit because he deserved it, point blank, twice to make sure, my ears deafened by the first shot hardly hearing the second, looked at the slumped, empty thing he had become with tears finally welling in my eyes, then got off the bus to find the waiting Hugo.

Although my shaking knees were threatening to drop me, I felt no shame. I did feel loss, though. Now he was gone, I recalled the dream from weeks before, full of loss, longing and pain, and it finally made sense... Love, hate, all confused into a little ball of life at its worst.

A man walking past stopped and looked at me in concern. "You all right, missus?" he asked.

I smiled weakly and he walked on. No one was bothered with our drama, I realised. Outside the tragedy unfolding within the bus, no one had even registered the shots. No one else cared about our little painful world.

"Bloody hell, that smarts," said a pained voice on the bus,

and I looked up in amazement to see George, alive, upright, one hand to his chest.

"Okay," Hugo said, stepping up to his partner, "I bet that bloody 'urt. You'll be 'aving a bruise the size of a dinner plate under there. I were wrong. You did need it."

"Need what?" I gasped. "What's going on?"

George opened his shirt with a pained flourish, grinning from ear to ear, showing a black vest of a kind I had only ever seen before on TV. "Bullet proof vest, Ms T. Like I said: *Just in case*. And now Hugs owes me fifty."

25. Homeward Bound

Stanley flew over the cliff in the rainstorm that blew in later that night. He hadn't earned his wings; it was only Hugo and George going, "One, two, three and away you go!" launching him into the dark night. We didn't think he'd earned any better way to be found than that of his victims.

Death was probably the best place for a confused man like him. I hoped Sarah gave him a hard a time in hell for 'loving' me, if he'd even understood what love was.

"Right," said George, all business like as we reboarded the bus. "First stop, somewhere to chuck the bloody carpet then, tomorrow, somewhere to buy new carpet."

I looked out of the window as the bus rumbled up Main Street and turned towards the by-pass, headlights illuminating the town, making it look far more interesting than it really was, thinking, 'Goodbye, Kerton, no thanks for all the memories,' then I yelled, "Stop!"

I jerked forward as the brakes jammed on.

"What's going on?" Hugo yelled from the driver's seat. "Forget yer toothbrush?"

"No," I said, half way to the door. "We left someone behind." I pressed the open button and called Misty, who I had seen running up the road. She galloped up to the steps, hesitated, then gingerly clambered on board.

I scooped her up. She purred and rubbed into my cheek. George practically grabbed her from me, but I said nothing.

"Okay..." Hugo said resignedly. "Any more passengers before I starts off again? No chickens or frogs or butterflies?"

I shook my head. "I think I have everything I want now, everything that makes my life, my life, though we'd better find an open pet-store for supplies for madam here."

"Supermarket," George said. "Twenty-four hour thingy, outskirts of Lyndhurst. Maybe 20 mins?"

"Lyndhurst? Where are we off to, then?"

"Surrey. Got some business in Bracknell."

We set off again, and I tried to imprison Stanley in the farthest reaches of my mind, hoping I'd forget him, like when I put the butter in the freezer by accident, or fed Misty Collin's cereal and him the dry cat food. But I know that deep down I won't forget the good feelings he gave me before I found out who he was. So I'm seventy something, does that mean I'm not allowed to love? At my age and after my life experiences, I think I need it, deserve it, am owed it by fate.

But for the moment I was home. It was a home aboard a converted bus with two petty criminals and my beloved cat, but June had been right. Friends are the best.

And friends that support you even when they know you're a murderer are even better. If you'd told me a few years ago that I would have had the strength to kill Stanley, I would have laughed and run away from you.

Is it strength, though, or more an indicator of how I am breaking inside? Doing things I would never have dreamed of doing a few years ago. Like Sarah, so blasé about having June and Lisa killed—just regular work to her. I hope I don't become like that, a completely broken soul, not recognising right from wrong.

I hid the gun away, only one bullet left in it, though I didn't doubt Hugo could get more if I asked, and deep in my bag under hankies and papers and granny-stuff it will shelter. If I have learned one thing from my adventures, it's that you never know when you might need a weapon. The knife from the cave episode was still in the cave somewhere, along with the lighter, but the gun... I would keep that safe, just in case my curse moved me to need it again.

Was I scared the lads or even the cat would succumb to the curse?

No, Misty still had eight of her nine lives, and Hugo and George were tough little gits who would protect me as fiercely as they had each other. I felt safe with them and could only hope they'd be safe with me.

'On the bright side,' I thought, feeling my death-defying humour begin to re-emerge as the bus bumped along, 'Little Kerton-on-Sea's going to be really popular this summer. After all those bodies turning up everywhere, it might have the biggest tourist boom ever... Every cloud, as they say.'

We hit the A35 minutes later. "Bus ho!" Hugo said with a gleeful air punch as he drove the three of us, battered and bruised in our bodies and hearts, on to a new adventure.

BOOK THREE

ST. AMELIA'S

"I love those who can smile in trouble,
who can gather strength from distress, and
grow brave by reflection."~ Leonardo da Vinci

1. What Did I Do?

Doused with freezing water, I gasped, screamed, curled into a ball and kept yelling as the liquid ran like melting snow over my head and shoulders. Hard hands pulled my naked body upright, fiery fingers burned my skin. Lashing out as hard as I could, I directed punches in the direction of assumed bodies, my eyes blurred by cold water and lack of spectacles. Voices invaded the place, echoing.

"She's back again," a young female voice stated as hands grabbed at mine, trying to stop my assault, but I hit harder, thinking this was torture and I needed to escape.

"Stop that!" ordered the harsh-accented voice of another woman, leaving me sitting in the bath, hands in the air as if beseeching an elder god to spare me as I twisted and shrieked. The ice water stopped falling, its job done. My body shaking with cold, I pulled in on myself, curling up like an assaulted caterpillar.

"Oopsie," said the first voice. "Yup. She's back with us, Mila. Get her dried. I'll go get Mrs Galyer."

Confused, shivering fit to fall apart, I jumped as a hazy woman in beige flung a towel around my shoulders. I hugged the warming cloth as she roughly rubbed me through it. I tried to make sense of what was going on and finally managed to say through castanet-chattering teeth, "Where the hell am I?"

I might not know where I was, or what the heck I was doing sat in a cold bath, but I did know one thing.

I was in trouble... again.

As another foggy shape entered the bathroom, I peered up blearily. The dark-blue figure of a woman loomed over me and said, "Now, now, Mary—"

"No," I growled, frowning in her direction. "I'm Molly."

The figure sighed. "Here we go again. Get her out of the bath. I'll talk to her afterwards."

Hands reached for me again.

"Gerroff." I twisted away from contact, grabbing at the vague modesty of the towel as the annoying hands persisted in drawing me up.

"Come on now, Mary," the first female voice said, cajoling and cheery and young. "We're going to hoist you out the bath and into your chair. Come on. You don't want to miss breakfast, do you?"

"Molly." I insisted. "Where are my spectacles?" I directed an accusing glare at the hazy shape as my shivering towel-draped form was hoisted from the bowels of the bath tub, down into a wheelchair, and hastily wheeled into a corridor, where with squinted eyes I made out doors extending down one wall, and a long row of curtained windows on the other.

My wheelchair was spun around into an open doorway fast enough to make me giddy. I heard a drawer slide open and close again. As I squeezed my eyes a bit, trying to focus, to make sense of things and failing, sharp vision blissfully returning as my spectacles were placed over my nose and I clearly saw the young woman attending me.

Short brown hair, bright blue eyes, a certain peeved twist to her lips. A pretty girl. One with the sort of long-legged coltish charm so many youngsters have but ruin the moment they open their mouths. I took in her pale beige tunic, the box of a room I was in: a bed, a wardrobe, a dresser, all magnolia walls and hideous puce curtains, and a toilet cubicle tucked in the corner.

"Nursing home?" I guessed dumbly, still trying to wrestle information from my clamped down brain as my heart ran in panic. What now? None of this was right.

Stress levels soaring, shaking from nerves and face getting hot, I shrugged off the damp towel and sat naked, thin as a rake. This wasn't my body. Not Molly's body. It was old and veiny and droopy.

Hastily replacing the towel around my quaking shoulders, the girl crouched and peered into my face. "Mary," she said in a soothing voice. "Relax. You're fine. You're safe. This is St Amelia's Nursing Home."

"What? How? Was there an accident or something? How did I get here?"

"Let's get you dressed and off to breakfast."

"No way!" I pulled back from her reaching hands. "I'm not doing anything until someone takes the time to explain why I'm here."

"I s'pose it is a bit confusing, but we're all here to help you, so let's get you dressed and I can explain."

I glared. She smiled back; a smile so sweet it relaxed me a little, so I let her help me dress in clothes I didn't recognise, my legs still feeling like rubber—from fear or some illness, I didn't know. I was pretty sure my legs had worked the last time I'd used them. My chest ached; I hoped they were giving me my meds properly.

I poked my thighs with a sharp finger that didn't look like mine. "What's wrong with them?" When the psycho-psychiatrist in Bournemouth had jabbed me with something so I couldn't run, it had deadened the leg—but these legs both had full sensation. I was thinking about them as though they were not mine. I didn't want them. I wanted back the ones I'd had before.

"You just haven't used them for a while," the girl said. "We'll get you some physio and you'll be right as rain in no time, you'll see. Right, so you won't need a nappy now you're awake." She dragged pants and slacks up my legs, shoved ill-fitting slippers onto my feet, tugged a button-less blouse over my head then swept a cardigan around my shoulders, starting to wrestle my arms into the sleeves as I struggled against her, against everything being forced on me, odd things making my senses beg for some normality. "Should've had a proper bath," she said. "You smell like an old dishrag."

"How rude," I said loudly, not noticing the door begin to open, "and let go of me. I'm not a bendy doll. My arms work simply fine."

A woman in the dark blue of a nurse's uniform entered. Tall and slim, hair in a modern short and spiky style, she had a good ten years on the lass wriggling my arms around like errant tentacles.

"Amber?" Ah, the woman in blue from the bathroom. She sounded cross. "What's going on? Who's being rude to Mary?"

I tutted, irritated by her air of authority. "You want to know what's going on? Well, I can assure you I do too."

"Interesting," the woman said quietly as we locked gazes. "Alright, Amber, find something else to do for five minutes."

As Amber left, the nurse stood close beside my wheelchair and looked down at me. "Mary," she began in a soft, persuasive voice no doubt designed to calm unreasonable old women, "I'm glad you're feeling so well today, but please don't fight the carers; they're here to help."

"Who's fighting?" I said in amazement. "I can put on my own clothes, thank you very much, and my name's not Mary, it's Molly, and I have no idea where I am and therefore every right, I am sure, to be a bit upset."

Unfazed, she said evenly. "You're Mary Cooper."

"Not unless I've been reincarnated, in which case it all went wrong and I want my money back."

Her face stayed calm. I supposed she had years of practice in dealing with oddballs like me, but she asked, "So, why do you think you're not Mary?"

The reasonable, suspicious-natured part of my brain finally kicked in and said it might not be wise to talk openly to this woman, especially considering how intelligent her eyes were, how it was obvious she was thinking deeply about some conundrum I posed for her. And, all of a sudden, like a vision, I remembered being in a Chinese takeaway with Hugo and we were going to take food back to the house, then...

Hazy memories came to me. Falling; blacking out before I'd hit the ground... as if my mind had drained away and the dark and nothingness wrapped around me like a huge blanket.

As I stared defiantly at the woman before me, I had a vague recall of being in bed and murmuring people wandering around me, the scent of disinfectant, the prick of a needle in my arm. But those were fuzzy impressions, more like a millisecond of being aware of one certain thing—the way a lump under my shoulder was making my arm ache so I wanted to shift it—and then I'd be gone again.

But now I was awake, and my body hurt, feeling bruised and aching, very weak, hunger and thirst clamouring in my belly as I sat there worried. Had someone whacked me over the head, drugged and kidnapped me? What had happened to Hugo?

"Your care was arranged with us a good two months ago, Mary," the nurse was saying. "You'd had a fall, stroked out and become unresponsive, so your son called. He wanted better care for you than his hospital could give." She raised her chin proudly. "We are an excellent, progressive facility."

"What was his name?"

"I'm sorry you don't remember your son's name. We'll help you with that."

I did remember Gavin but, after all the things that had happened to me in the past few years, I found it hard not to be suspicious. Had Gavin had really brought me in? Or had someone clobbered me and dumped me there to keep me out of the way? After all, how would Gavin have found me after I left Little Kerton with the lads?

"So who are you?" I asked. "And what was the name of the man who signed me in here?"

She drew a short breath as if I had annoyed her. "I'm Irene Galyer, the nurse-manager, and I can't actually remember who signed you in without looking it up. I have over forty residents and I can't remember every detail."

"Yeuk. Forty old people. How will I survive?"

She pursed her lips. "You are one of those valued residents, Mary."

I tried not to glower at her. "Can I really not walk?"

"Neither well nor steadily, no. You'd be surprised how quickly muscles atrophy when you're not using them. Use it or lose it, as—"

"Don't you lecture me!" That was enough to really annoy me. She had to stop me from trying to push up on the arms of the chair, to stand up, to prove her wrong. Of course I could walk! This was all a huge trick being played on me.

"Get off me." I wriggled, trying to get her hands away from me. "You're lying to me."

"Stop it, Mary." Hard palms clamped onto my resisting shoulders and held me down. "Calm down, sit down. Do things methodically, with help—"

"So you haven't been looking after me properly," I wheezed, breath shaking with anger. "I thought you were supposed to massage muscles to help them."

I heard an annoyed sigh and she came round to face me, her placid mask beginning to crack, lips pressed together, head raised high and arrogant, impressing on me that she was the boss.

Flicking a thread of errant hair back into place, she said, "You must understand, this is not the first time you have showed complete cognizance, but it's only lasted a few hours on the other occasions. Each time you've woken, I've explained the situation to you, like I will today when you're more settled. I'll go write my report now. I imagine your doctor may want to visit when I tell him you're back."

"Oh goody. I can't wait to meet him," I said, all the while thinking, *As long as his name isn't Dr psycho-Sanderson.* "And go check who's paying for all this, please."

Her eyebrows did a quick jog up and down and we looked at each other in mutual antagonism.

"Watch out," I said. "You frown too much. You'll need Botox to iron out those stress wrinkles."

She frowned even more then pulled herself straight and business-faced, turning back to the door and opening it.

"Amber!" she called. "Mary's ready for you."

"I'm Molly," I said firmly as Amber returned.

It was only then I noticed the plain gold wedding band snug on my finger. Stomach lurching in bewilderment, I remembered how I had taken it off after my husband's funeral years before, and lost it along with everything else in the house fire at Hartpury. So why should I be wearing it now?

2. Glad I'm Not You

I stared at the ring, dream-like, hearing Amber say, "I can call you a different name if you want. Makes no difference to how I bathe you."

"And what's with that anyway?" I said, looking at her sharply in disgust. "Why can't I shower *myself* with *hot* water?"

She laughed lightly. "What you doing, Mary? You love cold baths."

"I do *not*," I said loudly. "Whatever gave you that idea?"

Taken aback she stammered, "Well, it's in your notes, and we've given you quite a few 'cause they're supposed to be really good for you, so we was told, but 'cause you were out of it, it was hard to tell if you liked it or not. Now we know, it won't happen again."

I glanced at the ring again. Molly's or Mary's? There had to be an answer to all this.

"Did I really have a fall?" I asked as she proceeded to brush my hair with short strokes, patting it into shape as though I were a posh lady in her boudoir.

"Yeah, well, s'pose so. That's what it says in your notes. There's a scar on the back of your head here, so I s'pose that's it." She put the brush down and angled the chair to wheel me out of the door. I reached into my hair and she stopped a moment to move my hand to the long, hard line of a scar.

"So why can't I have a walking frame?" I asked. "Surely exercise would help? I don't need this silly old chair. It makes me feel decrepit."

"We've got loads of people to care for, Mary, and yes, you do need a chair 'cause you'd like as not slip and fall if you stand and I'd get into trouble 'cause I'd not followed procedure. Come on, breakfast is waiting and oh boy do I need a coffee."

Glancing up as we left the room, I saw the number on my door: 35, and a name written in neat capitals on the small whiteboard beside it: Mary Cooper. I stared, trying to psychically change the wording, but a silly thought jolted me. *What if I really am Mrs Cooper? Did I swap bodies in some heinous secret experiment the bad guys were carrying out?*

Outside my bedroom, the many-windowed connecting corridor ran straight to the left and the right, ending in more doors, and before Amber could stop me I tried to stand, failed, sat on the edge of the chair, lost purchase and slid gracelessly to the carpeted floor.

"What are you doing?" she squealed. "Did your ears not wake up with the rest of you?"

Another carer appeared from the next room. Dumpy, blonde hair so short it was almost invisible, her impression was that of a fierce little bull dog. "Help?" she asked in an accented voice identifying her as the other woman from the bathroom.

"Yeah, save me from this twit," Amber said. "Mary, behave yourself, please. Remember, you'll get *me* into trouble."

The two women lifted me back into the chair, the blonde spitefully digging her nails into my arms. I kicked at her shins. She swore in some other language and stalked away.

"Now, now," Amber cautioned me. "That's not nice."

"I was just warming my toes on her," I said.

"Well, you better watch out she don't warm her hands on you. Some of them carers are a bit handsy, you know."

"Disgraceful," I muttered. "Look, she pinched me, that's why I kicked. I suppose reporting her will fall on deaf ears or get you into trouble instead. I know something of how these hierarchies work."

"Yeah, cheap bloody labour," Amber complained as she touched my welts with kind fingers then wheeled me away. "Get a right lot of oddballs working here. There's a night nurse who's waiting to have her stomach stapled 'cause she eats too much. Go figure. Another who's working three jobs but got two kids and no hubby so don't ask me how she copes, and another woman who likes to ram you into the wall with her elbow if you don't get out her way in the corridors."

"Should you be telling me all this?"

She snorted softly. "To be honest, Mary, I don't reckon you're going to remember it later, though I'm not supposed to say that."

I held up my hands and stared at the skin. I am too old for faux modesty. The body ages. Nothing can be done about it, but I hadn't realised how old and thick-veined they were. I would never let my body fall into such disrepair. I am the one who refuses to age. There would be no chance of winning battles with this body. No way would I have the energy to try to dig myself out of a cave. I had to get to the bottom of this mystery before I faded away completely.

She wheeled me along to the connecting door, span the chair around and backed through the door. On the other side, the corridor did a sharp right turn. "Day room's here," Amber said.

Just before we got there, out of the window beside me I spotted swaying green treetops and a clear blue sky, rooks soaring high in the breeze.

"Help me up," I asked. "I want to see the view better."

Amber moved me past the dayroom door to a wall length window beside a fire door.

My eyes flickered over the evacuation diagram screwed to the wall, a very handy piece that showed all the rooms on the floor and the exits in case of fire, then I looked up to the obvious lock at the top of the door. The presence of a small light aperture suggested it was also an alarm. She must have noticed my gaze, as she said, "We don't want the residents getting out this way, do we?"

No, I bet you don't. This isn't a home; it's a prison.

She opened a smaller window and a crisp breeze blew in, kissing my face, lovely warm fresh air washing away the tang of nursing home, dull urine and faeces stink poorly disguised behind acrid faux-flower scents. Beyond the long window I could see a garden corralled by the four inside walls of the home, a lawn and well-tended flower beds, small trees and bushes, scattered benches for residents, and a small ornamental well.

On hearing squeaking like an excited guinea pig, I peered down. A man I assumed to be the gardener came into view from a corner underpass, pushing an old wheelbarrow with a dodgy, squealing wheel. He was a stooped chap with gardening gloves at the ready, wearing a garish red scarf on his head for sun-protection. I watched as he withdrew secateurs from the tub in the barrow and began to prune a Forsythia in a manner akin to butchering. I wondered why the home employed such an incompetent gardener. Simple finances, probably.

"And what's on the other side of the building?" I asked.

"Hang on an' I'll show you," Amber said with a tired sigh. She wheeled me through the swing doors of the dayroom right up to the far wall where another full length window showed lawns sloping down to a narrow, busy road, and beyond that a row of smart old houses stood, their red brick faces speaking of home, of happiness, of freedom. Middle class suburbia, I guessed. Then I spotted the stone wall with a sign: St Amelia's Dementia Care.

The cheek of it! Demented is the last thing I am.

The day room appeared to double-time as the dining room, wooden floored, comfy chairs set around, with seven people blankly sat in them. Not one of them showed a spark of life as other carers spooned food into flaccid mouths and the perfumes of zombieland descended on my trembling senses.

"Is this how I was?" I whispered to Amber as she parked the wheelchair and swung a side table across my lap.

She barely glanced at the other residents. "Yeah, just like that. You want feeding or going for it yourself? Save me some time."

I grabbed the spoon and fed myself from the bowl of offered cereal, watching those other poor souls all dribbly and empty-minded, dreading the idea I might pass back to that condition.

Some of them seemed far too young to be in a nursing home, but their declining states showed they needed to be. I suppose that should have been my first clue as to what was going on. I'd had some experience with dementia in Hartpury, the small town where I had lived for years, and those people had not been blank and static, they'd been confused but active; wandering even. I took it to mean the sad folk in the home were doped up to their eyeballs, a crime in its own way.

A television mumbled to itself half way up the wall so you couldn't reach to change the channel, though the carers did several times. I wondered if it was some kind of test; if you complained about them changing it, or wanted the channel changed, then you had some compos mentis left. I sat quietly, my eyes flitting from one silent, staring or dozing person to another.

July 10 showed in the corner of a weatherman's arm-waving introduction to the forecast for the week. So, Galyer had been telling the truth when she'd said I'd been out for two months. It had been a chilly May evening when Hugo and I had stopped for takeaway.

As I finished the cereal, I was thinking of Hugo again, my young knight in sullied armour who had been looking after me. Hopefully it had been he who had put me in the home. But, then, why was I Mary?

The carers left, a stillness fell.

The susurrus of the home's background noises had lulled me to the edge of sleep when a pyjama clad man got out of his chair with a lurch. He had the face of a man without hope as he walked purposefully to the other side of the room, drew the curtain back as far as it would go, opened the window wide and launched himself into the freedom of the blue.

3. I Am Not Me

"Nurse!" I shouted breathlessly, my arms reaching out as though I could arrest the deed, but the man had gone. "Amber! Help!"

Amber and an older woman rushed in to see what my fuss was. I pointed to the open window with a shaking finger and a shakier voice. "A man. A man just... jumped out."

They looked out of the window then back at me, jittering in my wheelchair as I attempted to move the wheels myself. The older woman, all make up and short fierce hair, her face twisted in contempt, scowled at me. "Not 'er again. You're trouble left, right and centre, you are. Amber, get 'er back to 'er room. Don't need this drama first thing in the morning."

"But the man," I protested. "He jumped."

"There's no one fallen," the woman said, all sharp and no-nonsense, marching up to me. "There is no one out there." She waggled an angry hand towards the window. "There's nothing to worry about."

"But ... but..." I looked at the empty chair. "He was sat right there, then—"

"Oh, gawd, she's a gabbler." The woman rubbed her forehead and exhaled deeply. "Move 'er out. I'll get Mrs Galyer give her more meds."

"The man..." I whimpered as I was smartly rolled away.

"Relax," Amber said, her voice soothing. "It'll all be fine."

I was still reeling with confusion and shock as I watched Amber make my bed quickly and expertly.

"I don't understand," I said; understatement of the year.

"Not to worry. Mrs Galyer will be here with something to calm you soon. She don't like trouble makers."

"Huh? I'll give her trouble," I said as frustration spilled out of me, and I put my hands on the chair arms, my slippered feet on the floor and pushed up. I tried to keep tall and straight and balanced but collapsed back into the chair, my jelly-legs refusing to hold me.

"Not again!" Amber said, rushing to grab me. "You are either mad determined or stupid silly. Listen, again, you'll get *me* into trouble, d'you want that?"

"No, but it's not fair," I grumped. "And whose clothes are these? I look like a female Guy Fawkes. Tatty."

Mrs Galyer appeared as suddenly as an unwanted zit. "Please don't make trouble, Mrs Cooper."

"Me? Never," said I.

She tutted. "Here." She handed me the paper cup she held. I saw two pink pills. Amber offered me a glass of water. I looked from offering to offering and said, "Sod that, there's nothing wrong with me. I saw a man jump out of the window. Isn't he splattered on the ground? Aren't you missing someone? Aren't you concerned?"

"Please take the tablets, Mrs Cooper. You will feel much better."

"Oh hell." I pretended to take them, sticking them up behind my gums, taking a slurp of water. "There. Satisfied?" I tossed the crumpled cup to the waste paper bin skulking in the corner and hit home. Yay; a tiny win for Molly.

"That's better," Mrs Galyer said. "Now, into bed with you. Believe me, you'll feel better after a little nap."

As I surrendered myself to the pillows, she stood beside me and said, "The man who signed you in here was Richard Cooper, your son. We'll talk more when you wake."

The name gave me a shock. *Richard* had sent me here? The dreaded Richard? Mind, I wouldn't put it past this being the dickhead's idea of a slow torture, shoving me into this place to have people convince me I was not Molly, leaving me to stew in a terribly perplexed state of mind. I'd bet I hadn't really 'fallen'. I'd wager I had been drugged, brought here, and more drugs had blanked my mind. Perhaps they had accidentally been allowed to wear off, or more likely they had stopped giving them to me so they could laugh at my confusion. Over and over again.

At that, I felt a jolt of hope that Hugo was also somewhere in the building, as befuddled as I was. Maybe I'd have to rescue *him*, if he couldn't rescue me.

Sitting back against the pillows and gazing straight ahead, I mulled over all this without a sound as the two women watched me. As I feigned sleepiness, guessing they'd tried to give me sedatives, Amber moved the pillows so my head slumped down and the watchers left silently. I prised the pills from my gums but they had already begun to dissolve and tasted vile. So I washed them down with water from the cup on the side table and began to day dream, trying to figure out what could be going on, but my thoughts quickly became unglued and I dozed.

~

I woke slowly, thick with sleep, scarecrow-headed. The wind called a gusty greeting at the window. My mouth tasted like I had eaten raw meat.

I didn't know the time, but it was July and still daylight, so could have been as much as nine at night. I buzzed the alarm for the toilet. I had to admit I couldn't get there safely on my own.

"Where exactly am I?" I asked the grumpy, hefty woman who came to my call. "And don't say England. That much is obvious."

"Woking," she said distractedly as she hoisted me out of bed and into the chair.

I wasn't familiar with the area but a nice walk would clear the cobwebs in my brain, help me to ponder who had put me there.

"I want to go for a walk outside," I said.

She frowned deeply. It did nothing for her severe face. "No today," she retorted. "Not this time. This night."

"Where's Amber?"

"She finish shift. Staff have homes and life, you know it?"

"So when can I go out, please? This place makes me feel like it's a prison. Some fresh air would be nice. You never know, it might improve my temperament."

Her eyes narrowed. She nodded but didn't speak for a moment then responded with, "Yeah. T'morrow. Where you want to going?"

"Nowhere in particular. A little look around. A little escape from four walls."

"Sonia!" Mrs Galyer's cautioning voce heralded her amazing *here I am* trick again, walking into the room and surprising us both. "I have told you before. *Two* people on a hoist."

Sonia said nothing as she went off, leaving me in the wheelchair. Mrs Galyer rolled her eyes and pulled a tightly apologetic smile, her voice softening as she stood beside me. "Now, Mary, it's good to see you so responsive, but—"

She exhaled, looking worried, eyes fixed on the floor.

"I know what you're going to say," I said, finding myself reassuring her when I was sure it should be the other way around. "You're worried my lucidity might run off again. You think I'm here because I have dementia—yes, I've seen the sign on the post outside—"

Then I stopped abruptly. What if this apparently caring woman was the one feeding me drugs? No, I *had* been drugged and was no longer, so that meant the drugger (if that's even a word) had to be out of the picture for some reason. "I do not have memory problems," I said emphatically. "I can remember very well that I need the toilet right now."

While that was dealt with, I contemplated what I was going to say. I wanted to say something along the lines of, *'I think I'm here because someone doesn't like me and thinks it's funny to keep me locked away.'* But that's paranoia if it's not true, and was unlikely to help my case.

As I lay back in bed again, Mrs Galyer gave a quick, sad smile. "We'll look after you, Mary. That's what we're here for. It's natural to be confused and afraid, but we're all on your side.

Now it's almost eight and I've had a long day and I wanted to try to explain this before I go home, so you have the rest of the evening to ponder on it." She drew in a tight breath, lips thin. "There is no easy way to put this. You are schizophrenic."

"What? No I am *not*, but I am a murderer so you really ought to call the police on me," I said hopefully. "Get me arrested and out of here."

She held up a tired hand. "I imagine it's hard to take in, but you first began to have delusions when you were a teenager. It would seem that, while in the altered state after your fall, you developed an alternate persona in your head. Think of it as... well, like you have been living in your own cosy cinema while your ordinary brain's been out of service. You have woken several times now, and each time you have declared yourself to be this Molly person."

"You're saying Molly's a figment of my imagination?"

"Exactly."

I frowned and laughed mockingly. "It's all made up?"

She nodded slowly, eyes on my face. "You seem more with it than you have been before, so maybe you'll stay with us this time. If so, would you like me to arrange a therapist for you?" She asked without a muscle out of place on her smooth condescending face as she lied to me.

Lord, how I hoped she was lying to me.

4. Molly No More

Mrs Galyer folded her arms, her gaze inscrutable. "In my opinion, your symptoms have progressed to the point where you're taking bits and pieces of information from multiple true events, along with a good dose of complete fiction, and creating new events that you are positive happened. You obviously feel persecuted and, you see, these fictitious events are almost always something the sufferer thinks someone has done to them. I *am* glad you've woken again, Mary, though I must warn you this Molly persona may still break through on occasions. But remember, please, she is not the real you."

She tried to take my hand but I pulled away sharply and sat on them, scowling at her.

"Mary," she said all persuasive and sweet, "you've always seen things. Your illness means you cannot *help* imagining things."

"Sure," I said with as much derision as I could muster.

"You said you saw a man jump out of the window." She looked at me kindly, quizzically, a mother asking her child for confirmation.

"He did."

"But he *didn't*." She touched a hand to her forehead. "Please think about this sensibly. How could a man fall from the window, and no one notice?"

I said nothing, just stared at my own window thinking that sometimes people don't see what's in front of their own darn noses, like drug dealing husbands and trickster beaus.

She tried to draw my attention back to her. "Mary, please listen for your own good. You have a mental problem where you cannot tell the real from the unreal, so your medicines will be adjusted as necessary, to keep you comfortable in your mind as well as your body. To help you see there is nothing to fear, you can depend on modern medicine. You are Mary Emmeline

Cooper, and you were a teacher. You had two children, one Richard who arranged your care, and a girl, sadly deceased some years ago. Your husband Conrad is also deceased, some years ago from an accident. You've had a long life, a lot of it on your own."

"I'm listening," I said after a minute of contemplating her words. Could this be true? Had there really been no major, no troubles at the seaside, people killed because of me? Had my poor old brain, stumbling around the corridors of my cortex, created a wide and exotic dream life to counter the boring truth? If it was all imagination, I couldn't help but think I should have made my adventures start a lot earlier in my life, not waited until my seventies.

Mrs Galyer folded her hands, looking down like a school marm about to lecture me. "All right. To business." She opened the bottom drawer of the dresser and took out a well-fed photo album, putting it on the bed. Beside it she placed a handbag I had never seen before in my life and a small red velvet jewellery box. "Look through these. They might help the true memories break through. All your effects should be in this room, or in the office locker. See if anything rings any bells." She pulled a slight, sympathetic smile.

"I suppose," I grumbled, not convinced, but reassured by the slim touch of humanity from her.

In the absence of my hands, she patted my knee. "Good god!" I yelped, shying like a horse. "Stop touching me unexpectedly. I don't like it. Put it in your notes somewhere. Spare me that, at least."

She restrained a sigh, bit back a reply, and left without another word, so I sat and stared at the items on the bed, the jewellery box, the bag, the fat red photo album, all lies, all waiting to draw me in; to make me feel I should be in this strange prison.

I didn't want to touch the album, to see the pictures or even smell them lest they told me my truth was not my truth. Awful though my times as Molly have been, I wanted them to be real. I wanted to not be ill. I was scared of not being Molly, but the task had to be done, so my hand reached out to the album and I pulled it onto my lap. It was a rough, aged thing, smelling of old lady perfume and threadbare on the spine. A well-loved item.

Inside the cover was a typewritten A4 page.

Mary Emmeline Cooper, I read. Address? Never heard of it. Widow. Husband died some twenty years earlier. Had we been happy together? If Molly had been a delusion, was the memory of Conrad's love what I had been searching for in my coma dreams?

But here was a smiling baby picture labelled Richard. A tremble of worry ran through me. Either my son Richard and I'd had a falling-out, something that would make him bad in my imagination, or this was all fabricated.

My fingers shook as I turned the pages. After the many doting photos of baby Richard, came those of a baby girl.

The photos, the room, everything faded into the distance as I saw her name and took in a shaky breath.

June.

When I'd recovered, I swiftly turned the pages until I stopped at one where June was a curly haired child of around eight or nine...

and the next picture showed a headstone with her name on it.

A daughter I had lost and didn't remember at all, though I had in my own way. My poorly mind had translated this tragic loss into my imaginary best friend June's demise. It was too much to take in.

And here was a Christmas photo labelled 'Conrad, Mary and Richard'. I stared closely at that photo of the couple stood with a teenage boy. Was that me? Twisting the wedding ring on my finger, I thought, 'Did you put this on my finger, Conrad Cooper? Were we happy? How many years did we have together before the accident took you from me?'

So I sat, and I read, and I teased pages back and forth

looking for inconsistencies. Here was a photo labelled 'Richard and Kelly'. A pretty brown-haired woman stood beside a heavily bearded man I had never seen before in my life, smiling as she looked at him with love reflected in her eyes. No wild daughter-in-law Vana existed in that album.

Eventually, I put the album back on the bed, opened the handbag, pulled out a scented handkerchief, a purse with a few coins in it, a small laminated picture of Conrad, nothing else there reminding me of anything. The jewellery was all tat, not even an engagement ring to shine in my world. I either had no taste or the good stuff was in the office locker.

I slid out of bed and stood carefully, balanced, ready for wobbles, looking across the room at the mirror above the whitewood dresser. A long, wrinkled and pale face stared back, hair short and curly and grey. It felt to be an unfamiliar visage, but so much was buzzing around in my head I wasn't sure of anything. I was thin, and surely Molly could never have been called 'thin'. Mary had married a nice man and had children. Mary was not a murderer; Molly was and regretted those deaths so, so much. I was happy to escape her, wanting to have had a man I loved. I wanted to remember it all, this Mary-life.

And what if I *had* imagined Molly? Why would I imagine such an awful person, such a terrible past? I was either psychotic, or it was all real.

I sat back and grabbed up the album again, opening it at the picture of smiling blonde-curled June. Touching the photo of my daughter, I smiled and felt a waterfall of loss pour over me. "June," I whispered. I could feel her in my arms at birth, bald-headed little waif, big blue eyes. Saw her toddling through a farmhouse kitchen. But Molly had never given birth to any child; the memories had to be false. 'Or maybe you did have a child,' said a little voice inside me.

No, I insisted. *You're making up all this as you go along. The more you think about it the more real she will become, the more you will remember because your over-active imagination will fill in the gaps.*

But abruptly—so abruptly I thought I felt my heart tear from the pain of it—I wanted to accept Mary, because what I was reading was a better life than Molly's, the lonely woman who had litter-picked around a village to make herself feel useful. And, the more I thought about it, I found I was quite looking forward to being someone else, like a fresh start washing away all the pain of Molly's past few years.

A little later, when the medicine trolley came round, when those hateful little tablets were placed into my hand, I took them with no qualms. What do they say in the movies? Shoot me up, doc.

So, when screaming broke into my slumber, I thought it was all in my Molly-dreams, and I curled up and wished it away.

5. Feeling Alive

July eleventh dawned, and I, Mary maybe Molly, was wrestled from sleep by Amber of the lovely smile, then placed in the day room where I slowly ate my cereal. My eyes were drawn many times to the window where I had (maybe) seen a man leap to his fate. Too many maybes were in my life.

I tried to find the jumper's face in my memory, remember what he had been wearing, where he had been sitting, but inside me only the fog of uncertainty swirled.

I had been told I imagined things; that I had imagined things since I was barely out of childhood. Was it true?

'Accept that you're Mary,' a voice seemed to whisper. 'Life will be so much nicer if you're not remembering killing people.'

But how do you accept you're not who you think you are, when most of you is convinced you *are* who you think you are? When you can remember your childhood, various schools, the stumbling teenage years of the awkward Molly Turner, how do you convince that person it's all unreal?

I didn't know how, and that was scary.

After breakfast, Amber took me for my wheelchair walk, hiding the door code behind a cupped hand, but smiling, smiling so sweetly all the while as she released me temporarily from prison.

She pushed me past the reign of the home's high boundary fence and into the sunlight on the pavement of the main road, the skies above us clear and bright, the breeze playing in the trees, leaves fluttering. A beautiful day, a whirlwind of gulls wheeling and crying above us in the warm air. In the distance I saw three towers looming, tall blocks of flats that seemed ill fitting in the countryside aspect of the place.

"Left or right," Amber said cheerily at the junction. "Left's the little local supermarket thingy, not much of a walk, and right's the High Street. I've taken you that way before. You said the shops reminded you of home."

I shiver ran through me. "I can't imagine falling asleep and not waking with memories. Was I just like this, those other times?"

"Yeah," Amber said as if she were trying to remember. "But this time you'll stay awake, you'll see.

She smartly bumped the wheelchair along the uneven path by the houses, bouncing me as merrily as a babe in a pushchair, stopping now and then to stare at her phone's face, scrolling, giving little laughs as she found things to amuse her in the cyber-world. It didn't worry me. It gave more time to think in the fresh air, to be out of that place where I felt locked up. Even the litter on the grass verges made me feel relaxed.

The shops did remind me of home. Old brick, converted from houses over the years, bay-windowed. How many times had she walked me there? I hoped she was right and I would not slip back into nothingness.

In a newsagent's window I spotted a somehow familiar toy for sale. I asked to stop and stare at it. Part of my memory told me I used to have a flouncy dressed stuffed fairy doll like that. On a whim, I asked, "Can I buy that pink fairy? The enormous one with long arms and legs."

"Sure," Amber said. "You always ask to stop and look at it, seems to me it's about time you bought it. You've got funds I can call on. As long as I get a receipt, I can get my money back from reception. Seems a funny thing for a lady of your age, though."

Is that why it looked familiar? Because of repeated exposure? Hadn't I had one like that lovely pink and soft creature when I was a child? Moments later I was hugging the fairy, my emotions all over the place. It meant something to me, but the specifics were lost in my head still.

"Wotcha going to call her?" Amber asked cheerily as we marched on, the wheelchair somewhat like a pushchair transporting an old child hugging her dolly.

"I will just call her Fairy," I replied. "The name seems to mean something to me. Maybe I had one as a toddler."

I suddenly realised we were on our way back. "Can we go up the next road?" I asked hopefully, wanting to prolong the experience. "I really like it out here. Such a gorgeous day. Makes me feel alive."

Amber glanced at her watch. "Nope, sorry, better go back or you'll miss tea and biscuits and it's my turn in the kitchen, so I'd get a rollicking if I was late."

"Has anyone visited me since I got here?" I asked.

"Don't recall, but there's lots of ins and outs and not many staff so I dunno. Anyway, it's sad but true that not everyone gets visitors. The kids: they get upset when their parents don't recognise them, you see, so you could have. You know you're a bit confused. People jumping out of windows, eh?"

"Pfft. Who gives out the drugs usually; mans the medicine trolley thing most of the time. That glowering nurse I saw last night?"

"The senior nurses take turns. You must be trained for it. Why? You want something? It's not the sort of thing I'm allowed to touch. I'd get fired on the spot."

"No, no, nothing like that. What I am wondering is, would you have any way of finding out what my meds are and when they were changed last?"

"I... suppose I might be able to find that out from your file in the office without being fired. But why?"

"Thank you. See what's changed recently. You know, what I was given, or had withdrawn from my chart, so that I woke that morning you told me I smelled like a wet dishcloth."

She gave a small laugh. "You smell much better now, but I doubt your waking had anything to do with meds. It's just... you know... it's the way you are now, Mary."

"No. I'm sure that medicine info might be useful for my doctor, whoever he is. And..." I looked around. "I have no idea where I am at all. That *is* disorientating and makes me feel even more lost, so pull up Google maps on your phone and home in on where we are."

"I'm glad you feel better, but you must realise this could be only temporary."

"I just said this is why I want the med details, right? So perhaps someone can figure out how to keep me awake permanently. Let's make the most of it while it lasts, eh?"

She stopped pushing me, put on the brake, stood in front of the chair, puffed up her cheeks and exhaled while I watched her eyes dancing around, deep thoughts being considered. "Okay," she relented, phone waggling thoughtfully in her hand. "That's Old Drive in front of us. I'll pull up the local area."

"Excellent," I said, interlocking my fingers around Fairy and wanting to cackle like an evil villain as their plan came together, though I had no plan yet.

She handed me the phone and I scrolled the map on the little screen gingerly. Old Drive: I pulled out a bit, tracing the way we had come. I could feel her eyes boring into me. I panned around a bit. There was no marked police station in the area. No bus station nearby, no train station...

Why was that man staring at us?

"No chippies in sight," I said, handing back the phone. "What a boring end of town this is. I fancied a takeaway."

"I could've told you that if you'd asked. Now, let's go back the short way, a fast and bumpy ride, madam, now you've held me up looking for chippies."

"I just love that salt and vinegar aroma. Evocative of childhood. Can I use the phone?" I asked.

"Like, for an actual call? No, I'm not allowed to let you do that. Any calls gotta be done at the home."

"Just one phone call, for heaven's sake." I found I was getting angry, and that man was still stood on the other side of the road, staring at us. "Even people in police custody are allowed a phone call. Who's going to know if you don't tell, and don't you think it's a tad suspicious that I can't have *one* call to the *one* number that I can actually remember?" I stopped dead.

I was thinking like Molly again, but if she was unreal there would be no answer to Gavin's house number, so that would settle things for me, wouldn't it?

"Don't be so dramatic!" Amber laughed. "You can call who you like from the home, just not from my personal phone, and I am not risking anything that threatens my job. So, now, off we go!"

She ran, pushing the chair before her like it was a toy car, going *vroom!* around the corners, and I had to admit it was fun.

Yet the man, still pretending to not look at us, followed close behind with his long-legged stride. I could see him reflected in the shop windows, hear the slap of his feet if I filtered out the other noises.

His presence annoyed me.

"Stop," I yelled.

Amber slowed, panting. "What now? If you need a wee, we gotta get a move on."

"I don't want to go back," I said loudly and tipped myself forwards out of the chair and onto the ground, where I raised my arms and peered at the watcher from under cover of my lacy cardigan.

His phone was up. He was filming us. And laughing.

"Not again!" wailed Amber as she hurried to my aid. "Not again. Gotta get you back in." She was panicking. "Anyone? Hello?" She called to a few passers-by as she heaved dramatically on my arms, but they looked and didn't aid.

'Come on, man with the camera,' I thought. 'I want to see you closer.'

I fussed and made things as awkward as I could.

Maybe I'll be on YouTube tonight, but I suspect it's something more heinous.

At last, a young man stopped to help lift-shove me back into the chair, and Amber, incandescent with rage—you could almost feel the chair vibrate with her anger—trotted us back to the home, while the watcher, maybe having found the amusement he craved, vanished into the streets.

6. Who's Playing Games?

The seething silence of Amber encompassed us for the rest of the way back, the girl too well trained to say what she thought of me. I was scanning images in my head to decide if I had seen the watcher before. That kind of covert observation was something that would happen to Molly, not Mary. The scales tipped slightly.

As we reached the home, I got the best view I'd had of it yet. It appeared to be modern four-sided building with little underpasses at the corners leading to and from the central garden. Amber saw me gazing up. "Three floors, each with ten bedrooms, its own dayroom and bathroom and kitchen. Okay? Now, back in another way. A quicker way, though thanks to you I doubt we'll make it in time. If only I could tell you what I really think of your shenanigans in town. If it feeds back it'll reflect badly on the whole staff, you realise?"

She wheeled me through the front gates, which appeared to be for ornamentation only, no locking mechanism in sight, to one of the corner underpasses. As we approached it, I thought, 'Ooh, nice. When my legs are working again, I can nip down the fire escape, sprint through the garden, bob along the underpass, and flit away like a fairy. Who needs a front door code?'

Then I saw the underpass had a single metal gate, code locked too. Bother.

Amber once again shielded her code inputting.

"Is it the same code for all the exits?" I asked. "Even the front door?"

"Why?" she snapped, swiftly wheeling me through. I heard the gate autolock behind us. "You planning on doing a runner in your speedo chair? Yeah, as it happens, it's the same code for everything. Don't think I'd be able to remember all of them if they were all different, would you? Gawd, just stop your fussing. I don't wanna be late."

She hurried us inside through the conservatory that jutted out into the garden, startling three old ladies sitting in basketwork chairs, then ran for the chair lift. "I'll just about make it in time." She panted. "No thanks to you."

As the lift, unable to feel Amber's urgency, dawdled upwards, she said in hushed tones as if someone could overhear her, "Sorry. It's not you winding me up, it's just that I had a showdown with Mila the other day over the way she was treating someone, and she went crying to Mrs Galyer and now I'm in her bad books and I feel a bit stressed. So I daren't get told off for anything. It ain't bloody fair. I need this job. I work my bollocks off and the night staff get away with sleeping on their shifts in the day room. I'm on my own and my boy's growing so fast—"

"You have a son? I'm sorry; I don't mean to be a bother."

'I am far too soft,' I thought as she parked me in the dayroom and rushed off. 'Because she has a child, I feel sympathy for her situation, but I am going to have to be tough to sort out who I am.'

Then, as I sat in the day room, patiently waiting for my delayed cup of tea, Misty ambled in.

I stared at my cat, doubting she was real. She sauntered with her fat cat wiggle to an empty chair, jumped up, curled up, began grooming her coat and didn't fade out.

Mila pushed in the tea trolley.

"Cat?" I waved my hand towards the chair, expecting dismissal of my words.

"Cat," she repeated, moving to scoot it out of the door.

My mouth bobbed open and shut. "What is the cat's name?" I asked warily.

The teacup was banged onto my table. "He Micky? Mitty?"

If Micky/Mitty was a boy, he wouldn't be my lovely old girl, Misty, but the name was so similar.

Anyway, I realised, if it had been Misty, surely she would

have come straight to me. They say cats are aloof and uncaring, but Misty had run to me on many occasions, sat on my lap, jumped into bed with me. I must be ill. I had transformed the home's cat into my own.

Amber, true to her word, and despite my high jinks, got me access to a phone call after the tea.

I sat beside her at the reception desk where a pretty, very blonde woman in smart ordinary clothes had, with no complaint or sign of deception, simply handed Amber an old dial-faced phone when Amber had said, "Mary wants to call her son."

"I'll look up the number," the receptionist said, turning to her computer.

"It's okay," Amber jumped in. "Mary knows the number."

With nervous fingers I dialled Gavin's home number in Kerton.

A woman answered, her voice soft, polite. "Vana?" I asked, though my sinking heart already knew it was not going to be her.

And that was the tone of the phone call. No one called Vana or Gavin had ever lived at that number, the polite lady assured me. She had been there almost five years. I hung up, almost in tears.

"Hey, it's alright, Mary," Amber said, rubbing my back while I was so numb with confusion that I didn't stop her. "You've just forgotten the number, that's all, but Sally's just gave me the right number." She dialled for me.

"Hell..oo?" a deep and cheery male voice answered almost instantly.

"Hello," I said slowly. "I... I want to talk to—"

"Mum?" the voice said with such sudden joy my fingers started twitching. "Mum? That really you?"

"Gavin?" I ventured in cautious excitement because it did not sound quite like him. "Did you move house?"

"Errr... no, Mum; this is Richard, you know; Tricky Dicky, you used to call me. Is there a nurse there? Let me talk to them."

So I handed the receiver to Amber, and sat like I was hypnotised, a single tear running down my cheek as my 'son' spoke to Amber and she reassured him, yes, I was awake again and, yes, visiting times were still open so when did he want to come?

"Mary? Mary?" Amber was staring into my face. "He's coming when he can get time off work, okay? He lives up in the Lake District and that's a fair way off, you know?"

In bed that night, I put my arms over my head and arched my back, feeling instantly better from the stretch as I thought, 'Okay, maybe the mad major and Gavin and Hugo were all figments of my imagination, and now I must wake fully from the dream. I am ill. I am in a remission. I don't need to escape. I am safe here and soon I will meet my son. My real son; Richard, the one I birthed.

~

Screams sat me up, shaking, panicking, wide awake. I was not imagining the male voice that intermittently yelled and begged from somewhere close by, muffled only by the door.

Legs now shaking from both fear and exertion, I somehow got myself into the chair, rolled to the door, opened it a crack and peered out. I moved out of the room cautiously, towards the recurring sounds. In alarm, I stopped and wanted to reverse as high-pitched wails ran up the corridor and into nightmares, then descended into sobbing, pitiful noises.

The subsiding noises came from the bathroom: now splashing, watery-gagging sounds, a male voice coughing. Could someone have got themselves into the bathroom and was now drowning?

That was possible. From what Amber had said, the night carers were more than likely sleeping in the day room on the far side of the floor, not listening for trouble as they should be. As far as I knew, there was nothing to stop a confused resident from wandering into a bathroom and drowning themselves.

At that jarring thought, I was about to intervene, but I

heard a door opening elsewhere and span the wheelchair into the nearest bedroom and sat there, panting in concern. Snores came from the sleeping resident behind me, but unhurried approaching footsteps in the corridor stopped, and I heard another door click open. I risked peering out to see the bathroom door ajar and...

"Is he cooperating?" asked a muted male voice that sliced my tension into ribbons of dread.

Through the pounding of my heartbeat in my ears, I didn't make out the reply.

"I'm not surprised," the man said. "Tough nut, this one. Another fifteen minutes then wipe and back to bed."

I quivered with the shock of the words; almost fell out of the chair. *You have to be joking. There can be no doubt now,* my poor mind yelled at me. My conviction had swung around again. I *was* Molly because, if I wasn't, why was I in a place where someone was being tortured for information in a bathroom, and a man had jumped out of a window to avoid his fate?

As Lewis Carroll said in Alice in Wonderland, *I know who I was this morning, but I've changed a few times since then.* Molly had killed a couple of men, unintentionally caused the deaths of a few other people; not the most outstanding life accomplishments but keeping oneself alive is a pretty important thing. And now I was Molly again I had to get back to my room, figure out how to walk properly, and get the hell out of there.

~

After unceremoniously ramming the deceitful wedding ring into the velvet box with the other things that were not mine, marking the transition back to my old life, I curled up in the foetal position in bed, hugging Fairy. The flowery perfume of the duvet cover was not reassuring. Nothing was. Warmth and comfort did not equal safety. The duvet's soft weight on me was nothing but another kind of prison.

7. Memory Time

After our escape from Kerton, the boys and I had galloped up the M3 to London in the converted house bus, because George's mother had contacted him to say she was ill and needed him back. She lived in an old Victorian terraced house in Barnes, not far from the railway bridge, so the bus had been parked elsewhere and the little Micra it towed used to go to her house.

Mrs Grosvenor, a large and larger-voiced lady, had greeted us with smiles and a bear hug for George, but was soon ranting about how he had been led into bad ways by Hugo, disapproving of their relationship.

We had been keen to leave after five minutes. She didn't appear ill at all, the shouting and lecturing going on and embarrassingly on, and I came to doubt she had any other voice than big, and no other person she worried about except herself.

So there was this large black lady whose rant had got around to telling us of the exorbitant prices of vegetables in the market, and I finally figured out she was not ill... that is, she had no illness other than the sickness of spending too much money and expecting your kids to pay for you. But even after George had transferred money to her via his phone's banking app, she was still going on and on; about me, her puzzlement at my existence. I suppose a bespectacled pensioner who was being extra polite in my frightfully posh English voice looked rather incongruous alongside one hefty bearded young man and her lanky black son.

To say her eyes were suspicious would have been an understatement, and Misty, my cat on her lead, had drawn even more puzzled looks as she cat-sniffed loudly around the room and kept sneezing.

"You done kidnap this lady?" Mrs Grosvenor had hooked

a rude, disbelieving thumb at me as she asked George the question.

Hugo had almost leapt off his chair. "Wot? No. What you think we are, Mrs G? This ere's me gran, Molly, out for some adventures, like. Eh, gran?" His eyes begged dishonest confirmation from me.

"Adventures?" Mrs Grosvenor roared in laughter. "What lady in her right mind want adventures wiv you two?"

I smiled sweetly. "Well, I'm—"

She barrelled on with, "You two ain't no angels. I know what circles you bin moving in; it all comes back to me ears and don't you imagine it don't. I reckon you holding her hostage for something you ain't telling me. That fine looking cat there; that a pedigree something worth a cool mill?" She stood with hands on hips glaring at the three of us.

I spluttered laughter into my hands and her face descended into even more fierceness.

"I'm not a prisoner," I assured her with a placating smile. "I'm here by choice, and the boys are looking after me until the current adventure ends, hopefully with a marriage where I shall be their bridesmaid."

Her breathing speeded up and I realised that might not have been the best thing to say to a woman who disapproved of her son's relationship, but she waved her hand dismissively. "Ooh, so you's a mad lady, then." Her voice was laden with sarcasm. "Mad cat lady. I shoulda seen it, lordy be."

Spotting Misty sniffing furiously around a flower pot with a large amount of greenery in it, she said curtly, "Get that cat out the yard afore he pees in here."

I introduced Misty to the back yard and left her investigating with the back door open. With her extending lead tied to a drain pipe, she couldn't go far.

"Is anyone hungry?" I asked as I came back in, hoping to soften the tight atmosphere with food. Mrs Grosvenor was in the kitchen, bent over the coffee cups but even her back looked angry. "I saw a takeaway as we turned in," I said encouragingly.

"Best nosh used to be just at the end of the road, by the bridge," George said. "You two go. I'd best wait here 'cause..." He discreetly pointed at his mother. "I'll keep an eye on Misty. Chips and pasty, Hugs. Same for Ma."

We went for the takeaway, passing the yellow Micra where he had parked at the end of the road, ambling along, chatting, for once not a care in the world, leaving George and his dragon for our half hour excursion into the bustle and noise of a London street.

Like I say, we were not gone long, but when we returned the front door was slightly ajar and the house empty to calls.

As Hugo bounded up the stairs to check, I darted into the backyard. Misty's lead had been untied from the drainpipe and there was no sign of her.

Hugo grabbed my arm, panic pushing him out of the house, dragging me behind him, out and down to the Micra.

As we flung ourselves into the car, Hugo said grimly, "I think we both know someone came and nabbed 'em when we nipped out. Just as well we did."

"George, yes, I can imagine they'd want him, but why Misty? Why his mum?"

He swung the Micra wide onto Mortlake High Street. "You 'ave to ask? After what they did to your grandkiddies? 'Cause they can, Ms T. Just 'cause the buggers can."

After a few miles of his crazy no-one's-going-to-track-me driving, we'd abandoned the Micra and hurried to the house-bus in the dark before scooting off towards Lightwater. I took over driving. Me, driving a bus, but surely safer in my unpractised hands than Hugo's shaking ones, as his state of mind had become worse by the minute.

So now my question was, if Misty really was living downstairs in the home, did that imply George and his mother might also be close at hand?

8. Storms And Steps

I had decided to play along and be Mary, if they so desperately wanted me to be Mary. I could pretend like the biggest pretender on the planet. I would be a meek and mild Mary whose son had still not shown his face, and while I simpered I would hide Molly as she planned the great escape.

On the practical side, I thought as I stumbled closer to sleep one night, I was quickly getting used to the awfulness of the place, the stingy food, the appalling attitudes of the carers. Amber was one of the happy exceptions. Most of the helpers were abrupt and not thoughtful at all, with little compassion, especially the brusque and rough night staff, some of whom were males who looked better suited to the profession of wrestlers. I called them 'night witches'; creatures who thought nothing of waking you from sleep to check if you were asleep.

I kept an eye out for my cat and checked every nook and cranny in my room. No bugs or cameras, I was sure, but I was delighted to find a compact little mechanical bedside clock in one drawer. My watch had not turned up in Mary's possessions and knowing the right time oriented me, so I set it ticking on the side and set it according to my old friend the weatherman.

I spied as much as I could, kept my ears and eyes open, did leg strengthening exercises as often as I could (since the promised physio had never appeared) and by the end of the week I could walk well enough; but whenever anyone else was around, I used the frame or stick.

I'd looked out of the window to see if there were any drainpipes I could use. There was one, but even looking at it made me feel ill with imagined catastrophe. Unless someone came after me with an axe, I was going to let that escape idea slide (pun).

Who was worthy of my suspicion? Who had arranged my addled captivity here? What was it all about?

Dr Richard Sanderson Jnr? Could this be his perverted idea of punishment for George's running over his aunt with an ambulance? And I had done something that had resulted in his uncle's death, that was true, but it hadn't been my fault.

Sarah Henders? Could she have survived the ambulance incident to come after me again? I would have to say, *Believe me, I really, really, really didn't want to kill your brother.* I couldn't in any way shape or form call it an accident, but it was something I would regret for the rest of my life. Not exactly my fault.

Henry, June's doting husband? Was he trying to punish me for the ills I had brought upon his family? My only mistake there was moving in with my son and thinking I was safe. Not my fault.

And my beloved son Gavin, or his wife Vana, could they be trying to get back at me because of my grandson Collin's injuries? Again, that accident was not my fault.

Nothing was my fault. It was all a horrid chain of events consisting of me being messed around by other people. If I wanted to blame anyone, I'd have to blame Hugo. His thievery started it all.

I was simply the poor schmuck who had to end it.

~

I found myself staring at the fire escape on the eighteenth of July, a bright morning, the birds twittering in the trees; my late sister's birthday, if I remembered correctly. I was contemplating how to get down those steps and away unseen, now I could walk so well with a stick to help. I realised that opening the exit would most likely set off an alarm somewhere and the horrid horde would rush to nab me, but how about I tried opening it few times then getting out of the way? Maybe if I triggered it enough times, they would think it was malfunctioning, crying wolf, and the problem would get shoved to the back of the queue of all the repairs that likely needed doing. Then, no one would take any notice of the alarm on the day I actually felt bold enough to go, because I knew it would be a dangerous move, with unimaginable consequences for me were I to be caught.

But opportunity hits at funny times, as does coincidence. Some hours later, as I looked up at the sky—only 8pm, but people already being put to bed so the evening carers could have earlier breaks—I could see the lowering black-purple clouds of a threatening summer storm. If there were to be thunder and lightning, that could help me on my way. The rain could mask me flitting across the front lawn like a terrified fairy, my walking stick my wand. Anyone alerted by the alarm might be reluctant to follow in the storm, thus giving me time to find someone to alert.

Then, from my lofty tower, serendipity be praised I could clearly see an underpass gate held open by a shovel, forgotten by the inept gardener. I was about to get him into trouble.

Hastily donning the thickest jumper I could find over top and trousers, since I did not appear to own a coat, I said goodbye to my doll, sent a whispered apology to Misty, took a deep breath and plunged straight into the escape.

I stretched to flip over the simple lock at the top of the fire door, then wrenched the bar to open it, letting in a wash of chilly air, but the anticipated alarm didn't sound. From the top platform I saw the vertiginous three storey drop and drew back a second; a second only because time was of the essence. On the wall behind me a silent alarm flashed blue, so down the metal stairway I went, with my fingers forbidden to betray me on the cold metal handrail. I imagined someone looking out of a window and seeing me, my being apprehended, dragged back in, all sorts, but no alerting calls came.

I moved to the underpass, went through the gate and, as I stopped at the front of the building to lean on my stick for a recovering second, the first rain fell. Petrichor perfumed the air, sharp and heavy. I took a deep breath; wet grass, remembrances of running in the rain as a child, laughing, jumping in puddles, and for a moment felt I had rediscovered the purpose of life: to live free, to love, to spend my days doing good... But that wasn't going to happen if I just stood there.

The storm broke loudly overhead as I finally escaped the grounds. Lightning flashed and rain pounded me as I walked as fast as I could along the public path with my stick's tap-tap turning into splash-splash in the puddles, cars passing and no one interested in me. I headed for the small supermarket Amber had mentioned, my clothes already drenched into wet T-shirt clinginess, and must have looked a sight when I staggered in as a small child standing by his mother pointed and shouted, "Zombie!"

"Thank you for making me feel so much better," I said to him, trying to swipe wet hair off my face with a wet hand. "Does anyone have a phone I could use, please?"

A shop assistant labelled Janice, a middle-aged woman wearing too much make up that spoiled what good looks she had left, rushed up to me. She put up her hands in a placating move and said all in a gabble, "It's all right. It's all right. Come on with you. This way." She took my arm with a gentle hand. "Just come and sit here."

"Jolly!" she called to someone else. "Going in the staff room."

She patted my shoulder. "You need a blanket or something, luv. You're right soaked."

Led out of public view, I said firmly, "I need a phone. I need to contact the police," then started shivering and was guided into a chair as though I were a piece of fine china, and the woman put something heavy and warm around my shoulders.

"There y'are, luv," Janice said. "Just rest. We'll get the police for you."

She went off for a few minutes, but as she came back in I asked, "Are they coming?" and her face crumpled with guilt as she muttered, "Well... er..."

"What did you do?" I asked, standing abruptly. "Did you call them or not?"

"I've never seen you round here and I figured from your clothes you're from St Amelia's, so I rang them instead."

"Gods, no!" I cried. "I need the police. I've been kidnapped."

I tried to leave the room but Jolly, a large man in blue overalls, blocked the way, arms folded, smiling but frowning at the same time so his face was all scrunched up.

"Poor dear," came Janice's voice from behind me. "Dementia's a cruel thing, innit? Kidnapped indeed."

"I am not demented," I said with as much righteous anger as I could manage, spinning to her, my angry finger stabbing the air. "The people running St Amelia's are corrupt. It's a house of crazy people alright, but the crazy ones are the staff, not the residents."

"See what you mean, Jan," Jolly said in a low voice.

"Oh Christ, oh God, no!" I sat back in the chair and hugged myself. "Please, for the love of everything sacred, don't make me go back there. I've only just managed to escape. You've no idea what they'll do to me."

Janice's warm hand touched my arm in an act of sympathy, but I flinched from its false comfort. "They'll dry you off," she said enthusiastically. "Give you a hot drink, make sure you're warm and safe and cosy."

I looked at her in denying horror. "No, they'll dunk me in a cold bath and laugh if I get pneumonia, then cure me 'cause they don't want me to die just yet."

Janice's face crumpled. "Oh, you poor, poor muddled dear."

I could feel the heat coming off her, so I reached out and hugged her, and I cried on her because there was no way I was going to convince her of the error of her ways, and no way to get the bulk of Jolly out of the doorway so I could make a run for it.

Use the walking stick. Threaten him; hit him; anything. Get arrested for assault and battery...

No. I was in big trouble. The night had come, and it

looked as dark as my imagination had made it. There would be pain for this, I was sure.

Except, when I was picked up (re-kidnapped) with smiles and thanks from the carers to the staff, I spotted the man, that man, the one with the phone who'd filmed me in the street, and I realised that no one had taken my escape seriously. He'd probably been there recording my flight down the stairs, giggled as I'd got soaked in the rain, guffawed as I had run into the supermarket thinking it a refuge, and that made me feel all the more that escape was, indeed, impossible.

So I sat on the damp ground by the van that had come for me, waving my stick like a weapon, and twisted and flailed and kicked, crying out in high pitched wails like a banshee, making sure they had one hell of a show and one heck of a time dragging me up before someone jabbed me into bewildered silence. But before I faded out, I had seen the faces of Jan and Jolly, utterly mortified by my behaviour and absolutely confident they'd done the right thing. Good solid citizens, the pair of them.

Other than being stripped, nappied, and put to bed with something that made me sleep for a long, long time, I was right; I wasn't harmed, more like handled with kid gloves, and that made me surer than ever that my life was just a joke to someone.

When I finally woke tucked in beside the fairy, and my brain caught up with the fact my walls were yellow, not magnolia, I realised I was in a different room and someone was finally taking me seriously because there were bars on the window and, when I moved to the door, I found it firmly locked.

9. Psycho Time

I stared at the barred windows. Did this infer I had missed an opportunity in room thirty-five and they were covering it here? Or was it simply that the door lock and the bars went together?

Thinking how incongruous it was to have a barred room with such pretty yellow walls, a jazzy yellow striped duvet cover and matching curtains, and merry pictures of the seaside on the wall, I jumped when the locked door snapped open.

A smart suited, bearded and lanky man came in, moving the padded easy chair so he could sit and face me as I sat on the bed. He just looked at me for a few moments, and I froze, staring back in disbelief.

It was the man the photo album had declared to be my son, but in real life I recognised him; my prime suspect, Richard Sanderson Junior, the psycho psychiatrist. Eyes glued to my face, doubtless looking to register the slightest hint of my understanding what was going on, he scratched his neck then asked in a cheerful voice, "How're you doing, old girl?"

Forcing my features into flat incomprehension, deciding to tread very cautiously, I asked, "Who are you?" making my voice feebler than it was already.

"Your son; Richard. You remember, right? I picked this place just for you, Mum. Nice and cheerful, eh?"

"Oh, thank you," I enthused. "It is pretty here."

He sat back even farther, biting his lip, frowning. I stroked the cheerful duvet cover lest I laughed while I wondered what he was hoping to achieve with this pretence.

Leaning forwards, he said in a kind voice, "Listen, Mum. They said you were lucid so I wanted to see you, but if this is lucid I would hate to see... well, I have seen. I'm so sorry. I love you, Mum," he said, trying to get eye contact with me. "Don't ever forget that."

He pulled a folded newspaper out of his pocket and placed it on the side table. "Got this for you. Know how much you like... liked... to keep up on things. Got a puzzle section too, when you're ready."

"I'm seventy-seven," I said proudly, "and I've still got all my own teeth. And you're scaring me, so go away."

"No, you're seventy-five. Why are you scared of me?"

You have to ask? What game is this we're playing?

"When can I go home?"

"Aren't you happy here?"

I gave a big smile. "Yes. I love the white cake, the icing is superb, and the fact that I can get breakfast in bed. That is divine, and—"

"So you're happier here, so stay and I promise I'll visit every week from now on, okay? I'll bring the twins next time. Would you like that?"

I opened my mouth to speak and stopped. I put my arms around myself and looked down then up, pathetically saying, "No, I don't like it here and they don't like me; the nurses, they don't!" I lurched forward and grabbed his hand. "I want to go home."

He removed my hand and I thought I detected the slightest smile.

"If you're a good girl, Mum. We'll have to see about it. You'll have to stop complaining."

I looked at his obnoxiously handsome face as if I were searching for something.

"Are you going to come again soon? I don't like it here. They don't give me enough cake and they keep giving me these awful cold baths."

"Cold baths?" He frowned, looking genuinely surprised for a second.

I started crying without even meaning too, a great well of miserable-ness spelling over me and I wiped my eyes on my sleeve.

"Now, now, Mum, it's not that bad. I'll ask them to get you more cake, okay? And to stop with the cold baths."

"Oh thank you," I blubbed, "and tell the witches to stop banging on my door."

"Witches?"

"Those two carers. At night they walk around and they're supposed to keep an eye on us, but they hammer on the doors to wake and scare us. *Banga banga bang*!" My fists hammered on my knees to demonstrate.

He took my left hand and angled my fingers. "You made a mistake when you took off the wedding ring," he said and shot up to grab my face with pinching fingers as I tried to jerk away. "I can see you in there, Molly. Now, tell me, what the fuck that was all about" He shook my head away as if he'd touched something contaminated.

I was exposed. Never mind, the ride had been fun. "I was hoping you'd go away. And shave off that beard; it's not flattering. And find some breath mints."

"Nice. You don't really think you're Mary Cooper, do you?"

"About as much as I believe you're my son."

"Damn, you lost a bet for me, you know. I said you'd cave and accept the idea. Gavin said you wouldn't."

"Gavin?"

"Yeah." He sat back. "I've got a use for you, you see. I need some info and I think you'll be just the right person to get it for me."

"Gavin," I repeated. "Whose side's he on?"

"The one that pays his bills. Now listen. There are two particular men here on level three, and both have stuff in their heads, stuff we want to know and have so far failed to get out of them. I don't like taking people to pieces to find out what they know, 'cause I know they too often lie. You've proven you're tough enough to help by not letting yourself get gas lighted by us."

"Actually, it was more the man screaming in the bath

that cinched it for me, but never mind. Carry on, dickhead."

He snorted a laugh. "We've let your real identity get leaked, so at some point these gents are going to approach you in the hopes you'll help them get out, and you're going to lead them on and find out what we want to know."

"And if I don't help?"

"Let's just say that Gavin thinks that being in with me keeps him safe, but it doesn't. Oh, it really doesn't, Molly. Cute creatures, those twins."

He took out his phone as I said, "Threatening children? How like dear Aunty Sarah."

He turned the phone screen to me. I saw photos of my grandchildren on the beach, laughing. Collin was there. I gulped. The boy had been languishing in a coma last I'd heard. It was so wonderful to see him well and happy that my eyes welled with tears.

As he put the phone away, Richard misunderstood the reason for my damp eyes. "So you see, I can do what I like with them."

I sniffed back a tear of mixed relief and worry. "How recent are those pictures?"

"Last week. Paid them a visit and built sandcastles with them. Vana bored me stiff maundering on about how sad she was, after having to chuck out their father and how—"

"She threw out Gavin?"

"Yes, and all the while I was choking with laughter inside because I was the one who'd hooked him into the business again."

"Well, a man can't afford to be unemployed in this day and age. Poor children."

"Don't worry." He leaned closer, conspiratorial. "He's working for me now; gets paid really well, and as for little lonely Vana... I got a date with her. Could end up as the kiddies' stepdaddy." He beamed. I stuck out my tongue.

"Okay." He slapped his thighs. "Back to business. Thing is, I think these guys might talk to you. The sweet li'l old lady factor, you understand."

I stared at the pastel yellow wall, seeing sandcastles and sunshine, then closed my eyes, breathing steadily. "I don't seem to have much choice but to try, though I might not be a good spy. And what then, Tricky Dicky? If I do get what you want, will you finally kill me like the disgusting creation you are?"

"Not sticking round if you're gonna insult me, Mum."

"And you can stop calling me mum, you... you... abject charlatan. And keep away from Vana. She's a cow but she doesn't deserve the likes of you."

"You've been a cow too. A right bloody nuisance, but I'm not into chopping up old ladies, just embarrassing them by filming their antics. We enjoyed your wheelchair tomfoolery, by the way. You were trying to get a look at the guy with the camera, right? That's when I knew you knew; that there was no residual problem from being knocked out."

"What?"

"You got hit over the head too hard after exiting the Chinese, so you really were out of everything for a few weeks, but I'm happy to see you awake and well."

"As if!"

"Anyway, I might, just might, be nice and let you go in the end. Be a shame to off someone as entertaining as you."

"And what are their names, these men? And what am I supposed to be finding out?"

"I'm sure you'll figure it all out," he said, and he was up and gone in an instant like he'd never been there, the door shutting on so many other questions I could have asked, and only the newspaper on the table showed he had ever been there.

I hadn't seen a newspaper for ages, only heard fractions of stories on the TV, so I grabbed and read it avidly.

Only a few pages in, I stopped and stared, my hackles rising as if a serpent were coiled in the pages.

A police report. A short and sad tale. A stolen car that

had crashed and both the driver and passenger died.

And one of the photos was of Hugo. I peered, I looked at the picture from all angles, I noted the crescent scar on his cheekbone, the way his hair swirled over his brow, the line of the beard...

It looked like him.

Dead, so the news said.

But if I have learned anything during my time dealing with bad guys, it's that dead doesn't always mean dead. Words are nothing. Show me his body, not even his grave, his cold dead body and I will believe you, newspaper, until then I will live in optimism. I have to.

I've put too much hope in the idea that you'll be able to track me down and rescue me, Hugo. I refuse to believe you're gone.

~

Mila came in and escorted me wordlessly to the day room where, over breakfast, I stared one by one at the afflicted gathered in the room's silent circle, guessed who the two men I had to talk to might be, and knew I had no coercive skills to get people to open up to me.

Overwhelmed, I loudly sniffed away an escaping tear and wiped my nose on the back of my hand. Someone in the room whimpered. It spread like Chinese Whispers until everyone had begun to sniffle or whine and the carers came back in to find the wicked emotional blighter who'd set off them all.

"It was me," I admitted. "I wanted to see if anyone else was alive. They are, you know."

"Okay," Amber said. "Enough of your little amusements. Back to your room. We can't have you upsetting the others. It makes too much work for us. Now, off we go."

I must have been a terrible let-down for the poor girl with my escaping and fussing and possibly getting her into trouble—all this assuming that she was innocent, not a paid henchman.

"It was nice to have a visitor," I said softly in my room.

"Even if it was a monster."

"That's an odd thing to say. You haven't had a visitor."

"He was here in my room just now. Look; that's the newspaper he brought for me."

She picked up the paper and riffled through it. "How did you get this?"

"I told you. The monster brought it in."

With a big sigh she said, "Well, if you say so, it must be true," then went out and closed my door with an irritated slam, clicking the lock on, leaving me wondering if it followed that, if she didn't know about Richard's visit, she didn't know about what was going on there. I hoped she didn't. I liked her.

Then I stopped liking her quite so much because I realised she'd run off with the newspaper and all the puzzle pages.

10. Two Good Men

As my little clock's hands wandered around to eleven and the room was dim and warm and cosy (a small mercy), I reclined in bed concentrating on counting the tick-tocks, something I had found calmed my galloping-rat brain as it tried to find a way out of the maze.

I had established that the window bars would not move in any way, machined all in one with the frame, not that I was into climbing out of windows. Maybe with all Richard's talk of psychological pressure, the bars were to make me feel totally incarcerated. It certainly felt like a cell. I couldn't even wander outside anymore with the door locked on me and, even if I had got out, my walking stick had gone walkies.

That room—number forty—was right at the far end of the corridor where the outside world would have shown the road curving away, so it was at least quieter than number thirty-five. So I jumped when my door lock clicked, the handle moved, and the door started to crawl open as if someone were creeping in, wanting to surprise me.

Now what? I swore inwardly, ready for the worst, sitting up.

"Who is it?" I demanded in a no-nonsense voice.

As I switched on the bedside light, the door swung fully open and a dishevelled man came in, hurriedly shutting the door behind him. He was a six-footer at least, but stooped as if ashamed to be tall. Far too young to be in a nursing home, his shaggy hair was muddy blond and his sharp face stubbled and leary; a face that would not have been amiss on a wanted poster.

He wore only striped pyjama trousers, and the way he was clutching the loose clothing made me tremble with imagined intent. "Go away," I hissed. "I'll scream. You'll get into trouble."

His head shook once before he collapsed into the easy chair in the corner with a weary sigh. "Need ya help," he said in a rough, quiet voice.

He frowned, looked away, and kept glancing at the door. "Y' can unlock it, y' know, from this side. Made you a key. Just shove this in yon gap there." He slipped something into the slightly open drawer beside him, then began chafing his hands together over and over.

"You made a key?"

"Yeah, it's not like it's fucking Fort Knox, y'know. So, you be tha' Molly Marshman," he went on. "Shoulda recognised the voice; kinda posh."

On hearing my married name, I became frightened and lifted the huge fairy to cradle in a comforting way. Although this man gave the impression of being tousled and tired, I was suddenly sure he was one of the men Richard had meant me to contact, and I had no idea how to deal with him. But he had asked for help and, you know me, I like to lend a hand. "So how can I assist, Mr...?"

"Barry. Just Barry, Ma'am, occupant of room 37." He tilted his head forwards as if he had failed to hear me correctly, peered at me from under heavy eyebrows and said in a pleading voice, "Y' can get us out, cancha?"

"Out of here? I would love to, but how do you think I can do that? Don't you know I failed earlier this week?"

"But y' got away from Sanderson, and y' escaped that cave—"

"How do you know about all that?" I demanded.

"S'pose you will na recognise me." He coughed a bitter laugh. "I was one of the gents grabbed y' outside Kerton Church. And y' got out the caves," he emphasised, sitting forward and looking at me earnestly, his face all admiration. "How'd y' do that? An' y' took down Stan-the-man. That's jest nothing short of a miracle."

"Stop right there. Don't you dare put me in the same class as Stanley."

"Aye, well, you may not want to be, Ma'am, but ye're quite the legend now."

"Is that why I'm in here, you think?"

He shrugged widely. "I can't tell y' that. I done some stuff, tha's true enough, but this is about the out, not the in."

I gave an exasperated sigh. Molly: the woman, the legend. Holy teacups. What next?

"The coast guard got us out of the cave," I said. "Nothing to do with me tunnelling out like Mr Mole, and I don't see how I can get anyone out of here. I've been thinking about it for ages and the only plan I tried, failed, because of stupid caring citizens."

"No," he moaned, cradling his head and theatrically shaking it from side to side. "I can't take much more. I can't, Ma'am. I'm half the man I used to be. I'll die of starvation soon."

"Hmpf," I said, sympathetic to the core. "Looks to me you could do with losing some weight."

"Ah was a heavy... that means ah was—"

"Yes, I get it, *heavy.* You should have made better life choices."

"Y' gotta help me! Ah need ideas from y'." He made an exasperated noise and stood up, wobbled and sat down with a thump. He was visibly shaking but pressed on with his faulty logic. "Y' know judo, karate, taekwondo?"

I snorted. "Any of that malarkey and I'd break a hip. Could we set off the fire alarm; get everyone evacuated? Surely they'd have to get everyone out?"

"For sure, ah'd love to have a good reason to set that alarm off for real, but they'd as likely leave us t' burn. The other floors are normal people, they don't deserve hell. Just us, the prisoners of floor three, for our sins." He buried his face in his hands again and I fought back the strange urge to give him a hug.

"Ah'm not ready t' die in here," he mumbled into his big hairy hands. Suddenly fierce, he glared at me. "Ah used to be somebody, somebody big. Someone important, and now ah have no dignity. They keep me so choked up ah don't know one day from t'other. They call me by an 'orrible name. They stick a nappy on me at night 'cause ah pisses meself. I canna live like this, Ma'am; you gotta think of something. What a fricking falafel!"

"I think you mean a frickin' palaver."

He began to gabble, sounding apologetic, hands clasped before him, begging. "I can change, become someone better, make meself over. Ah'm still young. Get me outta here, Ma'am, and ah'll be your slave for life, God's honest truth and ah means that. C'mon, we can help each other. Y' gotta help me. Or are you jest a pathetic old woman after all?"

In the distance I heard the unmistakeable snap of the connecting door opening. I glanced at the clock and...

Pressed the bell to call a carer.

Barry panicked, up and backing into the corner, slumping down on his haunches as he stared fearfully at the door then me, unable to conceal the fear choking his voice. "What y' done, you bloody bonkers old fart?"

"I have to pretend you shouldn't be here. It'll do neither of us any good to be found together."

"No, Christ, don't! They'll punish me, you crazy old broad; stick me in the hole for a week; more. I can't take it. You's killed me, Ma'am!"

The door flew open and one of the bulky male night carers stood there puffing like an irate bull.

"Nurse," I said anxiously, putting a tremor in my voice, "this man came in and he won't go away. Please get him out; he's scaring me."

Once Barry had been hauled out, I began to worry my actions might have really killed him. Now I felt guilty; sympathy for a felon, but my idea had been that Barry wouldn't think I had any connection to the doctor *because* I'd had him dragged out.

I blinked hard to keep back tears. This was about my survival, not Barry's; mine. I had to be tougher than I felt, cold hearted even. Gone was Molly who would give tramps money and rescue kittens. Here was Molly who would have wielded a Gatling gun to raze the building to the ground and not even worried about the other residents—they were all doomed anyway, one way or another.

Then old Molly came back and hated herself for changing so much.

When all was calm and dark, I tried using the credit-card sized sheet of hard plastic Barry had put in the drawer, wiggling it this way and that in the small gap of the door, but it took a few tries to master. I popped it in my dressing gown pocket and buried it in the tissues I found there.

I crept along to Barry's room and popped my head around the door like a neighbour coming in for a chat. His bed was empty. My heart sank.

Spurred on by guilt and a sudden surge of adrenaline, I got down the main stairs with little trouble thanks to my diligent exercises, almost made it to the front door, then had to hide in the bottom section of a louvred linen cupboard as footsteps came my way. I peeked through the gaps as the people passed.

An agitated man in PJs had come into view in the night-lit reception area, two male carers trying to grab him as he deftly avoided their clutches. With short, greying brown hair and a gingerish unshaven stubble, he was easy to recognise as one of the men I had seen in the dayroom. Past his best years but a rugged, strong man, with cords standing out on his thick neck, veins bulging on his forearms like a would-be Thor actor.

I would have called him handsome, but his eyes were too close together for my liking, or maybe that was an illusion because one of them was blackened with bruising.

"Let me the fuck out!" he yelled, randomly punching the front door's code reader before his hands were grabbed and held behind him. "You can't keep me in here," he raged. "Get off me."

"Quit that, Jerry," the larger carer said firmly. "Come on

now, mate, it's time for bed. You'll be disturbing everybody with this hullaballoo. Have some respect."

"Respect?" Jerry snorted. "No fucking respect in this place. Haven't you looked around?"

In a high voice vibrating with the edge of panic he yelled, "I'm not supposed to be here," and as he turned our gazes met through the gap of the louvres. His eyes widened. I froze.

He laughed, coughing and doubling up. "You dolts. Someone's gonna be held to task for whatever's going on." He leaned over farther, the men let go of him then, with an impressive swing, he brought up his fist and knocked one of the carers flying before the other reached into his pocket and stabbed the fighter with a syringe.

I watched in terrified silence as they half carried his floppy body away.

'I bet that's the other guy I'm supposed to find out about,' I thought. 'If so, I hope he doesn't realise what I'm up to because I really don't fancy being on the wrong end of that punch.'

11. Night Time Assignations

To my delight, the next day I was let into the dayroom for breakfast again, not that it was very exciting to be there but it's odd what simple things you miss when you can't have them.

I had inwardly sighed with relief when I saw Barry there but, despite pointedly looking across at him, he didn't so much as flicker his gaze my way. Who could blame him? He probably hated me now. He stared at his fingers, appearing to count them over and over; lost somewhere I couldn't help him escape from.

Only one other person showed any movement, a fuzzy-grey-haired woman who constantly nodded her head slightly, moving to some sound we lesser mortals could not hear. Her face was bland, neither happy nor sad, peacefully existing in that time and place. In one way I could have envied her. No worries beset her dormant soul. In another way she terrified me, as I saw in her the shades of what I could become.

Jerry sat beside her. He was the only one looking anywhere other than in front of him. He gazed up at the TV screen, where an old detective programme muttered.

There were no carers around so I said very quietly, "Anyone up for a game of escape from Colditz?"

Jerry's gaze instantly swivelled to the door, then to me. He looked straight at me, eyes wide, alarm on his face, but the tilt of his head made it a kind of hopeful, thoughtful alarm. I winked at him. After a thoughtful second he winked back. Now, how to talk to him properly? I listened warily to the noises outside the room.

Raising a hand casually to my chest, I pointed to myself, then to him as I mouthed widely, *Find you tonight.*

He made a fist on his lap, then put up the thumb and winked.

One a.m. My mouth moved wide, wordless. I held up one finger.

He winked again and, from the visible tightening of his jaw, appeared to be trying to resist smiling.

I eagerly put up with the day's boredom to await next morning's early assignation, hoping that all his winks were just code for OK, and not agreement to something else he'd thought I had been offering.

At one in the morning, I put on my dressing gown and practised my escapology again to make my way little by little along the corridor. At each door I stopped and peeked in. I found Jerry snoring in number thirty, the room next to mine if I'd only gone left past the office instead of right. I took it as a bad omen for the night and nearly left, but he would be expecting me.

I crept in cautiously and shut the door behind me with nary a click. As I put the central light's dimmer on half, he jerked awake into simply another confused, pyjama-wearing resident. The fright on his face said it all, then he hid under the covers like a terrified child and a voice heavy with suspicion asked, "Who's that?"

"Molly, from the day room," I said softly.

The blanket uncovered a black eye that peered at me in the half light. "Oh. You."

"Pleased to meet you too," I whispered.

The cover moved down and his one good eye narrowed with suspicion.

I held out a limp hand. "Molly," I repeated quietly, "though they call me Mary in here."

He looked at my hand as if I offered a dirty rag, and ignored it.

"Woke up on the wrong side of the bed?" I asked mildly.

"Wrong side the fucking planet," he snapped.

After a second's worth of decision making, he sat up, muttering, "Sorry, the old brain's pretty fogged up. Anyways, I'm Jeff Roman. Here, I'm Jerry. I don't know how they're doing it: the confusion, it's a nightmare. I'm Jeff but I'm like someone else too, my fake persona, like it's the twilight zone. I can feel —"

"I know, I know, so what can we do about it?"

I guessed he was bruised elsewhere as he laboriously twisted and turned before managing to sit on the side of the bed, long legs dangling, top open to show a broad hairy chest that had begun to shrink from lack of exercise and good food.

"Coupla months ago," he said in a bitter drawl, "I was still in the bye-bye business—"

"What's the bye-bye business?"

He huffed a mocking laugh. "Guess. And now I'm stuck in this here place, hyped up on some kind of muscle irritator so I constantly feel like shit, getting beaten up, half drowned... You got any clues what's going on? It's the UK, right, not the States?"

"England. Not far from London."

"Aw, hell," He sighed and rolled his shoulders. "I don't know what's real and what isn't anymore. We gotta find the combo for the front door, get Gwen a wheelchair and make a run for it."

"I'm up for elopement."

"Nothing to joke about!" he hissed, anger twisting his face into something alarming and fearful. "Gwen's my ol' lady. She's next door. We gotta get her out and get the cops, fast."

"It wasn't a joke. When someone gets out of a home like this, they call it eloping, not escaping. Makes it sound better in reports. I eloped to the supermarket and asked for the police but the staff put my panic down to dementia and called the home to get me back. Getting someone to believe you seems to be key."

"With three or four of us telling the same story? They'd bloody well better listen, lady. Okay, so you and me both, we got no mental infirmity and are being kept prisoners by drugs. The big question is, to what end?"

"I figure this is a place for people who've upset the cartel.

We're here to be psychologically tortured."

"You sure?" He looked me up and down but didn't ask how a granny had upset the big bad guys.

"I don't know for certain, but there was a man yelling in the bathroom one night. I heard them say he wouldn't talk. What do you think?"

He laughed weakly. "I think I was the bath man." He scratched his head. "I kinda remember it, like a nightmare. I gotta lot to say but I guess they're not getting it 'cause I'm still here." He looked me up and down. "Tip for you: fake responses, grunts and fearful looks get you a long way, should you ever cross them. It's easier to say nothing, 'cause the moment you speak all the other words come spilling out, like you broke the pledge and need to drink the bar."

"You're frightening me. They've not done much to me so far, except for locking me in a room with bars on the window."

"How'd you get *here* then?"

I told him about Barry. He nodded. "Listen, if you're scared, the cure for that is action. If we allow fear to paralyze us, we'll over-think and slow down. Don't succumb to fear, attack it." He waved a determined fist. "Don't run from your fears, embrace them, let them keep you sharp."

"Wow," I breathed, admiring how the befuddled man in pyjamas had transformed into a tiger. "Them's fighting words. Let's try to live up to them. And you said four. You, me, Gwen and who? Barry?"

"Yeah; Barry Hollister. Came to me one night and told me his story. He's Tony in here, the cry baby."

"Oh, come on, this place is enough to turn anyone into a cry baby, and men are allowed to show their emotions, you know?

"Whatever," he snorted. "Namby pamby bullshit." He lurched to his feet but sat back with a bouncy thump and a disgruntled sigh. "Tell me what you know," he said, so I sat on the easy chair and we chatted for a while, just like friendly neighbours stuck in a madhouse.

"How long've you been here?" I asked.

His mouth twisted. "Best I can tell, 'bout ten weeks, if that. Went to sleep at home, woke to an intruder who jabbed me, then woke here to be told I was this 'other' person. That my 'original' life was a deception of my own brain. That my lovely Gwen is someone called Angela and no way my wife; that it's another delusion."

"They're twisting us," I agreed. "Before this, did you have involvement with drugs?"

He hesitated, gave me a nasty look, then suddenly shot forwards with more energy than I would've given him credit for and grabbed my throat with one strong hand. My fingers scrabbled helplessly against his grip. Terror must have been written on my face as he leaned in to say in a calm and insulting drawl, "You a fuckin' stooge?"

"Neh," I managed to squeeze out. He let me go. "It's just —" I coughed. "I accidentally got involved with drug runners —"

He held up a silencing hand. "Don't tell me anything more. Now, no more time to chat with crazy meemaws."

"Weren't you supposed to say that in your head?" I asked in derision, rubbing my neck. "You're very rude. Any more sass and I'll put you on the naughty step."

"I need you to be serious for a feckin' minute."

"Whoa there, my sense of humour is a load-bearing coping mechanism and it's not going anywhere while I have to deal with the likes of you."

"Right. You use humour; I use anger to get me through. Now, since I was so rudely woken, I'm off to see Gwen."

He went to the door. I followed hissing, "What do you mean? 'Rudely woken'? You knew I was coming."

I suspected he was going to be an awkward man to deal with. And more than dangerous if he found out my task.

By then it was almost two in the morning, the time when the night carers who were supposed to be 'waking' night carers would be snoring in the day room, draped over chairs like blankets.

We stepped through the doorway of 38. As he put the lights on very low, I saw a thin lady asleep in the bed, her breathing hardly raising the bed clothes. She was the nodding lady with fuzzy-grey hair from the dayroom, sleeping as prettily as Sleeping Beauty with a softly angelic smile on her face. Jeff shook her gently, then a bit harder, then patted her cheek. She didn't wake. He stroked a hand across her brow and kissed her loose-skinned cheek. I saw his chin wobble as he straightened up, trying to keep in his emotions.

He looked at me sharply, and I think he realised he had shown me a chink in his armour. "That's the problem with being in a cage too long; your soul breaks. You can remember you had a home, you can feel it deep inside, all those memories of things I did... but..." He struggled for words. "I can remember the kids, but not where my house was. The dog, but not his name. This stuff they're giving me is making holes in my head." He gazed at Gwen. "I once read that love is a mental illness, but at the moment the idea of getting out with her is the only thing carrying me along."

He rubbed his hands over his face, trying to erase emotion. "She always was a fighter, so I reckon she made a racket when they grabbed her and they gave her something too strong to shut her up. And now she's permanently damaged."

I was so horrified at that idea, at that callous indifference to life which appeared to be copied in similar mindsets all over the building, that I suddenly desperately wanted to escape the room. "I'll leave you in peace. I'm off to look for a secret basement."

"Why the hell?"

"Because secret basements are always bad," I said, "and I wouldn't put it past this lot having one, would you?"

He frowned at me in the gloom.

"Access from outside?" I suggested. "Or via the wheelchair lift? Ever noticed any extra stops on it? Secret panels that could flip open?"

Scratching a hand through his hair in irritation, he said sharply, "Stop messing around." He took Gwen's unresponsive hand in a tightly desperate grip. "I know who she is and she's not a delusion. Twenty-five years of marriage is difficult to manufacture."

Again I tried to leave them together, to get away from a scenario making me emotionally uncomfortable, but he exited with me. He looked both ways along the corridor, the night lights glinting in his eyes. "The night crew'll be coming round at four. Plenty of time to do your thing."

"My thing?"

"Spying. I saw you in the linen cupboard. You're usefully weird."

I nodded in wordless agreement, happy that someone finally saw my inner soul, then went back to my prowling.

~

I'm not that brave though, and when I heard footsteps approaching I high-tailed it back to the safety of my room.

Suddenly, I felt too hot, stifled even, so I opened the window, letting in the cool night air. The wind sang a mournful tune in the tree branches, a melody punctuated with the whoosh of passing cars. As I leaned my hot brow against a metal bar, I looked out into the human-lit darkness and contemplated all the possible things I could do to get out, to get the others out. I only found one possible idea my head.

Turning back, I caught my face in the mirror; tense, wrinkled, pasty. I looked like a woman at death's door. My hair had become thinner and frizzier, my lips a pensive line. I hated that image. It made me wonder what I had left to battle for, but in the same instant I remembered it was not just me I should fight for—it was for all the other poor souls trapped there.

But now I had my 'associates'; Jeff, and hopefully Barry. They would be able to help me. I knew they would. If I couldn't get the mad doc's information *from* them, I was going to escape *with* them.

12. Molly?

Time rolled on to July twenty-second, only twelve weird days since I had first woken.

I saw Jeff in the day room, and I thought he gave me the slightest of nods. Gwen was beside him, awake but staring blankly into space. The TV burbled a quiz show, its fractured laughter the only sound in the room.

In total bewilderment, I tried to imagine how I could be expected to get a man like Jeff to help me, when bathroom torture and drugs had failed to get information from him. Say 'pretty please'? I was fooling myself if I thought this little plan of mine was going to be easy.

As I sat there, a panicky feeling enveloped me as if I was drowning. My heart raced, my hands became clammy at the idea of the task before me. Self-doubt was rampant, its horses running up and down my spine with hard hooves. I couldn't do this.

I looked around at all the sad, empty faces, and it was if I had entered purgatory, that odd place between the calm of heaven and the chaos of hell, and I suddenly wasn't sure which realm I should be in with my past mistakes and errors weighing so heavily on me. Did I deserve peace?

So many things had gone weird so fast, that all I could do was feel my way along slowly, groping like a blind man in an unfamiliar room; an unknown room; a crazy room.

Staying awake at night did nothing for my mindset either. I was worried enough already and roaming the corridors like a wraith, looking for anything useful, avoiding contact with carers, was stressful. I was not cut out to be a spy.

And the biggest problem was that lack of night sleep resulted in day time torpidity, where I dozed deeply and became unaware of what was going on.

On one occasion, I woke in the dayroom to the clatter

of my lunch being removed from the table across my lap, the carer walking off with my plate of untouched food. "Hey," I called weakly, because that was how I felt, "I was going to eat that. Leave it."

The woman barely cast a glance over me. "Eat it now, you'll get food poisoning. Stay awake next time."

Off she went with my food despite my angry calls. I hoped a proper nurse might pop up and tell the obnoxious lunch lady to bring the food back. I doubted it'd give me poisoning, but lack of food was not going to do my constitution any good. I imagined coffee with cream, toast dripping with butter and marmalade, and wished I hadn't because my stomach growled louder until I began to feel queasy. *Maybe I should give Dr Evil a call. I'm not going to be of any use if I'm half starved.* How exactly was I supposed to contact him?

Angry, I walked stiffly to the corner office, but no one was there and they were not quite daft enough to leave the door unlocked. But that meant no one was by the stairs to stop me, and the gate was so simple a two-year-old could have mastered the locking mechanism, so I went down to the next level where floor two's office was hosting a small meeting of five. A poster on the half open door said, "It's important for somebody with dementia to feel they're being listened to and understood. Show patience with our patients". They sounded nicer than the lot upstairs, so I interrupted the talk, hunger making me bold.

"Excuse me, but I've had no lunch," I said loudly. The obvious head of the group was a petite dark-haired nurse with gaunt features, sitting at a cramped desk while the others stood around. She gave me a look to wilt garlic.

"God's sake," she exploded, making me take a step back in alarm. "It's gone midday. You'll have been fed already, you stupid woman."

I noticed a couple of the other carers glance at each other in puzzled concern, taken aback at her rudeness.

"Just shut up and go back to bed," she carried on, nose pinched between thumb and forefinger. I must have really been stressing out the poor dear.

But it was hard not to respond, hard to bite back on the comments thrown at me.

"Go away," she ordered again. She huffed and scowled so deeply her face was like an angry carved pumpkin. A flapping hand waved me away. "We are busy," she spat. "No lounging around for us."

"I was asleep, and no one woke me for lunch, so I missed it," I stated.

"That's your look out," she muttered and turned back to the carers. "Wish I could get enough sleep," she said bitterly. She flipped the pages of notes before her. "Where were we before that interruption?"

"You shouldn't be so rude," I said, disgusted by the scorn visited on me. "You're setting an incredibly bad example to the youngsters. So much for showing patience with the patients. Anyway, I thought we were supposed to be called residents."

"Which room are you?" she demanded; eyes narrowed.

"I'm not a room, I'm a person, and I want to call my doctor to complain about my treatment."

She sat back, some recognition coming into her face, and swore under her breath before turning to the others. "She's from upstairs," she said evenly, but her eyes flickered to me then away. "I always said they needed to lock the bloody stairs more securely. Quick, let's get her back up."

"I don't understand," a girl in the group said. "Why's this so bad?"

"Which proves you haven't been listening. Upstairs is the psych ward. Now come on, Mandy, help me get this one into the lift. You never know what they might be capable of. Quickly, but constrain her gently, or we'll all be in trouble."

~

Reaching my floor, I was shoved out of the lift by the women who were obviously panicking, and I found coldness creep along the gloomy corridor, a subtle breeze carrying unpleasant mixed scents of cabbage, cookies, disinfectant.

The psych ward, was it? They could call it what they liked, but it wasn't like any psychiatric ward I had ever seen on TV, and I doubted it merited the title.

Undeterred however, my stomach calling for attention, I ambled off towards the kitchen. Full of chatting staff, the afternoon coffee and biscuit fest was well under way, all the chocolate and cream varieties from the boxes bought for the residents disappearing into their own gullets. I stopped in the doorway and called out, asking for replacement of a lost lunch, hoping someone there had the kindness to feed me.

Amber stood up from the back, shoved half a chocolate cream into her mouth and said, "I'll deal with her. Back in a mo," and escorted me back to my room. When we got there, she poured me a glass of water and emptied her pockets of eight fat Bourbon biscuits. "There," she said. "Keep you going 'til teatime? How'd you get out the room? You're s'posed to be locked in?"

"No one put me back after lunch," I pointed out.

"Gawd-useless lot," she muttered. "Okay, I'm on lunches tomorrow. I'll come make sure you get yours, okay?"

"You are so kind, Amber dear, not like most of them here. Though, you do owe me a newspaper."

"Oh yeah, I just can't resist puzzles; sorry. I'll get you a proper book next time I'm out, okay? Anyway, I'd leave this mouldy place if I could, but I need the money and the pay's really good."

I wonder why that should be? To keep your mouth shut, perhaps?

"You said you have a son?" I said.

"Yeah: Earl. Curly Early I call him 'cause of all his curly hair. He's a darling but kids are so expensive. But..." She shrugged and gave a cute little smile. "Maybe I got a nice bloke in my life now." Her gaze drifted absently through the window.

The old envy sprang up. She had a man; a nice man.

Envious to the end; eh, Molly?

"I hope he's nice," I said, "or I'll kick him in the balls for you."

She laughed gaily. "You are a funny one. Guess that's why I like you." Lowering her voice, she said, "It's the gardener: Red. That's not his real name, it's 'cause he laughs and says we can't pronounce his proper name right, so we all calls him Red like that scarf he wears all the time, see?"

"Should at least be a good garden produce provider," I said. "Good luck with him."

"I'm teaching him to read and write proper," she said with a proud air. "He said he kinda missed out on that when he was moving around as a kid. He's a pretty quick learn and we kinda bonded over the lessons."

I am not envious. I am not envious. Yes, I am.

She peered out of my window, tapped on the glass and waved. "Oh good, he's out the front." She opened the window and blew the man far below some kisses, laughing lightly, such happiness on her face that it doubled my envy.

"I'd like to contact my son again," I said, interrupting her happiness in a slight mood of unkindness. "If that's possible."

She looked back at me then shut the window. "Okay, I'll go ask Sally, but you do realise, don't you, that elopement might've revoked some of your privileges?"

"I would've called phone calls *rights*." I huffed. "Maybe I should sneak down there at night and just use it."

She chuckled. "It won't work at night. I heard a night carer was caught calling her bloke in France for hours at a time. Ran up a mega bill. Got the sack. Now Sally locks it when she leaves."

"And if there's an emergency?"

She shrugged. "Who hasn't got a mobile nowadays?"

"Another question. Why do floor two's staff act like floor three's full of toxic psychotic monsters?"

"You went down there an' got caught?" she gasped. "Your wandering's really gonna get you into trouble. Never mind

bars on windows and locked doors, they might put you in the h
—" She clapped her mouth shut and moved away.

"Trouble's my middle name. *Might put me in the...* what were you going to say? Hole?"

"Oh... Molly, you—"

"*Molly?*"

She bit her lip. "I mean Mary. Of course I mean Mary."

"Be careful, dear," I said, staring at her meaningfully as her movements became erratic and she couldn't look at me. "Your cover's slipping."

"Oh shit!" she cried, and left faster than I had ever seen someone move, leaving me with a puzzled little smile. What had that all been about? She knew more about me than she said. This could be interesting.

13. Hope

Amber didn't turn up for her shift the next morning, which upset me. I was scared I had frightened her away and lost a friend; an ally even.

Instead, a new woman woke me on the first day of August, when I had begun to feel I would be in that place forever.

"Hello," I said cheerily as I sat up. "Nice to meet you, but where's Amber today? I hope she's all right."

"No idea," she said briskly in a *how the hell would I know* way. "I'm Margaret and I don't know who I'm replacing 'cause I'm bank, but come on, up with you. Breakfast. Do you walk or ride or what?"

"I like to use a stick but someone swiped mine. And I prefer to make work for people, so can I have my breakfast in here, please?"

"I dunno." She scowled. "I'll ask."

Five minutes later she brought me a breakfast tray.

"Here you are, your ladyship; as requested."

"There's no need to be rude. Anyway, you forgot the flower in a vase. No decent breakfast tray would be seen dead without a flower."

She looked at me funny. "Yeah, right. Why don't you want it in the dayroom?"

"Because all the other residents are empty, and you know what I mean. I have a soul still; compos mentis. It depresses me to see the empty others."

"Why're you in here if you're such a smarty?"

"I suppose you don't know anything?"

She put her hands on her hips. "And what's that supposed to mean?"

"I don't mean you're not smart, I mean this is a corrupt institution and you'd do well to get out before you fall in too far."

"Well..." She fussed with the bed sheets then turned to the door saying sarcastically, "I must say, I wish I didn't have so much work to do, so I could hear *all* about this exciting world in your head."

"Then come back after breakfast," was my riposte. "There's much to tell. Bring me a stick and your coffee and biscuits and enjoy the show." I smiled gently.

She frowned. "Hmph. Well, what more should I expect. It's common knowledge dementia patients lose their inhibitions, get all talkative and spill all their made-up secrets in a really serious way, so you don't know if they're for real or just messing with you."

"I've met dementia patients and I don't think anyone on this floor acts like one."

She gave me the side-eye but went on, "This lady one floor down, she told me some outrageous stuff that sounded like a movie I saw a while back—she sort of turned it into her life. Bit like you, so I've been told. *Watch out for that Mary*, they said to me. *Good imagination on that one.*"

"How insulting. Still, I'll look on the bright side. At least I don't have to worry about phone scammers in here."

That elicited a wanly curious smile, then she startled me by saying, "You're getting a moustache, Mary."

"How rude and irrelevant!"

"No, it's a fact. Look in the mirror. Want me to help pull them?"

"It may be a fact, my dear, but you do not have to point it out. How would you like it if I said you're getting grey hairs?"

Giving an angry pout, her hands shot to her hair; a mane so black and shiny it was like a cap on her head.

"Really? You're just getting at me now, aren't you?"

I nodded. "And it's not nice, is it? Now, tell me the truth, why did you say all that before? Was it a sort of non-dementia test?"

"Could've been. There are certain patterns we're trained

to look for, and you're not exhibiting any of them."

"Good," I said, finding a chink in her armour. "So come back with your coffee and I'll tell you what happened—but don't mention it to anyone else—and then you can go home and read all about it on your computer. It'll all check out. There should be pictures of me in my former glory too."

She stood with one hand on the open door, gazing at me with puzzled eyes, then shrugged and went away. About an hour later she came back with a walking stick for me and her coffee. She sat and listened as I told her an abbreviated version of everything that had happened to me in the past few years, then she nodded, said, "Okay," and left.

~

In the night, I had a very unsettling experience. I woke to hands dragging me out of bed; angry male voices cussing me for wetting the bed. Someone ripped Fairy from my grasp then pulled off my nightdress and had me squealing in fear, then almost threw me into the easy chair. I sat shivering, watching as hazy people stripped the covers off the bed and marched off, leaving me naked and scared and shaking.

It seemed to take ages for them to come back and make the bed, and all the while I sat and shivered. Again, so roughly I couldn't believe these men deserved to be called carers, I was wrestled into a nightdress and placed in the freshly sheeted bed.

"Where's my fairy?" I asked. My request was met with snorts of derision, and they moved on. I got up. I looked around. Fairy was nowhere to be seen and I realised the chances were he was in with the bedding, in the laundry. I'd ask about him in the morning.

~

In the morning I was woken by Mrs Galyer of The Face of Thunder. A face condemning me for something. "Whatever's the problem?" I asked, getting up on my elbows, peering at her blearily. "What have I done now?"

"One of the residents has been attacked," she said. "And I

think it might have been you."

"What?" I said in astonishment.

"Your toy fairy was found in the room with the victim."

"So you're saying my fairy attacked him? Stabbed him with her little plastic wand?"

"How did you know it was a man and that he'd been stabbed?"

"I didn't. I was being facetious. Look, I've just woken up. I need to pee. I'm starving hungry, and I can't go around at night attacking people. The door's locked, for heaven's sake."

"I will have to call the police. I will have to give your doll in evidence."

"Go ahead," I said. "Explain to them how a woman in a locked room did the deed. Maybe Fairy did it on her own, but if she isn't holding a knife, I would assume she was innocent."

I told her about the night carers who I suspected had taken the fairy, and she frowned at me in a disbelieving and intimidating way. Then she rolled her eyes, gave a sharp exclamation of disgust, span on her heel and went out.

What were they trying to pull now? Stealing my fairy to place it at the scene of a crime was just ridiculous. And I was sure if they actually did bother to call the police, and I doubted that they would—considering the nature of the place—no one could possibly suspect me of an attack (on who, I wondered?) based on a fairy-doll's location. One thing was certain though, I would never see Fairy again. Little by little, they were wearing me down. Maybe I should pretend to be upset. Give them the satisfaction of hearing me cry. But there was just something in me that wouldn't let me do that. To Hell with them all.

~

At eight sharp, Margaret came straight to my room, glancing fearfully behind her at the closed door, then me, her fingers clenching and unclenching on a small piece of paper.

"I'm going to have a severe migraine," she said softly, "and leave and never come back. I read, I learned, I put together a bit more than two and two and I don't want to be involved in this place anymore, and I'm not willing to contact police 'cause that'll direct it back to me, but if it'll help you; here." She shoved the paper into my hand. "Memorise it then eat it or something, but don't ever let them—" She pointed over her shoulder. "—know it was me. Here, you didn't really attack that Mr Dan, did you? No, no." She waggled her hands in disbelief at her own question. "Sorry I asked. This is a very peculiar place."

As I looked at the door code on the paper, as potent as a magic spell, she said something that instantly made me tear-up: "Good luck, Molly Turner."

After lunch, I asked where the nice temporary carer had got to, because I thought it was less suspicious than not asking, but my query was met with shrugs. I knew, even if they didn't. She had found the truth and was keeping out of the way for her own safety.

I decided not to pass the code to the men immediately. If we escaped using that code, it would be obvious someone had given it to us, and Margaret, being someone new who hadn't lasted five minutes, might well be suspected and put in danger. I really didn't want any more innocents hurt because of me.

14. Runaway Gran

I was never interviewed by police (big surprise) but Amber came back after three days, much to my delight and relief.

Her sudden absence had not had anything to do with me. Earl had been rushed into hospital with appendicitis and she'd needed emergency time off to care for him.

It had been the most fortunate appendicitis anyone had ever had, as far as I was concerned, as I might never have got the door code otherwise. And it had incidentally helped her too.

Red had been so worried about Earl, she said, that the whole situation had gone a bit comical, like a Laurel and Hardy film where people (namely him) had been running around like headless chickens not knowing what to do. She hadn't been sure which of the two males in her life had needed most comforting, but it had proven to her that Red—kind, considerate and bush-butchering Red—was the man for her.

"Right," she said after breakfast, a conspiratorial glint in her eyes. "I need *you* to cover for *me* today. *You* asked for a ride out, right? So we're off down the road at *your* request, if anyone asks. I want to pop home, just to check on Earl. He's home but still feeling a bit poorly."

"If you want more time, let me walk," I suggested, keen for the activity. "One stick, two sticks, a frame? All nice and slow and careful."

She shook her head. "No sticks and supports allowed outside the home. Wheelchairs only. Come on. Nice day for a pretty dress, I think. An' if you behave yourself we'll stop and get you a nice puzzle book, okay?"

"So you lock me up in here, but I am free to go out. This is a place of contradictions."

She laughed. "Life's a bloody contradictory thing if you

ask me. C'mon, let's get you ready."

Outside, I breathed easy, wearing a dress in a bright flower-print (a dress I had never seen before in my life), the sunshine and birdsong filled me, life magically slipping to normal as she trundled me down the road in my chariot.

"Now tell me," I said. "Is this trip really so you can talk to me about why you called me Molly the other day?"

"I don't remember doing that. Sit back and admire the scenery. Just look at that pink flowery bush."

"I remember it well. I'm the prisoner. Are you my hope?"

"Another word and I'll turn round and take Mr Potts out instead. It was Mr Dan's turn but…"

"Indeed. You can't take Mr Dan out. I was accused of his attack, you know. My fairy was found in his room."

"I heard. No one got any idea who did it. He weren't a very nice man."

I had a sudden idea. Had someone attacked him so he'd be taken to hospital, so be out of there?

"How is he now?" I asked, expecting no more than to be told he'd vanished.

"Oh, he's carked it," Amber said calmly.

"What?"

"Yeah, didn't you know? I thought the whole home must."

I fell silent.

"You okay, Mary?"

I told her how I had been treated by the night carers and that I suspected them of stealing Fairy to frame me for murder.

She sighed heavily. "Maybe. I'd rather not be accusing anyone though."

I shrugged in resignation. "Okay. How old is Earl?"

"Older and wiser than the hills" she said flippantly. "So he says, the cheeky little bugger."

"Home alone?"

"Nooo… got a friend watching him."

"That's a relief."

"You think I'd leave a kid on his own? When he's just come out the hospital? Come on, Mary, give me some credit."

Her house was a small, mid-terrace, run-down building with peeling paintwork and a forecourt of chipped stone. On the driveway sat a car, an old brown Range Rover, a large and muddy vehicle that looked like it had yomped through winter fields then collapsed for a long sleep.

She saw my head turn to evaluate it.

"Red bought it for me. It's a bit crap, but don't look a gift horse in the mouth, kind of thing. He was a dear for getting it. It's all legal and goes like a bomb to the shops, but why drive to work when I can walk on these lovely days, eh?"

"Indeed. And a vehicle of such innate charm. Why bother to wash it?"

"You're in no position to be a critic, so shut up," she snapped as I touched a sensitive spot. She must really like the man. Parking the wheelchair on the path, she put on the brakes then unlocked the faded blue front door.

A curly-headed poppet instantly clamped himself onto her leg with a whimper of, "Mummy, Mummy, Janny said I have to do some practice spellings but I still feel really sick, I really do."

Amber gave a heavy sigh, one that spoke of parental responsibilities vying with work's requirements. "Just be a minute, Mary. Stay put, please!" She vanished into the house leaving me in a nice patch of sunshine that made me sleepy.

I rubbed the itchy needle marks high on my upper arm. I had only noticed them the last couple of days, sure I was being doped again, perhaps a needle slipped into my arm as I slept. What for, though?

'Maybe,' I thought, 'if I walk off really fast I can escape down the road, turn the corner, vanish.' Sure it would get the girl into big trouble, and I was sorry about that, but I had to think of myself first, and she had Red to help her should she get dismissed.

So I stood up, got to the end of the path, then walked

down the slight slope of the lane with one hand on a wire mesh fence to keep me steady. I was doing pretty well until I moved too fast on a tight corner and found my feet crossing over each other. My heart began to thump, I lost control of my legs and careened into a thick garden hedge. As I tried to extricate myself I checked around for the man with the camera but he wasn't in attendance that day. Angry Amber cries came from behind me, and she grabbed my arms to help my balance as I plonked myself down on the path with no measure of grace.

"Sometimes I think you're bloody bonkers," she gasped. "You need a watcher as much as Earl does 'cause you just have to get yourself into trouble. I told you to stay."

"I'm not a dog," I grumped, quite comfortable on the warm tarmac. "I am a cat, and I shall go wheresoever I wish. Unless you tell me why you called me Molly."

She pulled a peeved face. "Nutter. Because you kept saying that was your real name, right? So it just slipped out, okay? Now shut up about that and *stay here* while I get the wheelchair, and never let on this happened." She waggled a warning finger at me. "You know all this stuff you pull doesn't just have consequences for you, don't you? Think of little Earl with an unemployed mum and how hard it'd be for us if Red don't stick around, and it'd all be your fault, okay?"

"Some things are definitely my fault," I said quietly, believing it. "Shouldn't have taken the short cut at uni, shouldn't have let myself be duped by good looking men, and shouldn't have led children into trouble with me."

"Now what you going on about? You're safe as long as you do what I say. Now stay here and don't crawl off or something equally ridiculous." She backed away up the rise, looking daggers at me all the time, grabbed the wheelchair and ran back with it. "Sit!"

"Still not a dog," I said, but I wilted into the chair, for some reason once again plagued by all the awfulness of my past, playing and replaying scenes in my head as the view of the lane and houses around me seemed to tremble like a heat haze. I rubbed my arm again. "Who's been jabbing me? Tablets *and* injections? What are they for?"

"I dunno. I did check up on your meds; you know, like you asked me to. Nothing odd that I can see. You've been on the same stuff for ages, but no injections."

"What are these, then?" I demanded, hitching up my sleeve to show the offending marks. "If they're not injection marks, are you suggesting they're mosquito bites?"

Amber stopped pushing and ran a delicate hand over the sore area. "That is sort of odd," she agreed. "Maybe you *have* been scratching some bites. They weren't there when I dressed you earlier."

"Yes, they were. They've been there a few days."

"I can't believe I wouldn't have noticed them."

"You haven't been here the past few days, and I mainly dress myself, so be useful and look up my meds again. There's something odd going on here." I fixed her gaze. "And I think you know it."

"All I know is you're a naughty one, so no puzzle book for you. Straight back to St Amelia's."

~

Back home at the 'home', I walked out of the dayroom with my stick and gazed fondly down at the central garden in the glory of midday sun. The cat lounged in the shade of a bush, stretched out to her full luxurious length. I wanted to go and pet that white floofy tummy, smoothing my cares away in the act.

A tall black carer helped a tottering female resident using a walking frame to sit on a bench in the shade of a tree, then sat with her, leaning close, the resident smiling happily at whatever she was being told. 'That's the way it should be,' I thought.

Meanwhile, the gardener, head shaded Bedouin-style with his red scarf, showed a chubby shaven face as he tended to the straggly branches of a Philadelphus bush—though tend was not the right word for the secateur-hacking that I witnessed. I wanted to open the window and yell, 'You're doing it all wrong'. I wanted to go down and show him how it was done properly. I could only hope for Amber's sake he was better with vegetables than he was with flowers, dear me.

From the milky haze of the hot day, a figure emerged from behind the cherry tree and stepped between the rose bushes. Big and bushy bearded, I gasped in sharp recognition as he walked up behind Red in three long strides, grabbed the shovel out of the barrow and bashed him across the back of the head—

I rapped madly on the window. "Up here. Up here!" I called. Hugo had come for me.

"What you seeing, Mum?" The familiar voice made me jump and I turned to see Barry lounging nearby on a walking stick, peering out of the window, trying to follow my gaze.

"Good heavens," I said. "I'm going to have to get you a collar and bell or you'll give me a heart attack."

Looking back to where Red was still snipping at the bush, I realised no attack had occurred, just some weird illusion had afflicted me, and I found myself happy for Amber that her beau was still alive, and crippling despair for me. No Hugo in white knight mode.

"I thought I saw something odd," I said. "How are you? So sorry about you know what."

"Guess you 'ad to do it. Jest one night in the hole. Had worse."

I wasn't sure I wanted to know exactly what form of punishment the hole was.

"You didn't bump off Mr Dan, then?"

"Nah, funny thing that, but don't mourn him. Were a real nasty bloke."

"I imagined we were all good guys caught by the bad guys."

"Kinda, but not all."

Moving down the corridor with him shadowing close behind, I asked, "Any brilliant escape plans concocted yet?" I smacked my lips. "There's a funny taste in my mouth. I think I'm being given a little *extra*, if you know what I mean."

Why drug me? Surely they need me alert to pry into the minds of the men?

He shook his head morosely. "I think the three of us need to rub heads a wee bit more. Great minds, and all that."

From down the corridor laughter echoed, the carers with their complex lives of families and fun and freedom, but not for me, not for any of us in the home. I wanted to cry for all of us.

We walked slowly back to my room, like two old codgers with stooped backs, walking sticks tapping beside us. The place was affecting us badly. Barry had to be a good twenty years younger than me, but he was as frail as an autumn leaf, just hanging on until the wind of evil intent blew him away.

"Never doubt your own eyes," whispered a disembodied voice, and with a start I thought I saw a grinning effigy of the major stepping back through a closed door.

"You alright, Mum?" Barry asked, frowning, looking where my gaze was focussed in despair.

"I'm hallucinating." My lower lip began to tremble. I opened my door and hobbled to the bed, no deceit in my gait. "We can't even try to escape unless I am one hundred percent sure I'm lucid, balanced, clear headed enough to go." The room did a slow ballet around me as I gently lowered myself to the bed. A high-pitched whine rang in my head, in my ears, through my body.

Barry's concerned face loomed over me like the moon, then went away along with everything else.

~

I woke tucked up in bed in my darkened room, the only sign of movement the curtains playing in the breeze from the open window. I had no recollection of being put in my nightclothes; nothing. A big horrible blank.

Thirsty, I reached for the bedside cup and found it empty so stood up carefully, then I thought I saw the major standing up from the easy chair, an image that flickered and faded as I realised I had no glasses on and it was Barry in the half light.

"Water," I said simply, turning slowly back to the bed; turning, turning, almost falling, until Barry was behind me, holding my upper arms in a firm and supportive grip.

"Get y'self down on that bed again," he insisted. "Y' shaking. Rest up. We'll talk soon enough. I'm jest going to stay here a while longer, keep an eye on you, Mum."

"Why're you calling me mum?"

"Yer nice like a mum, see?"

So I lay back as he got me some water. Comforted by the idea that someone cared enough to call me mum and look out for me, I closed my eyes and remembered what Hugo and I had got up to after Barnes; things I was sure had happened, no illusions, no lies; truths.

15. Pond Wishes

Hugo and I had taken the essentials off the house bus and dumped it just like we had the Micra, then bought a car under a false name to wander around the lesser roads of Britain for a week or two, not admiring the views but trying to get our heads into a place where we could decide on the next course of action.

Hugo had been in a bad place mentally, and me too in my own way. I had already lost so much at Hartpury, then Kerton, and now my cat had vanished too, not to mention that Hugo had lost his partner of many years. Not knowing where someone is, is far worse than the finality of death. So although Hugo picked fights with me over silly things, I guessed it was only his stress showing, and I treated him kindly so a strong bond grew between us in those grieving days.

Eventually, I had spotted an advert for a resident cook and handyman for a lady. Former employers' references faked with ease—I may have missed my calling—we got the job in a not so built-up village. Just what we needed. A little dilapidated garden for me to play with, an overgrown pond, a collapsing greenhouse, and a kind gentlewoman who paid us for our work and let us live in her annexe. It was exactly the kind of thing I could get my organising teeth into; get my mind into a better place, get it firing on all cylinders again.

Hugo, not so dumb as he sometimes sounded, got books and tools off the Internet and learned DIY.

We had almost a year of lovely peace and quiet. Despite the obvious age difference, Hugo was on the cuff of being a late child for me, and no one asked. He had even taken to calling me Mum. I had liked that. Those were good days. I remembered them with affection, but I thought it both odd and sad that I had come to trust Hugo more than I did Gavin, my officially adopted—

"Mary, it's time to get up."

Yanked back painfully from the time when I had been happy and hale and hearty, I woke back in the body of the old woman. I could feel my mind whirring with confusion, images of Hugo and rose bushes mixing on the plain yellow walls around me like flickering scenes from an old cinema, telling me I was drugged again. Even moving my arms was hard.

Amber's smiling face swam into view. "Nice cup of tea for you, Mary, and a little surprise. Look. Brought you a packet of choccy biccies. Keep them hidden, okay?"

She helped me to sit up then breezed out. I looked at the pack of biscuits with a wordless gratitude, then stared at the cup of tea on my bed tray and wondered what subtle poison might lurk in its murky depths... Contradictions. One carer who cared and others who might well cheer if I passed away.

~

I'd found tarnished coins while cleaning out the lady's pond. She said the local children threw them in, using it as a wishing well. When I told Hugo, he had solemnly thrown in a shiny silver fifty pence.

"Oi, you," I said playfully. "I'm trying to get stuff out, not in."

"Jest wishing," he said, face solemn, thoughts hidden behind his bushy beard.

"What are you wishing for?"

"Don't come true if you tell, right?"

"I think that refers to wishing on birthday candles."

"Thinking we can't stay 'ere forever, Mum. Don't get me wrong, I likes it, but wishing for things to move on. It's not the future I'd imagined."

Later, when the cleaning out had been accomplished, I fed Hugo's coin back to the pond fairies and added a copper-silver pound of my own, wishing for him to find the peace I had wrongly assumed he had. A young man's dreams are not going to be the same as an old woman's.

"Mary. Time to getting up," chirped Mila's voice.

I woke with a start. *What? Not again!*

How many days were passing as I existed, half asleep, half awake, barely aware of them, losing any details that might have happened in those incognizant states? If this was someone's idea of torment, it was working. How could I get out of its vicious cycle? *Have I upset Richard with my lack of progress? Is this some kind of punishment from him?*

Staggering to the toilet, I washed away the tea, and I felt better for doing that but still felt I was going crazy like that popular poster which says, 'You don't have to be mad to work here but it helps'.

My poster would say, 'If you're not mad when you come here, you soon will be'.

I had lost, according to the helpful TV, only three muddled days. It was now the beginning of August, hot and sticky, and I was not, to the best of my knowledge, insane just yet.

I was very surprised later to hear the cat scratching at my door. I unlocked it and she pushed in, curling around my legs with affectionate noises. As I crouched and stroked her silky head, I saw with a joyous little gulp the slight trace of tiger stripes in the fur between her ears; stripes that confirmed her identity as much as her asking to come in. She purred and licked my hand, then put her front paws up on my leg and snuffled into my dressing gown pocket, remembering the treats I used to keep in other dressing gowns, in other towns, other lives.

"Oh, Misty," I whispered, tears clouding my eyes. I wiped them with the tissues from the other pocket. "I knew it was you. There are no cat-nibbles in these pockets, I'm afraid."

I wanted to grab her, to claim her as mine again, but I was afraid that if I did that someone would make her go away permanently. So I kissed her little ears and was about to persuade her to leave when the door moved and Barry's voice hissed, "Ey up?" as he came in.

"New friend?" he asked with a touch of amusement when he spied the cat. "Lord knows we need some."

"My cat; Misty," I said. "These weirdos are not beneath kidnapping cats too."

He stroked her long body. She meowed at him. "Nice little moggy," he said. "I like cats." He straightened up. "You open for visitors? Got some things t' say. You've been out of it for a while. We could tell."

"Sure, but do me a favour. Take Misty and put her on the stair-side of the connecting door. I don't think it's safe for her to be seen with me."

"Right-o." He scooped her up delicately and walked off cradling her like a baby.

When he came back he said, "Could hear her calling from behind it. She likes you a fair bit."

"Used to follow me through the fields when I walked," I said in fond remembrance, "back in the good old days. Now, what do you need to say because I am really tired again, though it is nice to see you. You and Jeff been messed around again, too?"

"Been messed around bad, now I'm jest lonely," he said, as miserable for company as Misty had been. "Thought we could 'ave a natter."

"Just a natter? Thought it might be something important. If you're caught in here again, I'll have to deny you again."

"Aye, Miss Perfect, you follow the rules, be a good girl, dontcha worry 'bout us."

"We have to look out for ourselves."

He flopped onto the floor, back to the bed like a dog that is refusing to go out, so I didn't shoo him.

After a moment he said, "You like me, don't you? I'm not shit in yer eyes?"

"I don't *dislike* you. What are you getting at?"

"Me mum, she told me to get lost." He made an odd little

noise like a sob. "Afore I got in here, she wouldna talk to me; called me a stinkin' criminal. If she'd a-liked me a bit more I reckon I'd a never gone that way."

The bed frame trembled as he began to cry silently.

"Dammit," I said, and I slipped out of bed to sit by him and held him while he had a good bawl and told me of his rotten life and kept calling me mum, until he felt better and I began to wish he'd let go.

Then his mood turned about and he started telling jokes as we sat there in the almost dark, making me laugh a little as he chuckled quietly at his own bad jokes, trying to lift both our spirits. I was cheerful enough with him, but caution kept me from calling him a real friend, afraid he'd turn out to have done something terrible, so I asked him straight out why he thought he was there, what awful thing had he done in the past to bring such ire down on him. He went silent for a moment before he said, "If ah tell you, you won't ever talk t' me again."

I snorted. "My trust in humanity has eroded to emptiness, so nothing would surprise or shock me anymore. What dire thing did you do?"

I had hoped, of course, that his answer would be whatever the doctor wanted to hear, but all he said was...

"Ah lost a dug."

"Dug?"

"Aye, this total soppy lass, Karen was. Crosswell Lady Karen something or t'other. Woulda gone with anyone."

"Oh, Karen's a dog. Whose was she?"

"Weird chap named Doc Sanderson. The major's boy, you know?"

"Oh lord; yes, I do. I can imagine that would get you into trouble with him. Couldn't you get Karen back, then?"

He shook his head, hair flopping like spaniel's ears. "Ah was s'posed to be exercising her, but I oped the car door and off she went trotting into the sunset. Her, her pedigree, the pups she were carrying... all gone. Tried everything: dog homes, Facebook, Twitter, poliss, no luck." He gave me a distressed, tortured smile, full of regret and pain. "That dug were pain in ma backside, but I'd never hurt her. And the Doc, he went mental an' shoved me in here."

"That man is mental at the best of times. I wouldn't be surprised if he thinks you dognapped Karin to get the revenue from the pups."

"That'd be a bad move if I had! Who'd be feeding her wiv me in here? More harm than good." He shook his head. "Stupid man's off his trolley."

"I can't imagine why you think losing a dog's bad enough for me to stop talking to you."

"Cause anything coulda happened to her. Anything, and... Guess I'm ashamed; 'specting to be hated."

I almost laughed aloud. Barry was the opposite of a hard man, as soppy as the dog. *Richard, if all you need to know from this man is the whereabouts of your expensive lady dog, I think you are going to be very much out of luck. Regret and remorse, yes, you'll get that, but I don't think he knows where Lady Karen is.*

"Oooh, I nearly forgot. I got ya a gift." Barry beamed as he handed me a snooker ball from his pocket. I rolled its smooth red coldness in my hands.

"Thank you. Just what I've always wanted."

He huffed a laugh. "Got it from the ground floor's table. Put it in a sock or summit; make a cosh."

"A weapon? How thoughtful." I tapped its solid hardness on my head. "I haven't got any socks, only tights. Would it kill?"

"You want it to?"

"No, no, just inquiring."

"I sees you Molly," he laughed. "Reckon we've got more in common than many would think."

I grinned back. He had me sussed. The way I felt about some of the people in that place, being whopped with a ball in a sock might be a good cure for their heartlessness.

~

The next night, both Barry and Jeff both crept in and the three of us bandied around escape ideas, but I discovered Jeff was angry with me. He'd overheard that my little jaunt to the supermarket was going to result in CCTV cameras being set up at exits, making any escape plans harder.

"But why?" I complained, trying to defend myself. "We can't be the only ones who've tried to escape. How come they're only installing cameras now? You'd think they'd be *de rigueur* in a place like this."

"De riggy-what?" Barry asked. I waved a dismissive hand. We weren't there for lessons in language.

After a moment's thought Jeff said, "That's not the issue. Maybe they *have* escaped. Staff wouldn't advertise it, but it's us that gotta escape before new feckin' cameras watch us all the time, so *think*."

"More to the point," Barry jumped in, "is how come just we three en't permanently drugged anymore? Some of the others may be not so deep in shit as they look, but it's just us who are up to wandering at night, isn't it?"

I could guess the answer to the *not-drugged* question, though I wouldn't tell them. It was probably because, if the men were out of it, they couldn't tell me anything. I didn't like that line of thought. I felt so vulnerable. If I told the truth, would Barry be using snooker balls in socks on me? Would Jeff use those big hands to...?

I pretended to feel sicker than I did, and they left.

~

In the day room I would stare at the other residents and hope they'd look back, but the only person who had even a glint of life in his eye was a fairly young man with a long ponytail, whose bedroom door I had seen labelled: Mr A Potts. On that occasion, he was awake and moaning softly to himself like a child having a dream. He caught my eye and smiled slowly and thoughtfully then looked away again then, with considered and slow movements, he untied his dressing gown belt, put both hands on the arms of the chair, stood and let the gown fall in a heap at his feet. I watched in fascination, half expecting him to take the belt and hang himself. Ready to stop him if he tried.

But he simply wobbled and unbuttoned his pyjama jacket, let it slip to the floor too, and finally dropped his trousers so he stood naked, trembling, though I had looked away by then. "Wa hay," someone said *sotto voce* and, to my amazement, Barry started to undress too, then Jeff, in a slow strip with no reason behind it. An elderly, bearded man smiled broadly and began to undress too, then another man shifted, looked up and began to wrestle with his gown like it was a straitjacket, and I wondered if the group action was serving to break through some of the dulling effects of whatever they were kept down with.

Soon there were seven naked men wandering around the dayroom like zombies, colliding with each other, some part of their minds awake but others still asleep, and they stumbled and tripped and one fell into my lap so I shrieked, and Barry—ooh, I could not look—but he hauled the man off my lap. My skin was crawling. I managed to scoop up a discarded dressing gown and covered myself with it, barely tolerating the pungent man-smell of it, putting up a woolly wall against the weird display, not willing to try to get back to my room while the walking dead trundled slowly around and around.

No staff showed for quite a few minutes, then Mila swung open the door and took a reverse step in alarm, yelling backwards for help, and the room became a kind of Dodgems stage with staff trying to catch bare arms and zombies almost knocking carers over, their faces shining with the joy of their game.

In all the chaos, Barry and Jeff sat down, put their PJs back on, and Barry winked broadly across at me, at which point I realised it was some plan they had actioned.

By the time the other naked walkers had been sedated and felled, Barry and Jeff were sitting in quiet innocence.

The almost empty dayroom slumped back into a calm but satisfied gloom, and the carers who had wrestled clothing back onto its owners left scowling, as if that was our punishment.

16. A Hole In One

The same day as the stripping incident, I was off for my nightly look-round, peering out through the curtains now and then, when movement in the darkened garden caught my eye. A man was approaching the well. From the outline I saw as my eyes adjusted, I guessed it was the gardener.

Yes, it was Red walking across the crazy paving, with big spades resting over his shoulders... no, one was a pickaxe. He approached the bench closest to the well, lodged the pickaxe into something on the ground and elevated the end of the bench up to about forty-five degrees, then used the spade to hold it up.

He stepped back, took off his scarf and wiped his brow, looked around then strode off towards one of the corner tunnels.

I stayed still, watching, puzzled heart beating hard, ears tuned to the possible sound of doors.

Five minutes later Red reappeared, dragging along a male body by its feet.

From the evidence of the dangling pony tail, I realised it was Mr Potts.

Red hauled the poor man along the path and rolled him inelegantly into the hole, eased the bench back to level and ambled off, shovel and pick axe over his shoulders again, and I could imagine him whistling, *Hi ho, hi ho!* like some evil dwarf.

That was my first view of what they called the hole, but all I could think was, *Poor Amber; she doesn't know what Red is like at all. Though, if he's in on the shenanigans going on here, is she too? That would explain why she called me Molly.*

Oh dear. Has another possible ally bitten the dust?

Barry made me jump as he walked up beside me, soft-footed as a cat.

"I really am going to get you a blooming bell," I declared,

one hand to my heart. "Say *Hi* or *Oi* or something before you startle elderly ladies. And you can only come into my room if you promise to keep your clothes on."

In the safety of my room, I asked, "That hole under the bench. Is that where they put the naughty boys and girls? If so, I'm sorry you had to suffer it for a night because of me. And why'd Mr Potts do all that run around in your birthday suit palaver when he'd have known, wouldn't he, that they'd shove him in there? And what about the other strippers?"

"They mess wiv us, we mess wiv them. Be another chap's turn in t' hole tomorra. Fun, though, weren't it?" He gave a broad, big toothed smile, then leaned forwards and rubbed his eyes. "Doubt it'll be the last lot of shenanigans while we have any fight left in us. Sides, you notice how many peeps were in and outta that room?"

"What do you mean?"

"While all the dancing and wobbling were going on, pockets got themselves pinched. Purloining, to put it politely, several items of interest." He grinned victoriously.

"I did wonder what it was all about."

"You'd be amazed how thick some of the uniforms are. They notice something missing, they're too scared to admit it. Win-win for Alfred Potts and the rest of the gang. That's why they don't do pass-cards. We'd 've nicked one as quick as you can say what's yer fancy." He yawned widely and noisily. "I canna sleep. But I'm so tired."

"I appear to be doing the opposite. Can't stop falling asleep."

He laughed. "It's in the coffee, it's in the tea, it's in the dinner, we canna escape. Drugs... they're all around us!" He sounded a tad crazy and suddenly grabbed my hand and pulled me into a bear hug that scared me.

I drew back quickly. "I have to ask you something," I said cautiously. "Jeff said you attacked a girl."

"Nah," he said, disgust on his face from the question or the memory, I couldn't tell which. "Freakin' bitch said she'd yell rape if I didn't give her more money. I didn't, she did. Long time ago. Learned from it."

I had witnessed something similar happen with Hugo, all lies from the female, so I wanted to trust and believe in Barry just like I had Hugo. "Okay, now you can hug me."

"Don't let Jeff hug y', though. He's the one y' gotta look out for. Cold blooded killer he is. Only person he's ever cared for's that there Gwen."

"Hmm... thanks for the warning." I didn't have to like him, and he didn't have to like me. We just had to help each other get out.

Barry managed to pull at my heartstrings, though. He was suffering and he needed a cuddle, that was all, so I let him hug me until he broke away of his own accord, swiped a hand across his eyes and muttered, "Sorry, Mum."

"Any time you have your clothes on," I said.

He chuckled, waved and went off, and I wondered how the big lumbering man had cured my fear of being touched. Life certainly did work in odd ways.

I went to see Jeff's wife; found Jeff coming out of her room. We both jumped. He relaxed, let out a sigh and leaned back against the closed door.

"No change," he said, his voice deep with whispering. He looked over his shoulder as if he could see through the door; see Gwen in the room. "I dunno what they've done to her; or if she's got real aging problems. All I know is, she was fine before all this started."

"She'll wake, Jeff," I said as encouragingly as I could, though not believing my own words. "You'll see, when I manage to get out and get the troops it will all be okay."

"What *troops*?" he mocked. "The cops'll laugh and bring you back with a bow on."

I huffed. "Give me some hope! If I don't try, I won't know, and I've got friends out there—" I realised I had little chance of finding Hugo on my own but I had sparked a glimmer of hope in Jeff so I barrelled on. "Well, contacts anyway, and they'll help as soon as I can alert them, you'll see."

"I hope you're right. I really do."

His eyes were deep in their red brown sockets, painted with all the pain he must be feeling. But he snorted cynically and continued scanning the corridors like he was John Wick.

Hairs pickled on my neck at a distant sound. "Someone's coming."

He looked at me with a frown, disbelieving, then moving, indicating for me to follow. We managed to get to the ground floor and the small unlit conservatory, exit doors locked of course.

"Listen..." The word hissed in that gloomy, glassy place. "You have to go back to being dumb. Play your game. Wait for me to tell you what to do, not all this wandering around on your own. Some of the staff are armed," he went on. "Not guns; needles. You show you know too much and they'll jab you. Write it in the day book for the big man to laugh as he reads."

"Big man?"

"Yeah." His head bobbed in the dimness. "We're a circus act, Molly. Here for someone's fun, so we are kept down defenceless and embarrassed, so he can laugh when he reads that you shat your pants or fell in the corridor or didn't get rations."

"You know this for a fact, or it's your theory?"

"Half way between," he replied.

I told him about being filmed.

"Proves one of my theories, then," he said. "You sure the asshole was related to this place?"

"Yes, because I've seen him more than once. I reckoned they're laughing at the Candid Camera shots over their coffee."

He wiped his face with his hands. "God is gone," he said dramatically with an unwarranted glare at me. "His angels have fallen, the devils rise and there is no hope here unless we can find some fucking weapons and work out how to get rid of everyone who stands in our way."

"I wouldn't know how to plot to kill anyone. I killed the

major by accident, another man in an emotional moment, but to contemplate murder coldly and slowly, that's not me."

"They used to call me the canyon cowboy," he said.

"Why?"

"Because I chucked people off mesas. Bad guys; fun times. Best days of my life." He smiled lopsidedly then winked at me. "Apart from the honeymoon."

I was about to reply with an ill-considered response, when he said, "By the way, it was me stole your fairy."

I glared. "Why were you trying to frame me?"

His eyes were fixed on my frowning face. "I didn't trust you. Why should I? Figured if you were on the other side, they'd not make a fuss 'bout you offing someone, but it caused a real ruckus so obviously—"

"You despicable—"

"Hey, shut it. He was a monster; had it coming. You seem to live in a black and white world—"

"Hardly."

"But Mr Dan, as they called him, he was shit and I wiped the world's ass for it."

"How kind of you," I began, ready to drown him in sarcasm, but he suddenly held up a finger for silence and mouthed widely, 'Someone's out there.'

After a few minutes silence we exited the room and parted. He clapped me on the back. I suppose it was meant to be reassuring, and in a way it was, as I felt not only a painful slap but a final acceptance that I was one of the team.

I would say I have seen more darkness in these last few years than at any other time in my life, times that taught me it's safer to be my own motivator, have to find my own way, my own stepping stones, being the only person I know I can depend on no matter what others might claim, but that mind set was fading as I was only too glad to have Jeff and Barry beside me, dog-losers, thieves and murderers or whatever they might be.

17. Confession

I experienced an incredible lurch of my heart and more resolve to get the hell out when I saw Mr Potts being wheeled into the day room. There was a disturbed look about him. Not the slightest bit blank, his eyes flitted around the room as if searching for escape, lips trembling, hands clasping and unclasping. His eyes met mine with nervous twitches and he looked away, shifting sideways in his chair to avoid my gaze.

As I sipped my insipid tea, I found myself thinking about the hole, wondering if I could stand it, were I to be punished that way.

Shortly, I asked if I could sit in the garden, even the idea of the hole giving me claustrophobic thoughts, and once out there I chose the bench closest to the well. I peered over the low wall, seeing grass less than three feet down and a small grille in the side below ground level, a drain I supposed. Though not designed to hold water, the well still made me shudder with remembrances of another stinky well some years before, so I turned my face to the sun and let it warm me.

When a tall, well-groomed and neatly dressed man exited the conservatory door and walked smartly towards me, I doubted my eyes. My heart stopped, then sprang into palpitations as he took a seat beside me.

"Gavin?" I reached for my son, my *real* son, excited, fearing an illusion. "Are you here? Are you really here? Are you going to take me home? Please take me back. I'm sorry I left. You won't believe what's going on in this place."

"Mum, shush," he said, looking around. "Yes, I know what's going on here, it's all Doc Richard's mucking about, but you'll have to put up with it for a while longer, capeesh? You have to get something he wants, or you'll put me in a bit of a bind. Listen, I told him you could do this, so do it, and we can be a family again."

I sat back, furious. "You are my son. You should be defending me, not letting me be manipulated by a loony like him!"

He drew in a huge breath and held it so I hastened on with, "And if he's the boss, and he wants me to do this stuff, why doesn't he stop them shoving gunk into my veins. I feel awful; sick. I've lost so much weight. My hair's falling out. I hallucinate."

"Well, that's the...umm."

"What?"

"The meds you have to take."

"What? My heart pills? They never did anything like that to me before."

He looked at me furtively. "No one's told you, have they?" He turned away and muttered, "Buggers're leaving it to me."

"What? Sit up and speak clearly."

"You've got cancer. You haven't much time to—"

I held up a silencing hand. "Don't worry, I'm used to the idea already. It might be a release. Might stop all this idiocy."

"Mum." He grabbed my hand. "You have to try for *us*. For me and Vana and the kids. You don't know what Richard—"

"Of course I know what he's like. I know what the whole sordid business is like better than anyone."

"So be a good mum and do what they say. Don't take too long, then we can be together again for as much time as you've got, with the family that loves you."

"Visit more. It'll make it bearable. Why haven't you visited before?"

He shook his head condescendingly. "I've visited a few times. You were out of it, so I guess you just don't remember."

I stared. "Yes, I can believe that, so I will try to be busy and patient *and* tolerant. Now, tell me, how are the children?"

"Collin's improving gradually. Still in the General. The girls miss you. They'll be glad to see you back after this. Okay, sorry for the quick visit but I have to go. Okay? Love you. Bye." He gave me a peck on the cheek and left me hot and flushed at his words.

Something's so wrong here. Prickles had been running up and down my spine since he had mentioned Vana. Richard had said she'd chucked out Gavin, and shown me the picture of the very much not-comatose sandcastle-building Collin. Also, Gavin never kissed me. He barely ever returned my 'love yous'.

So now what the hell was going on? Was that man with the camera watching? Did they want me to bellow insanely and thrash around again for their viewing pleasure? Did they want to see me in frustrated agony from being told I was dying —which I wasn't too worried about considering my current problems, and maybe wasn't even true. So, to make them happy, and in case Gavin was still somewhere close enough to hear, I put my head back and let out one long loud wail that echoed off the walls, sent some jackdaws cackling skywards, and I felt so much better for it.

~

"I have a confession," I said to the men as I sat in bed propped up by pillows, trying to look like a harmless little old lady. Jeff was seated on my chair and Barry on the floor, his long legs stretched out before him. The room still held the warmth of twilight, and the overhead lamp dimmer was on its lowest setting. Such a cosy setting for such a difficult confession.

"Go ahead, Mum," Barry said.

I wished Jeff wasn't sitting so close but, if I were dying, maybe his anger would see me out quicker. It's not easy for me to live a lie, no matter how simple the bad guys make it look.

"Do you know who Doctor Richard Sanderson is?" I asked Jeff and braced myself.

It was Barry who replied, "Major Sanderson's lad; nasty piece o' work. You know I lost his dug."

"Never heard of him," said Jeff. "Why?"

Here we go. "He's asked me to spy on you two."

Jeff got up with a jerky hurriedness that almost knocked the chair over.

I jumped despite my preparation, but he stopped, folded his arms and glowered down at me. "He *what*?"

"He thought you'd spill the beans to a little old lady but I've not even told him that we're in contact, but I'll feed him false info if you think it's a good idea."

"So why the fuck're you telling us?" Jeff asked. His arms were still folded but I could see his fists clenching and unclenching. "I knew there was something off about you."

"I'm trusting he won't find out I've told you. Look, I've been told I'm on the way out. There's hard working tired, and then there's drugged tired, and I'm in the latter state. Whatever I've got, they're either trying to hit it hard so I can spy for the doctor, or it's part of his plan—that you two feel lulled into complacency by my illness; that you'll open up to me if I'm enfeebled. I'm sick to my stomach, my head thumps and my muscles don't always work properly. It's hard to pretend anything."

They were staring at me. I sniffed and sighed heavily. Weary again.

"Anyway, that's why I decided I would rather risk your wrath and have you kill me, than live like that. I want us to be able to trust each other with no secrets."

"You'd best be glad you're a senior citizen," Jeff said. "I think I might be letting you have a second chance."

"Yes," I smiled wanly. "Your fists have been telling me that for a few minutes now. I think you now know the answer to why just we three are fully awake. Any other questions I can answer? Barry? You've been very quiet."

He got up like a spider unravelling its legs and opened his arms to me, hugged me and cried while Jeff looked on with a mix of disgust and humour on his face.

"Oh, Mum, Mum," the smelly man-child Barry gasped against my ear. "We'll look out fer you. Don't y' worry."

I pushed him off gently. "I have the door code," I said, but I didn't say how long I'd had it.

"Give." Jeff held out a weary, demanding hand.

"It's in my head. I made a rhyme of it."

"You better be right."

"Gratitude oozes from your every pore," I said, and recited the rhyme to him.

He repeated it twice then said. "If they think this one's been compromised, they'll re-set all the doors so we have to choose a good time to go."

"I'll leave it in your capable hands then," I said, "because I think by the time we escape I'll be too weak to walk. Look, please, find me some not-so-important secret I can pass to the horrid doctor. Something that'll take him a while to verify or I'll be in even more trouble for not giving him anything."

Then the effort of speaking and hoping, and the relief of not being killed by the men I was supposed to betray, dragged my mind down into an exhausted sleep again, but it was nice to feel cared for, to feel Barry's arms hold onto me again as I began to slip, down, down, into blissful nothingness.

18. Who Doesn't Lie?

I woke to an empty room and a wonderful feeling of freedom. Now free from the worry of deceiving the men, I hadn't realised how much it had weighed on me, but all happiness slipped away as medicine was brought to me before breakfast.

"Down the hatch, Mary," the obnoxious medicine-bearer said, forcing the paper cup into my hand and scrutinizing my actions as I raised it to my lips. "In they go," she went on. "Now take a big gulp of water and swallow them down like a good girl." She examined my mouth with unkind hands. "Good," she said curtly and marched out.

After a moment, making sure she wasn't going to come back and catch me in the act, I dashed—okay, I wobble-stumbled—to the toilet and tried hard to make myself throw up. It was a ghastly feeling and I failed.

"Insert your fingers deeper," said a refined male voice and I span around to look in horror at an image of the major looming over me, fedora at a jaunty angle. "It's too late, Molly," he said, shaking his head patronisingly. "Far too late. It's in your system already, isn't it? Altering your perceptions."

"Piss off," I said to the illusion, though to be fair I've never spoken like that to anyone in my life, not even the bad guys, and some weird, ingrained politeness would not have let me talk to the murderous major like that had he been real.

"Happy to meet me in your last moments, my dear?" he asked sweetly.

"These are not my last moments. You are a delusional illusion and it's almost time for breakfast, so go away."

Darkness was beginning to spread around the room, his hideous smile the last thing I would see unless I looked into the toilet bowl and, *Oh look, he's here too—not my reflection; his.*

Black clouds were growing, the ceiling writhing with

shapes.

From outside, distant devastated cries sounded. Someone was in the bath again. But this time high pitched female screams came too, a wail and lamentation mixed with an agonised woman's disconsolate crying, the like of which I had not heard for many years, and I realised the sounds were mine.

"I'll meet you in the in-between," the major's voice broke in. "That space between awake and asleep where your mind is suspended, malleable, burning and writhing. And there will be more pain when you wake, of that I'll make sure."

As he faded out like the Cheshire cat, his bearded grin echoing in my mind, I slumped to the floor a weak mess of a woman, crying for those who cried outside, or inside, or anywhere.

~

We had liked living in the annexe of the well-to-do lady's house. I'd felt safer than I had for ages, and Hugo recovered slowly, day by day working through his grief and confusion at the loss of George. As I'd always felt with my own son, not knowing where someone is, not knowing if they're alive or dead, is worse torture than knowing they're deceased.

However, after a month or so, Hugo was dating. A girl first, then another girl, then a young man, and although I had no doubt no one would replace George, like no one could ever replace Stanley for me, Hugo at least seemed happy. We were up and away, shady pasts left firmly behind. Life was normal.

But then he found a girl who was the epitome of 'the only fly in the ointment'.

The fly's name had been Graziella, a pretty name for a girl with striking good looks, tall, slim and heavily made up, dyed blonde hair with stylish dark streaks, swooping eyelashes totally fake, but the overall effect was stunning. She worked in the teashop next village over, and I had to wonder how Hugo, my big bearded and shaggy-haired Hugo who looked like a young gorilla with his beetling brow, had managed to attract a girl like her. I will shrug there. Opposites attract.

But he was happy, and I wasn't going to knock that, so I was polite when I met her although I thought she had a mean glint in her eyes, and I watched out for him in true Mama Bear fashion.

Once, you see, she hit Hugo, and he was ashamed to show me the mark. He hadn't done anything to her, he assured me, and I believed him and became even more wary of a woman who'd resort to violence to make her point.

They made up and all was well for a fortnight, but one day I happened to hear them arguing in the back garden, so I softly opened the window a smidge in case I could hear something I could help them with.

What I heard horrified me so much, I instantly began to record it on my phone.

A furious Graziella was telling Hugo in no uncertain terms that he was a liar. He had never had access to a trust fund, and he'd led her on to expect more than he could give financially.

Hugo countered calmly with he'd never said he had money, that his mum (me) had it, but on folding her arms she stood firm and said, "If you don't get me ten grand by tomorra, I'm gonna to say you attacked me. Don't think I won't. I'll scratch meslef, all that lark, and no one will ever want you again with a police record!"

She turned and stormed off round to the side gate.

I intercepted her on the front drive, gave her marching orders while waggling the video in her face, then went to Hugo who sat on the garden bench looking as lost as the day we'd escaped Kerton.

But when I told him what I'd done, he hit the roof.

I had expected gratitude, but in the ensuing argument I discovered that Hugo really didn't think much of himself as a ladies' man. He was so terrified of being partner-less he wanted to find a way to make up with her.

"She'll always be after something," I cautioned him.

"Shaking the money tree to see what drops."

"I really like her. She got spirit, that's all. I wanna provide for her," he said firmly. "Marry her, have a babby or two, bring 'em up proper like I weren't."

"Oh Hugo!" I could have cried at his misplaced trust, his innocent view of love and parenthood. "The path to love is not the one you're on with her."

"Says the one wot fell for Stan whisker-face," he snapped.

"Yes, I admit he duped me and, I say this kindly, as your almost-mother, I think Graziella is duping *you*."

"Nah, she prob'ly having her monthly or summit. She'll calm down, you'll see."

"And if she doesn't? You do *not* want to get hit with the coppers investigating you over an assault claim, Hugo, or they'll find out who you really are and we'll have to move again... if you aren't arrested."

He knew I was right as he grumped off, stomping along the crazy paving in his work boots, hunched over like a small ogre, muttering something to himself, my words having hit the spot, but he didn't want to admit it.

A few days later he was happily going off to the pub to meet a lass called Corinne, or maybe it was a lad called Corin. I couldn't keep up with him, but he seemed happy enough again, so I was too.

~

Strong and firm digging fingers were hurting my skinny arms as I was dragged up from the floor where I had passed out, and the hoist hauled me into bed. They were arguing, those so-called carers, cussing each other for not checking on me sooner, and I laughed out loud... or in my head, I didn't know which. They were going to have to drug me a lot more to keep my nature down.

As they left, I seemed to hear the major's horrid voice hissing in my ears. 'They will kill you, Molly, just like they killed all the others; ignominiously, shamefully, pissing their

345

pants and soiling themselves at the end of their time.'

"Oh dear," I said quietly, unfazed. "That's a rather dramatic prediction, but it worries me not a fiddle, you know, because you're an illusion. I want to sleep. Have peaceful dreams. Go away."

He moved closer, the bedside cupboard becoming his body. 'When someone as innocent as you kills, Molly, you will always have nightmares; always, because something changes inside you. Breaks. Messes up your soul. Believe me.'

He might be right at that.

~

The bedroom door abruptly swung wide. With a start I came to, blinking at the carer with the breakfast trolley. How I hated this hip hopping of days.

"Come on, Mary," the dark eyed woman said; someone new, yet again. The turnover of staff must be furious. This one had a let's-get-everyone-sorted–so-I-can-get-my coffee briskness to her moves. She raised the bed head and helped me to sit up; swung the bed table over my lap and plonked a plate of culinary goodness in front of me: two slices of half burned toast with a scraping of marmalade. "Lucky you, brekkie in bed. Alright for some, innit?" She smirked as she placed a bowl of soggy cereal and a spoon beside the toast.

Yes, so lucky. Alright for those who haven't had their freedom taken from them.

"Got any sherry?" I asked.

She snorted and left. I looked at the rations and thought of my dear friend June. *Tea on her seaside balcony, the playful sea breeze messing with our hair as we laughed, eating freshly picked raspberries with the fading warmth of the sun on them...*

I felt shipwrecked, lost in both time and place.

Barely had the toast met my lips when the door opened and Gavin came in—but not my darling Gavin, no; the Gavin his ill-chosen life had turned him into.

He grabbed the back of the easy chair and almost threw it across the room to sit by the bed, hunched forwards, tension in every part of his body as he snapped, "What're you playing at?"

"Wha—?"

"You know what I mean! You gotta find out what Rich wants. The pressure's on me, Mum. You've got to get that info or you'll kill us all. All of us, Vana, the girls, Collin—think how vulnerable he is in hospital. I know you and Vana didn't get on, but do you really want to see her dead?"

There had been so many lies in that speech I didn't know how to respond.

"I'm sick. It's hard."

"Stop making it all about you," he said, voice spiked with ice. "Think of someone else for a change."

"Okay," I said cautiously. "You can tell Doctor Evil that I have made contact, and please, please ask him to stop with the poison. I'm finding it difficult to stay awake, to think straight. How would you fare at work with that stuff in you?"

"He's trying to keep you alive long enough to do the work, for god's sake. Afterwards you can go to a nice *real* nursing home and be looked after by fairy-tale nurses until you cark it."

I waved a hand. "Whatever. Go away. I don't like seeing you like this. It breaks my heart."

"Yeah, sure." He raged out.

19. Fight Night

To my delight, Amber came in after breakfast. Seeing her cheery, pretty face wreathed in smiles wiped away some of the gloom from Gavin's tirade. "Glad to see you looking bright," she said. "Been worried about you."

"Hello, dear, I've been worried about me too. Going to the day room, are we? What's the date?"

"August twelfth. Time really does fly, and no, you have to stay in here in case you get another fainting fit. Oh my gosh, what's these marks on your arms? They shouldn't handle you so rough."

"Good grief, dear, I've been telling you for days, haven't I? The way people are treated here is downright diabolical."

As she folded down the sheets, she glanced back at me. "I haven't seen anything going on—"

"And you can't do anything unless you witness it personally? Look at these finger marks. I can't have done them to myself, can I? And the needle marks are still appearing. What do you say about that? Report them. It's the night carers who are the bad guys."

"Seen personally; that's the rules. I can't be here off my shift and no way am I gonna to pull a night shift just for you, cute little old lady that you are." She smiled down at me and I felt like crying.

"You could at least report Mila," I suggested. "Whenever she's near me—well, no she goes out of her way to torment me, crosses the room to flick me on the head, poke me in the ribs, she even slapped me for no reason the other day."

Amber had paused and was staring at me with sadness in her eyes. "I believe that, I really do, but I—"

"Didn't witness it," I finished for her. "Lord above. Alright then, how's the boyfriend?" I asked, abandoning hope for the moment.

She hesitated and I was afraid I'd upset her. She didn't look up for almost half a minute, instead fussing with the bed covers. "He's fine," she said eventually, slowly, "but the old one —Earl's dad—showed up the other day and Red beat him up."

"Isn't that good?" I asked. "Macho. Defending his woman."

She shrugged. "I s'pose Ralph deserved it. Just felt like I might be going into the fire from the frying pan. Red scared me. I thought..."

Another hesitation, so I jumped in with, "Thought Red might hit *you*?"

"Yeah," she said anxious faced. "That all men might be nutters in their own ways. Earl's dad were drug dealing. I'd wondered where the money was coming from and once I found out I didn't wanna know, so I left. Literally packed our bags and left the flat there and then."

"I am so sorry," I said sincerely.

"So I'm playing it real cautious with Red now, though he swears he wouldn't hurt a hair on my head, it's best to be careful, innit?" I nodded sombrely but she dashed on with envious eyes, "But you wouldn't know what it's like, would you, Mary? I don't suppose you had to bother much about that drug thing in your day."

And I couldn't tell her, could I.

I waited until she had gone, then went into the toilet. The face reflected in the tiny, mirrored cabinet above the basin wasn't me; wasn't Molly in her prime. It was a wrinkly woman with shadows of defeat under her eyes where there should have been fight, determination, the attitude of I shall never grow old. But it had all gone.

It didn't help that, when I exited the toilet, I found the major sat on the end of the bed. I climbed under the comforting duvet, ignoring his image, and found a sheet of paper between the covers. I hadn't noticed the door opening and closing, but someone had to have come in to place it there.

The words didn't make much sense to me, just as likely

because of the state I was in, but I assumed it was information to occupy Richard for a while.

It had been delivered in the nick of time. At one o'clock, my hardly-touched lunch tray had only just been removed when Richard came in. I was cold in bed despite wearing both my nightie and dressing gown, feeling sick and hardly containing enough energy to be surprised any more. "Lucky me. To what do I owe this honour, dickhead?"

His smile melted away, his mouth becoming a thin flat line, and a slight twitch was tickling his eye. "I see what uncle Stan meant now. An ugly old woman with a lovely sense of humour. That's how he described you, believe it or not."

"Ugly? I'd imagined he might be kinder than that."

"Does nothing fucking faze you? This English stiff upper lip act is amazing. So bear this in mind. I could've had you beaten with bats, kneecapped or lobotomized, but this way is more fun. I am familiar with the damage confusion, uncertainty, deception and lies can do to a mind, and I immersed you in it: not knowing what was going on when, what time it was or even which day or even if you'd be alive the next day."

"Do you want a medal for it?"

"You could at least thank me for looking after your miserable cat."

"And George Grosvenor?"

He shrugged. "The intent was to get all of you in one fell swoop. To only get the poof was disappointing, so we took the cat to upset you."

"Where is George now? And Hugo? He was with me when you grabbed me."

Head on one side, his eyes glimmered. "I don't know. I handed that issue to someone closer to the problem."

"You're lying. If they're dead, just tell me."

"But that would be a kindness, and I am not known for such things. Far more painful for you to sit and wonder where your little boyfriends are. But, to the matter in hand. Gavin

350

said you had some words from the two wise men. Hope my trip here wasn't for nothing."

I handed him the sheet of paper. He frowned then got up wordlessly, still staring at it.

"Are you poisoning me?" I asked as he headed for the door. "Is Gavin telling the truth when he says I have cancer? Or are you playing with me?"

He turned back. "You're not ill that I know of. Maybe it's just a reaction to something."

"Really?" I sighed. "Or you could be lying again and again and again. Go away before I vomit on you."

"That bad?" He looked concerned and stepped back to the bed, staring into my eyes, taking my wrist pulse with cold fingers. I shrugged my arm out of the dressing gown and drew up the sleeve on my nightie to show him the offending needle marks. He looked, exhaled sharply, took out his phone, and dialled as he kept glancing at me.

"Irene," he said, "what's this about Mrs Cooper's meds upsetting her? Yes, I see. I know she keeps running, but that's your fucked up security. I need her lucid. Now." He took in a sharp, angry breath and glared at the window. "We had an agreement, Irene," he said in a warning voice. I wondered who Irene was then recalled the first time I had met Mrs Galyer.

He hung up. "That should fix it. They were trying to keep you down when I had asked for you to be kept up. Simple misunderstanding. You should stop trying to escape."

"Mrs Galyer," I said. "And you, and Gavin, all in cahoots, who would have thought it?"

He cackled; an unseemly noise for a man. "Now you can enjoy your stay and, don't fret, we will look after you exceptionally well. Now you're working, you're worth keeping." He waved the piece of paper. "Get me more. I don't want to kill anyone else until I'm certain they're guilty."

I snorted. He was making me angry. Like Stanley had make me angry. Thinking about all the people he was hurting like it was some fun game.

"Shove off, dickhead," I growled, sagging back into the bed, then thinking of something and making my eyes peek over the top of the cover like a child playing. "Hey, wait, I forgot. I have something else for you. Come here and see." I waggled my eyebrows up and down as I imagined what I was going to do...

Maybe he was an educated man with doctorates and all that stuff, but he was still thick enough to approach the bed, so I reared up and thumped him hard with the billiard ball. He yelped, recoiled, then dragged me out of bed by my nightdress, ripping it. I didn't yell, I did struggle. He dropped me to the floor, the items on the bedside table falling all of a clatter around me, and then he kicked my side so I doubled up and squealed, regretting my life choices as he stood over me panting with anger.

He touched where I had bashed his skull. I was so weak I doubted it had damaged him.

"How quickly you forget I control your life, your drugs, your food, your comfort," he snarled. "Don't try to play games or I'll prescribe something that'll make you throw up your guts every five minutes."

"Haven't you done enough?" I whimpered, holding my side as I cowered on the floor. "It was Hugo's fault, you must know that. He's the one that started everything. Leave me alone. I tremble constantly—"

He picked up the offensive ball and left, the door slamming after him.

"Ooh, Mary, did you fall out of bed?" Amber cried as she came in a few minutes later and I was still on the floor.

"Can I kill him?" I asked.

"Who?" Amber said as she helped me up to the chair.

"Richard."

"Your son? Why do you want to kill him?"

I gave her a baleful, questioning look. "Can you really not tell that the doctor and my son are two separate people?"

"Are they? Are you sure?"

"Oh Gawd, don't you start. I think we both need to escape these mind games."

"Mind games?"

"This is why I want to kill him." I showed her my bruised side, my torn nightie. "He did this. He's the one trying to tell me I'm not Molly. He's the one arranging all this not-so-subtle torture."

Her cool fingers examined where he had kicked me, but all she said was, "Whatever did you hit yourself on when you fell out the bed? That clock of yours?"

Give up, Molly. You might as well talk to the wall.

"I'll get something to put on that bruise," Amber said, breezing out as I began to cry, filled with pain both physical and mental.

20. Scoot!

I still hadn't fully recovered from Richard's visit when I went to bed later that evening and looked in my bedside drawer for a tissue, and gasped when I saw a mobile phone nestled there.

After a second's disbelief, I leapt upon the phone in excitement. Had it been left for me or lost? No; no one loses a phone in a bedside drawer. I had spent the rest of the day recovering from my bruised side in the day room, trying to think as the TV lulled me into a false sense of security. The phone could have been there for hours.

Then I realised whose it must be, and I put it down as if I had accidentally picked up a venomous snake, terrified. With all the things I had seen on films about people being tracked by mobile phones, now I had finally got my wish for a phone I couldn't risk implicating Amber, bless her heart for trying to help me.

'What a useless, cowardly drip you are,' I yelled at myself. 'Keep it and give it to Jeff. He'll know how to use it.'

But Amber... But Earl...

Who mattered more? Two men with dubious pasts and an old woman with no future, or the bright-eyed lass with her new future waiting? Had she really considered the risks when she'd put the phone in my drawer? I thought not.

I unlocked the door, put the phone on the windowsill behind the curtain, gazed up at the uncaring, beautiful stars, went back to bed and fashioned a weapon, of sorts.

I stopped wanting to eat, but I also stopped feeling sick, so it was a two way street. No more needle sticks appeared on my arm, but I still felt like I was at death's door, not convinced I would ever get out of there. I would never see my grandchildren again. Richard would go through with his date-threat, seduce and marry Vana—they were actually a good match—becoming a stepfather who encouraged the children into his heinous ways. I would rather die than see that happen.

Disappearing into many hours of oblivion, I came-to in my sunny room, clock showing 10am, a saline drip in my arm, a nappy you know where. I wanted to scratch my head, but found my hands were strapped to the bed frame. An itch I couldn't scratch; a different kind of hell.

I floated half in and half out of death's doorway, giving up on myself. No one was going to help me. Hugo wasn't going to ride in on a white horse. He was probably really dead.

Amber came in some time later, a shaft of sunlight turning her hair into the red-gold halo of an angel.

"How are you?" she whispered furtively, and I guessed she shouldn't be there.

"I don't like these restraints. What do they think I'm going to do? I'm too weak to elope."

"It's so you don't take out the drip." Her voice dipped lower. "We 'ad someone a while back stab a member of staff with the needle."

"So have you any fluffy handcuffs, perchance?"

She grinned cautiously. "Still very much with it, then. You've got to fight this. I've seen too many just give up, even in the time I've been here."

"Scratch my head, would you? This itch is the worst torture I've had so far."

Directed to the offending area, she scratched my head for welcome, blissful relief.

"Surely you could untie just one hand?" I suggested.

"I'd get into trouble."

"That's what you always say."

"Well, it's true. I would."

"I bet you'd do it for Red if you found *him* all tied up."

"If he were all tied up..." She pulled a cheeky face. "It'd likely be with the fluffy handcuffs."

I chuckled.

"That's better." She smiled delicately, not sure she'd won the battle, and she hadn't.

"I don't want to recover," I said. "I want to go. Everything's too hard. I can't get out. I can't win, 'cause even if I get out what will I face? Hunted forever? A life of running, hiding, worrying?"

"You can't quit now. After all you've gone through, you can't just give up now." She took my hand, squeezed it and I saw tears well in her eyes, causing them to spring into mine too. It was touching that someone liked me so much to try so hard; to take risks for me.

"Did you get your phone back safely?" I asked.

She gave me the look of a startled doe.

"I didn't use it," I said. "I didn't want to put you in danger."

She bit her lip and let go of my hand, tears forming again. "I... I better go."

She moved to leave then stopped midstride, turning slightly to say apologetically, "I do want to help. I really do. It's just so difficult. I wasn't made for this game."

"What 'game', dear?"

"Will you fight if I say the magic words?"

I smiled at her; so pretty, so delicate, a flower already marred by evils of the world.

"Are the words 'pretty please'?" I asked.

"No." She rested her brow on the door for a moment then looked round, exhaling, looking so worried I wondered what was coming, but what she said just before she went out made my heart jump so much she nearly killed me anyway. But it had the desired effect, instantly turning my thoughts away from rapping on Death's door.

"Hugo's alive."

I would have called her back, asked her to stay and tell me what was going on, but I was pretty sure that the words were only something she'd said as a last resort and then regretted, but oh my heart, they had done the trick.

~

Later, a nurse replaced the drip in frigid silence. I turned my face from her, let my lips tremble and ignored the hands that attended to my needs. She made no effort to communicate and left when the tasks were done.

No one fed me, unfortunately, as the idea of Amber knowing the truth was piquing my appetite at last.

In the gloaming, the door opened silently and Barry appeared like a hulking wraith beside the bed.

"How're you doing, Mum?" His voice was full of concern. "Yer not dying, are you? Figured they'd jest taken you down a bit."

"I was trying to catch up on my beauty sleep."

"Like you need it."

"Why, thank you, dear. Can you undo these things?" I pulled against the straps.

He undid them both.

"And take out the cannula," I asked.

"Ah canna," he said. "Blood's not ma thing."

"You're joking, surely?" I removed the tape on the drip cannula, gritted my teeth and slid it out. The grossed-out expression on Barry's face was priceless. I wondered how he'd coped with being a bad guy who couldn't face blood. "Help me sit up. Open the window. Let's have a breeze. Where's my hairbrush? I must look a sight."

"Brought you supper," he said, and took three biscuits from his pocket. Ravenous now, I fell on the treats like the proverbial starving man. "So good," I said in chocolate ecstasy, taking a drink of water. "Help me stand. I'm a wee bit giddy."

He tried to haul me upright but, somehow, we both slipped. I fell back and Barry tripped forwards and ended up between my legs on the bed in a very heavy and uncomfortable pose. "Get off!" I squealed.

It was at that moment Jeff opened the door, saw what he thought was going on, grabbed Barry by the collar of his PJs and threw him onto the floor, hissing, "Leave the lady alone!"

"He was helping me," I yelped in horror, secretly delighted to have such a knight on my team.

"Gah; sorry, pal." Jeff extended a hand to Barry and helped him up. "Just reacting."

Barry rubbed his backside with both hands. "No 'ard feelings."

It must have been the sugar rush, but an idea had spiked into me. If Amber really knew who I was, she'd understand the need. "What if I got you to a car? Can you break in quietly, hot wire and so on?"

"Yeah," Barry said, cautious. "Depends how old the car is, mind. Modern computer-y ones are really hard to hot wire or I'd a had a go already with this lots'."

"I know where we can get an old car."

"How come? How far?" Jeff demanded.

"It's a carer's. She's on our side—well, on my side at least —only lives about ten minutes away; less if we hurry. Does the name Hugo Jenkins mean anything to you?"

Barry nodded. "Young punk-arse git. Thought he were dead."

"He's supposed to be, so I want to pay a visit to both get the car and see what she meant by Hugo's alive. He was a good friend of mine."

"Need all the bloody help we can get," Jeff said. "But I've decided it's time to make a move. The play in the dayroom scored us some scooter keys." He proudly held them up. "I left it a while to see if anyone made a hoo-ha, and no one has, so I'm using the code and getting out tonight."

"But..." I said, "I'm know I'm muddled, but if you have the keys, aren't they just waiting for you to make a move so they can nab you? And how do you even know any bike out there is the one the keys belong to? You don't want to waste the —"

"I went down and had a look-see," he broke in, his tone implying my stupidity. "The reg number's on the ring; see?" He shoved it into my face. "So I'm off to try your pass code and my luck."

"Want a pillion?" Barry offered.

"No, take me," I said eagerly. "I'm much lighter."

"Negative. I'm gonna do this on my own. You'll hear what happened one way or the other."

"Ah'll keep an eye out for you from the top window," Barry offered.

"Gwen..." I said. "You don't think they'll take it out on her if you're missing?"

He drew in a resigned breath. "I'm not convinced she's in there anymore. That's the only reason I'm risking it."

"Good luck," I said, and he left, Barry close behind.

I grabbed my stick, toddled out after them then went into Gwen's room... where I stopped dead.

She was in the bed and looking at me, eyes bright in the low-light. She didn't acknowledge my presence at first, just staring with wide owl eyes, but then a haunted look of mingled fear and anxiety ran over her face and, frowning, she said in a hoarse whisper, "Where am I?"

"Er... it's a kind of prison," I said, a finger to my lips to quieten her, "but you've woken just in time because we're getting out tonight. I think I'll take you to another room, though, because the bad guys might come for you when they find your hubby gone."

I helped her into the wheelchair that had been folded against the wall, and pushed her back to my room, arms aching, wishing I was the one in the seat.

Somewhere in the home there was a ruckus going on, doors slamming, raised voices. Had Jeff's escape been detected already? Hadn't Barry been spotting for him? I'd go look as soon as Gwen was settled.

"You'll be safe in here," I said hopefully as I parked her chair facing the radiator.

"I'm cold," she said feebly. "What's going on? Where's Jeff?"

"He'll be here soon." I lied to keep her happy. "Here..." I

wrapped a scarf around her neck. She tugged on the duvet so I wrapped that around her too. She hunched up as though she were freezing, and I left her like that as I crept out, then sprang back in as heavy footsteps echoed down the corridor, more doors slammed nearby, and footsteps finally retreated.

I looked out cautiously. Silence. I got to Barry's room and found him dressed in top and jeans and pulling on some trainers.

"What's going on?" I asked. "You going off with Jeff after all? What was all that fuss I heard?"

"Yeah, poor old codger didn't get too far," Barry said with the hint of a grin. "He took a tumble down the stairs afore he even got out the building. Floor two shoved him back up in the lift and he's in his room nursing a duff leg."

"Am I allowed to laugh?"

"As long as he don't hear it, reckon it'd be safe enough. Time to try fer the car, I reckon."

"So, we're going to drag him off on his poorly leg?"

He sniggered. "You got a mean streak, Mum. I'll go have a natter, see how bashed he is, if he's up fer it. Fer now, you get yerself some outside clothes 'cause I'm sure up fer finding that car."

The door opened and there was Jeff, almost falling into Barry's room, his gait pained and face contorted. He staggered to the bed and sat heavily. "I failed," he growled. "I'm nothing but a fucking old man, falling down the fucking stairs!"

"Jeff!" I began in great excitement, but Barry butted in with talk of trying for the car and the next thing I knew they were staggering out again, seeming to forget I was the one they had to follow. Men! I had to tell Jeff about Gwen. I had to change my clothes.

My luck had held so well I shouldn't have been surprised when, as I crept along the corridor after them, I sensed more than heard someone behind me.

I was about to turn when I felt the needle in my neck, and off I went to la-la land.

21. A Fate Deserved

I didn't know how much time had elapsed when I came-to, but my first thought was that I had let the team down. They didn't know where Amber's car was.

I was in a dark, cramped space. It felt like ice covered my skin, pressure was all around me, no room to stretch out, the smell of damp earth heavy in my lungs in the darkness. Light; a sliver from behind me, pale as a moonbeam. Hard to move... rocks pressing into my side painfully. Ah, I knew where I was... the hole. I was in the hole under the bench, the light coming in through the grille in the well shaft.

I lay there for long minutes, no energy to call out, cold creeping over me, slippered toes frozen and legs aching with the strain of being curled up, trying to shift away from things poking and paining me, hurting me all the more.

A hoarse whisper came through the grille, accented, female, familiar. "Serve you right."

"Mila?" I struggled to move. "What'd I do to you?"

I heard the murmur of a deep voice before she said, "He say, not me, *he* say it your fault; all your fault."

"Who's there? What's my fault?"

"He say, everything you touch dies, you are... what the word?" she asked someone. "Ah, he say, you plague."

"I say he's somewhat overly dramatic." I wondered how to play things. Be a mouse or be a lion? Beg or demand?

I doubted I'd fade out and die on a warm summer night, but one never knew. I couldn't see that I deserved it, though. It wasn't my fault that anything had happened. Thieving Hugo had started it all back in Hartpury; been the cause of all the deaths. I wondered what the scales of justice would say—my fault, his fault? The webs of Fate had crossed and recrossed to produce this horrible mishmash of accusations and declarations.

I mean, I knew I must die eventually, but not there, not then, not on the verge of finally escaping with my two new boys. No, that would be no good at all. Most unfair. Not that life was fair in any shape or form. I decide to go with anger. It had served Jeff well.

I drew in a deep breath and hollered, "When I get out of here and find out who you are, I am going to rip off your fingers, one by one!"

I heard a startled breath, like the hiss of Darth Vader.

"He say, you choose wrong words."

"Tell him he is a dick more than a dick is, and I will wrap *his* dick around his neck and strangle him with it!"

Mila stammered, "H... he hear." Her voice quietened as she turned away. "I can no say all this, sir, this hard to me."

"And tell him he's a fucking coward or he'd face me himself!"

A scuffling sound.

"Get out the way," the horrifyingly familiar voice said to Mila, and I imagined him shoving her roughly aside, her ratty English having failed her. Heard her scampering away, probably threatened into silence.

"Tell you this, Mum, I'm the one whose ass you gotta kiss t' get outta there, and I'll also say you're not getting outta here. Ever. This is the last place you'll ever see."

"Gavin, why? Was I that awful a mother?" I asked in horrified bemusement. "We did the best we could for you, your father and I. We loved you. Yes, even he loved you, in his own way."

"And what a way that was."

"What do you mean? Did he hurt you when my back was turned? If he did, I couldn't stop—"

"Shut up," he ordered in a tired voice. "Quit with the games. You knew, didn't you?"

"If you're going to be cryptic—"

"You knew who my real parents were."

I faltered. "No. Not in the least. Never."

"Richard told me. Said I deserved to know the truth."

"If your father knew who your parents were, he kept it from me. Like the fact he was the local drug kingpin. You know, little things like that."

"I don't believe you. You've known all along, haven't you? Admit it."

"Are you a Hitler clone?" I asked. "I think that'd explain a lot; both terrible attitude and foul temper. So come one, you obviously know more than I do. Who are your parents and what's all this lunacy about?"

"You killed my real father."

"Eeh?" I frowned deeply, thinking of anyone I'd encountered that was old enough. "The Major?"

"No, you moron! *Stanley.*"

I held my breath in shock, trying the get the cogs winding to a logical conclusion.

"So, Sarah was your mother?" I asked hesitantly. "Stanley said she hated children, so I suppose it makes sense that she'd want to get rid of—"

"No. Stanley had an affair. I was the result. My mother died—"

"Suspiciously, I'm sure."

"Then Stanley had me handed over to Oswald when he heard you wanted a kid."

"That must be why Ozzie said he'd sorted the adoption papers."

"You don't sound surprised at all. I repeat; *did you know*?"

"None of it, I can assure you." But something sang in my memory. A birthday party in Kerton, Stanley looking at the children playing and saying something about his wife hadn't wanted children. And, later, on the bus, he had referred to himself as 'grandfather', which it now became apparent he was. Grandfather to Gavin's children...

"Actually," I said, "I'm impressed you set up all this crazy just for little old me because I killed your father, a mad man who would likely have made me vanish too, the moment he tired of me."

"Not just that! You've messed up everything. Every fucking thing!"

I could hear him getting more and more agitated with every sentence, and there was another noise up there, Misty calling to me.

"Don't be cryptic," I said as calmly as I could, a mother trying to appease an errant, whining, adult child, "You're not six years old."

"Vana chucked me out when I told her the truth. I haven't seen the kids since she convinced a lawyer I wasn't a fit father 'cause of my history with the cartel."

"Hardly my fault what you were involved in. You're a grown man, the choices were yours. Shame on you. You didn't get that from my parental guidance."

He snorted derision. "You big headed bragger, everything's about you, not interested in hearing anything about anyone else. Any time I tried to have my say as a kid you'd interrupt or zone out until you could say something else about you." I heard Misty give an aggrieved yowl. "Get away from me you bloody cat, you're as much a pain as she is."

"That's not fair. I tried to take care of you. To direct you, to help. And you told me I was dying. How cruel is that?" The tears came as I broke to pieces inside, his words cruelty unmatched, my own son working against me; too much for me. My son, not my son. "I'd put myself in the line of fire to protect you," I said, closing my eyes, wanting to un-hear his words. "Let me out, please. You're just an angry little boy. Maybe I wasn't the best mum, but I loved you!"

"Shurrup!" he yelled fit to wake the whole home. "Now you've caused another mess that I have to clean up. You're fucking impossible to kill. Thought I had you in your bedroom, but that wasn't you. How do you manage it? Deal with the devil?"

"What? Gwen? No!"

"Old lady in a wheelchair in your room... of course I

thought it was you. You all look the same; old, wrinkly, grey, smelly."

There was a sudden commotion up there; grunts, tussling.

"Hey!" I yelled, straining to hear. Then it all stopped and the world was silent again.

There came a scraping noise and pale light come down from above me. The bench was being levered up.

Barry leaned in, reaching for me, but it was hard to grab his hand with my cold and aching fingers. He struggled to get a hold on me, but Jeff's critical voice encouraged him. Finally, he grabbed my dressing gown sleeve and began to draw me out inch by inch as I pushed with numbed feet. As my head emerged into the fresh air, there was an odd sound behind us but Barry said in a harsh whisper, "Don't look."

"Is that Jeff? What's he doing?"

"Jest dealing with a problem. Okay, come on. Up you get. You can walk. Remember *you're* resilient, Mum."

"I don't want to be resilient. I want someone to help me, to hold me up, to look after me. I am too old for all this. Find me a warm bed and leave me in it."

Misty nuzzled up to me in cat-sympathy. I reached round her for a lovely smooth stone off the rockery and pocketed it.

"Nah, got a million years left in you yet, *Mum. C*ome on." Barry supported me as we went back through the garden, through the unlocked underpass gate and out to the road, where I collapsed in a cold heap, my dressing gown looking like a child had used it as the tablecloth for a mud-pie picnic. I was too cold to take it off.

"Yer not getting off that lightly," Barry said. "C'mon. Up y'get." He turned his broad back to me.

"I bet you haven't the strength to carry me for ten minutes. That's how far it is to the car."

"Aye, well, let's see," he said and bent down so I could piggy back on him. "Ah once carried a lass three miles on my back, back in Leeds."

"Well done. I trust she was grateful?"

"Nooo, Mum, we were kidnapping her, but the point was that I did the carrying. Don't ignore that."

I didn't know whether to laugh or cry.

Barry marched along the darkened deserted pavements along with his old lady burden in the direction I had shown him, Misty diligently tagging along.

"What about Jeff?" I asked in panic before we'd gone too far. "He won't know the way."

"Arranged a pickup point when we've got the car. Relax, Mum. All sorted."

Either Barry had the strength of a small horse despite his trials in the home, or I was half the woman I had been. I think it was probably a bit of both, but onwards he plodded. If we heard a car, he stood very still facing the road, with me hidden in the darkness behind him.

"Wow, this is fun," I said as the roll of his gait made my hips creak unpleasantly.

"Really?"

"No hell no. I'm going to ache like I'd ridden a horse."

"Ah'll take that as a compliment," he laughed. "Much farther?"

"No, not really." The road had few streetlights, and it looked quite different in the dark from the sunny walk I'd had with Amber. I wasn't even sure for a second it was the right one.

"Did Jeff ever mention a bloke named Hallshaw?" Barry asked conversationally. "He were a mate o' mine, kinda moving in the same circles as Jeff. Jest wondered if anything had come to light of him."

"You can ask him yourself when we pick him up," I said. "Oh gosh, put me down at this bus stop. I'm getting very uncomfy."

He dropped me onto the bench of the bus stop where the folding seat was almost as uncomfortable as his back. "Jest a moment," he cautioned gazing out at the dusky surroundings, "then we got to get on our way agen."

Misty, who had followed us all the way, meeping now and then, jumped up and settled down on the bench as if it were the comfiest cushion in the world. Under the dull light of the shelter, her fur glistened.

Minutes dragged by as I rubbed my aching thighs. Overhanging branches tapping the bus shelter canopy sounded like a grandfather clock ticking. Few cars passed. Waste paper scuttled past in the breeze. I grabbed it and put it in the bin to one side then massaged my legs again.

"I am so unfit," I muttered. "I'd never manage to deal with my grandchildren like this."

"Better get word to the family to skedaddle after this. Don't need Rich-Dick after them, or you'll never get to play with 'em again."

My heart skipped a beat. "Do you really think he's nasty enough to take out his ire on little children?"

"He said he would, Mum, and we both know what he's like."

What I felt in that moment was certainty of deceit. Here was Barry—big old dependable hugging Barry—talking about Richard threatening my family when I knew, I absolutely knew, I had not shared that detail with either of the men.

What was he up to? Was the Hallshaw character's location what they wanted from Jeff? Someone must suspect me of getting information I hadn't got. Did that mean Barry was one of Richard's agents? And did that also mean Jeff wasn't waiting back at the home, but captive again because Barry wanted me to himself, to question?

Although I didn't think I had named her, I was leading him straight to Amber's house, putting her in harm's way. And if she knew where Hugo was, and Barry honestly believed he was dead, did that mean he *wanted him dead*?

What had I done?

Any of those scenarios meant Barry was a bad guy.

Maybe I could pretend to faint, to have a heart attack,

something to get me taken back to the home, but tomorrow the codes would have been changed and I'd be back to square one. As all those thoughts buzzed through my mind, I wished I still had the red ball. I could have taken off a sock and made a cosh as Barry had suggested, knocked him out and waddled to Amber's... I couldn't simply run from him. Was a bus due in the next few minutes that I could push him under? And all the time I was hating myself because here I was again, in a situation where I might have to harm someone I had liked. Then I remembered what I had seen minutes before. It was now or never.

"Do you have children, Barry?" I asked, begging Fate to aid me in my dreadful decision. I had to hit him hard enough to knock him out, and I didn't want to do it. If he answered *yes* I'd pretend I'd forgotten the way to Amber's, if *no*...

"Not on yer Nellie," he retorted.

When I look back on it, it certainly was like Fate offered him up to me because, at that moment, he leaned over to re-tie his trainers' laces, giving me the exact opportunity to raise my green-glass weapon from the bin, stand to get the right angle, and to swing hard...

But it took more than one thwack. It took another and yet another before he was down and out. I panted, hating myself, dropping the bottle back into the bin. *Needs must,* I kept telling myself as I rolled his unconscious body into the dark and scraggly bushes behind the bus stop.

The sky billowed heavy clouds above me, the temperature dipped and I shivered, the adrenaline rush fading out and tiring me. I wished for the rain to hit and wash out my guilt, but it didn't oblige.

I plodded resolutely, and a little sadly up the road because, more fool me, I had been duped into liking another man. Followed by a patiently pattering calico cat, we drew closer to where the car waited.

When I finally reached Amber's house, I looked at the muddy Range Rover and patted its bonnet like an old friend—

my escape vehicle only if Amber let it escape with me, since there was no Barry to set it free and, somewhere back at the home, hopefully Jeff would be waiting for a pickup, if Barry hadn't done something to him. I felt everything was falling apart, so I rang the bell expecting police to answer; sighed deeply, then rang it again.

Amber eventually answered in her nightclothes, my apologies for disturbing her poised on my lips, but her bed-wrinkled face gaped in oddly relieved disbelief as she said, "Molly! What took you so long?"

"What do you mean?" I asked, as she took my arm and pulled me in, Misty sniffing her approval at the door. "What took me so long?"

"Hook by the door; teddy bear keyring," Amber pointed to the car keys then gave me a tiny smile and petted Misty. "Who do you think's been helping your mummy?" she asked the cat.

"I have no idea," I said.

"Pfft, yeah, well, he's upstairs. Go see. Be warned, he's like a bear with a sore head when he gets woke early, but I 'spect you knew that."

Baffled, I headed up the stairs, then I stopped midstride, thinking who I had known in the mornings; who had woken beside me? Not Ozzy. God no; not my supposedly deceased husband, though that was another body I had never seen. I took a step backwards. If he was 'helping' me, I didn't want to know. But base curiosity saw me stepping up again, and there was the only other man I have ever woken near to.

He was sitting up in the rumpled double bed, scratching his head and yawning, red scarf resting with his clothes on the bedside chair. "Just a mo," he said. "Let me get me 'ead in the moment. What time of day does you call this, Mum?"

I slumped onto the bed. "You old young bastard. They fooled me into thinking you were dead, but all this time you've been hiding in plain sight." Then all my anger at how he had caused everything dissolved in the sublime relief of seeing

Hugo alive and well.

22. New Son For Old

Hugo clambered out of bed and sat heavily on the chair, on the clothes, a useful ironing effect set in motion. "I weren't gonna mess with the likes o' Doctor Dick," he said. "Thought it best I just snoop around until you came back into your right mind. Didn't reckon it'd take so long."

Sitting on the bed end, I said in wonder, "I can't believe I didn't recognise you. You've lost weight."

He rubbed the stubble on his chin. "No beard's better 'cause it don't itch, and short hair's good for aerating the brain, so my nursey Amber says. Don't worry, she was in it with me from the moment I told her about you."

"And putting people in that hole?"

He grimaced. "I had to do what they told me. 'Sides, I'd done it to a few and they were all fine after."

"Okay, what about Amber? I love your chat up line. 'I not English. Need help learn reading and writing'. Haha."

"Didn't really do that. Told her straight out what I was up to. We needed a cover, though. And I tried to help you, Mum —left the side gate open, got Amber to leave the phone." He laughed. "Figured you'd be better at escaping than you were."

"Thank you, but simply the door code would've helped a ton."

"I had it left it in yer way twice," he said with a hint of despair.

"Where?" I couldn't believe I'd been so daft as not to notice it.

"In yer dressing gown pocket."

"Fail," I said. "So near but so far. I found tissues and binned them. Didn't see them as note paper, you numpty."

"Ere, don't you go blaming me. I tried and you obviously got it eventually. There was a limit to what I'd ask Amber to do. I was scared she'd get all squirrely and give herself away, and

I weren't risking that. She's preggers. When you're well away, we'll wait a week or so then pack up and go live someplace else."

"Finally got what you wanted; family on the way. I'm happy for you, but what about George?" I asked carefully.

"The call to Barnes was a setup. Mrs G didn't like George being with me. Planned to split us by any means. Hated you 'cause you said about being a bridesmaid."

"So you've seen her?"

"She was very apologetic, Mum. That's how I knew to come 'ere. She admitted she'd asked Doc Dick to sort you out."

"I feel so hated all of a sudden."

"She won't be 'urting anyone anymore."

"You didn't ditch her in the Thames, I hope?"

I heard the answer in his momentary silence, the blank stare of a man wondering if he should lie or not. "She sent my Georgie to the States; the cow." His face crumpled. "Some kinda programme to de-gay people, of all feckin' ignorant ideas."

I patted his knee sympathetically. "Barry Hollister. Another man in the home. Name ring a bell? Said he knew you."

"Bloody hell." He gaped. "Keep away from him."

"He was coming here with me to help steal the car so we could escape, but he knew something he shouldn't, so he's... been incapacitated."

"Close shave that. Remember Ginge? Nasty lad with ginger beard back in Hartpury? That were Barry's little bro."

I made a disgusted noise. "I am always fooled by bad guys pretending to be nice. How about Jeff Roman, the American man in the home, with a wife, Gwen?"

"Don't know nothing about no yanks."

"He's sarcastic and rude, so I'll guess he's not a baddie too. Assuming he's out of the home and not locked up again, he and I are going to alert the authorities, so watch out. Thanks for everything and the best of luck. Oh, do me a favour? Can Misty stay here? Earl would love her, I'm sure. She's downstairs right now. I was afraid she'd come to some harm in revenge for my escape if I left her at the home. Let her live here with a nice family, and when the baby's born put an advertisement in... I don't know, let's say The Times. Something not too cryptic. Red plus Amber equals blue—or pink. You get it?"

He had suddenly paled. I think the full import of going to be a father, no matter how much he had wanted a family, had only just hit him. I gave him a peck on a stunned cheek, a quick hug, then left him sitting there staring into space, lost in whatever future scenario he was envisaging.

Amber took my muddied and bloodied dressing gown and gave me an overcoat, told me the car was fully fuelled, and there were snacks and bottled water in the boot. They'd anticipated my running to hers when she'd used my real name in error and got the car ready. She apologised for all the times she'd had to lie to me. A man really had jumped out of the dayroom window, but staff had been pressured to cover it up. Hugo had told her to act like I was an ordinary resident, to cover her back, so that's what she'd done. I laughed, forgave her lies, hugged her like a daughter and off I went.

I drove away at a snail's pace, getting a feel for the vehicle.

I hadn't said goodbye to Misty, and I felt sad about that. The cat had been with me through all my adventures. I hoped she'd be happy with the little family.

As I came up to the bus stop my headlights hit the red-black smear on the ground by the bench and a sob caught in my throat. I hadn't even noticed it at the time. *Don't stop, don't stop, don't check, don't even think about him.* The next moment the heavy summer rain began to fall, a blessing at last. As the wipers swept back and forth in their hypnotic way, all I could hope was that the water would wash away the blood stain I had just driven past.

I drove slowly past the home, dull lights showing behind some of the curtained windows, my skin prickling. If Jeff was still inside, how could I get him out?

But suddenly, there he was at the road side, waving me down. His leg obviously paining him, he heaved himself in, dripping wet, hair plastered on his head like a grey pancake.

"Call this a car?" he said. "Where's Barry?"

I told him what had happened. When he heard the name Hallshaw he slammed a fist onto the dash. "Fucking fucks!" he shouted. "There I was thinking you were the spy and it was him all along."

He looked across at the wide-eyed insulted face I gave him. "Hallshaw's the guy they wanted info on. Well done, Molly."

"Well done for maybe killing another man?"

"Waste of space."

"I'm sure he had his merits."

"I'm not. Thinking back, I'm almost certain he made me trip down the stairs, then he left me to be hauled up again. Then after we got you out the hole he said he was going back inside but snuck off with you. Thought it was a mistake made in the moment, that he'd come back for me. Now I reckon he just left me. Period. They still wanted to pick my brains."

"You need to get dried out."

He looked at the SatNav. "There's a superstore ahead. Stop, sort some clothes, and we'll have a little talk about your son and my wife."

"Adopted son," I corrected him as my nervous grip tightened on the wheel.

~

With us both clothed in motley items scavenged from a charity bin behind the store, and eating snacks from the back of the car, we had our little talk.

As I had already guessed, Gavin had killed Gwen, mistaking her for me.

Not knowing I had been nabbed by Gavin, Jeff and Barry had hunted for me, initially suspecting me—me, for heaven's sake—of killing Gwen. But while peering out into the darkened garden, they had noticed Misty walking around the edge of the well, then Gavin hidden to one side, and Barry had guessed from Misty's behaviour where I might be.

Sneaking out in the dark and quiet garden they'd heard enough of the conversation to realise Gavin was the murderer.

As I was being rescued by Barry, Jeff had dealt with Gavin.

At this point he abruptly stopped talking and I knew he'd killed him.

I began to cry bitter tears while Jeff munched crisps and I wondered what he planned for me. I sniffed, blew my nose, and said, "I don't blame you, Jeff. Don't think I won't miss him, though. I raised the child and I loved him like my own, but in a way Gavin was doomed. His real father sealed his fate the day he made him, giving him a murderer's genes. No matter what my husband and I did to make him feel loved, nature won out over nurture."

His hand came onto my shoulder and I jumped. "Poor old girl," he said and patted me. "You've been through the wringer. I had to suspect you, it's the way I'm wired. Suspect everyone. But now I see you're in the muck and need rescuing, I'll not let you fall by the wayside. I'll look after you."

He grinned, wafting the pungent smell of salt and vinegar crisps my way, a homely scent reminding me of my cottage and takeaways at the seaside, and something hit me right in my emotional gut and told me I was close to home; close to safety again.

"How frightfully civil of you. Maybe you're a gentleman after all." I sniffled, then tears of relief, of rescue, of hope finally realised, gushed from me like a waterfall, and strong arms reached for me.

23. Molly's End

It's been a cold and winding road to get me here. The innocent Molly of Hartpury is gone, replaced by a broken, world weary and hardened woman who expects to die every day. I am years of pain and disappointment all scabbed over and the slightest knock makes me bleed again. I don't know when I will truly heal.

Jeff has been my rock, my guide, my mentor in this strange new world I am living in. We stuck together. It just seemed to work. Our combined mix of cynicism, humour and determination could reorder the world. This is not quite the kind of love I yearned for, but he makes me happy. Molly's end has come, and now I am Mary, Jeff's wife in name only, though I wear a lovely gold band I chose for myself, a bit fancier than my original ring.

Jeff got his contacts on the case and the home was cleared of all residents. Mrs Galyer was arrested, but most of the carers just vanished. Richard? Well, he's on Jeff's list to catch up with one deadly day, and Barry's never going to cause anyone trouble again.

A fake ID on social media means I can keep an eye on Vana and the children, and they appear to be doing alright. She seems to think Gavin's done a runner, not knowing she's a widow. I wonder what became of his body, though? For years I had mourned his death, and now I am none the wiser as to where his earthly remains are, all over again. But then, what became of the man who jumped from the window, and Mr Dan, and Gwen? The home obviously had a very efficient evidence removal system in place.

I have never had the guts to tell Jeff that Gwen had been cognizant at the time of her death. I don't think he needs to know now. I think it would break him. He would never have considered leaving, had he known she was awake. He has relegated her absence to a sad, tight little corner of his mind, and lets me fill the rest of it. Fine by me. We all have little corners filled with things we don't want to remember, yet cannot bear to forget.

Guessing on the time frame, I kept my eyes on The Times and spotted 'Red plus amber makes pink and blue'.

Either the dolt had completely misunderstood my instructions—they had been rather hastily given in that bedroom—or Amber and he had twins. I've looked around online but he's hidden his family well. Good for him. I hope he can bring up a child to be a better person than he was in his early years. I knew that was his wish but, after my experience with Gavin, maybe that's not as easy as I had assumed.

I used to think I had the rest of my life to discover my place in the world, one just for me labelled 'Here is Molly and she tries so damn hard', but everything has come to this, and I am oddly good at it. We live out of suitcases, travelling all over as work calls, never boring, sometimes a little too exciting for the old pitter-patter of my heart.

What are we are doing nowadays, you ask? Do you read the news?

Last week we were in a town bordered by a fast flowing, green watered river, spanned by a wide two-lane bridge, with a footbridge underneath, all held up with wide, graffitied concrete pillars.

I skulked on the footpath under the bridge. We knew from research he liked to come that way after work, the peace of the riverside walks somehow resting his corrupt soul. As he approached, I stumbled and dropped my shopping bag, loose potatoes spilling out. I gave a little squeal. The man stopped as I looked up with begging eyes.

"I wouldn't normally ask a stranger," I said in a crackly old lady's voice, "but can help, please? It's my poor old knees, you see."

It wouldn't have mattered if he'd helped or not. Jeff, already in position, darted out and the man didn't stand a chance—very much like his victims had not stood a chance. I didn't help roll him into the accommodating river, I had done my part, so I picked up my spilled shopping and walked on.

The news said, "Police confirm man drowned in River Lamar was missing paedophile wanted for questioning about attack on local child."

Yes, that was it; that was us. I know I should feel guilty that my whole trying-to-do-good life has come down to this, but I am not a monster. All those who tried to harm me created this woman I am now. Broke me apart and patched me together again.

But then I think...

Actually, I'm being helpful.

It is, in the end, a very special kind of litter-picking.

THE END

Printed in Great Britain
by Amazon